THE ORPHAN KING

created by
TYLER CHIN-TANNER
and
JAMES BOYLE

Tyler Chin-Tanner
writer

James Boyle
artist

Andrew Dalhouse
colorist – chapters 3, 4, & 5

Pete Carlsson
letterer

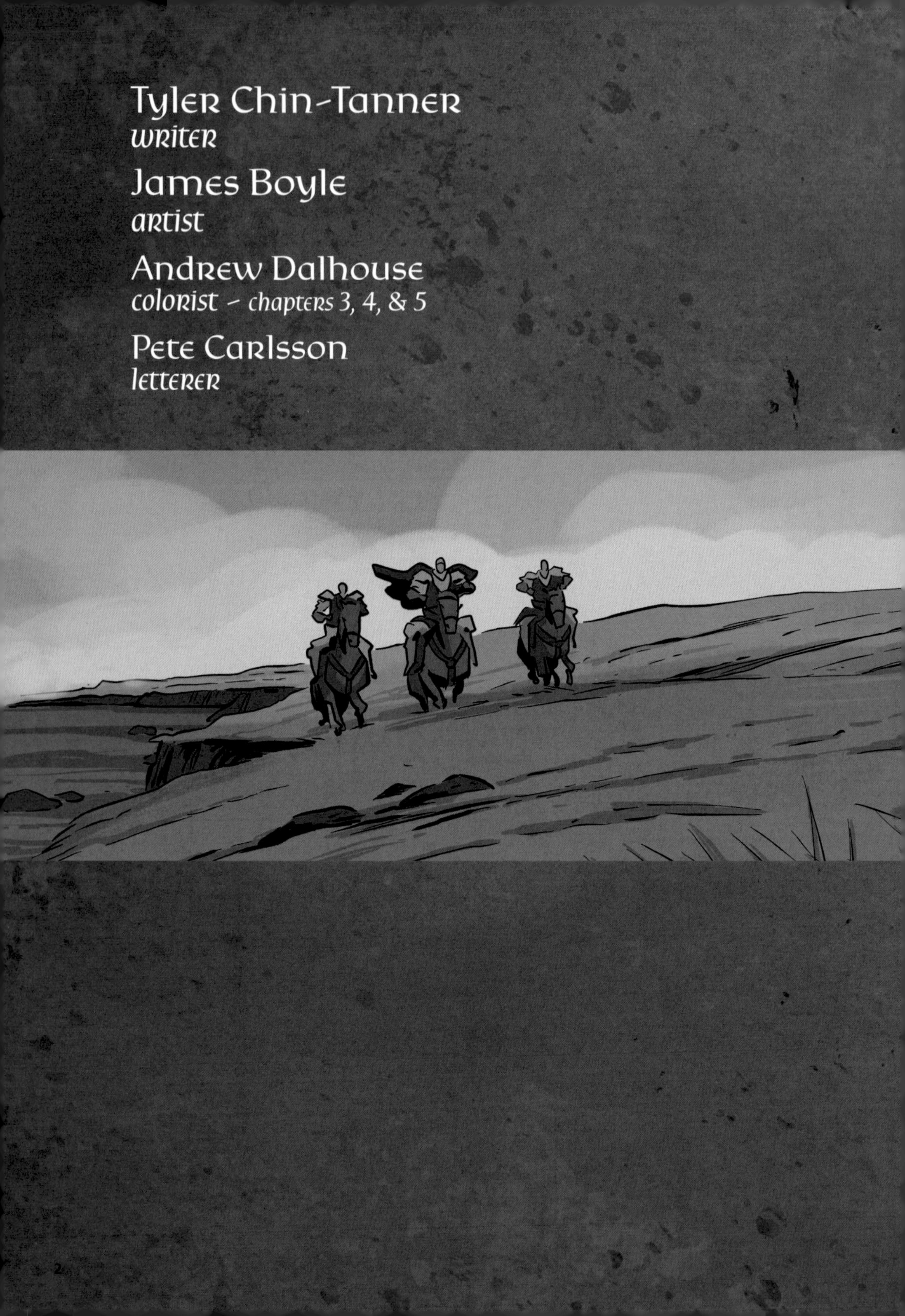

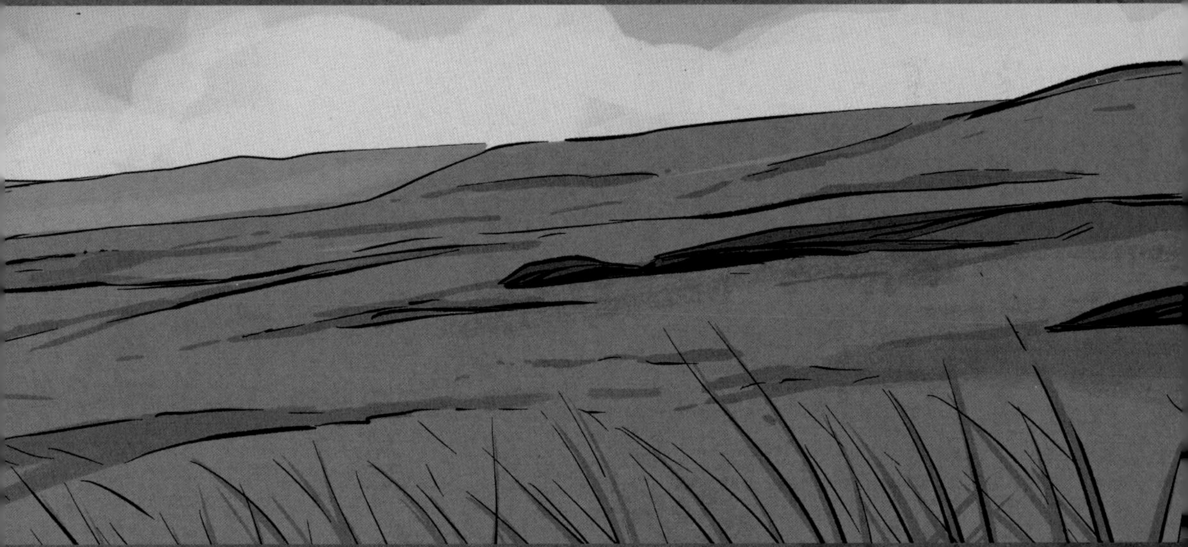

script editor:
Wendy Chin-Tanner

editorial contributor:
Joseph Illidge

cover illustration:
James Boyle

logo design:
Nicola Black Design, LLC

book design:
Pete Carlsson

Tyler Chin-Tanner
Co-Publisher

Wendy Chin-Tanner
Co-Publisher

Pete Carlsson
Production Designer

Diana Kou
director of marketing

Jesse Post
Book Publicist

Hazel Newlevant
Social Media Coordinator

ISBN 978-1-949518-14-6 Printed in Canada

AWBW.com

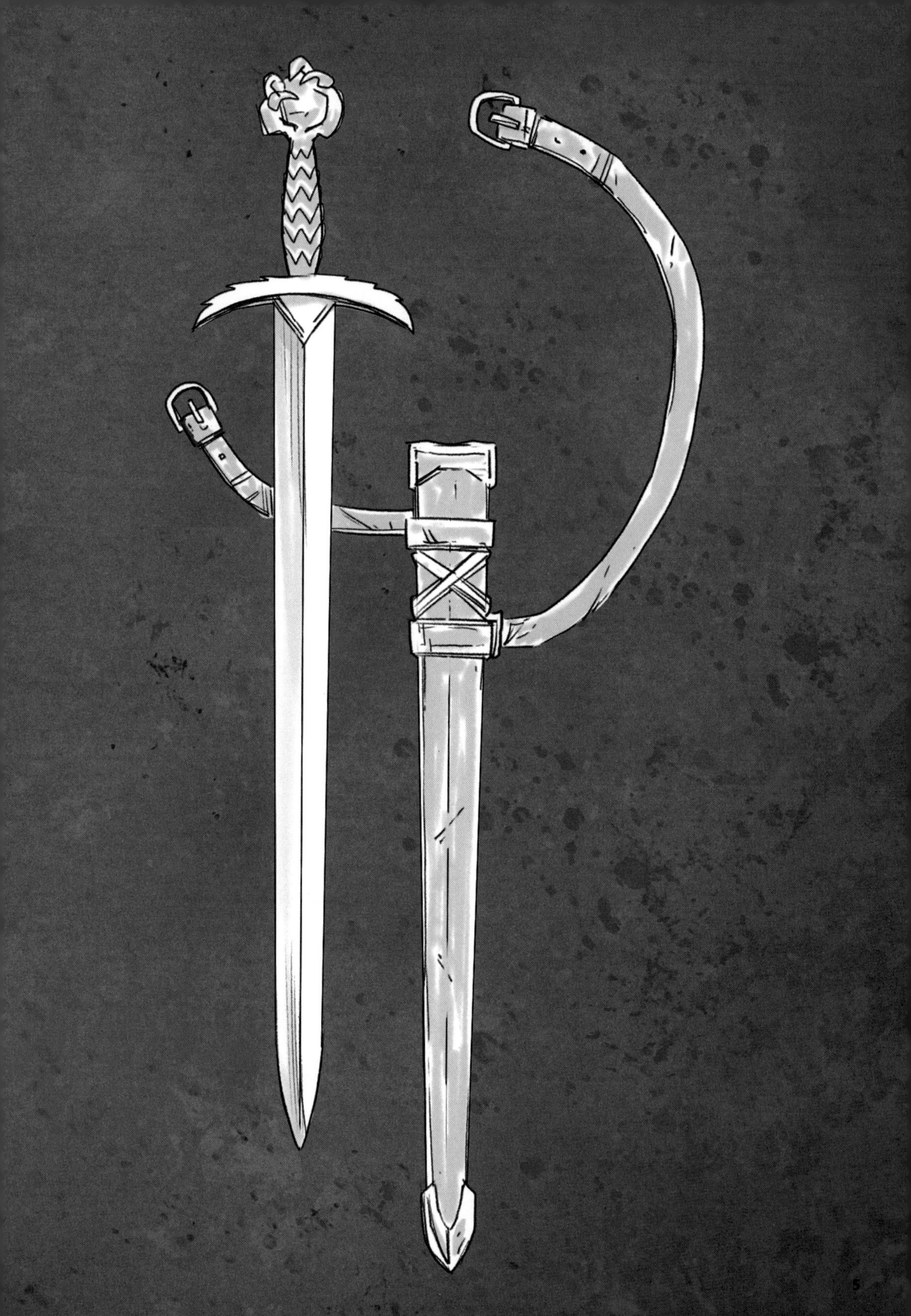

Publisher's Cataloging-In-Publication Data
(Prepared by The Donohue Group, Inc.)

Names: Chin-Tanner, Tyler, author. | Boyle, James, 1982- illustrator. | Dalhouse, Andrew, colorist. | Carlsson, Pete,
    letterer, designer. | Chin-Tanner, Wendy, editor.
Title: The orphan king / created by Tyler Chin-Tanner [writer] and James Boyle [artist] ; [Andrew Dalhouse, colorist
    (chapters 3, 4, & 5) ; Pete Carlsson, letterer ; script editor: Wendy Chin-Tanner ; cover illustration: James Boyle ;
    logo design: Nicola Black Design, LLC ; book design: Pete Carlsson].
Description: [Rhinebeck, New York] : A Wave Blue World, Inc., 2021. | Interest age level: 013-018. | Summary:
    "In a retelling of the Arthurian legends that upends the traditional notions of birthright, a young prince is
    orphaned during his training and now must fight his way back home with the help of a band of outlaws."--
    Provided by publisher.
Identifiers: ISBN 9781949518146 (trade paperback)
Subjects: LCSH: Princes--Comic books, strips, etc. | Orphans--Comic books, strips, etc. | Outlaws--Comic books, strips,
    etc. | CYAC: Princes--Fiction. | Orphans--Fiction. | Robbers and outlaws--Fiction. | LCGFT: Fantasy fiction. | Action
    and adventure comics. | Graphic novels.
Classification: LCC PZ7.7.C45 Or 2021 | DDC 741.5973 [Fic]--dc23

For Maddy and Lucy, who inspire me
with their joy and wonder.

- Tyler (Dad)

For Wren and Sidney. May you always
find your way home.

- J. B.

Chapter 01

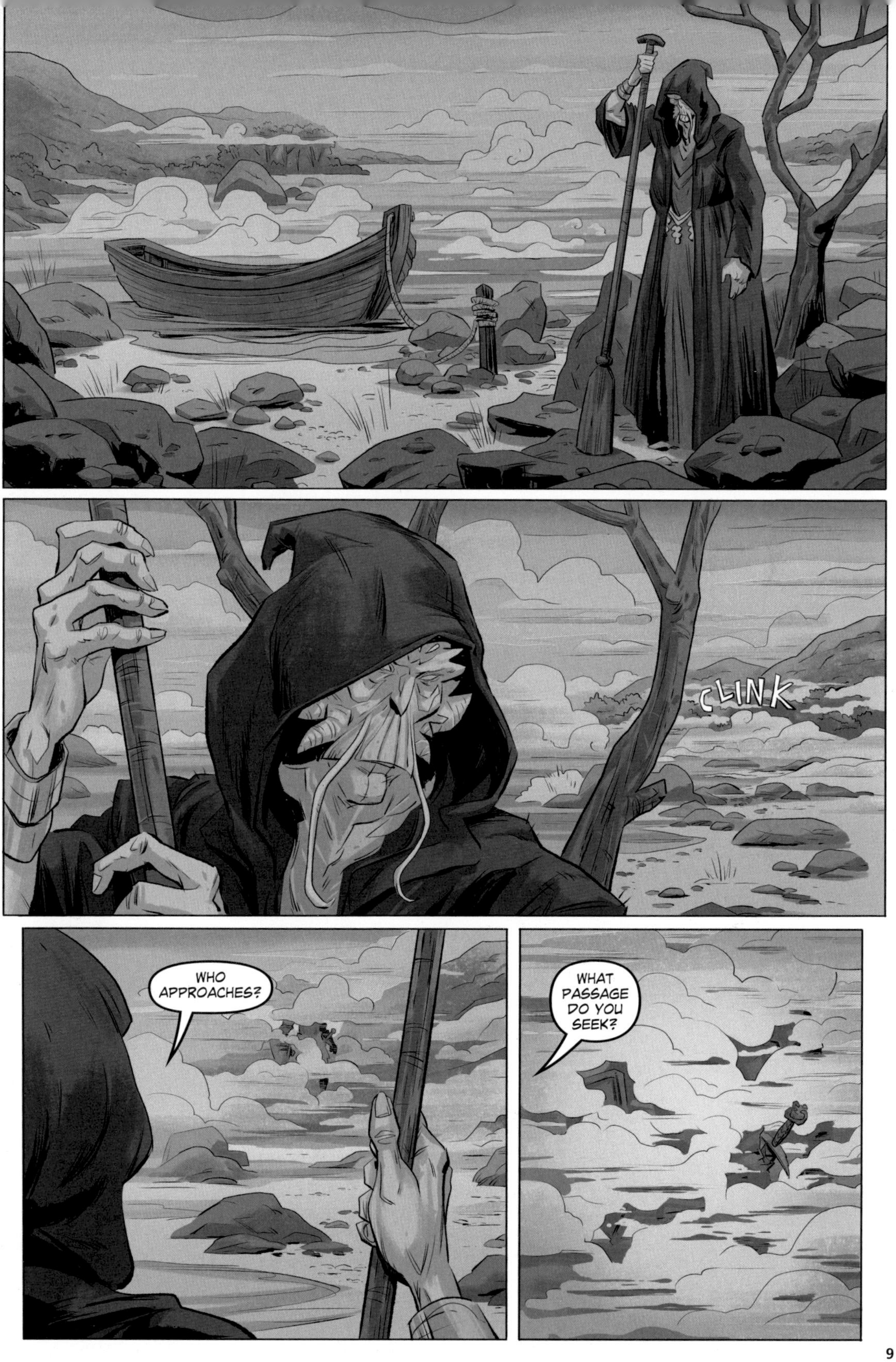
CLINK
WHO APPROACHES?
WHAT PASSAGE DO YOU SEEK?

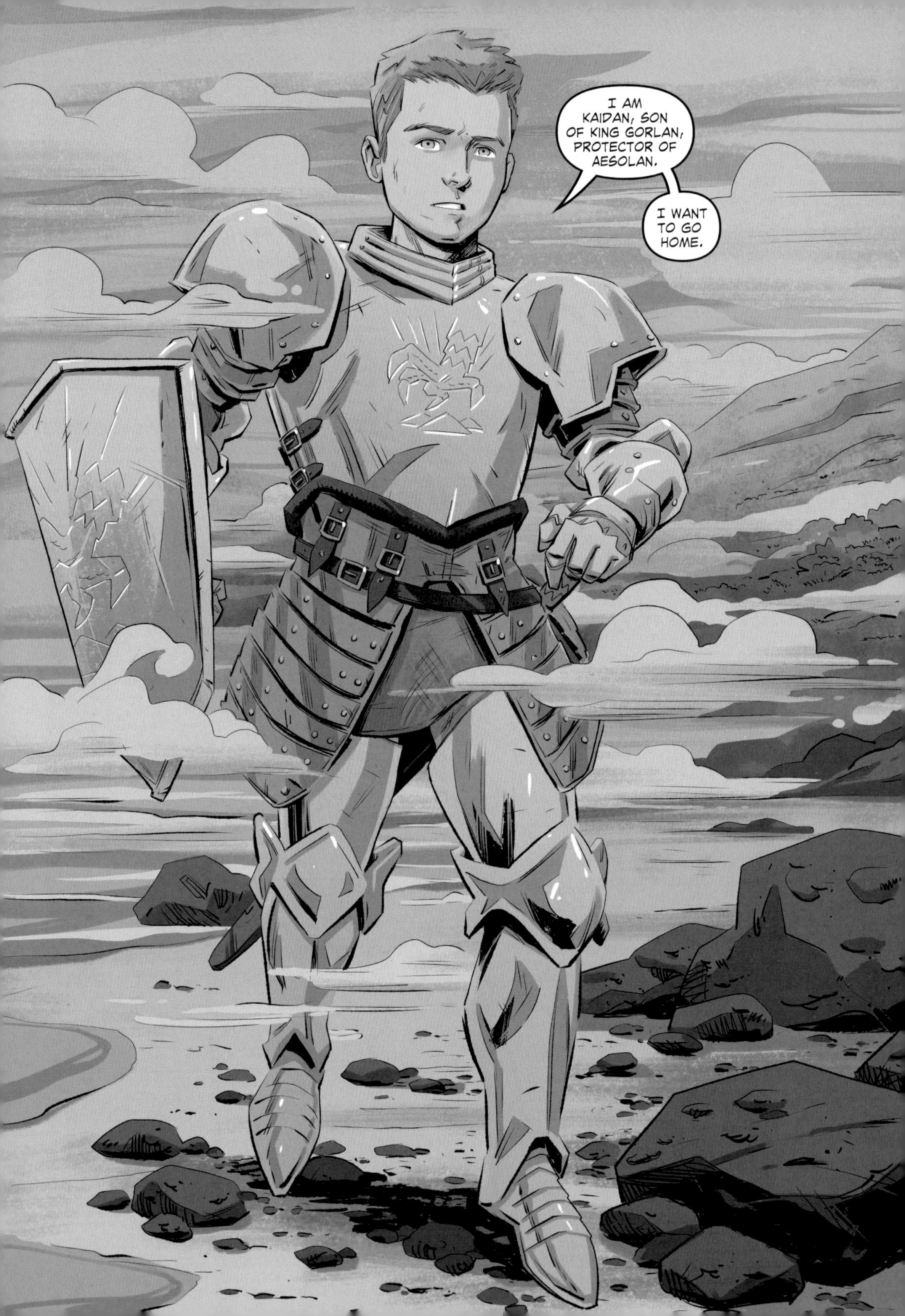
I AM KAIDAN, SON OF KING GORLAN, PROTECTOR OF AESOLAN.
I WANT TO GO HOME.

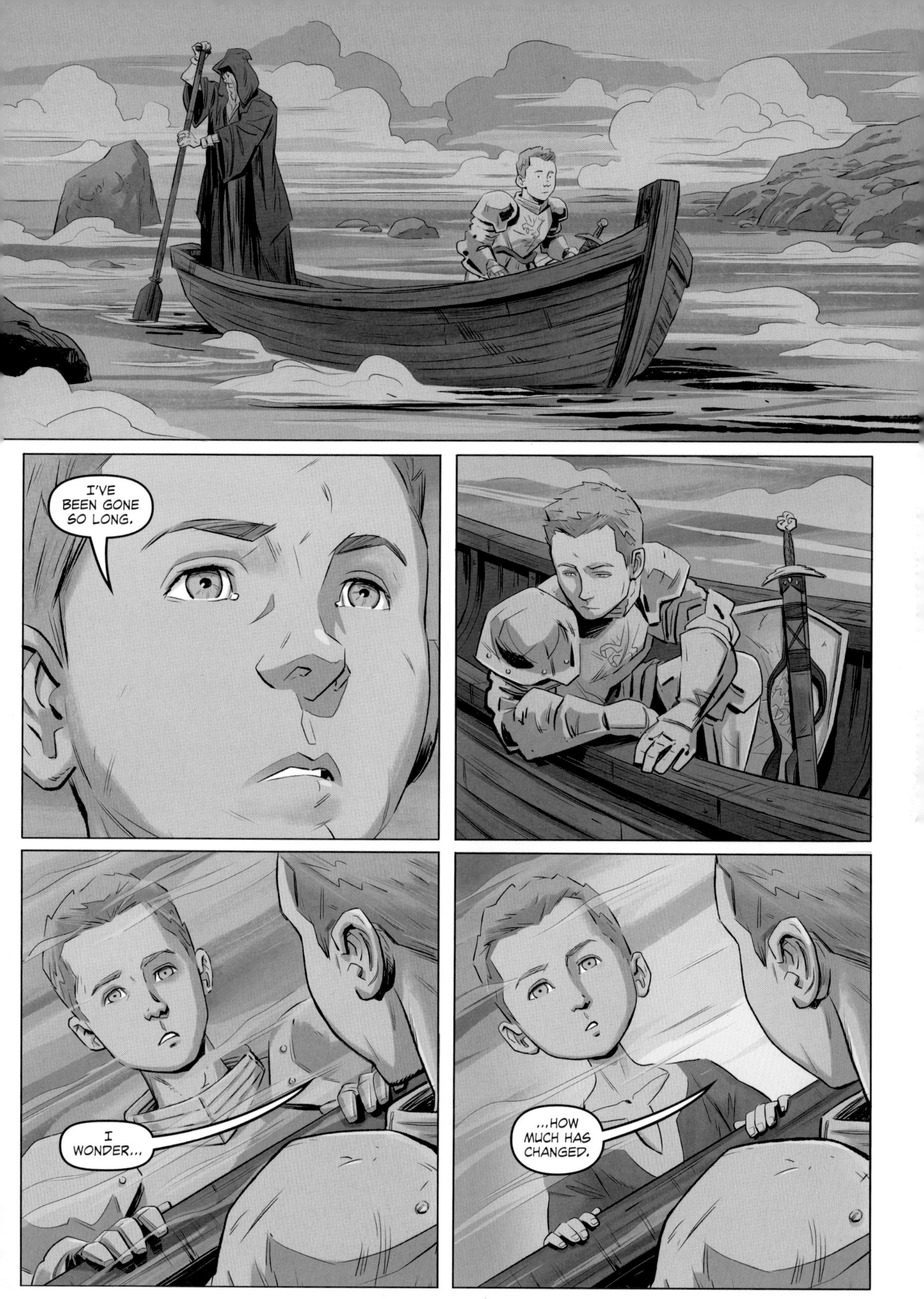
I'VE BEEN GONE SO LONG.
I WONDER...
...HOW MUCH HAS CHANGED.

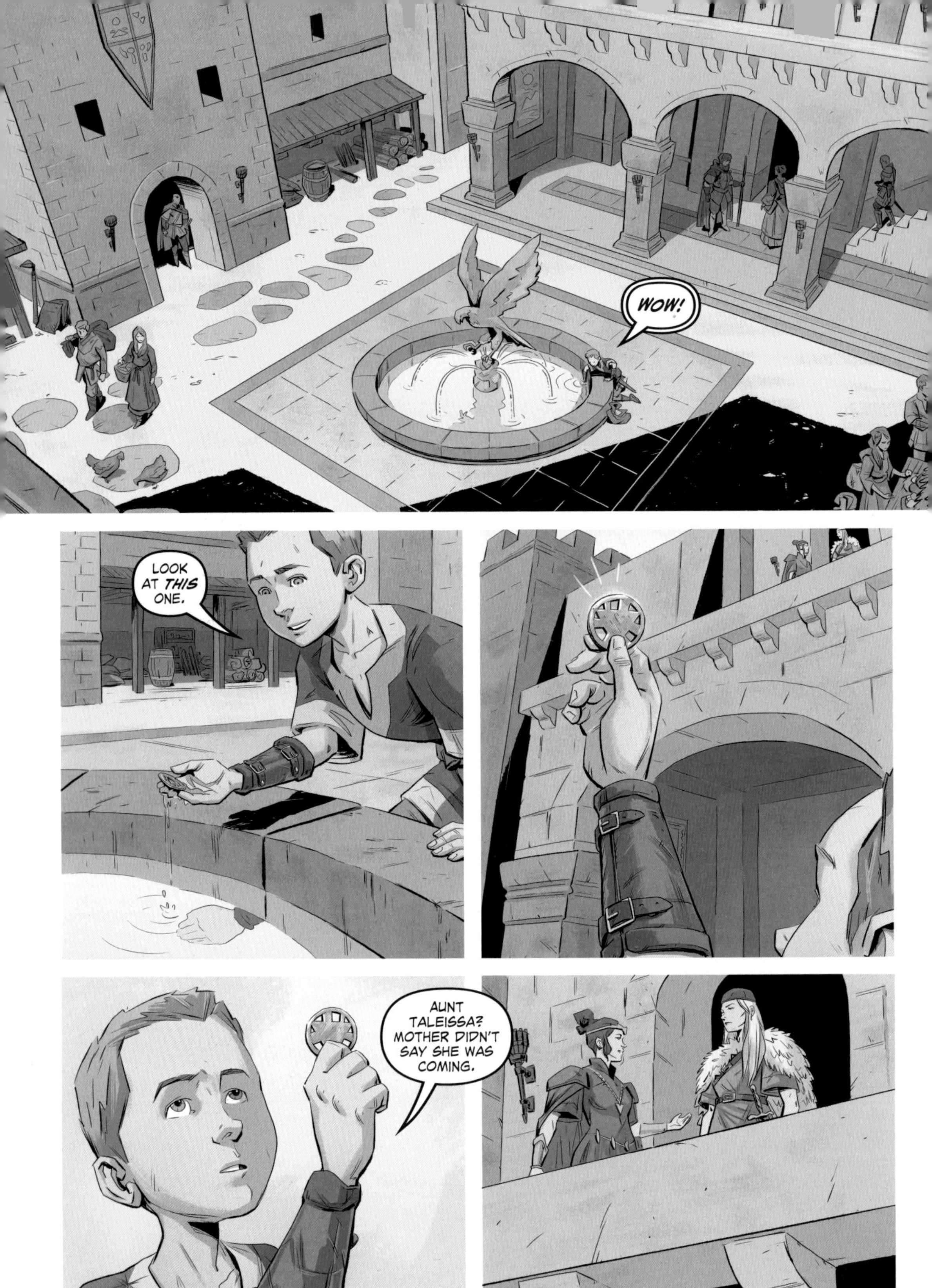
WOW!
LOOK AT *THIS* ONE.
AUNT TALEISSA? MOTHER DIDN'T SAY SHE WAS COMING.

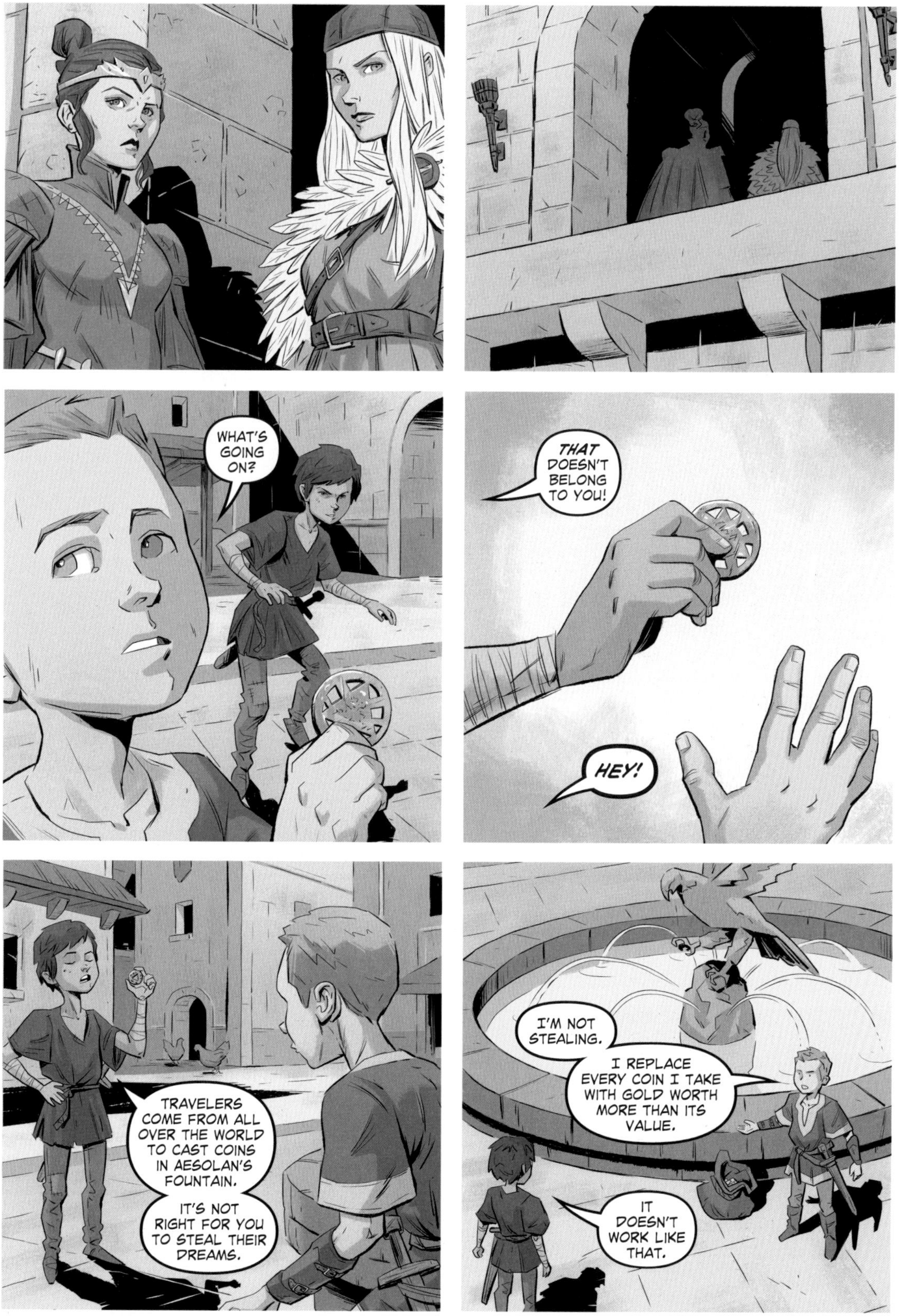
WHAT'S GOING ON?
THAT DOESN'T BELONG TO YOU!
HEY!
TRAVELERS COME FROM ALL OVER THE WORLD TO CAST COINS IN AESOLAN'S FOUNTAIN.
IT'S NOT RIGHT FOR YOU TO STEAL THEIR DREAMS.
I'M NOT STEALING.
I REPLACE EVERY COIN I TAKE WITH GOLD WORTH MORE THAN ITS VALUE.
IT DOESN'T WORK LIKE THAT.

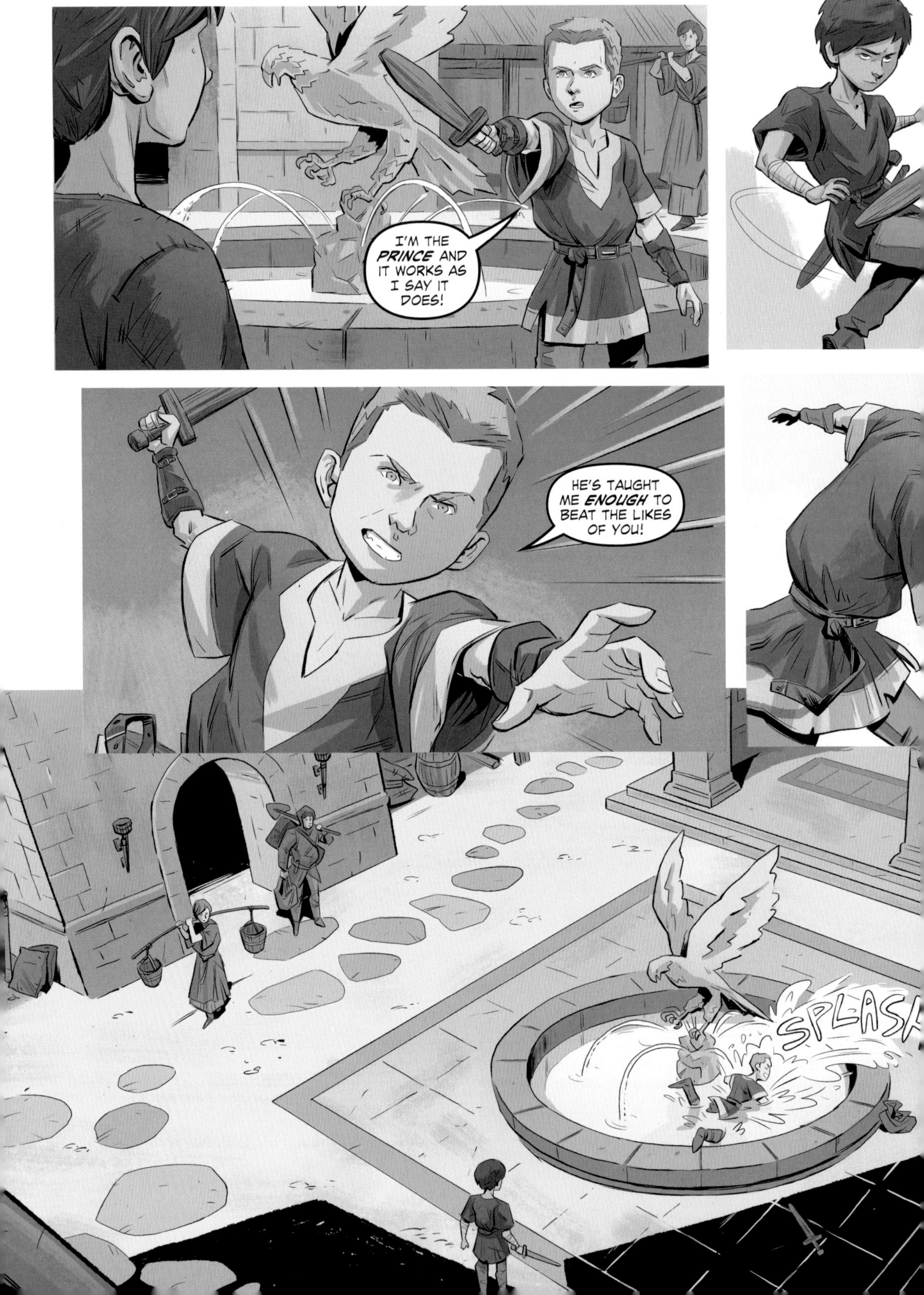
I'M THE PRINCE AND IT WORKS AS I SAY IT DOES!
HE'S TAUGHT ME ENOUGH TO BEAT THE LIKES OF YOU!
SPLASH

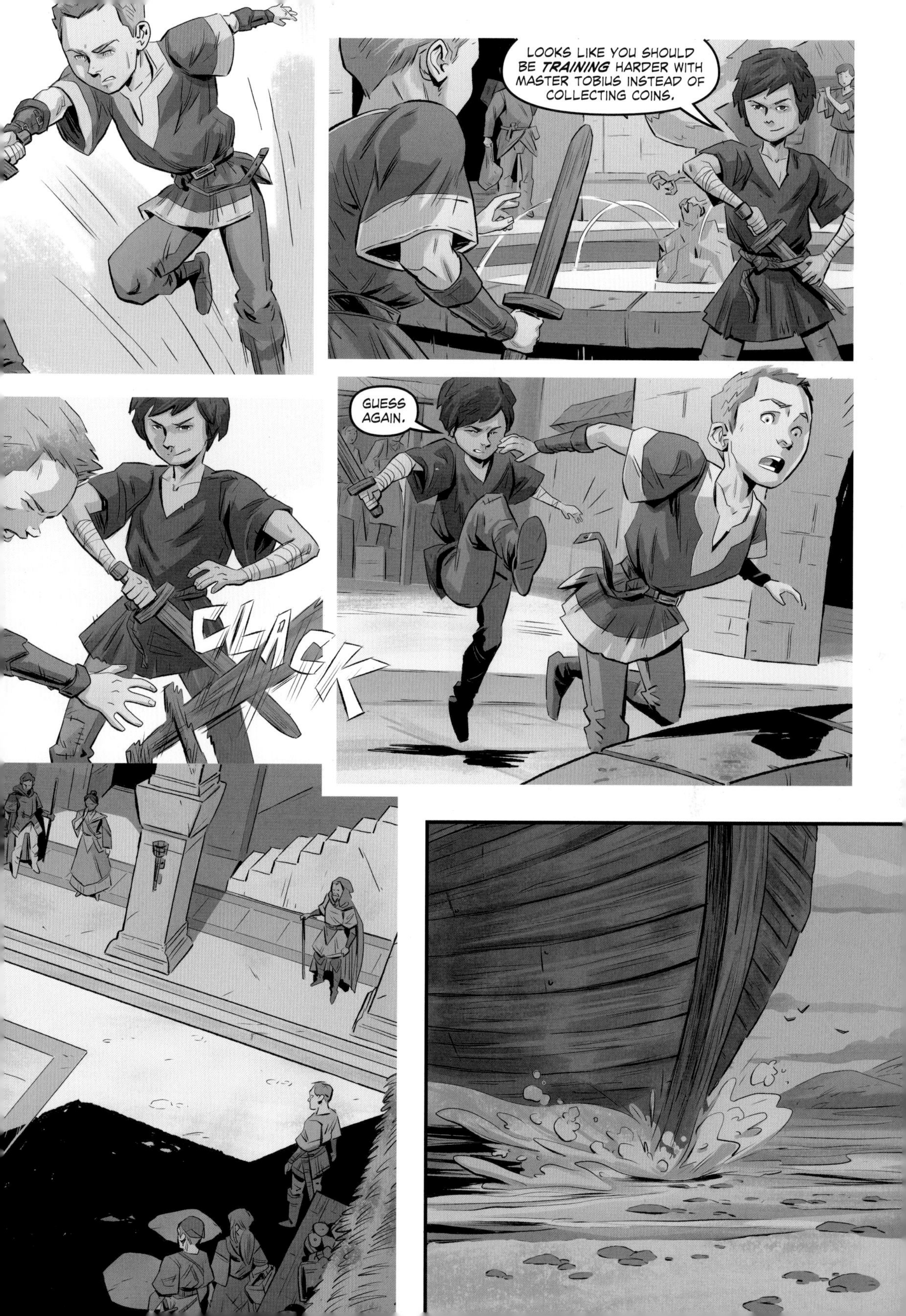
LOOKS LIKE YOU SHOULD BE ***TRAINING*** HARDER WITH MASTER TOBIUS INSTEAD OF COLLECTING COINS.
CLACK
GUESS AGAIN.

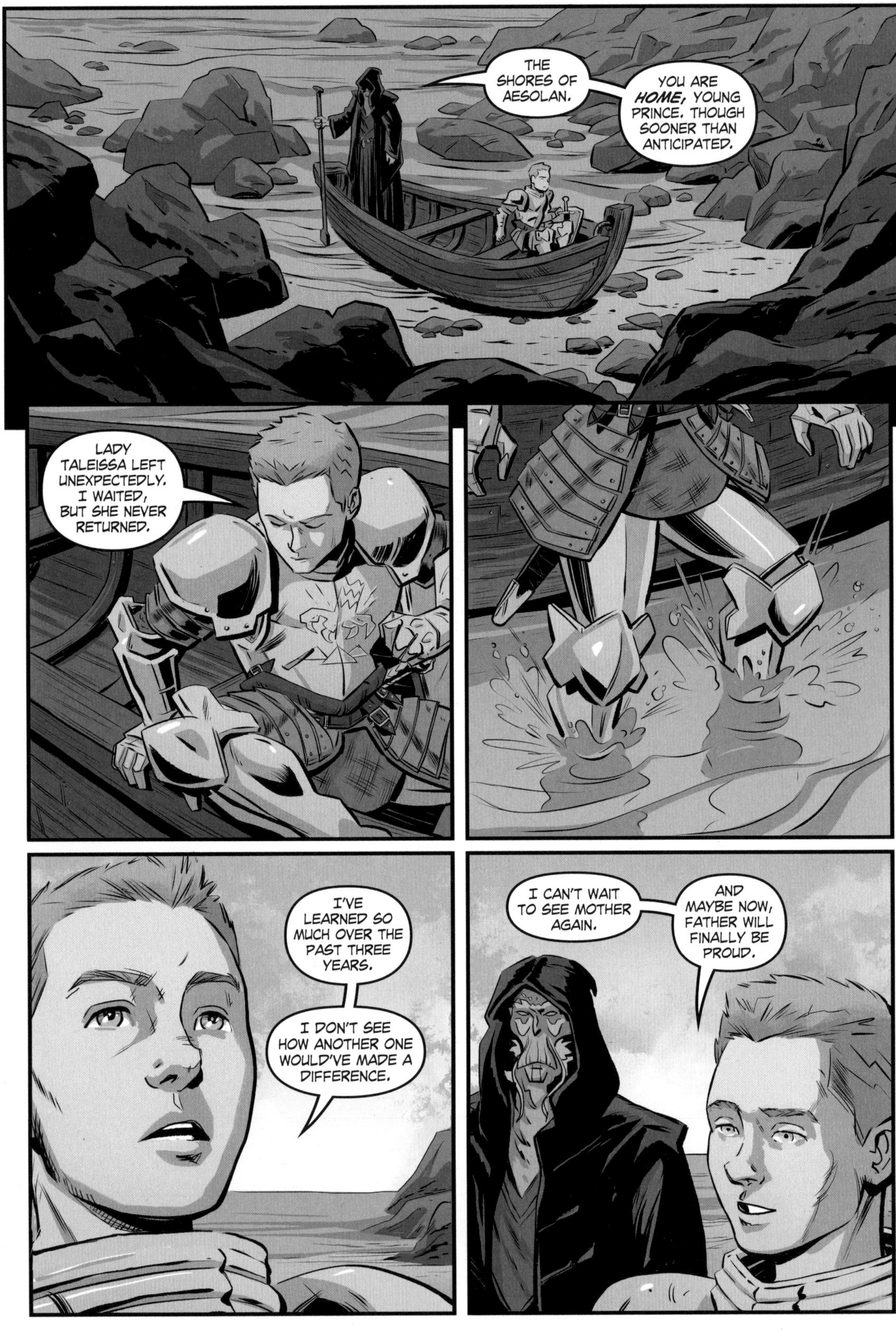
THE SHORES OF AESOLAN.
YOU ARE **HOME,** YOUNG PRINCE. THOUGH SOONER THAN ANTICIPATED.
LADY TALEISSA LEFT UNEXPECTEDLY. I WAITED, BUT SHE NEVER RETURNED.
I'VE LEARNED SO MUCH OVER THE PAST THREE YEARS.
I DON'T SEE HOW ANOTHER ONE WOULD'VE MADE A DIFFERENCE.
I CAN'T WAIT TO SEE MOTHER AGAIN.
AND MAYBE NOW, FATHER WILL FINALLY BE PROUD.

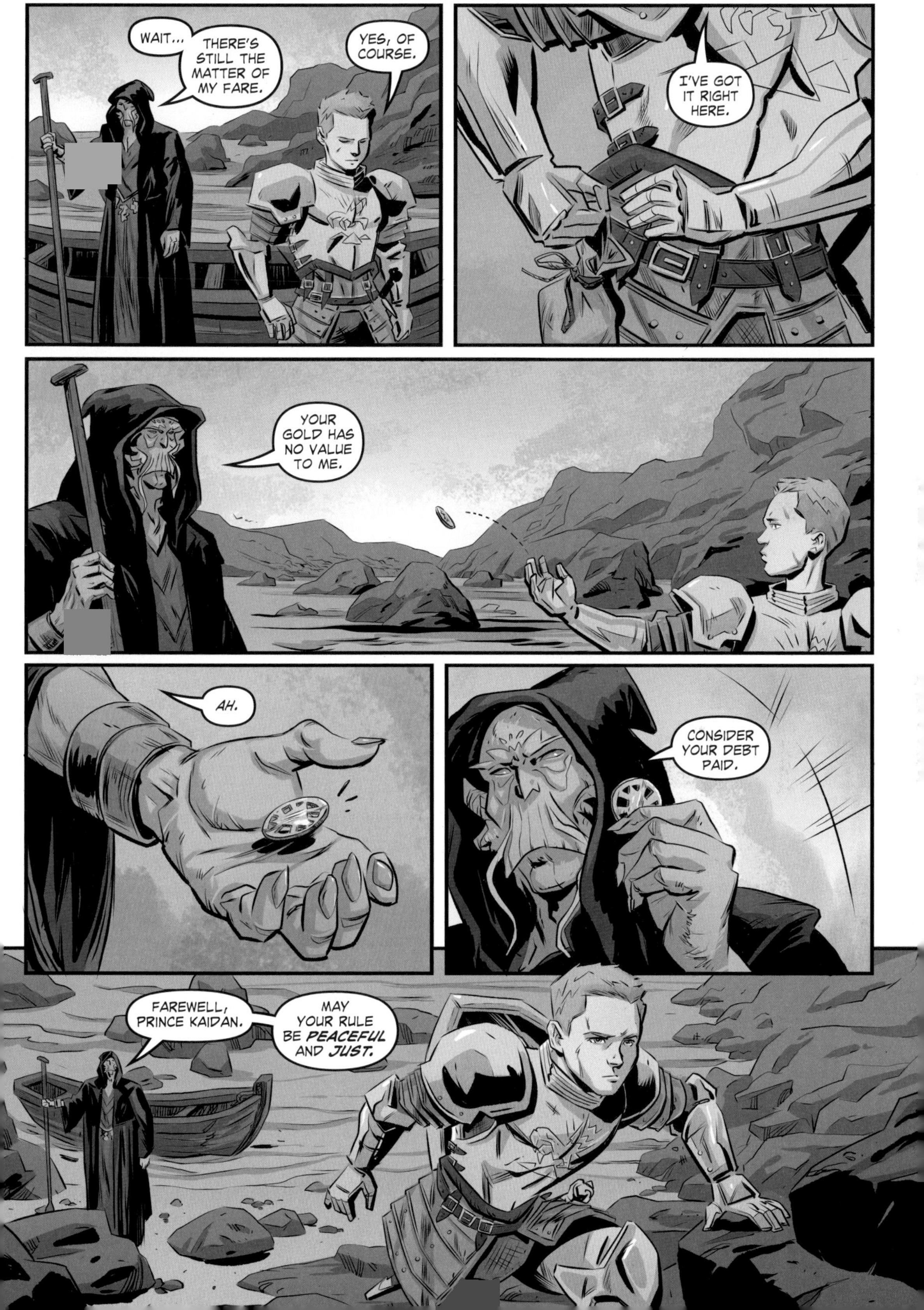
WAIT...
THERE'S STILL THE MATTER OF MY FARE.
YES, OF COURSE.
I'VE GOT IT RIGHT HERE.
YOUR GOLD HAS NO VALUE TO ME.
AH.
CONSIDER YOUR DEBT PAID.
FAREWELL, PRINCE KAIDAN.
MAY YOUR RULE BE *PEACEFUL* AND *JUST.*

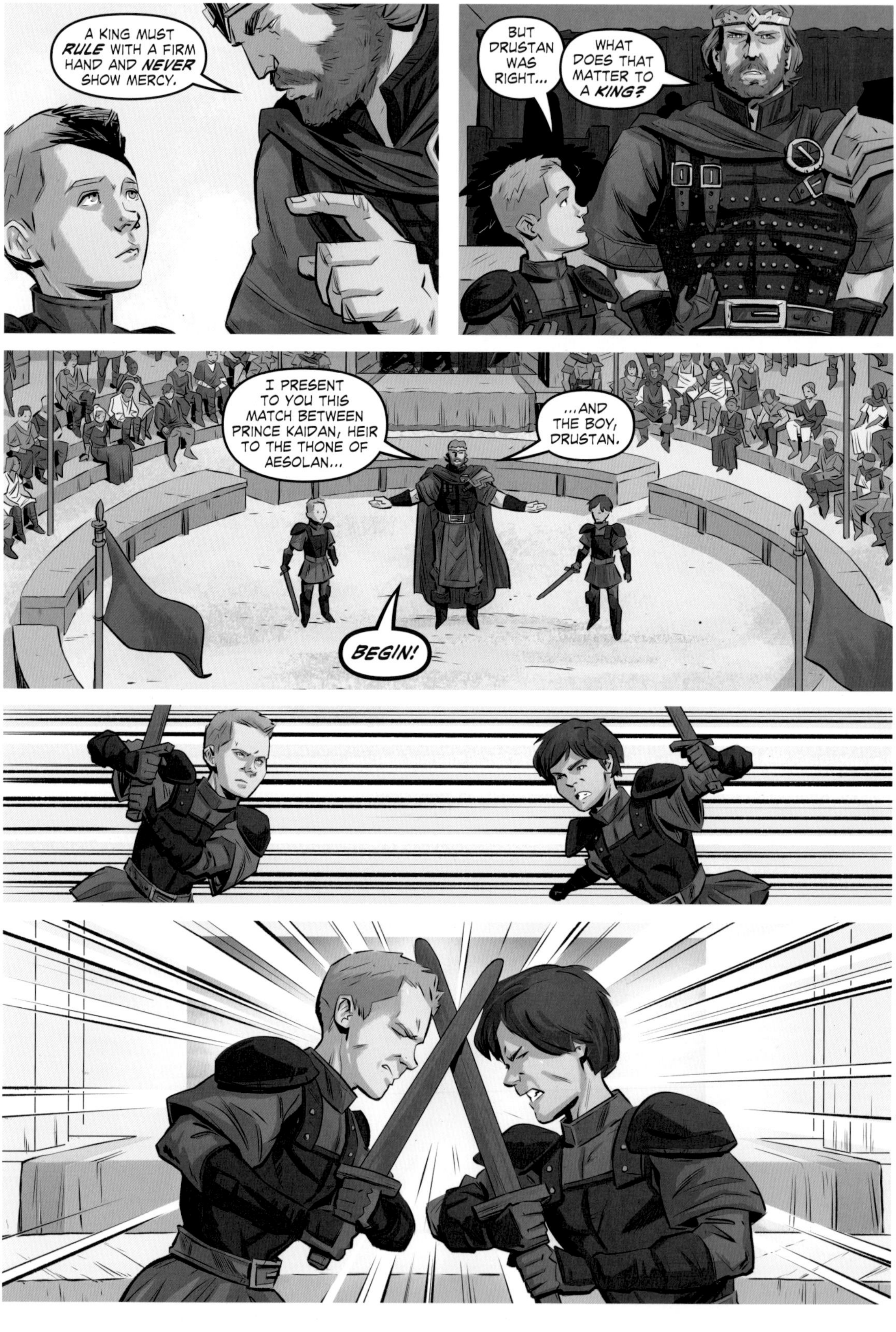
A KING MUST RULE WITH A FIRM HAND AND NEVER SHOW MERCY.
BUT DRUSTAN WAS RIGHT...
WHAT DOES THAT MATTER TO A KING?
I PRESENT TO YOU THIS MATCH BETWEEN PRINCE KAIDAN, HEIR TO THE THONE OF AESOLAN...
...AND THE BOY, DRUSTAN.
BEGIN!

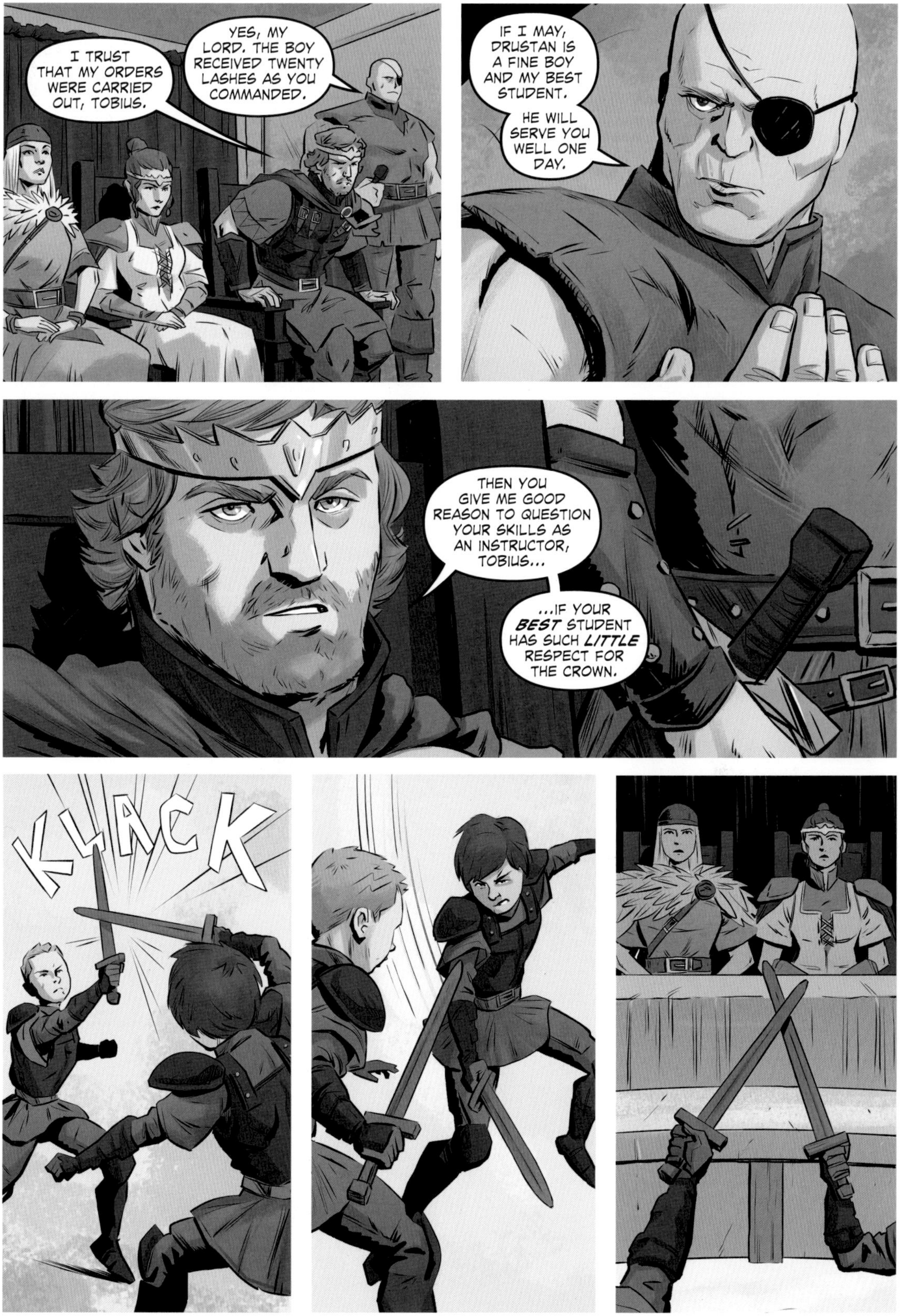
I TRUST THAT MY ORDERS WERE CARRIED OUT, TOBIUS.
YES, MY LORD. THE BOY RECEIVED TWENTY LASHES AS YOU COMMANDED.
IF I MAY, DRUSTAN IS A FINE BOY AND MY BEST STUDENT.
HE WILL SERVE YOU WELL ONE DAY.
THEN YOU GIVE ME GOOD REASON TO QUESTION YOUR SKILLS AS AN INSTRUCTOR, TOBIUS...
...IF YOUR ***BEST*** STUDENT HAS SUCH ***LITTLE*** RESPECT FOR THE CROWN.
KLACK

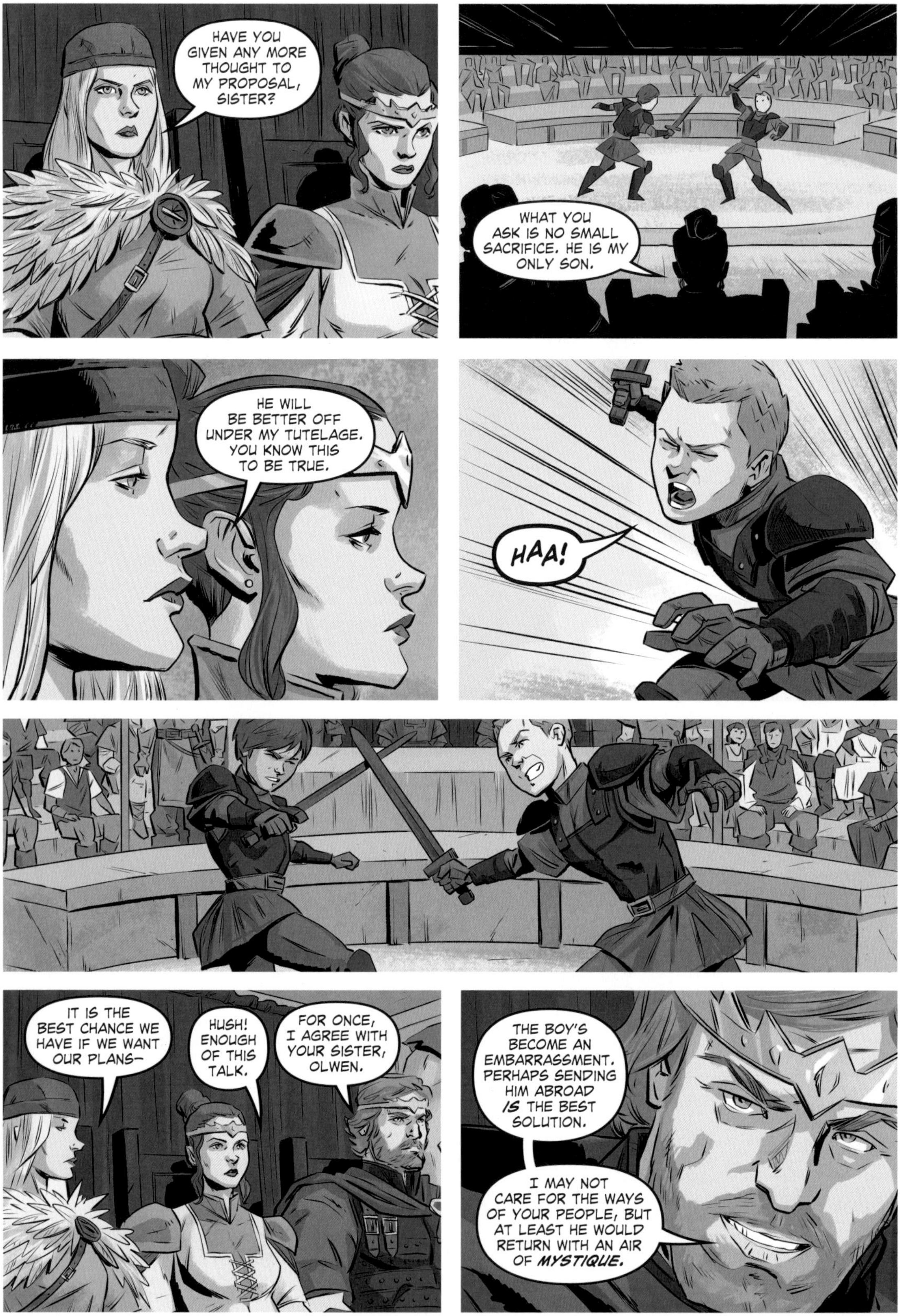
HAVE YOU GIVEN ANY MORE THOUGHT TO MY PROPOSAL, SISTER?
WHAT YOU ASK IS NO SMALL SACRIFICE. HE IS MY ONLY SON.
HE WILL BE BETTER OFF UNDER MY TUTELAGE. YOU KNOW THIS TO BE TRUE.
HAA!
IT IS THE BEST CHANCE WE HAVE IF WE WANT OUR PLANS—
HUSH! ENOUGH OF THIS TALK.
FOR ONCE, I AGREE WITH YOUR SISTER, OLWEN.
THE BOY'S BECOME AN EMBARRASSMENT. PERHAPS SENDING HIM ABROAD *IS* THE BEST SOLUTION.
I MAY NOT CARE FOR THE WAYS OF YOUR PEOPLE, BUT AT LEAST HE WOULD RETURN WITH AN AIR OF ***MYSTIQUE.***

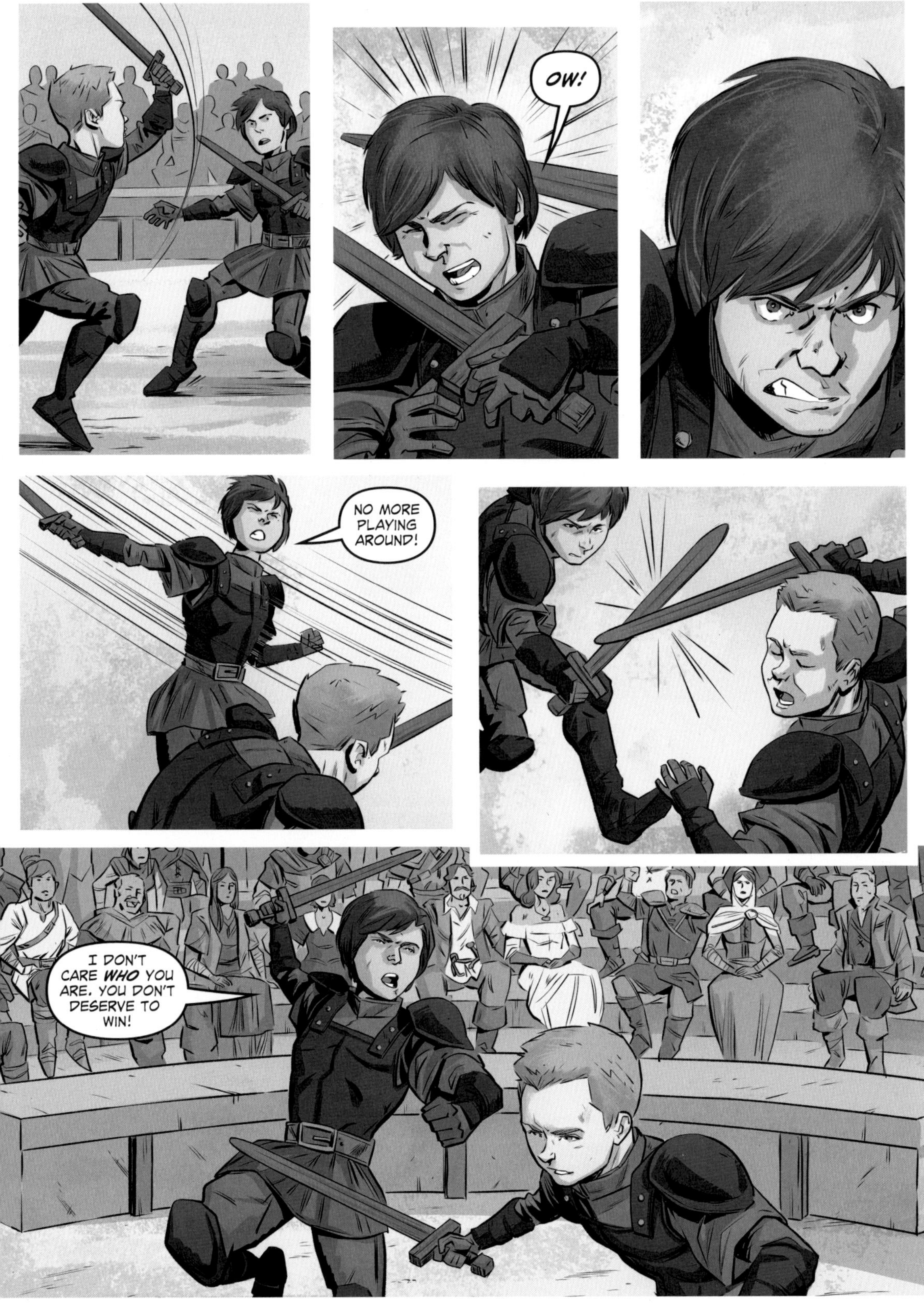
OW!
NO MORE PLAYING AROUND!
I DON'T CARE **WHO** YOU ARE. YOU DON'T DESERVE TO WIN!

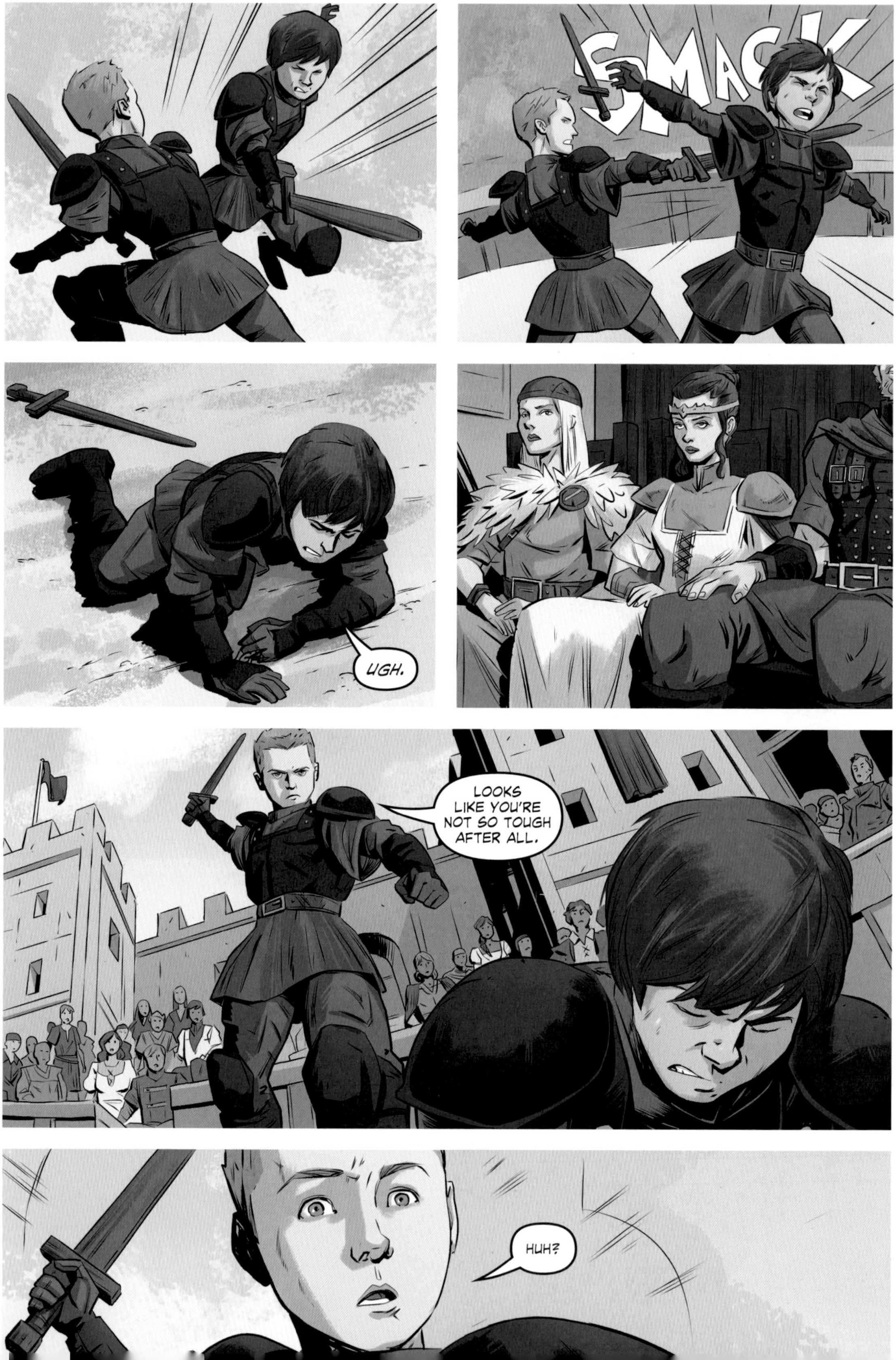
SMACK
UGH.
LOOKS LIKE YOU'RE NOT SO TOUGH AFTER ALL.
HUH?

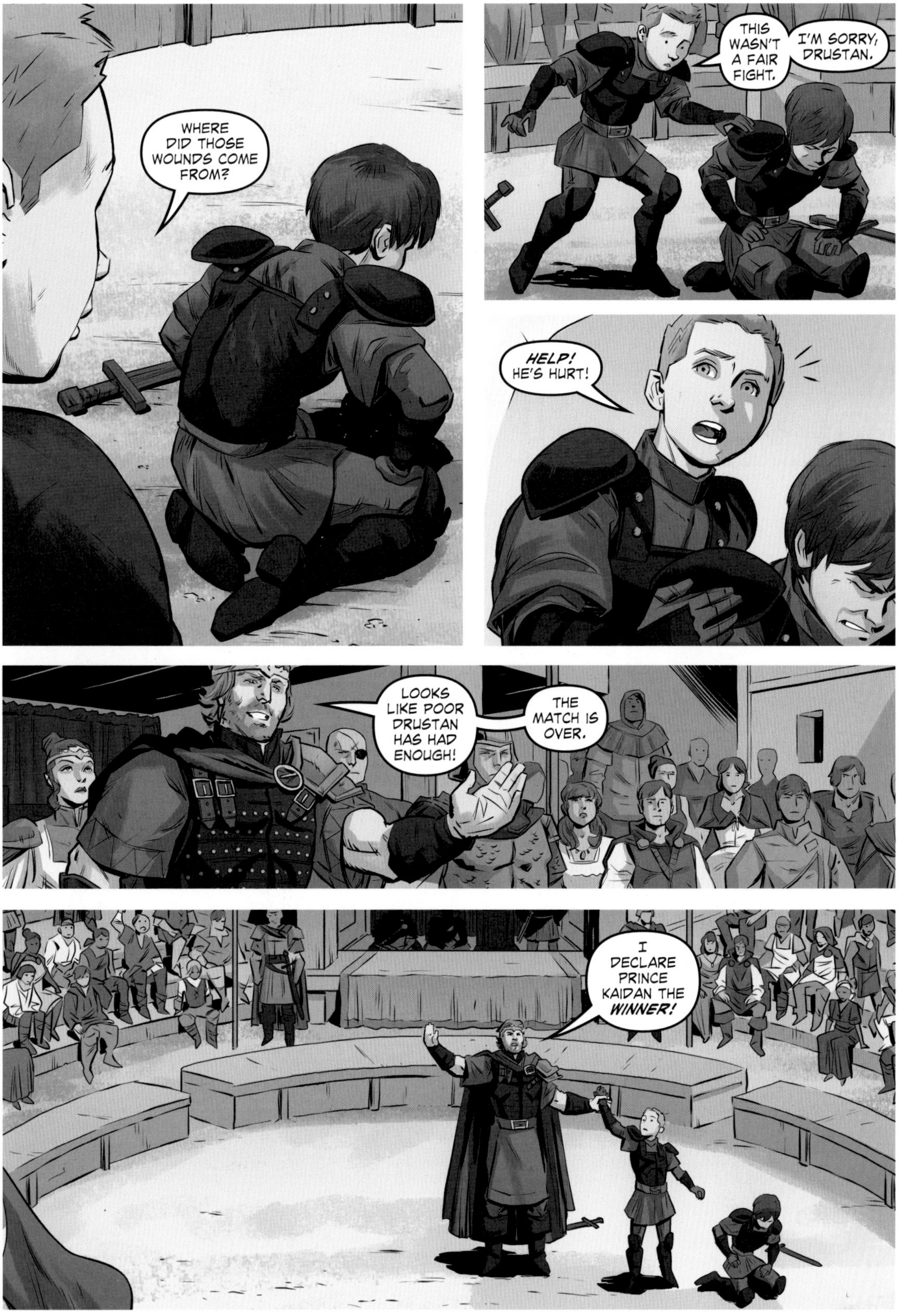
WHERE DID THOSE WOUNDS COME FROM?
THIS WASN'T A FAIR FIGHT.
I'M SORRY, DRUSTAN.
HELP! HE'S HURT!
LOOKS LIKE POOR DRUSTAN HAS HAD ENOUGH!
THE MATCH IS OVER.
I DECLARE PRINCE KAIDAN THE *WINNER!*

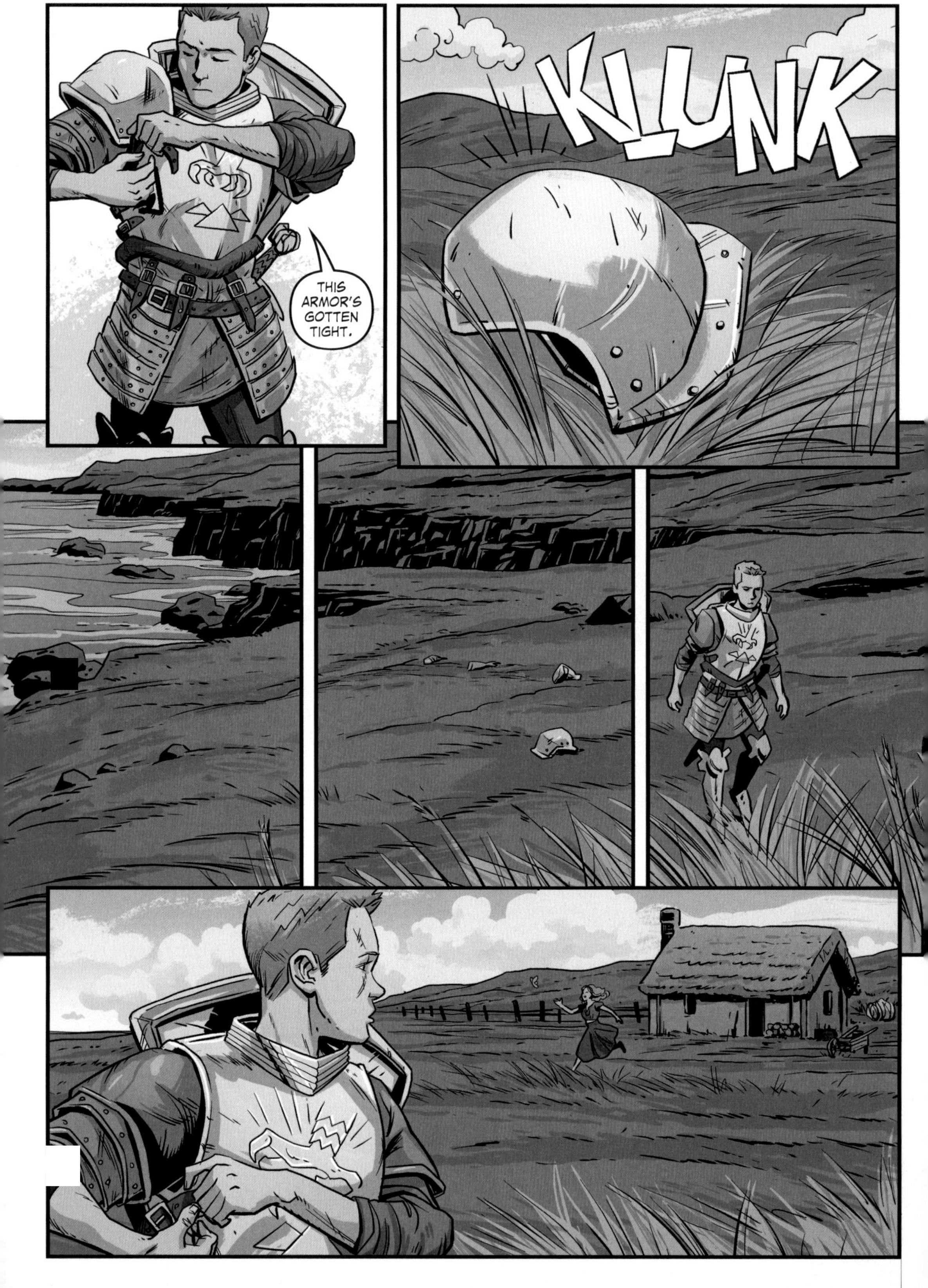
THIS ARMOR'S GOTTEN TIGHT.
KLUNK

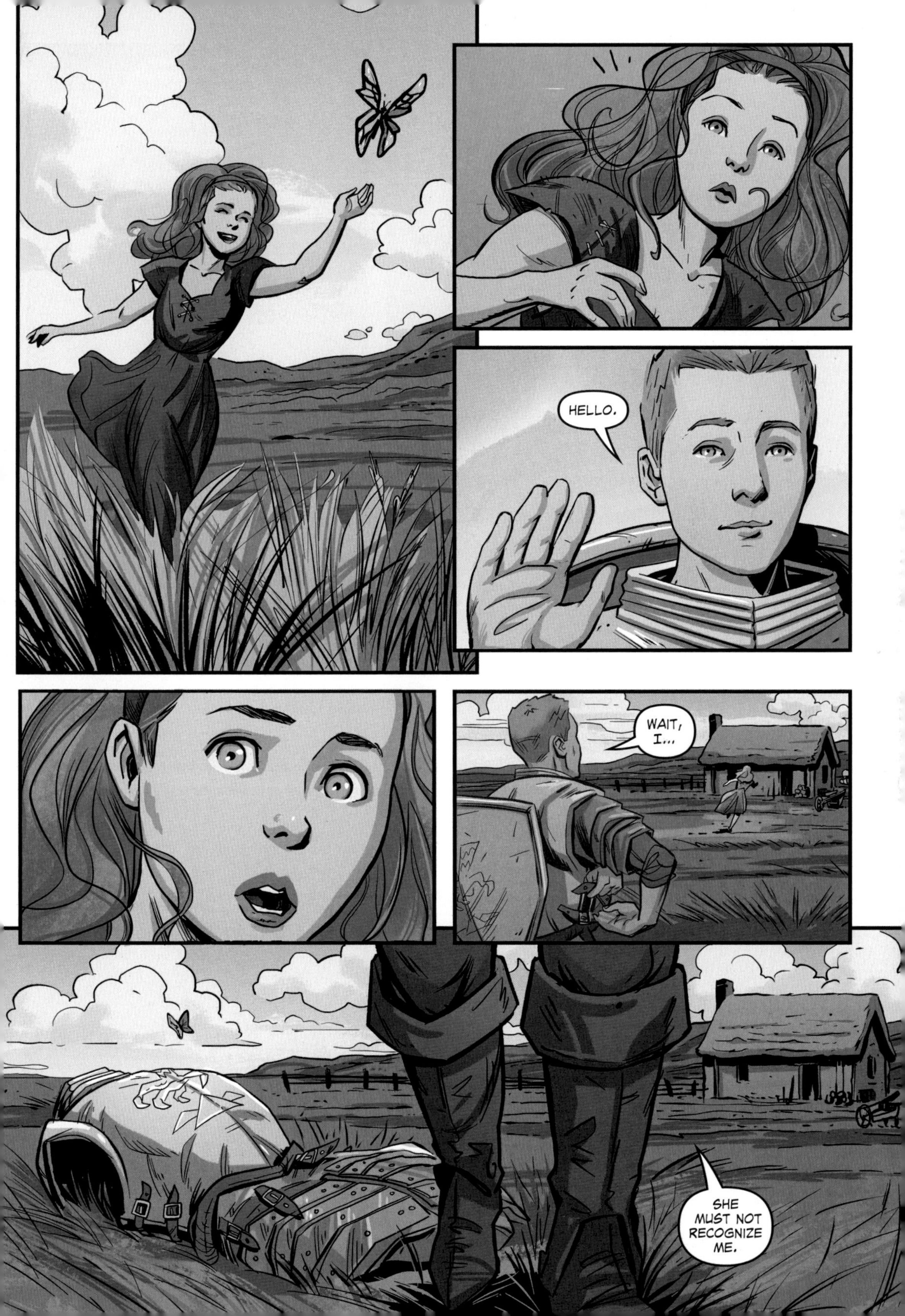
HELLO.
WAIT, I...
SHE MUST NOT RECOGNIZE ME.

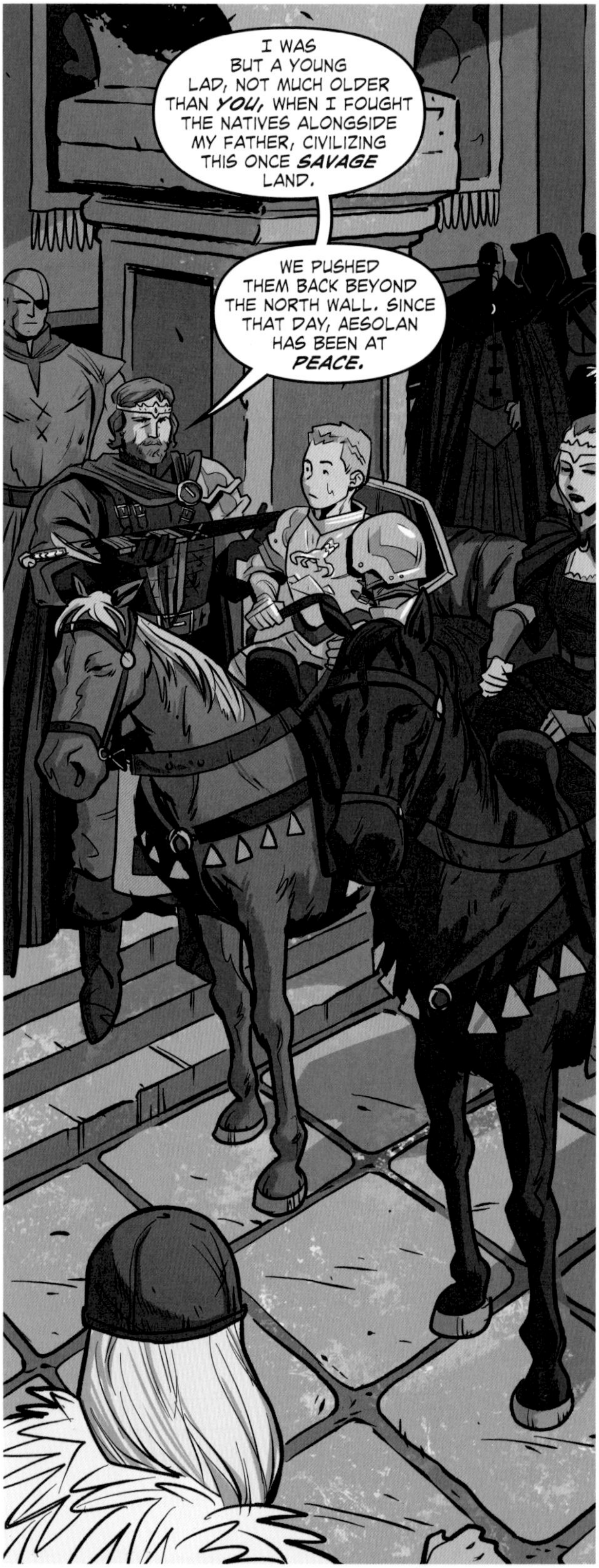
I WAS BUT A YOUNG LAD, NOT MUCH OLDER THAN *YOU,* WHEN I FOUGHT THE NATIVES ALONGSIDE MY FATHER, CIVILIZING THIS ONCE *SAVAGE* LAND.
WE PUSHED THEM BACK BEYOND THE NORTH WALL. SINCE THAT DAY, AESOLAN HAS BEEN AT *PEACE.*

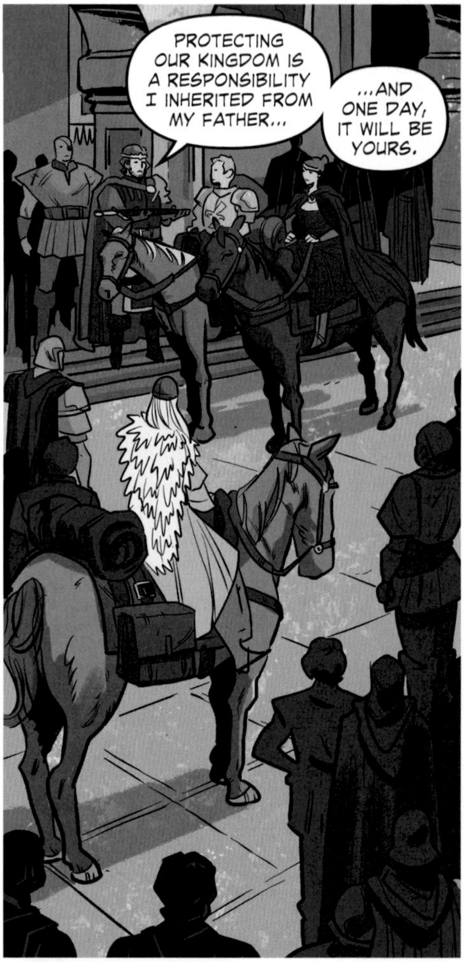
PROTECTING OUR KINGDOM IS A RESPONSIBILITY I INHERITED FROM MY FATHER...
...AND ONE DAY, IT WILL BE YOURS.

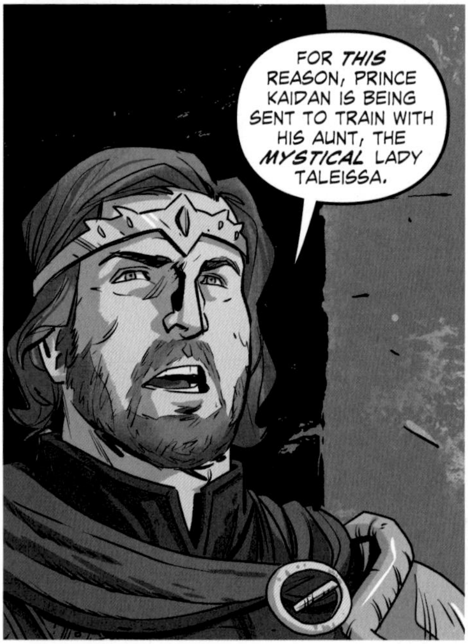
FOR *THIS* REASON, PRINCE KAIDAN IS BEING SENT TO TRAIN WITH HIS AUNT, THE *MYSTICAL* LADY TALEISSA.

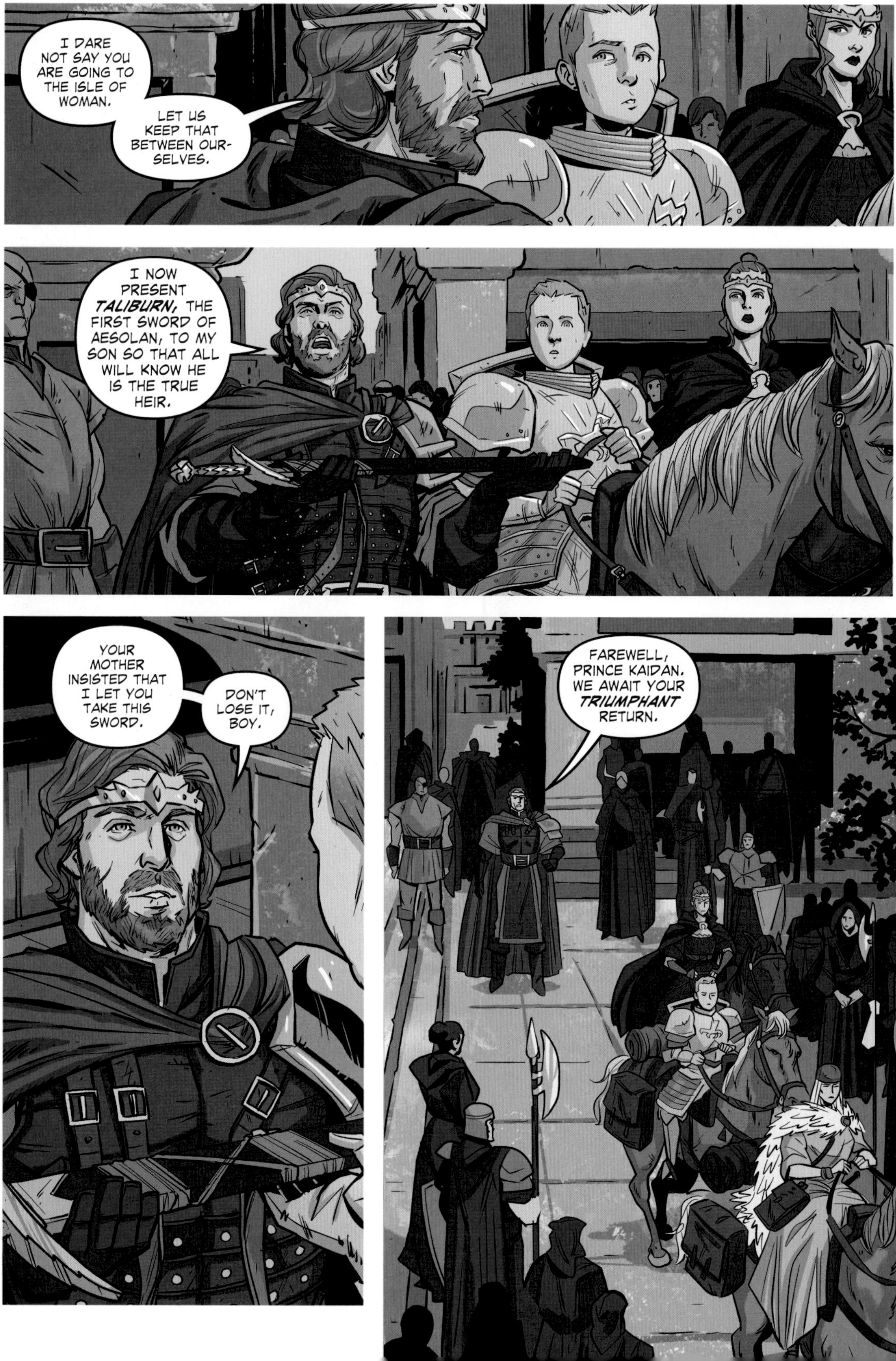
I DARE NOT SAY YOU ARE GOING TO THE ISLE OF WOMAN.
LET US KEEP THAT BETWEEN OURSELVES.
I NOW PRESENT *TALIBURN,* THE FIRST SWORD OF AESOLAN, TO MY SON SO THAT ALL WILL KNOW HE IS THE TRUE HEIR.
YOUR MOTHER INSISTED THAT I LET YOU TAKE THIS SWORD.
DON'T LOSE IT, BOY.
FAREWELL, PRINCE KAIDAN. WE AWAIT YOUR *TRIUMPHANT* RETURN.

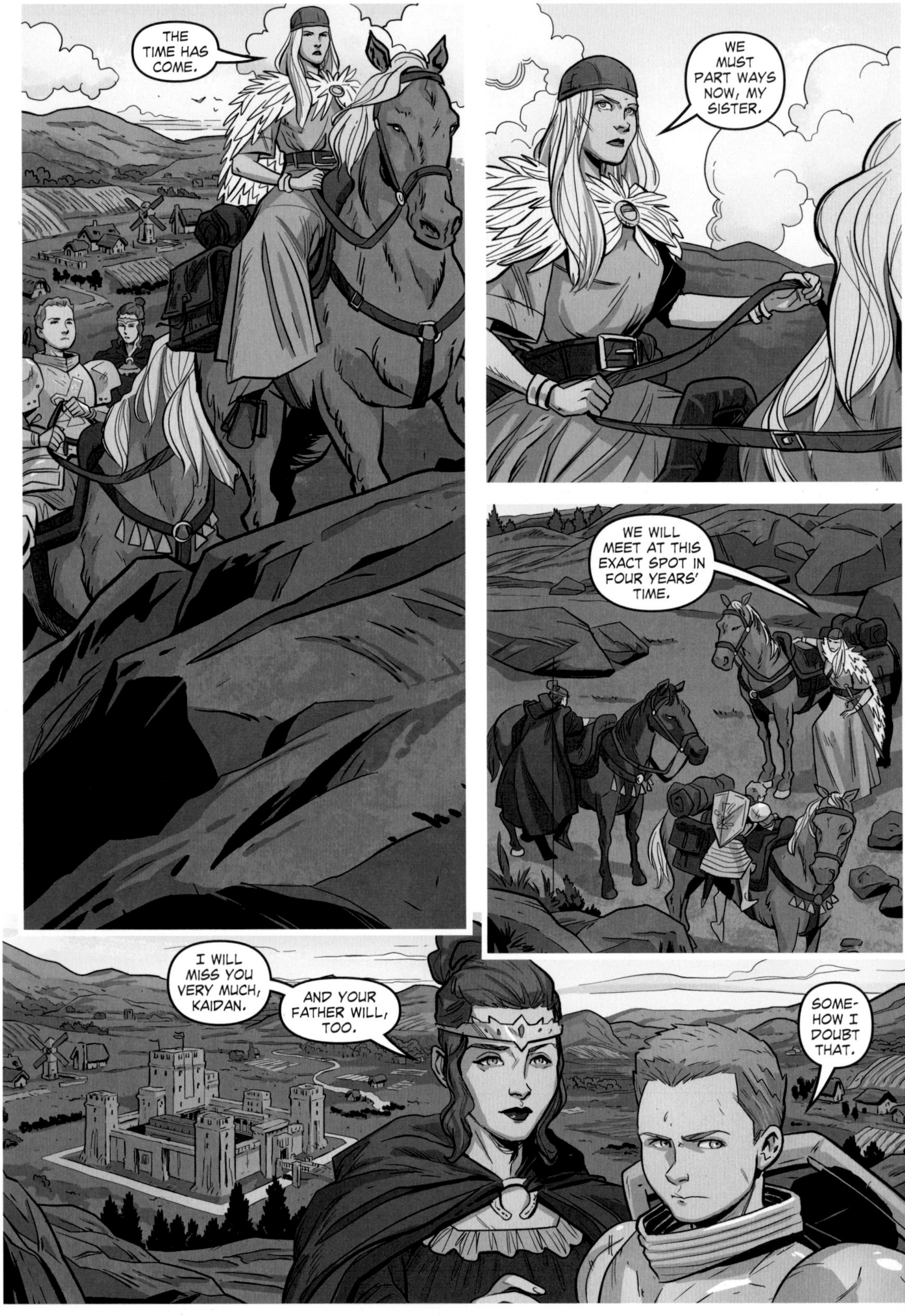
THE TIME HAS COME.
WE MUST PART WAYS NOW, MY SISTER.
WE WILL MEET AT THIS EXACT SPOT IN FOUR YEARS' TIME.
I WILL MISS YOU VERY MUCH, KAIDAN.
AND YOUR FATHER WILL, TOO.
SOME-HOW I DOUBT THAT.

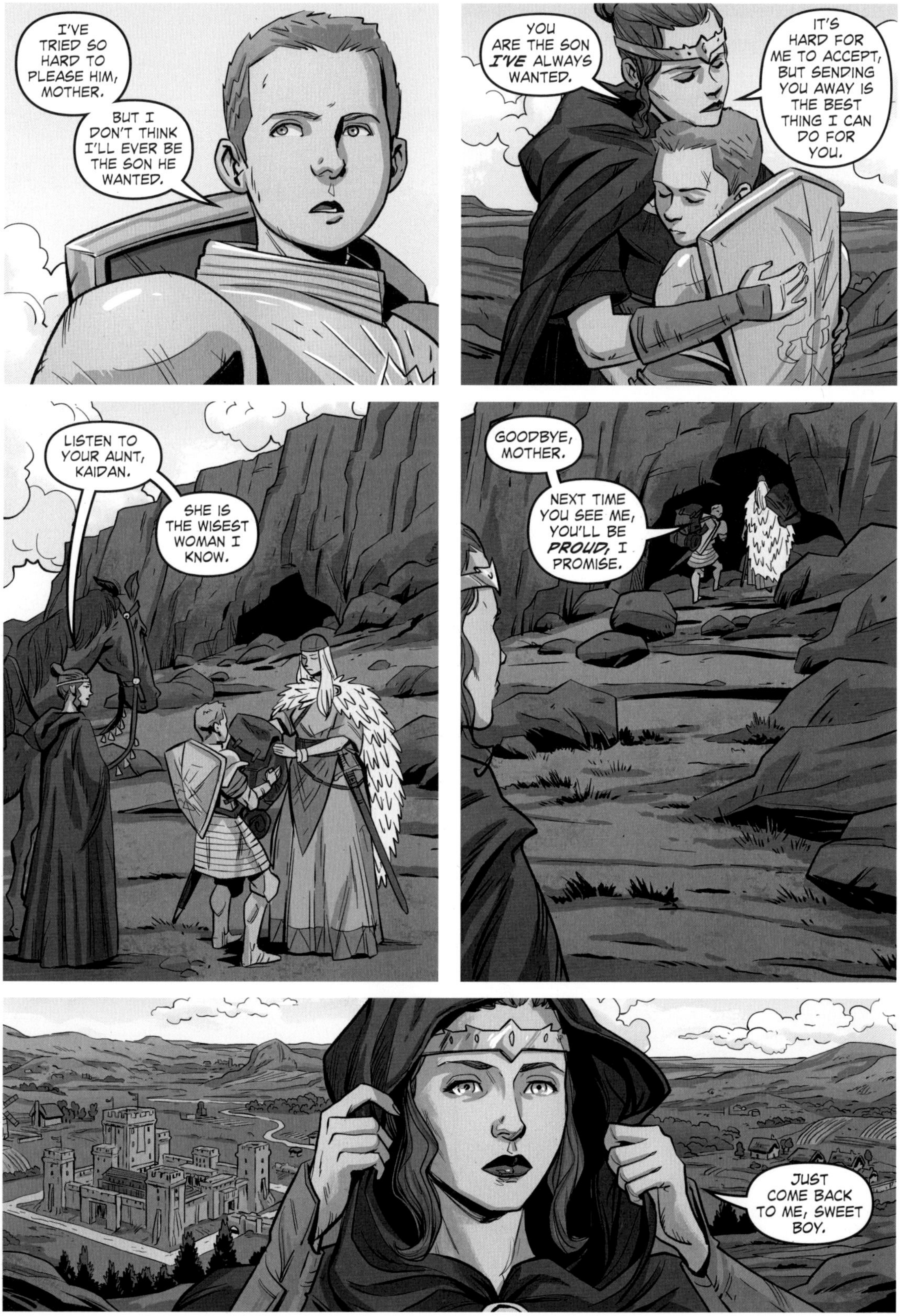
I'VE TRIED SO HARD TO PLEASE HIM, MOTHER.
BUT I DON'T THINK I'LL EVER BE THE SON HE WANTED.
YOU ARE THE SON I'VE ALWAYS WANTED.
IT'S HARD FOR ME TO ACCEPT, BUT SENDING YOU AWAY IS THE BEST THING I CAN DO FOR YOU.
LISTEN TO YOUR AUNT, KAIDAN.
SHE IS THE WISEST WOMAN I KNOW.
GOODBYE, MOTHER.
NEXT TIME YOU SEE ME, YOU'LL BE PROUD, I PROMISE.
JUST COME BACK TO ME, SWEET BOY.

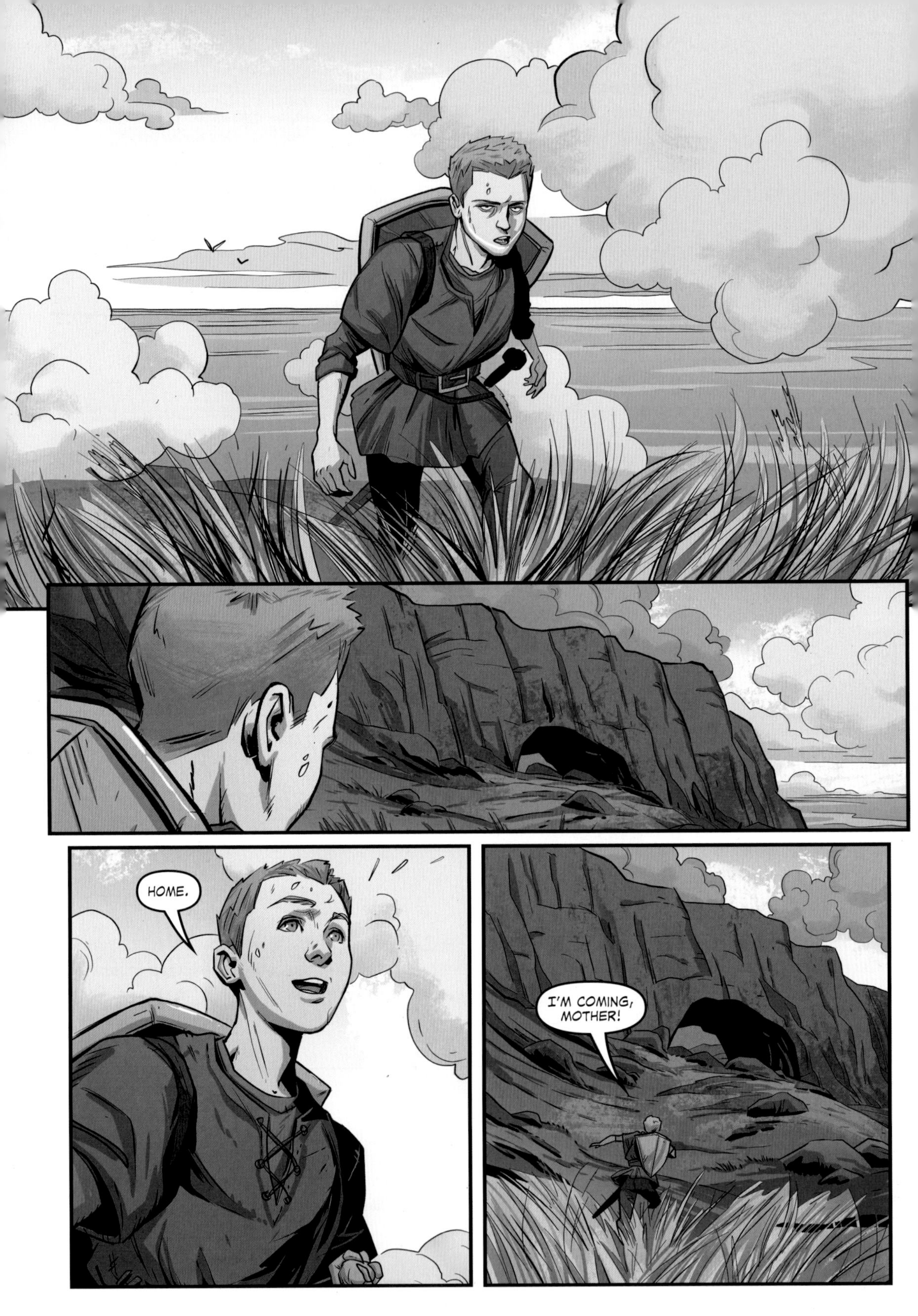
HOME.
I'M COMING, MOTHER!

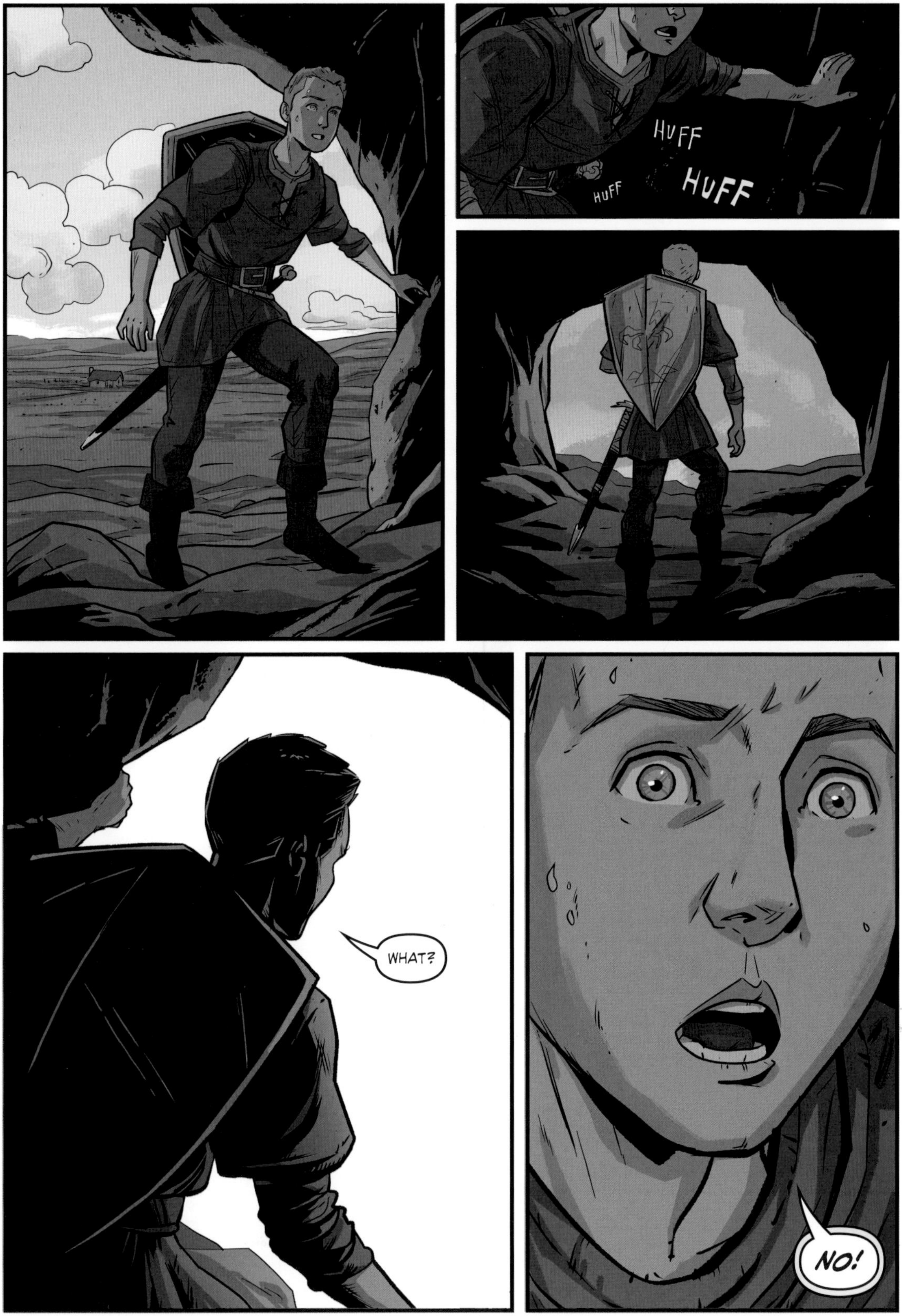
HUFF
HUFF
HUFF
WHAT?
NO!

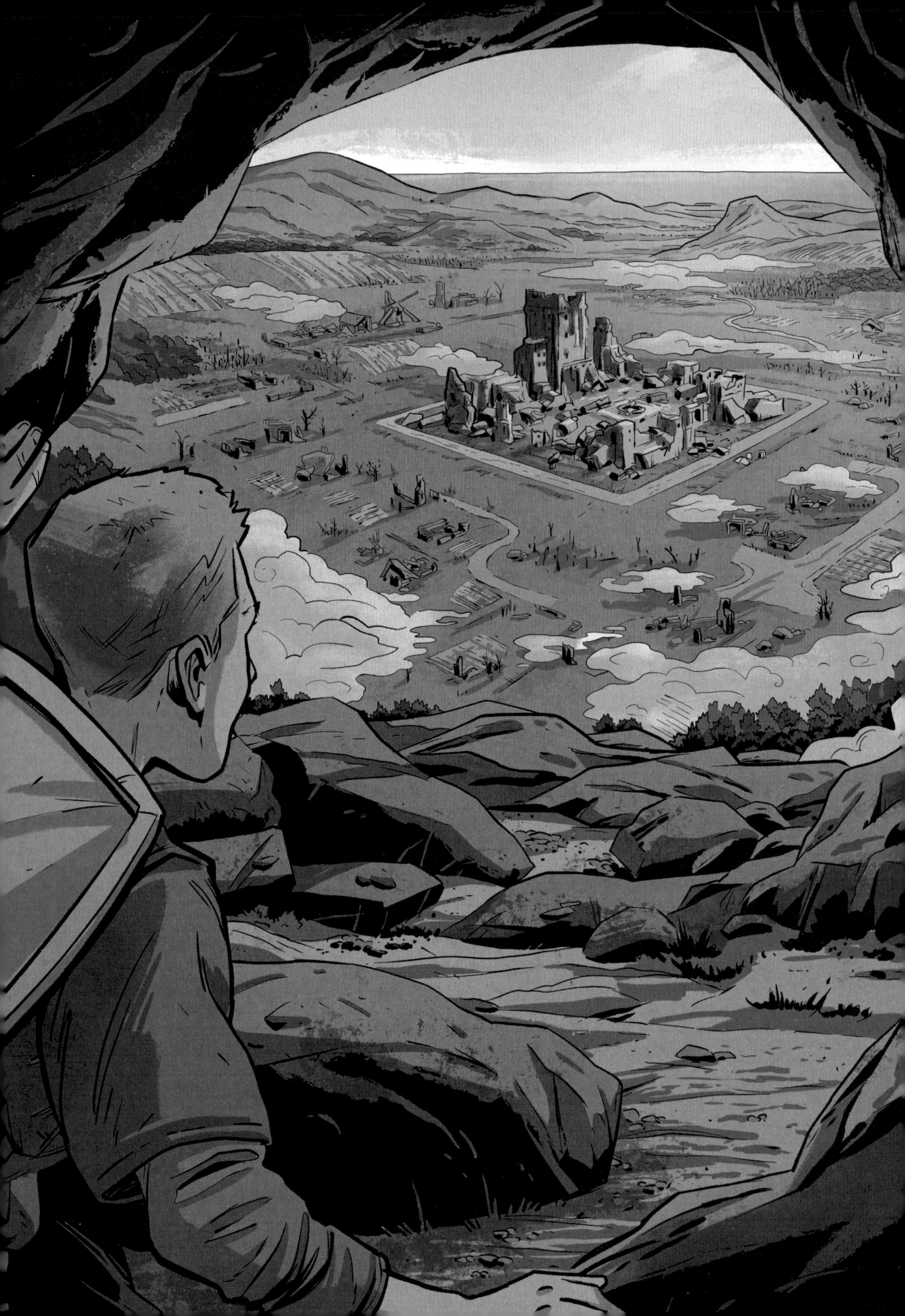

Chapter 2

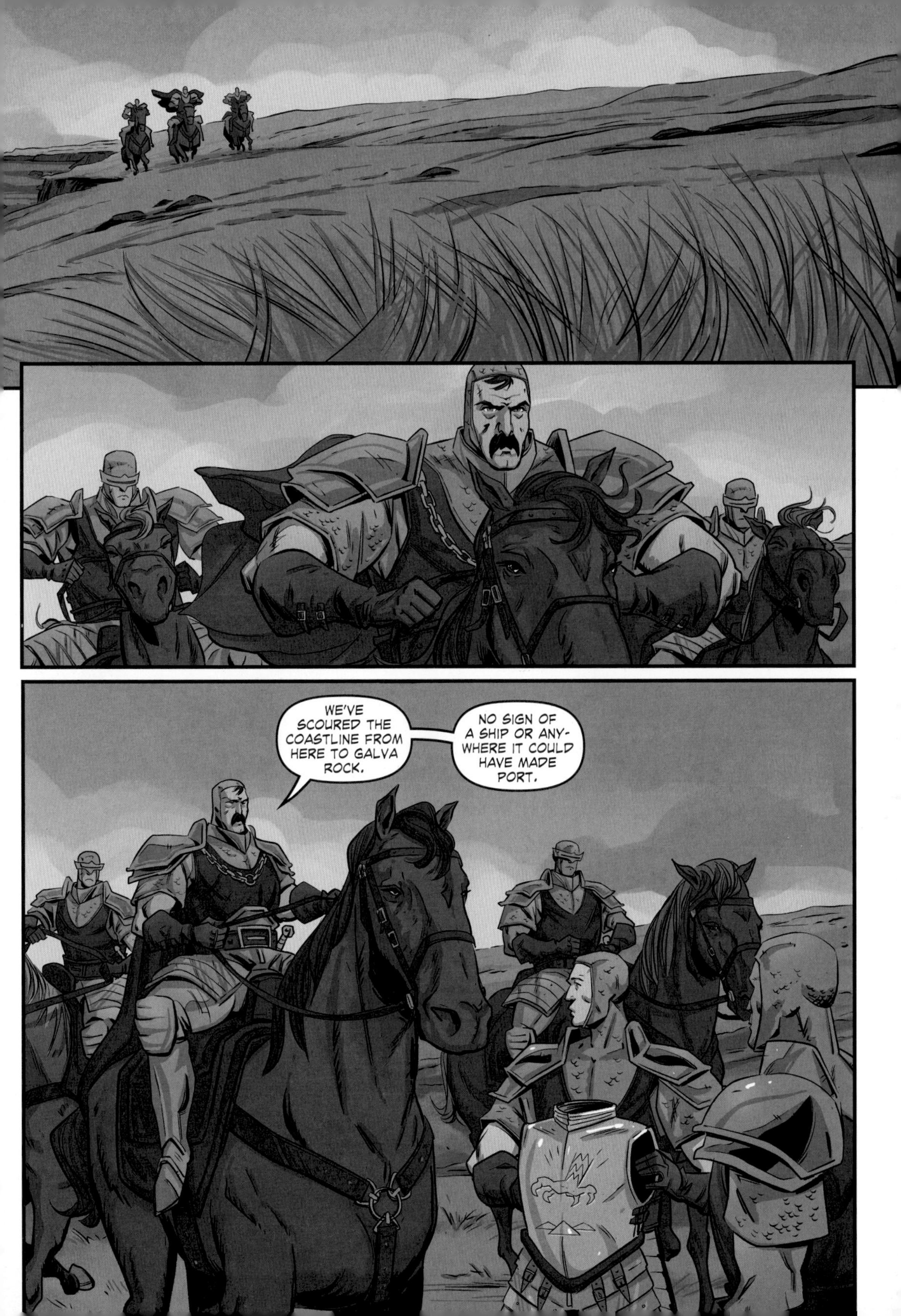
WE'VE SCOURED THE COASTLINE FROM HERE TO GALVA ROCK.
NO SIGN OF A SHIP OR ANY-WHERE IT COULD HAVE MADE PORT.

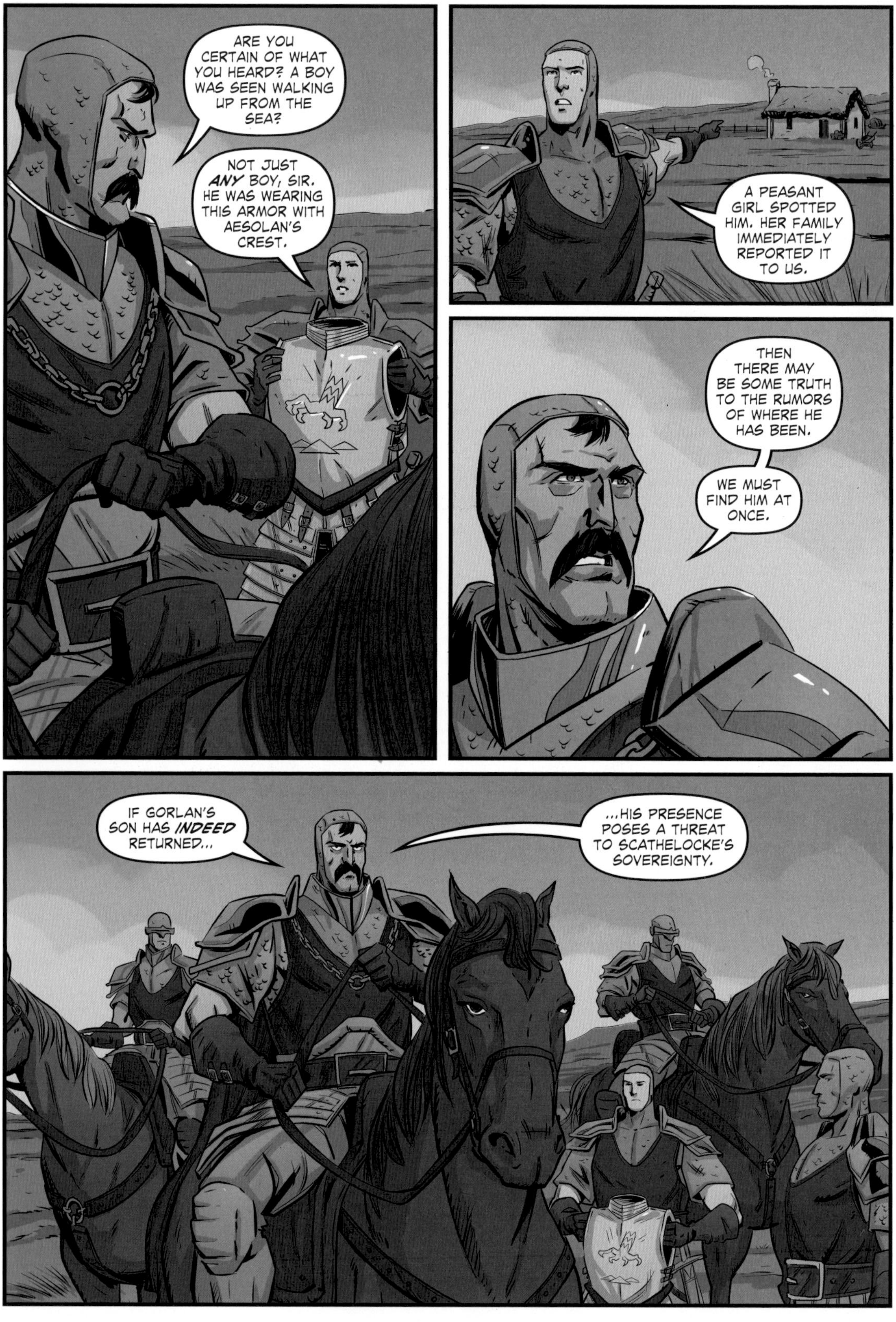
ARE YOU CERTAIN OF WHAT YOU HEARD? A BOY WAS SEEN WALKING UP FROM THE SEA?
NOT JUST *ANY* BOY, SIR. HE WAS WEARING THIS ARMOR WITH AESOLAN'S CREST.
A PEASANT GIRL SPOTTED HIM. HER FAMILY IMMEDIATELY REPORTED IT TO US.
THEN THERE MAY BE SOME TRUTH TO THE RUMORS OF WHERE HE HAS BEEN.
WE MUST FIND HIM AT ONCE.
IF GORLAN'S SON HAS *INDEED* RETURNED...
...HIS PRESENCE POSES A THREAT TO SCATHELOCKE'S SOVEREIGNTY.

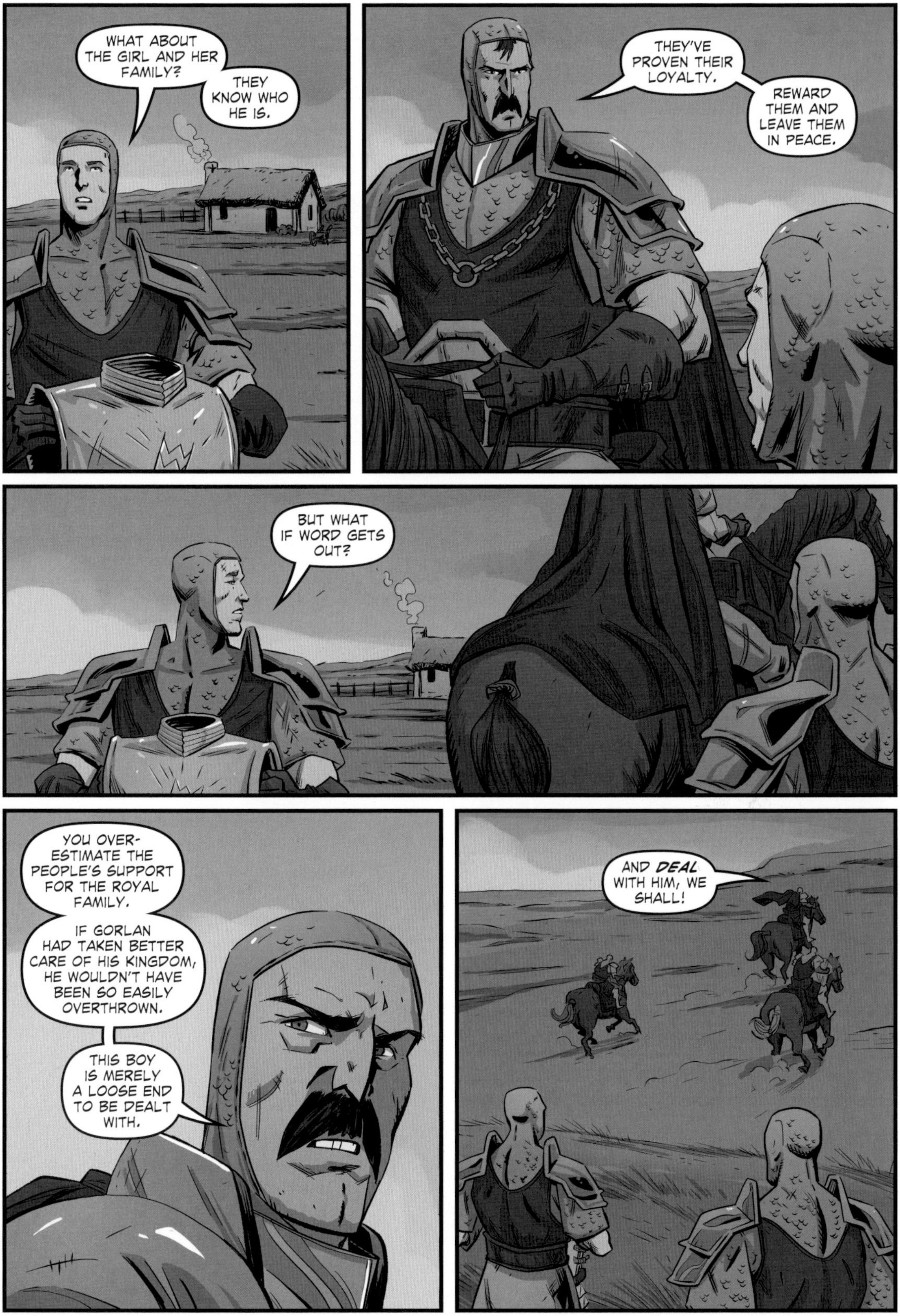
WHAT ABOUT THE GIRL AND HER FAMILY?
THEY KNOW WHO HE IS.
THEY'VE PROVEN THEIR LOYALTY.
REWARD THEM AND LEAVE THEM IN PEACE.
BUT WHAT IF WORD GETS OUT?
YOU OVER-ESTIMATE THE PEOPLE'S SUPPORT FOR THE ROYAL FAMILY.
IF GORLAN HAD TAKEN BETTER CARE OF HIS KINGDOM, HE WOULDN'T HAVE BEEN SO EASILY OVERTHROWN.
THIS BOY IS MERELY A LOOSE END TO BE DEALT WITH.
AND DEAL WITH HIM, WE SHALL!

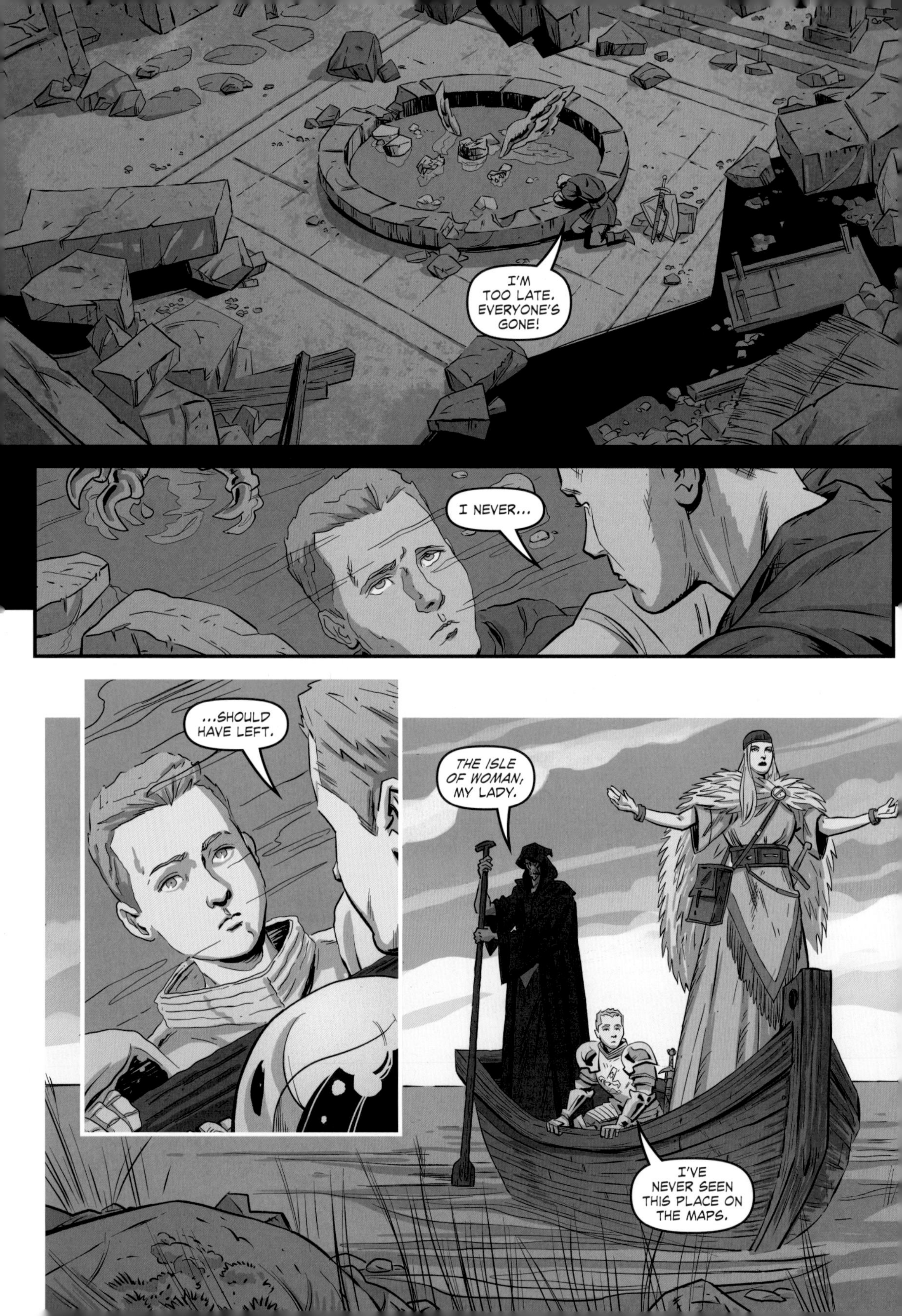
I'M TOO LATE. EVERYONE'S GONE!
I NEVER...
...SHOULD HAVE LEFT.
THE ISLE OF WOMAN, MY LADY.
I'VE NEVER SEEN THIS PLACE ON THE MAPS.

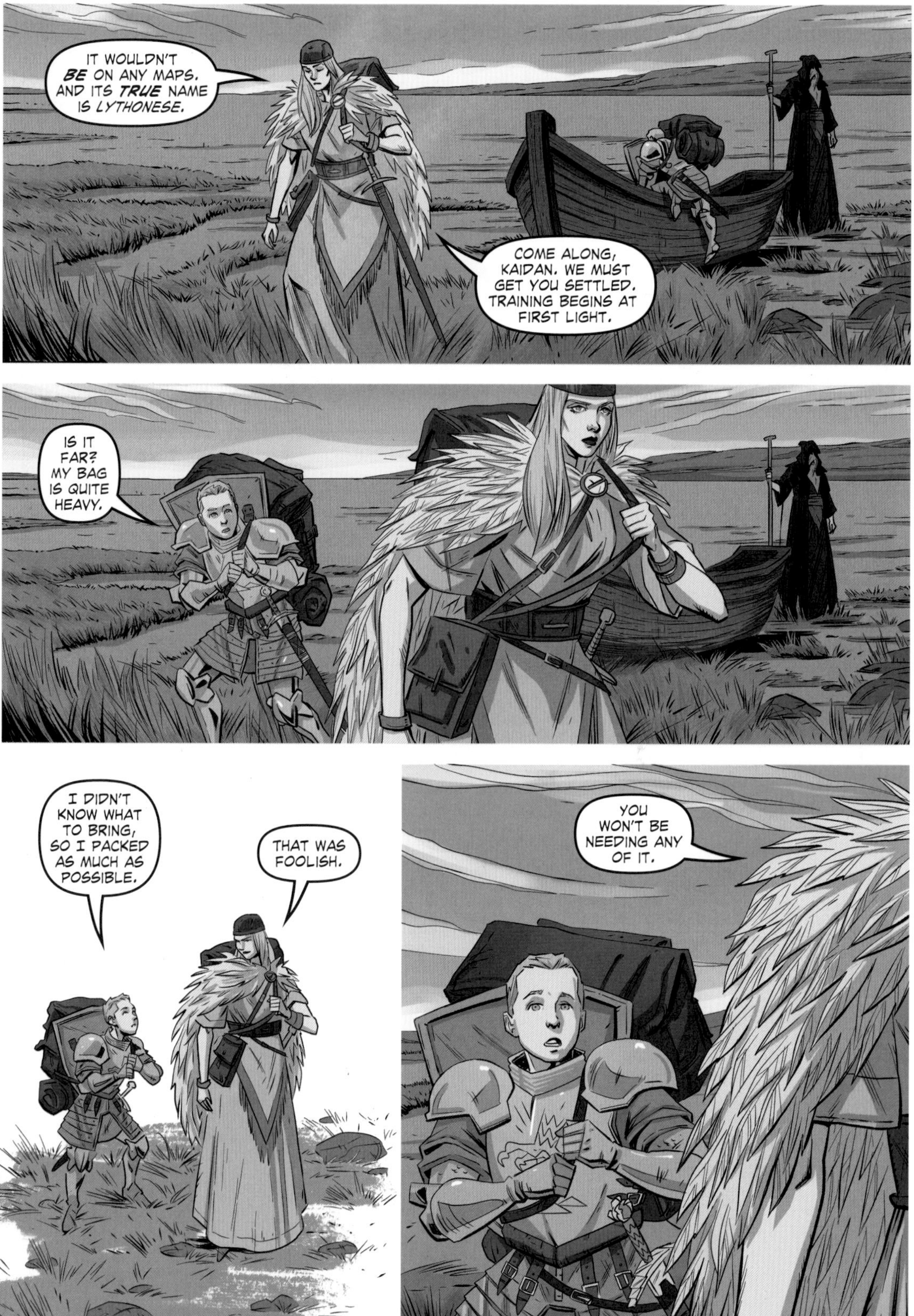
IT WOULDN'T *BE* ON ANY MAPS. AND ITS *TRUE* NAME IS *LYTHONESE.*
COME ALONG, KAIDAN. WE MUST GET YOU SETTLED. TRAINING BEGINS AT FIRST LIGHT.
IS IT FAR? MY BAG IS QUITE HEAVY.
I DIDN'T KNOW WHAT TO BRING, SO I PACKED AS MUCH AS POSSIBLE.
THAT WAS FOOLISH.
YOU WON'T BE NEEDING ANY OF IT.

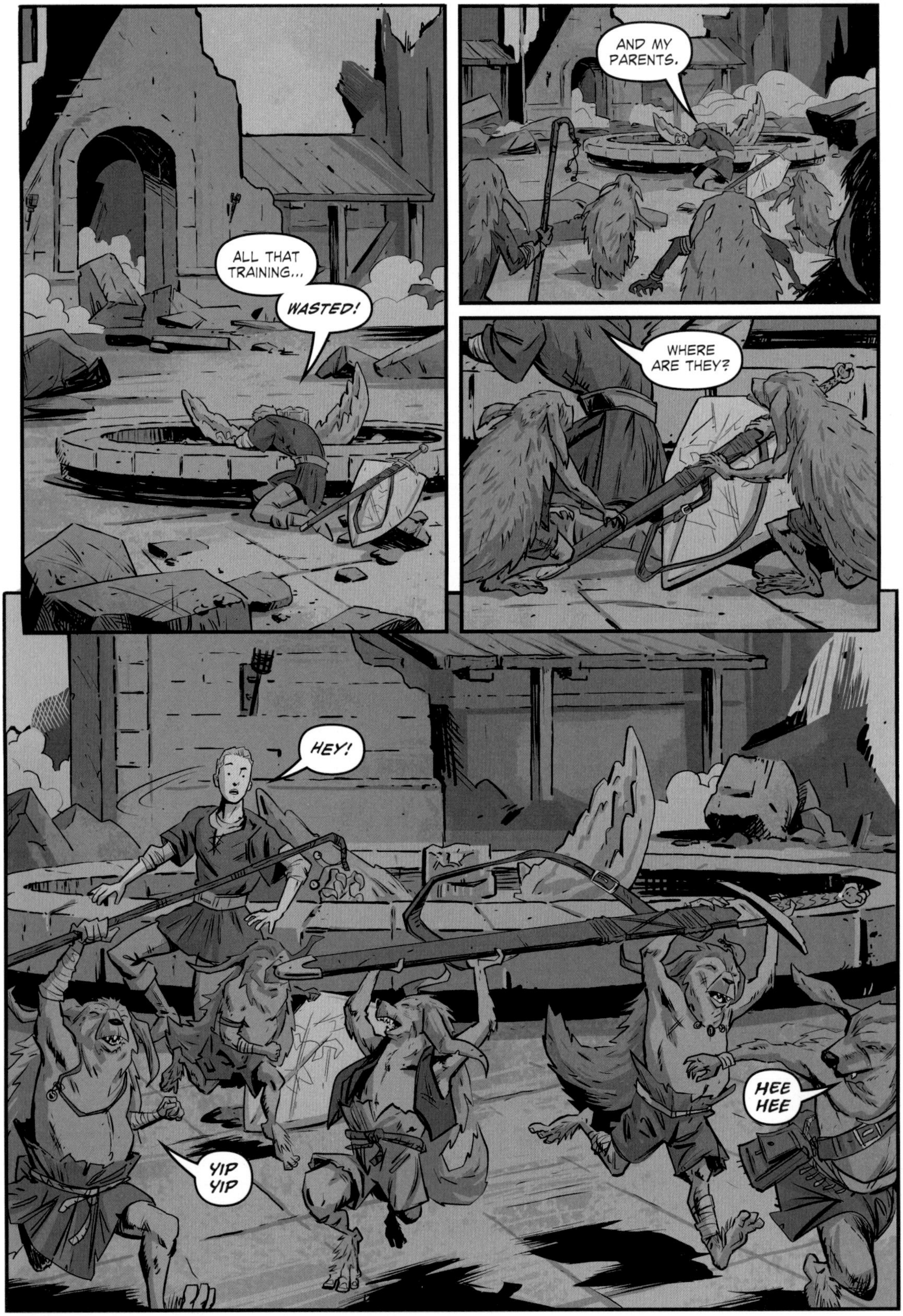

ALL THAT TRAINING...
WASTED!
AND MY PARENTS.
WHERE ARE THEY?
HEY!
YIP YIP
HEE HEE

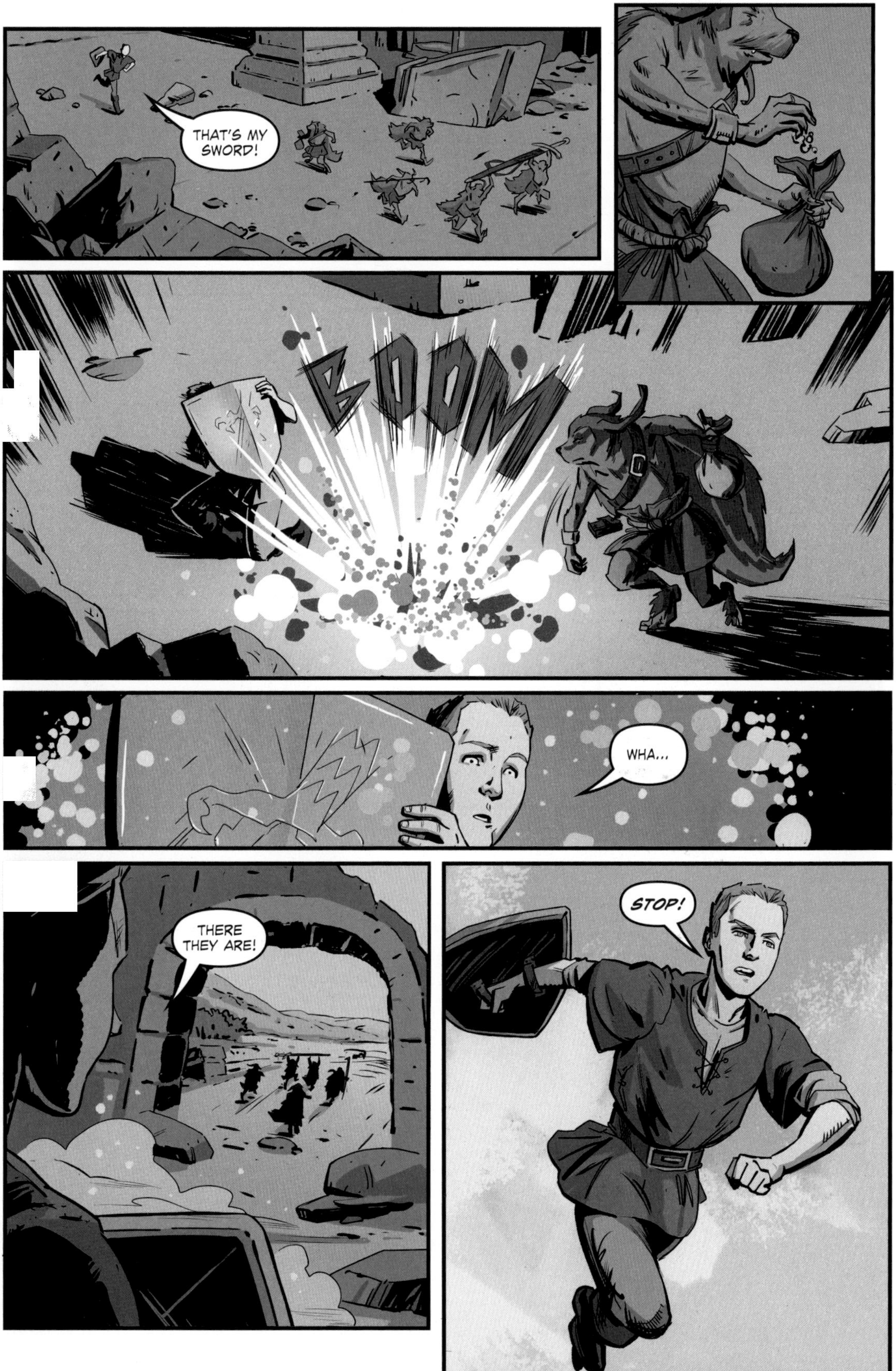
THAT'S MY SWORD!
BOOM
WHA...
THERE THEY ARE!
STOP!

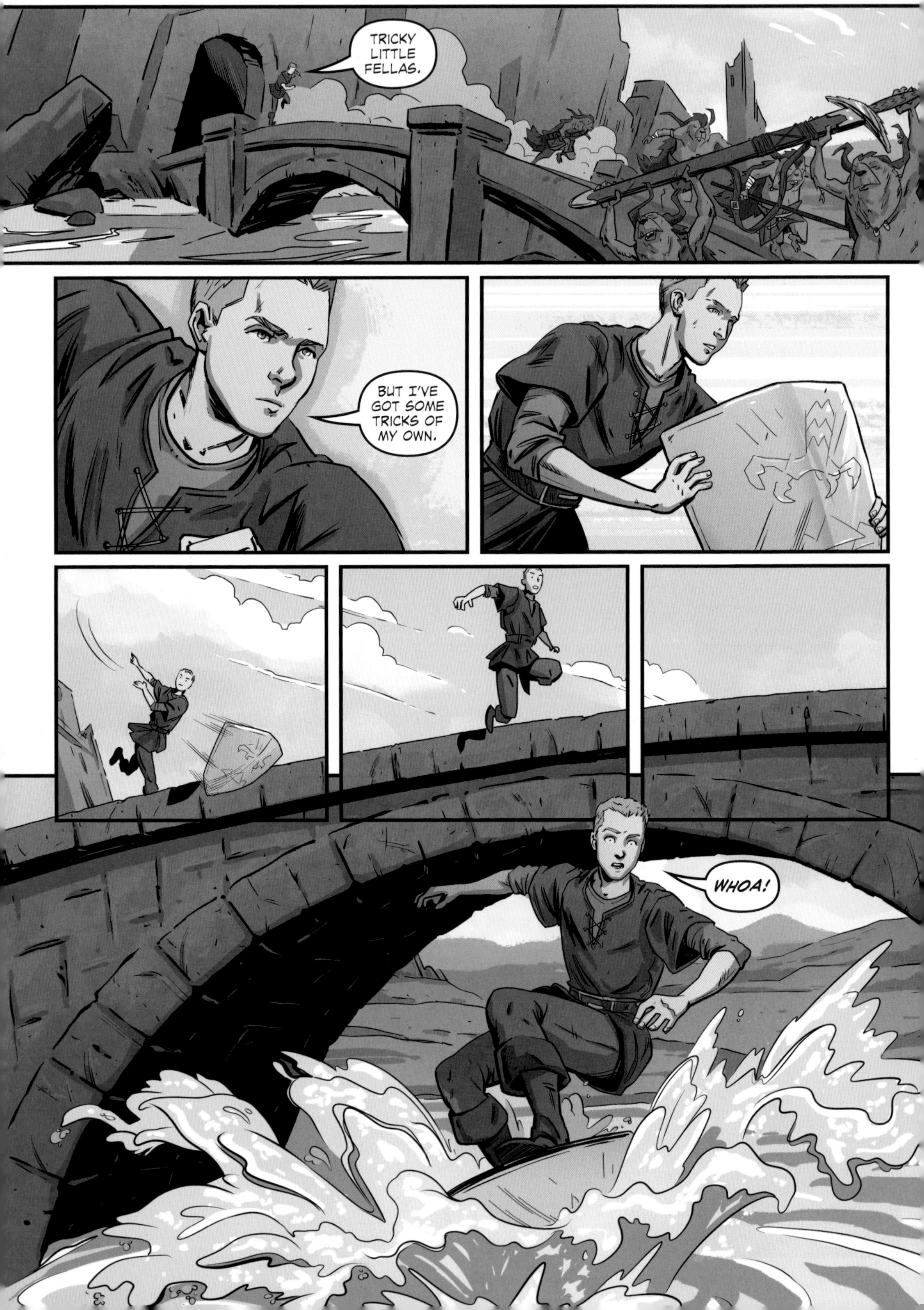

TRICKY LITTLE FELLAS.
BUT I'VE GOT SOME TRICKS OF MY OWN.
WHOA!

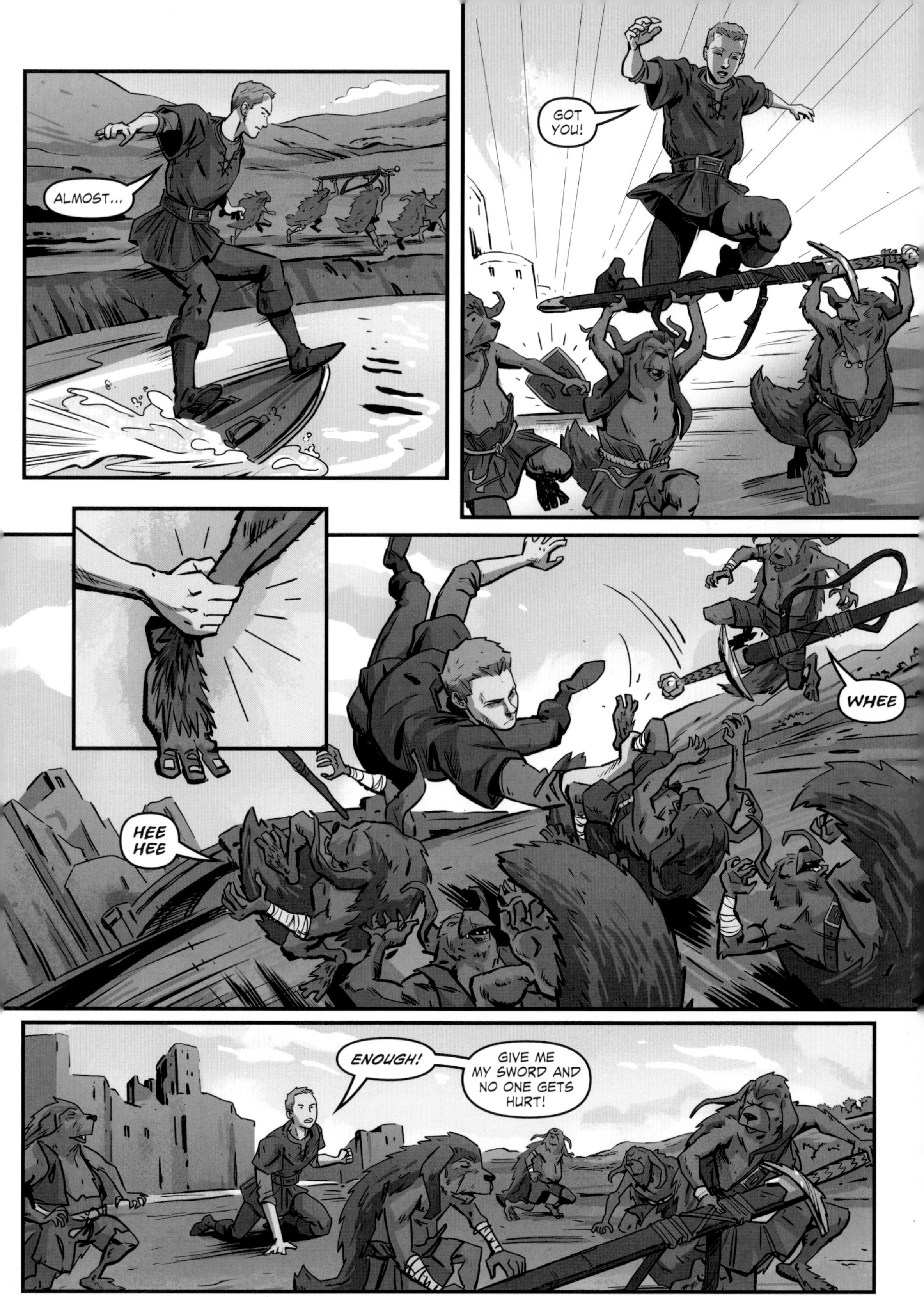
ALMOST...
GOT YOU!
WHEE
HEE HEE
ENOUGH!
GIVE ME MY SWORD AND NO ONE GETS HURT!

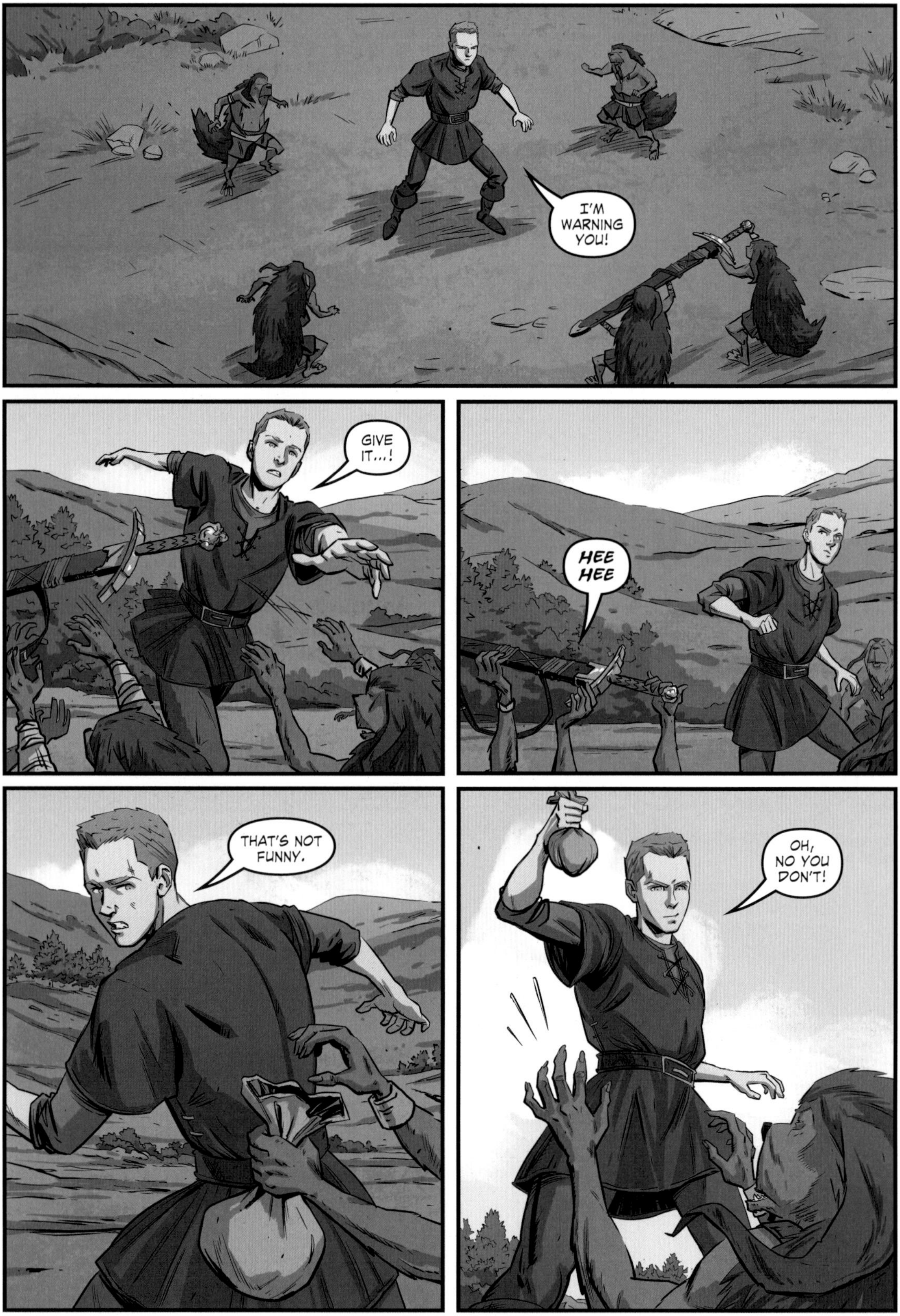
I'M WARNING YOU!
GIVE IT...!
HEE HEE
THAT'S NOT FUNNY.
OH, NO YOU DON'T!

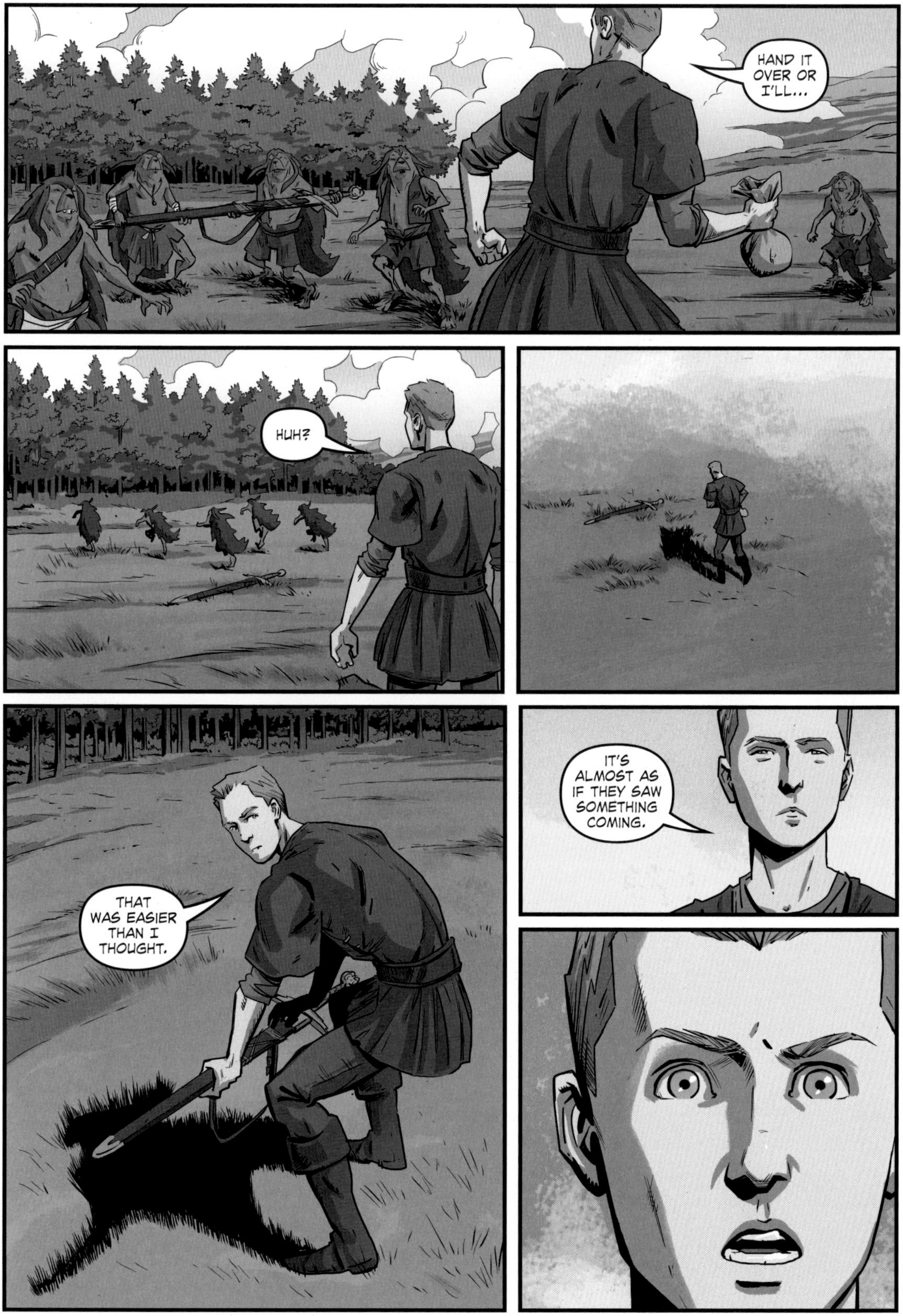
HAND IT OVER OR I'LL...
HUH?
THAT WAS EASIER THAN I THOUGHT.
IT'S ALMOST AS IF THEY SAW SOMETHING COMING.

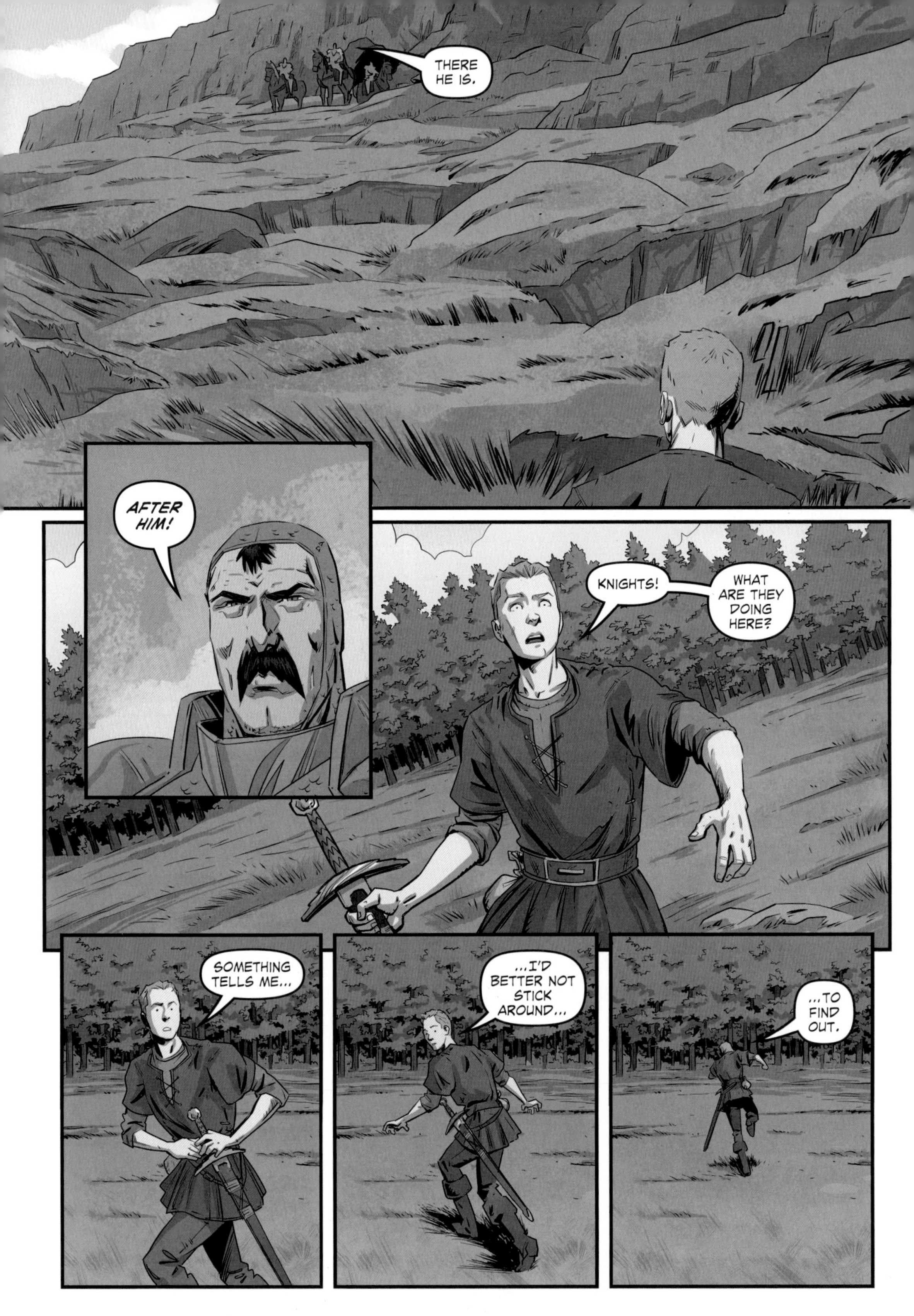
THERE HE IS.
AFTER HIM!
KNIGHTS!
WHAT ARE THEY DOING HERE?
SOMETHING TELLS ME...
...I'D BETTER NOT STICK AROUND...
...TO FIND OUT.

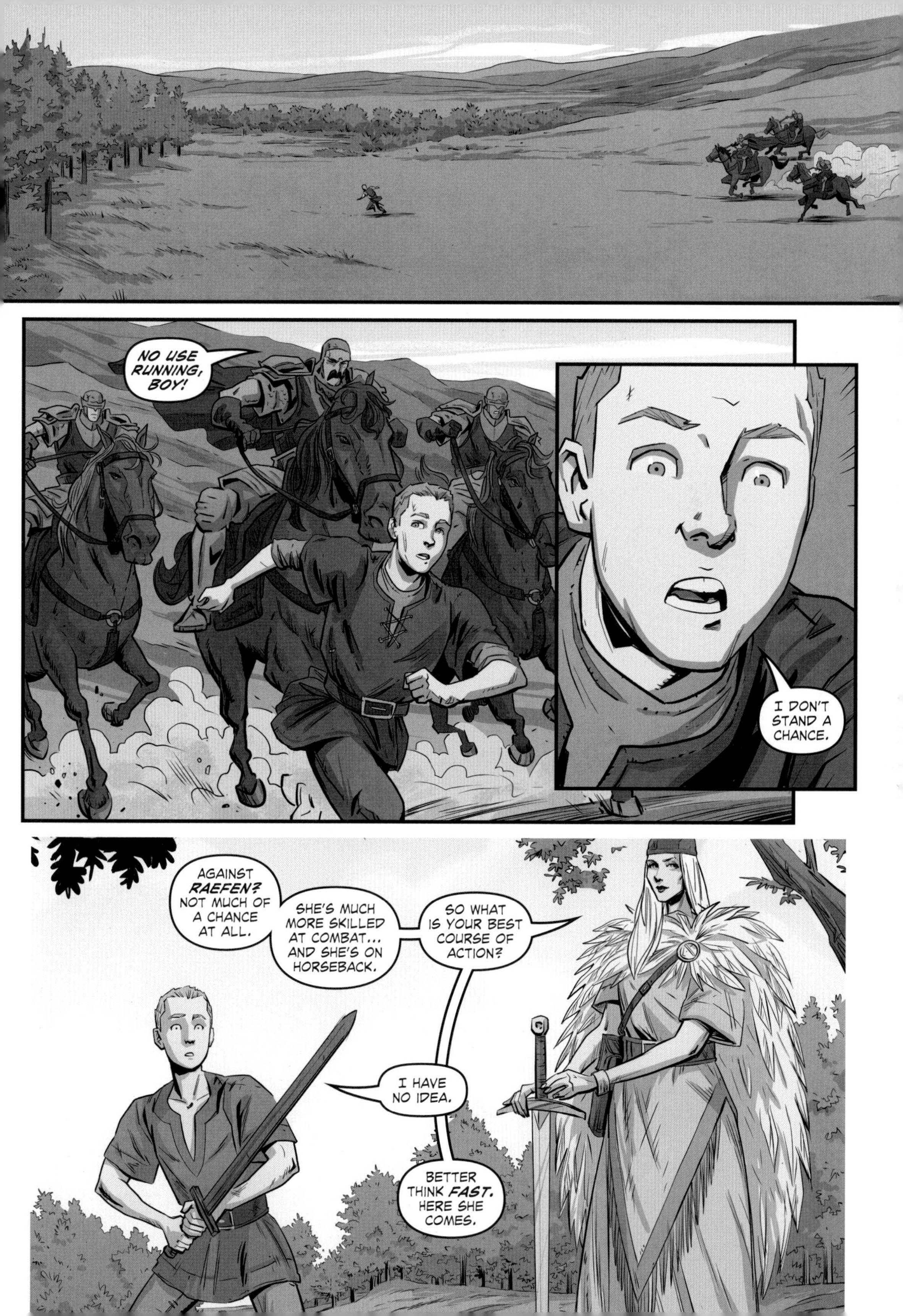
NO USE RUNNING, BOY!
I DON'T STAND A CHANCE.
AGAINST RAEFEN? NOT MUCH OF A CHANCE AT ALL.
SHE'S MUCH MORE SKILLED AT COMBAT... AND SHE'S ON HORSEBACK.
SO WHAT IS YOUR BEST COURSE OF ACTION?
I HAVE NO IDEA.
BETTER THINK FAST. HERE SHE COMES.

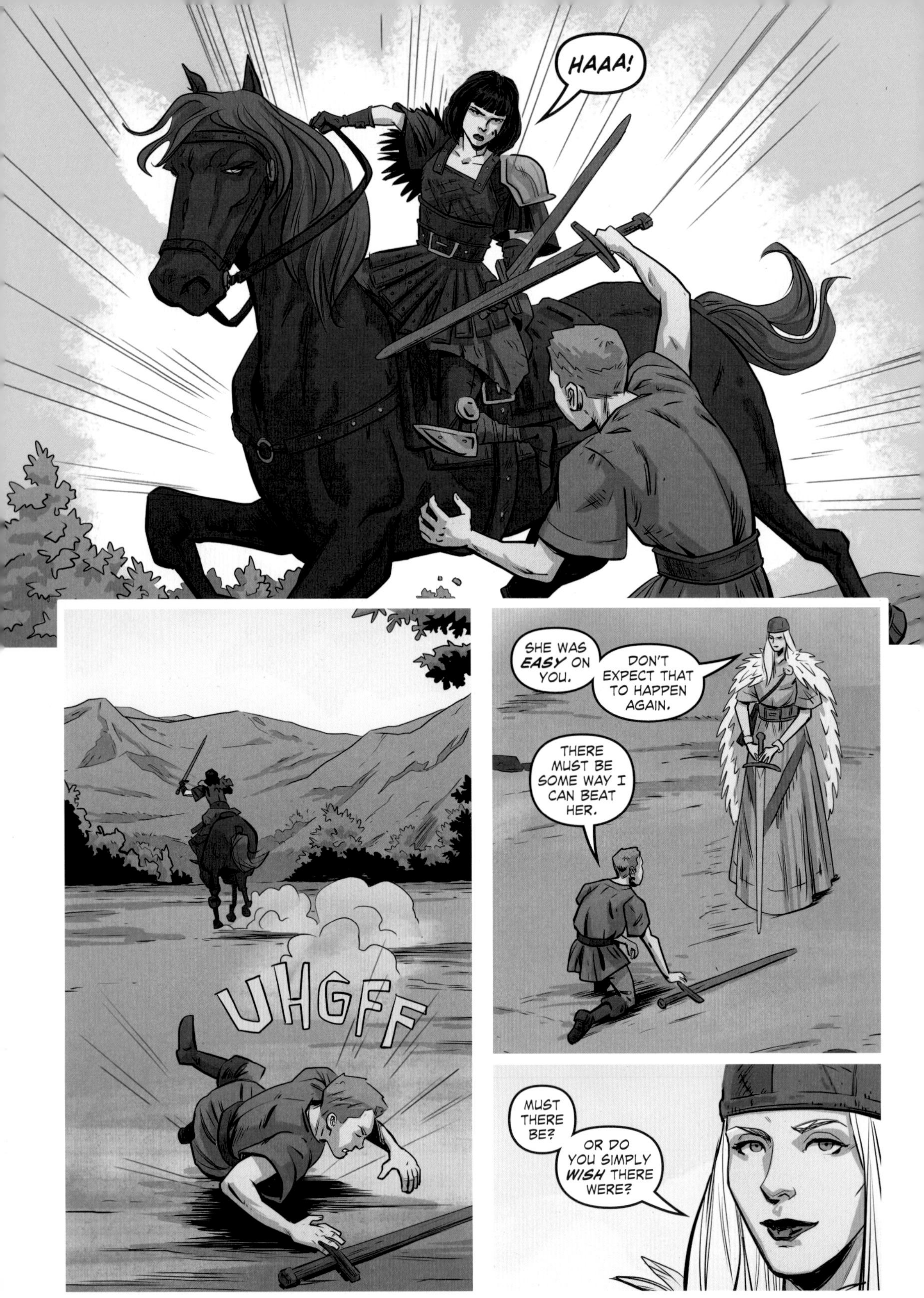
HAAA!
UHGFF
SHE WAS EASY ON YOU.
DON'T EXPECT THAT TO HAPPEN AGAIN.
THERE MUST BE SOME WAY I CAN BEAT HER.
MUST THERE BE?
OR DO YOU SIMPLY WISH THERE WERE?

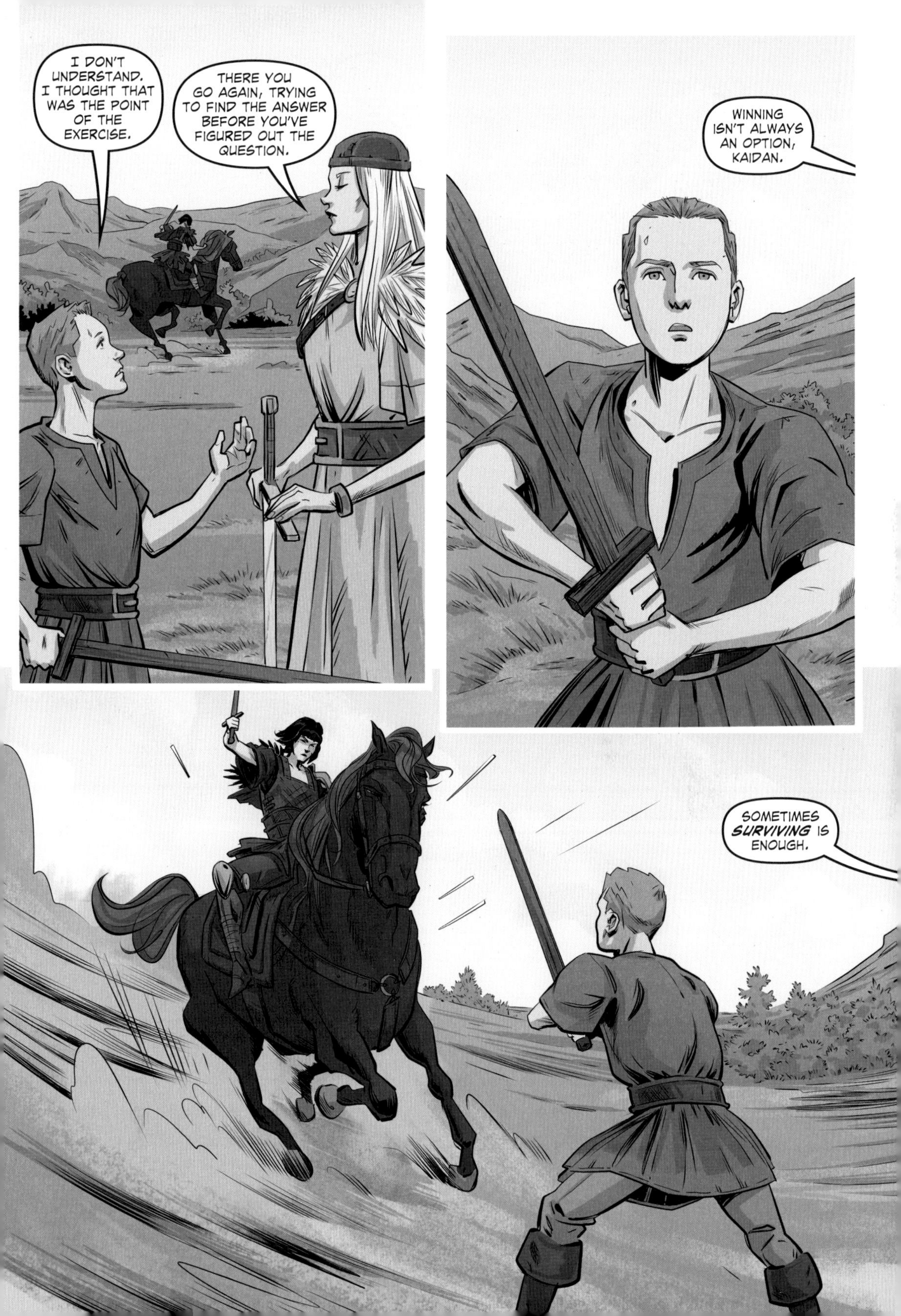
I DON'T UNDERSTAND. I THOUGHT THAT WAS THE POINT OF THE EXERCISE.
THERE YOU GO AGAIN, TRYING TO FIND THE ANSWER BEFORE YOU'VE FIGURED OUT THE QUESTION.
WINNING ISN'T ALWAYS AN OPTION, KAIDAN.
SOMETIMES *SURVIVING* IS ENOUGH.

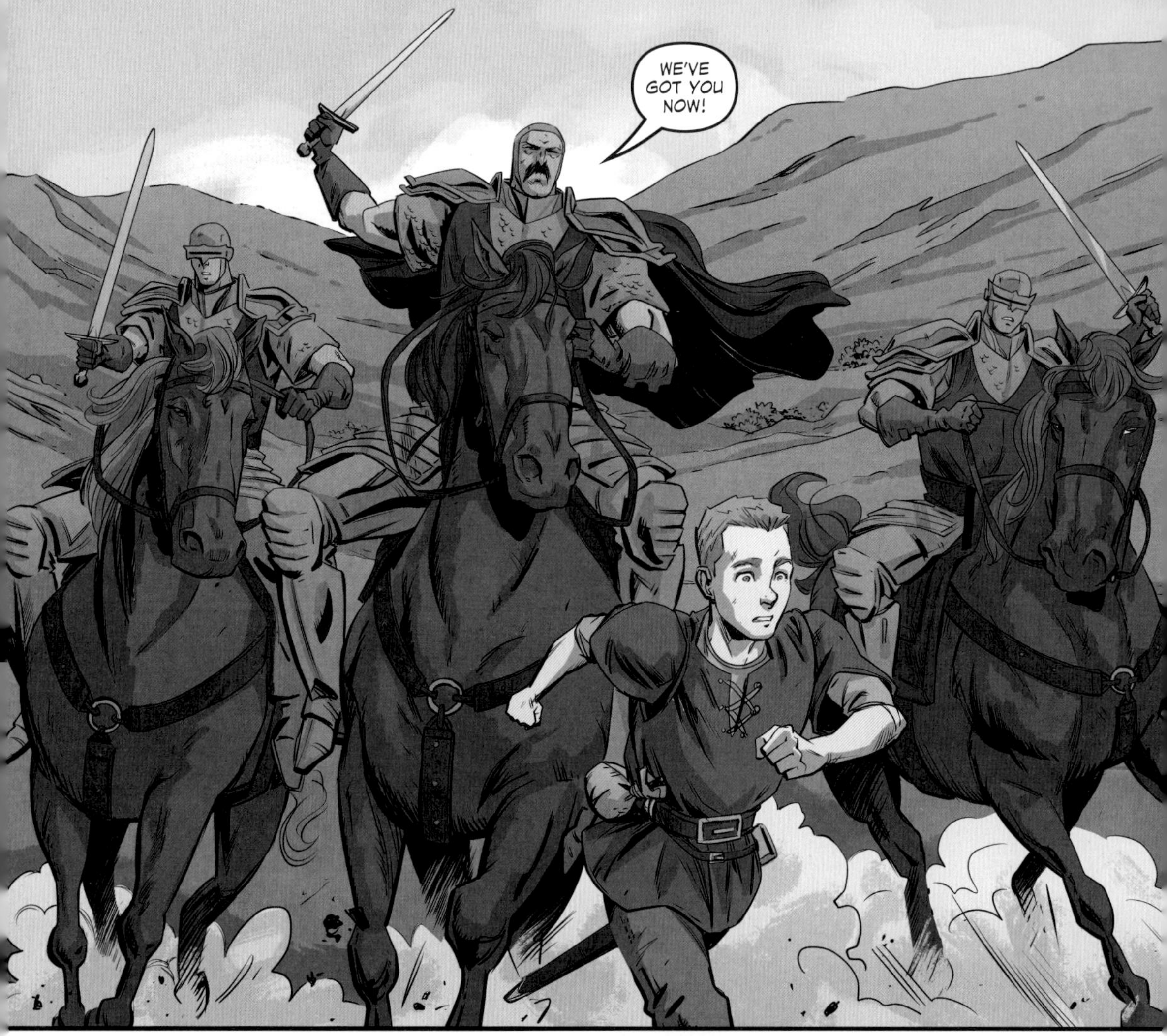
WE'VE GOT YOU NOW!

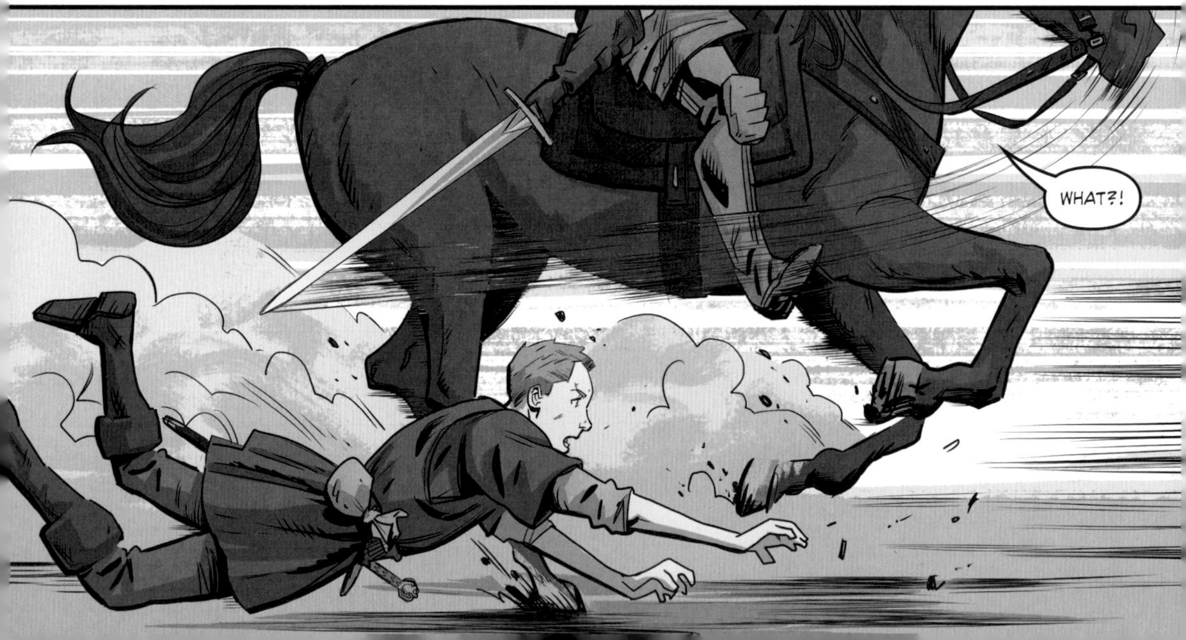
WHAT?!

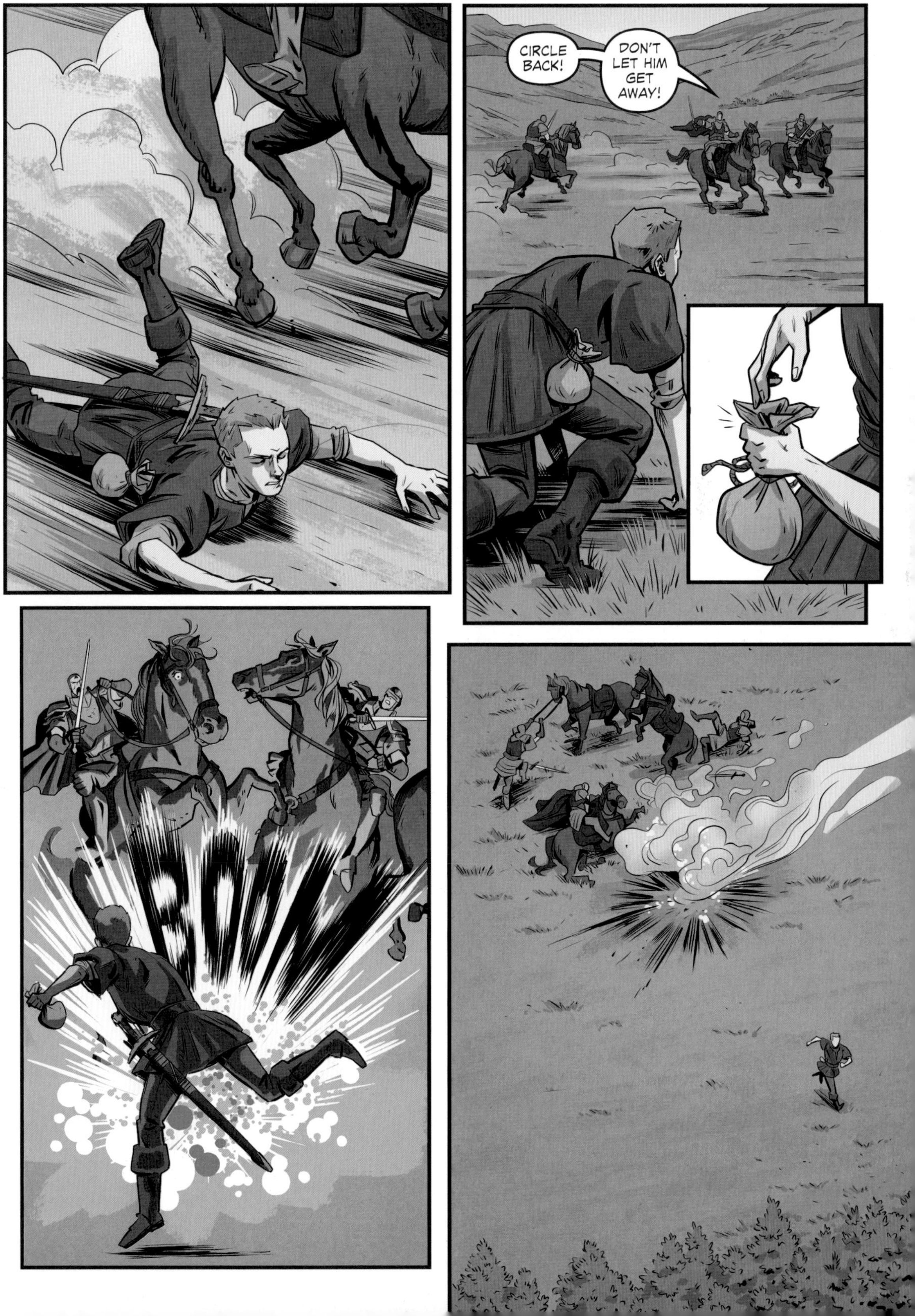
CIRCLE BACK!
DON'T LET HIM GET AWAY!

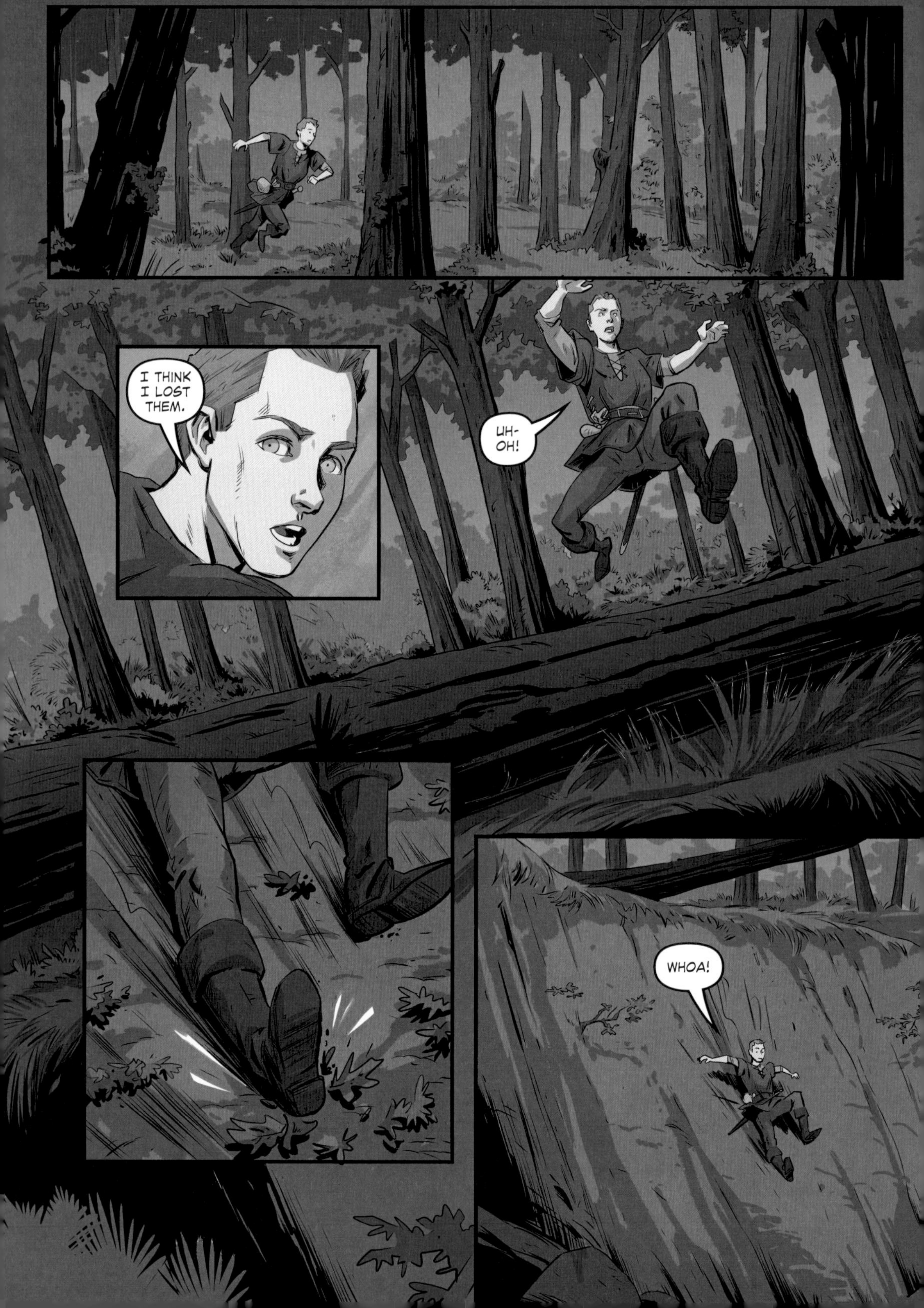
I THINK I LOST THEM.
UH-OH!
WHOA!

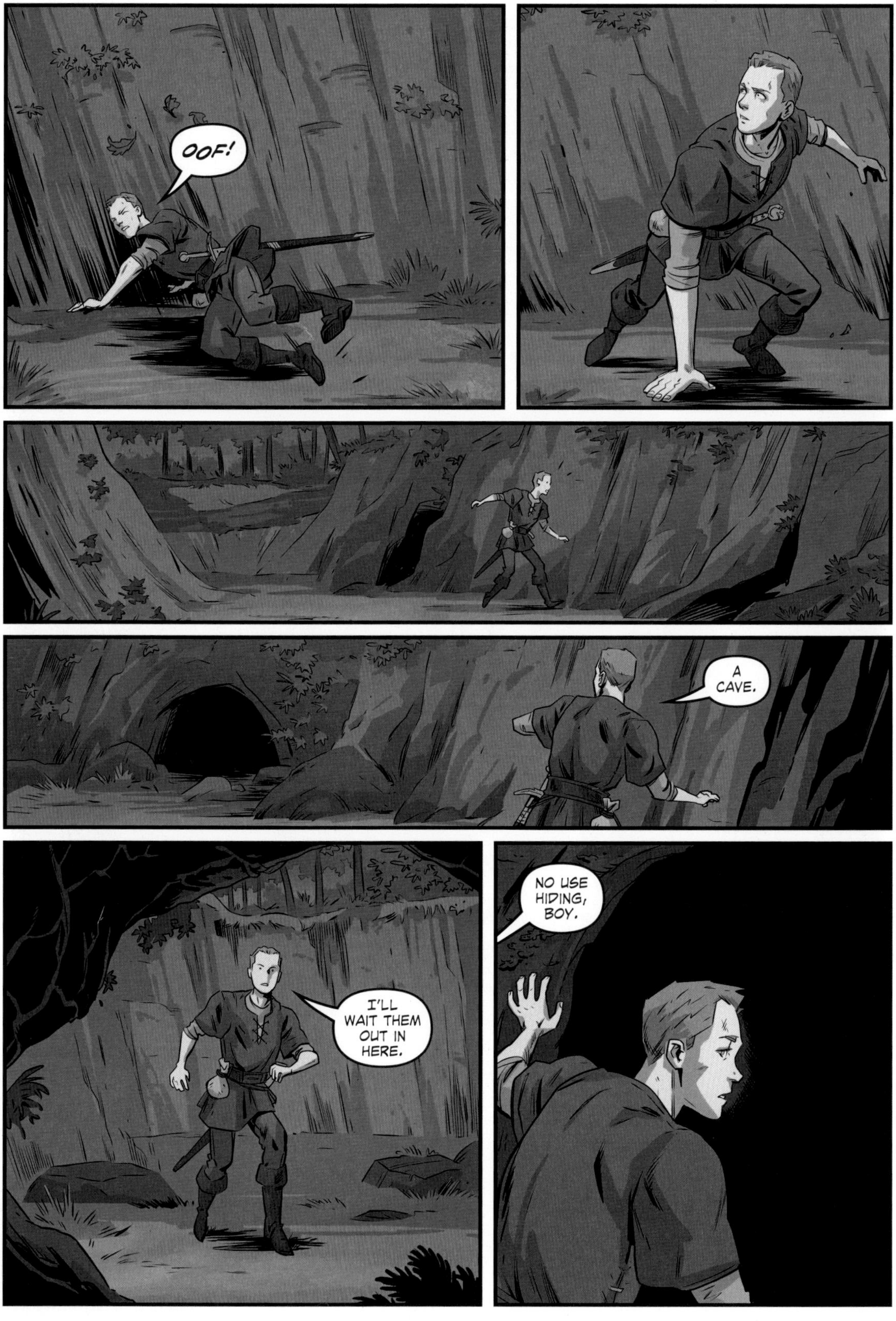
OOF!
A CAVE.
I'LL WAIT THEM OUT IN HERE.
NO USE HIDING, BOY.

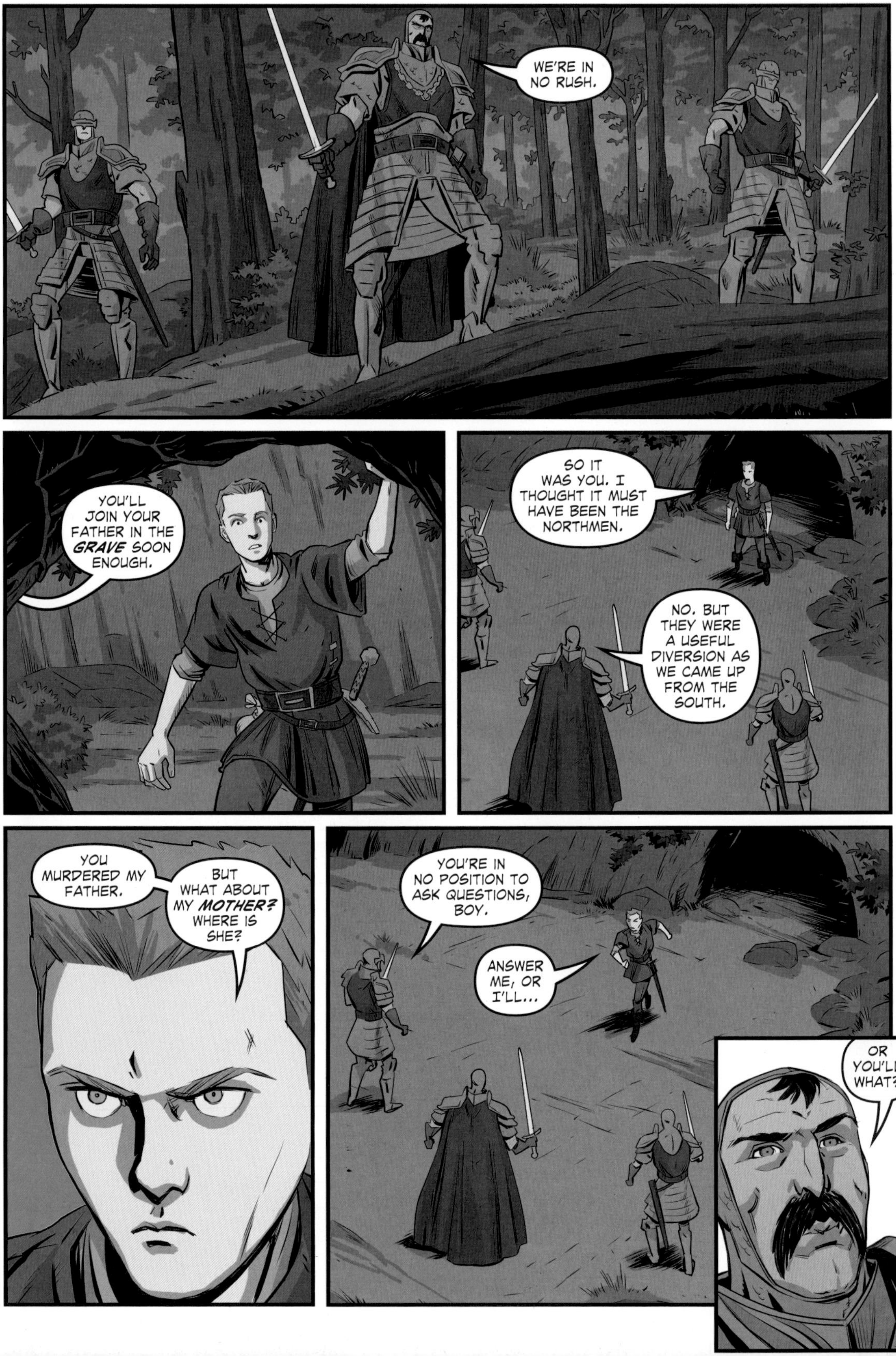
WE'RE IN NO RUSH.
YOU'LL JOIN YOUR FATHER IN THE ***GRAVE*** SOON ENOUGH.
SO IT WAS YOU. I THOUGHT IT MUST HAVE BEEN THE NORTHMEN.
NO. BUT THEY WERE A USEFUL DIVERSION AS WE CAME UP FROM THE SOUTH.
YOU MURDERED MY FATHER.
BUT WHAT ABOUT MY ***MOTHER?*** WHERE IS SHE?
YOU'RE IN NO POSITION TO ASK QUESTIONS, BOY.
ANSWER ME, OR I'LL...
OR YOU'LL WHAT?

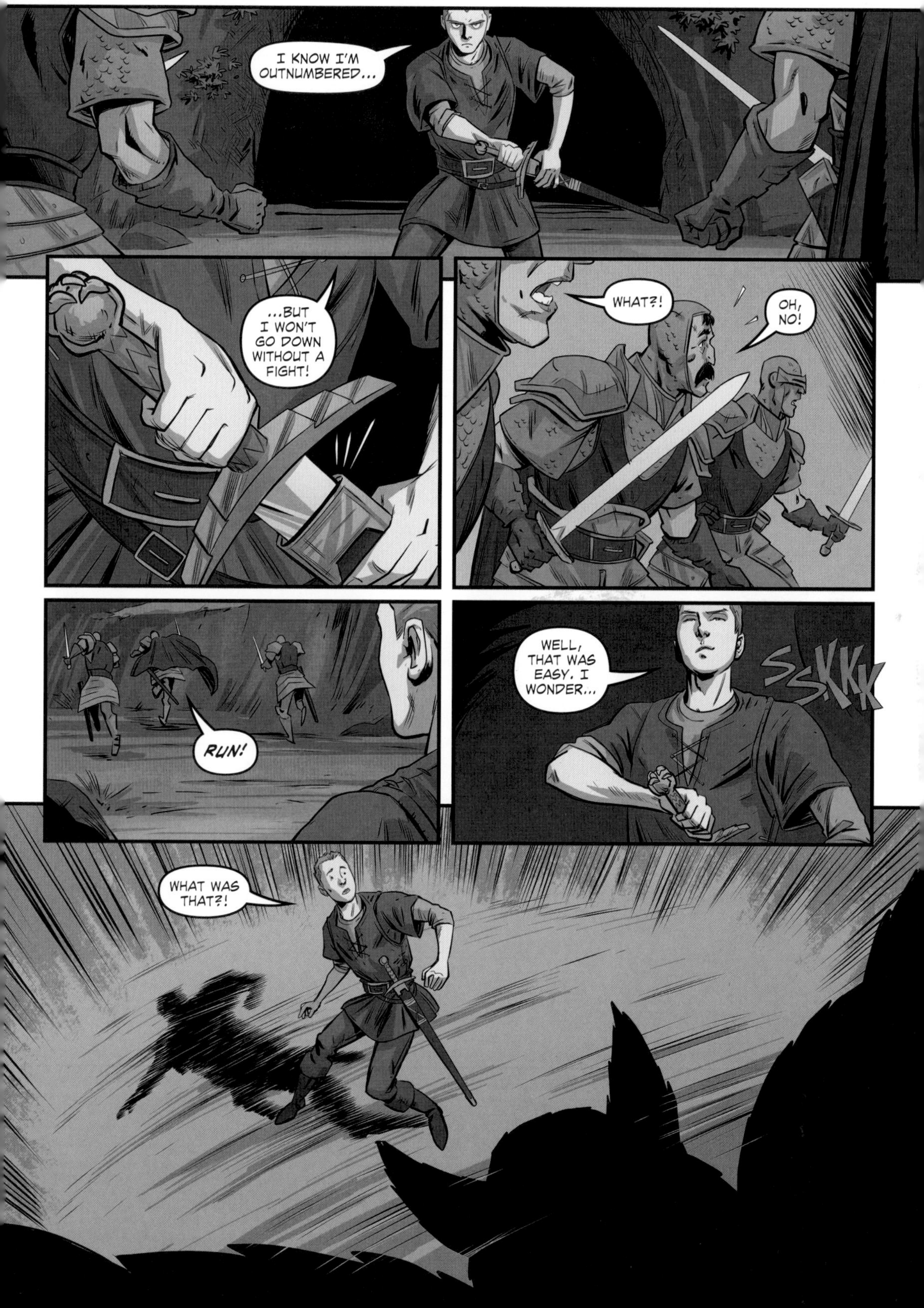
I KNOW I'M OUTNUMBERED...
...BUT I WON'T GO DOWN WITHOUT A FIGHT!
WHAT?!
OH, NO!
RUN!
WELL, THAT WAS EASY. I WONDER...
SSKKK
WHAT WAS THAT?!

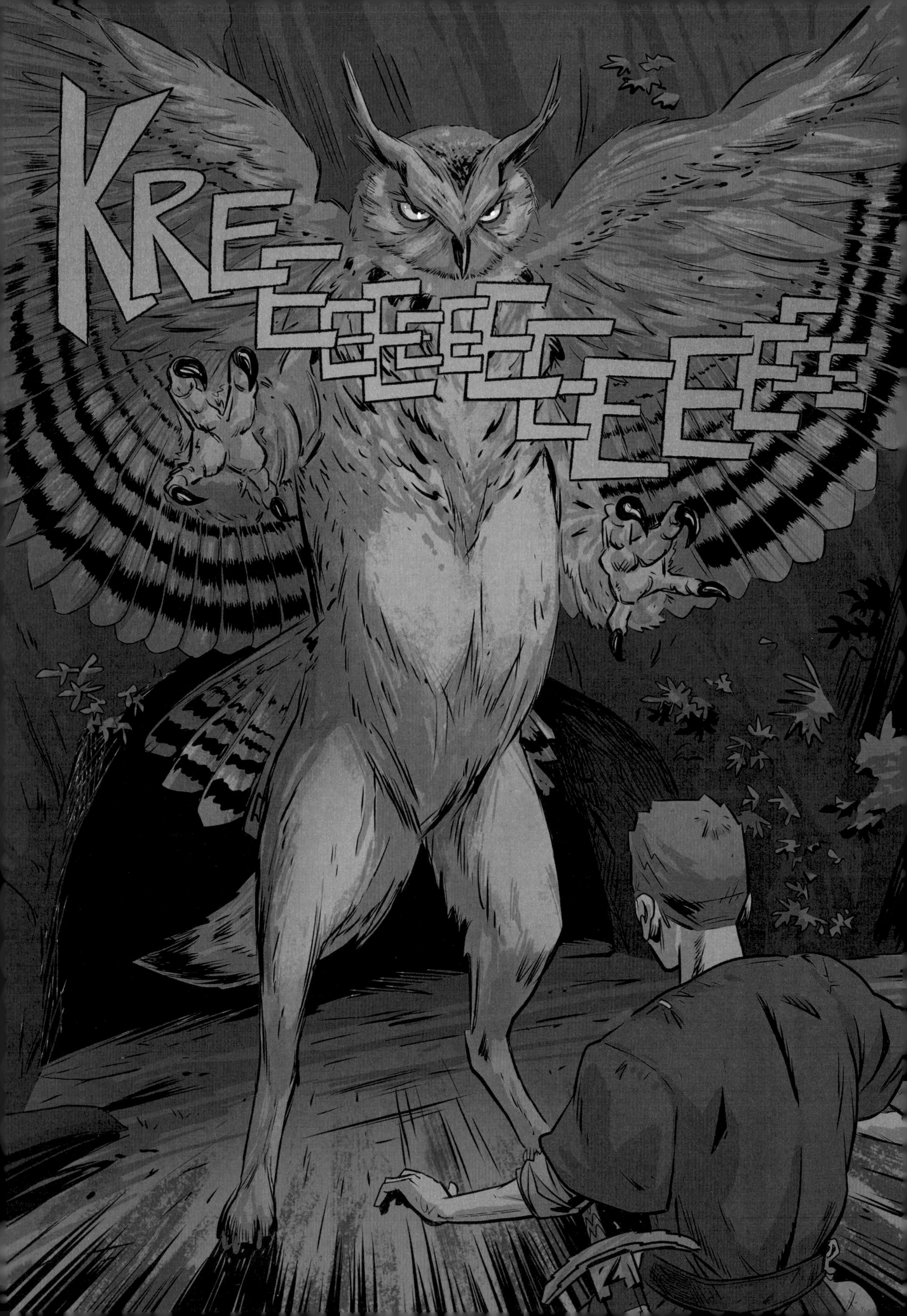
KREEEEEEEEEEEEEEEEE

Chapter 3

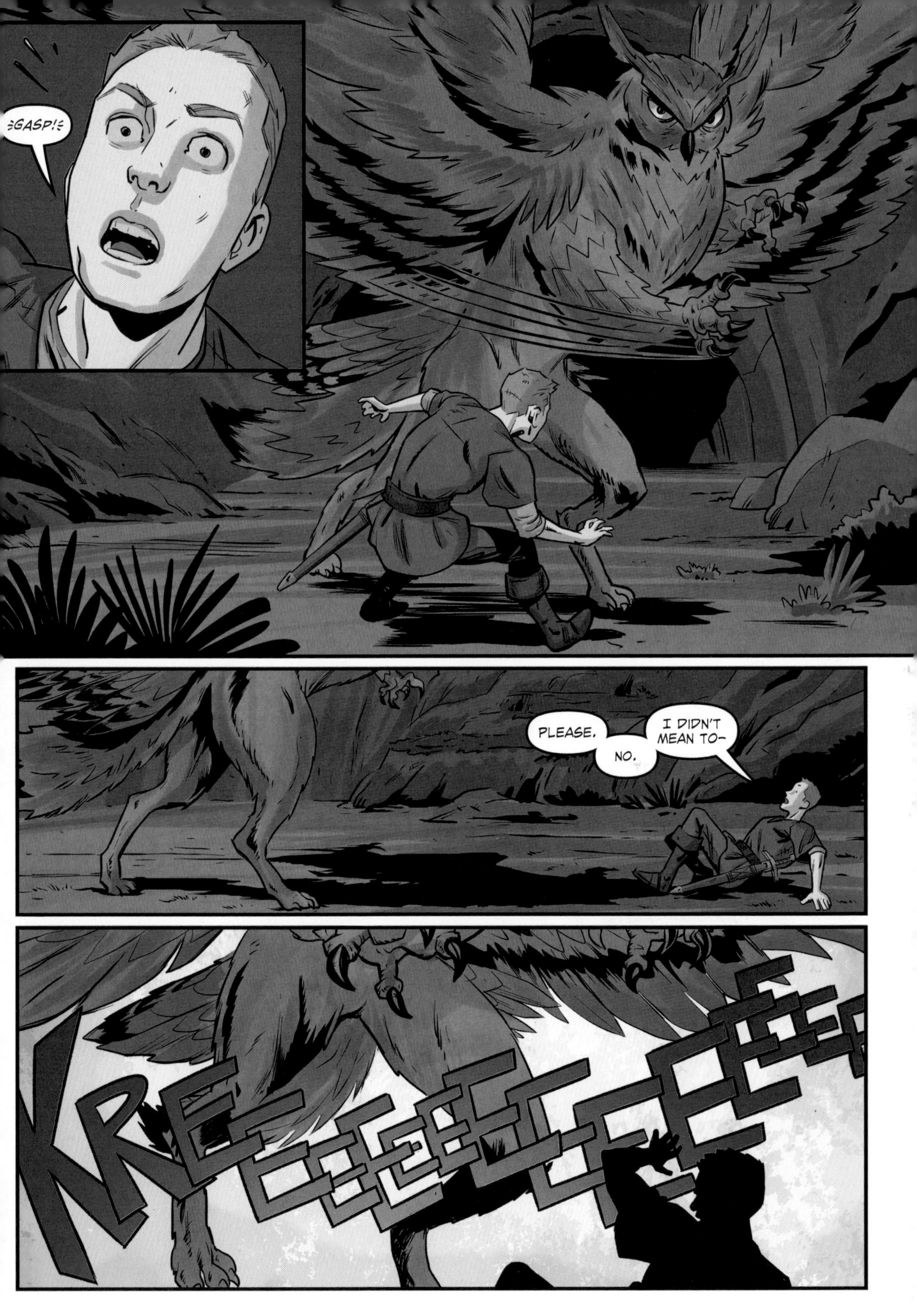
GASP!
PLEASE.
NO.
I DIDN'T MEAN TO–
KREEEEEEEEEEEEEE

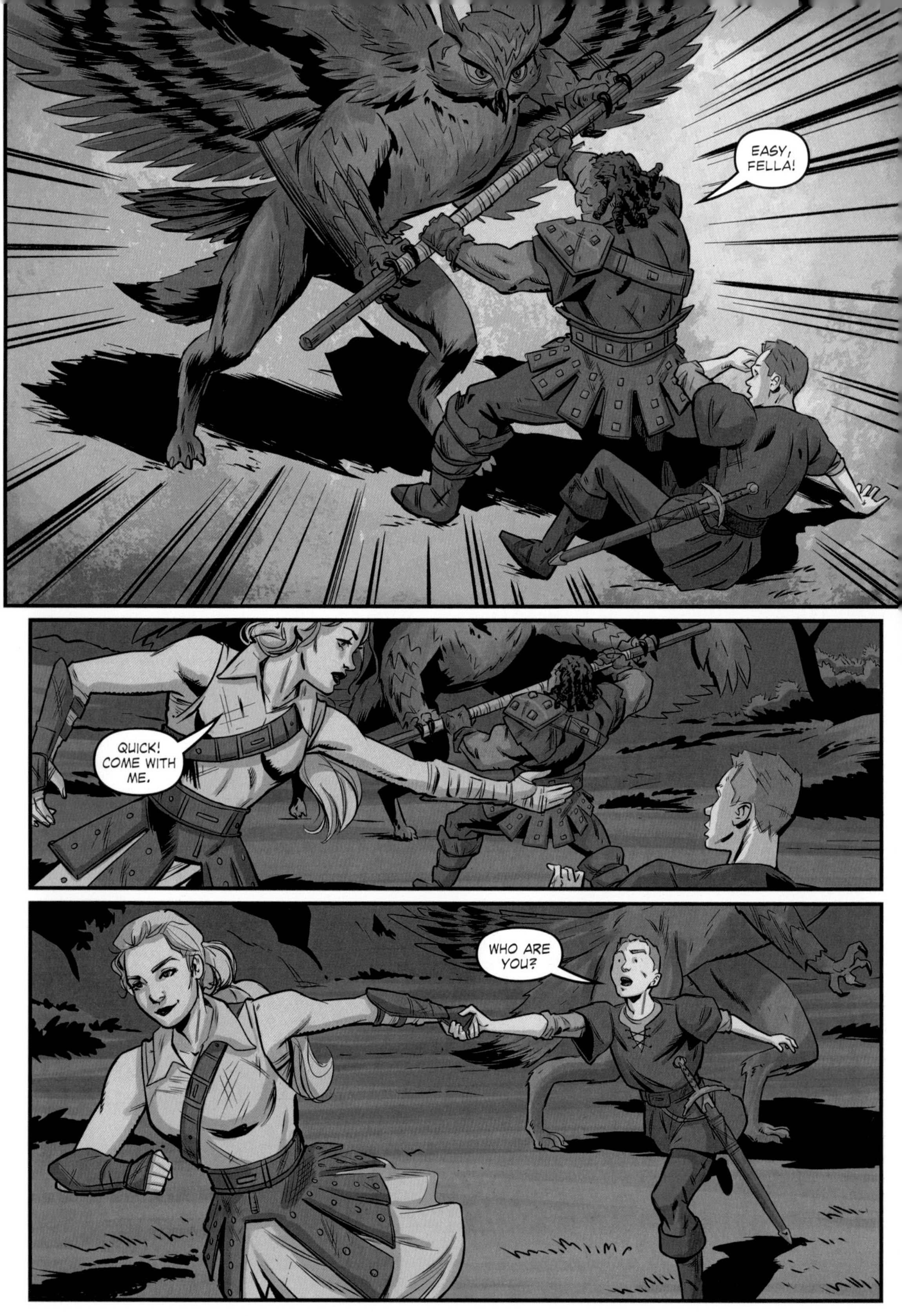
EASY, FELLA!
QUICK! COME WITH ME.
WHO ARE YOU?

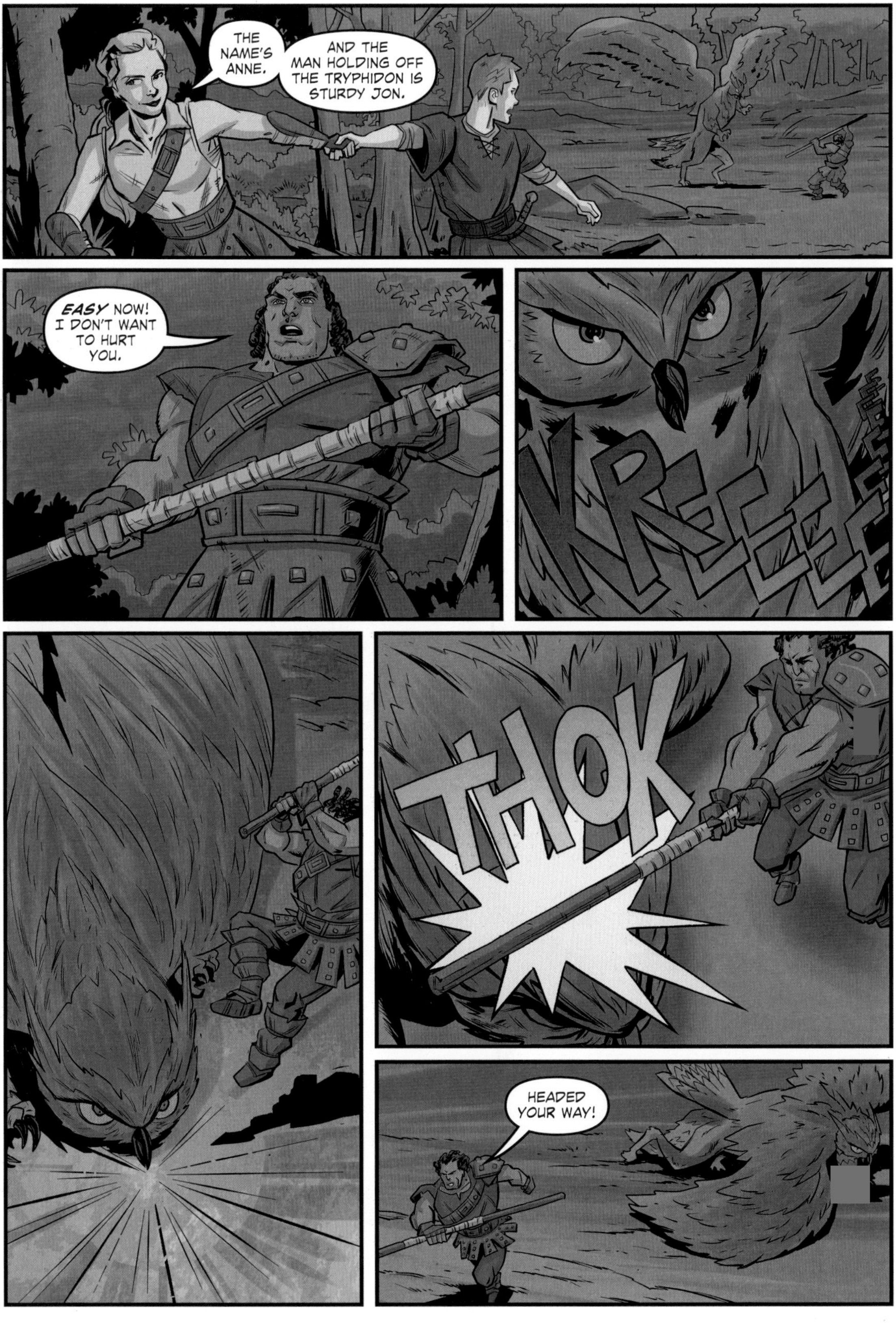
THE NAME'S ANNE.
AND THE MAN HOLDING OFF THE TRYPHIDON IS STURDY JON.
EASY NOW! I DON'T WANT TO HURT YOU.
KREEEEE
THOK
HEADED YOUR WAY!

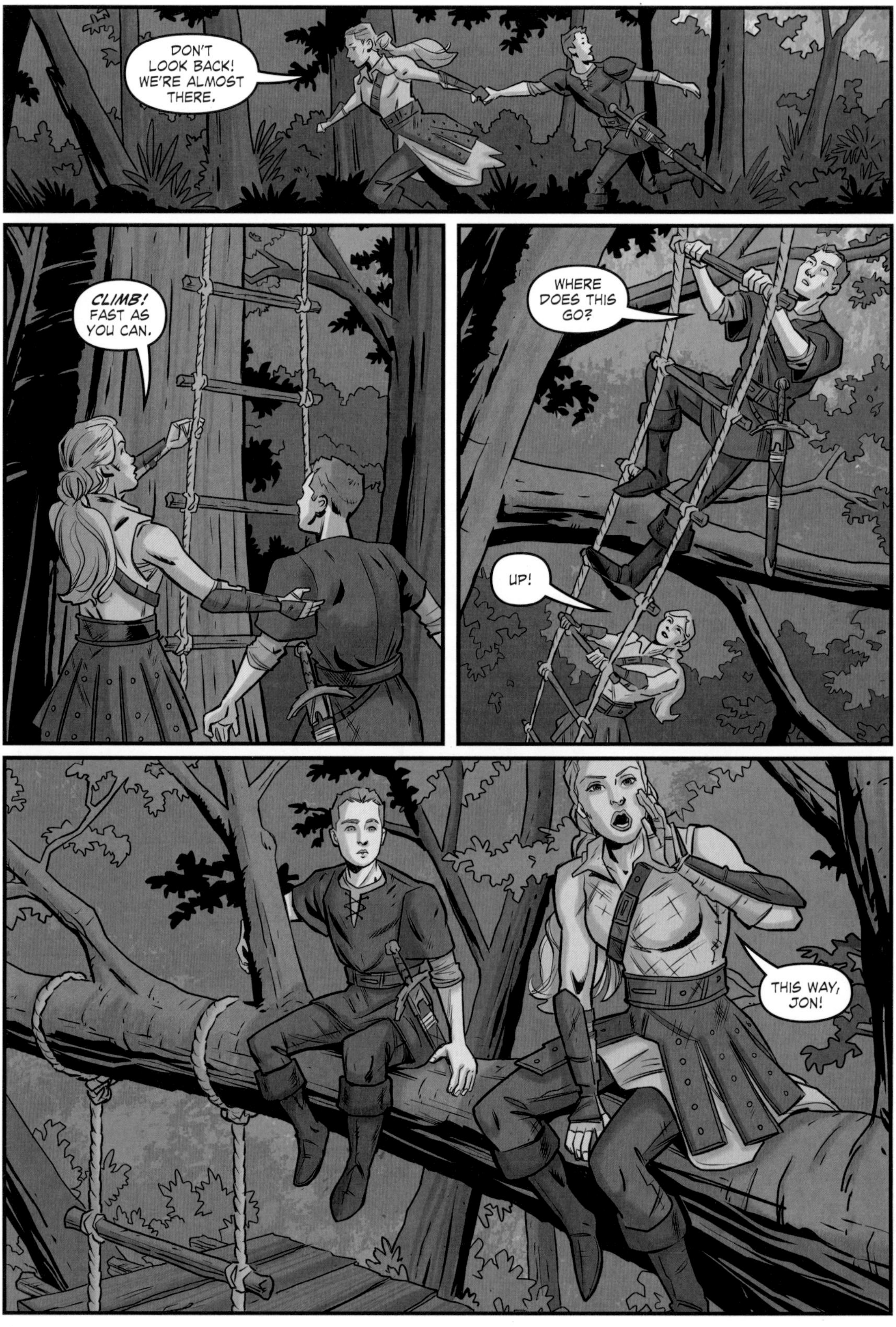
DON'T LOOK BACK! WE'RE ALMOST THERE.
CLIMB! FAST AS YOU CAN.
WHERE DOES THIS GO?
UP!
THIS WAY, JON!

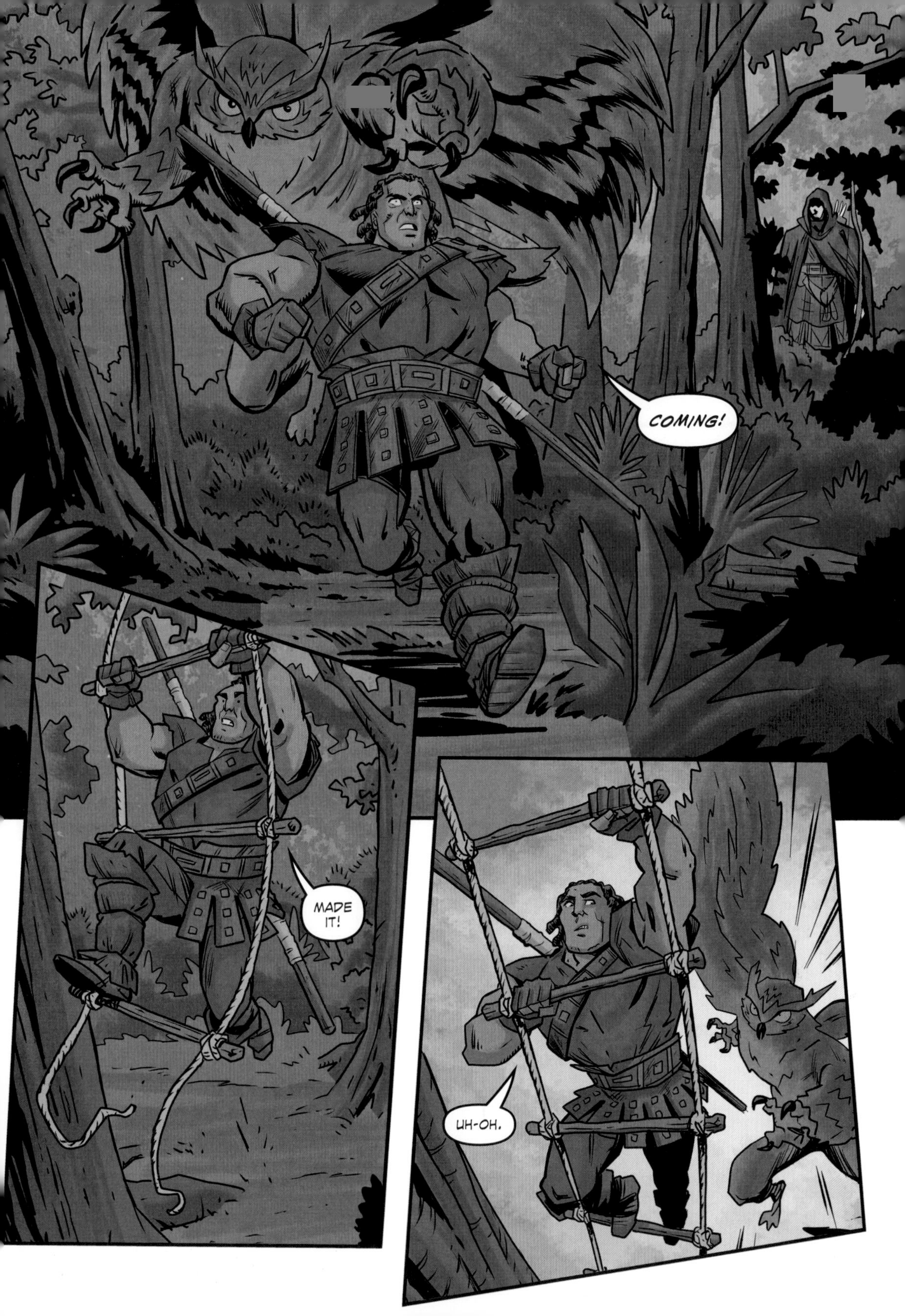
COMING!
MADE IT!
UH-OH.

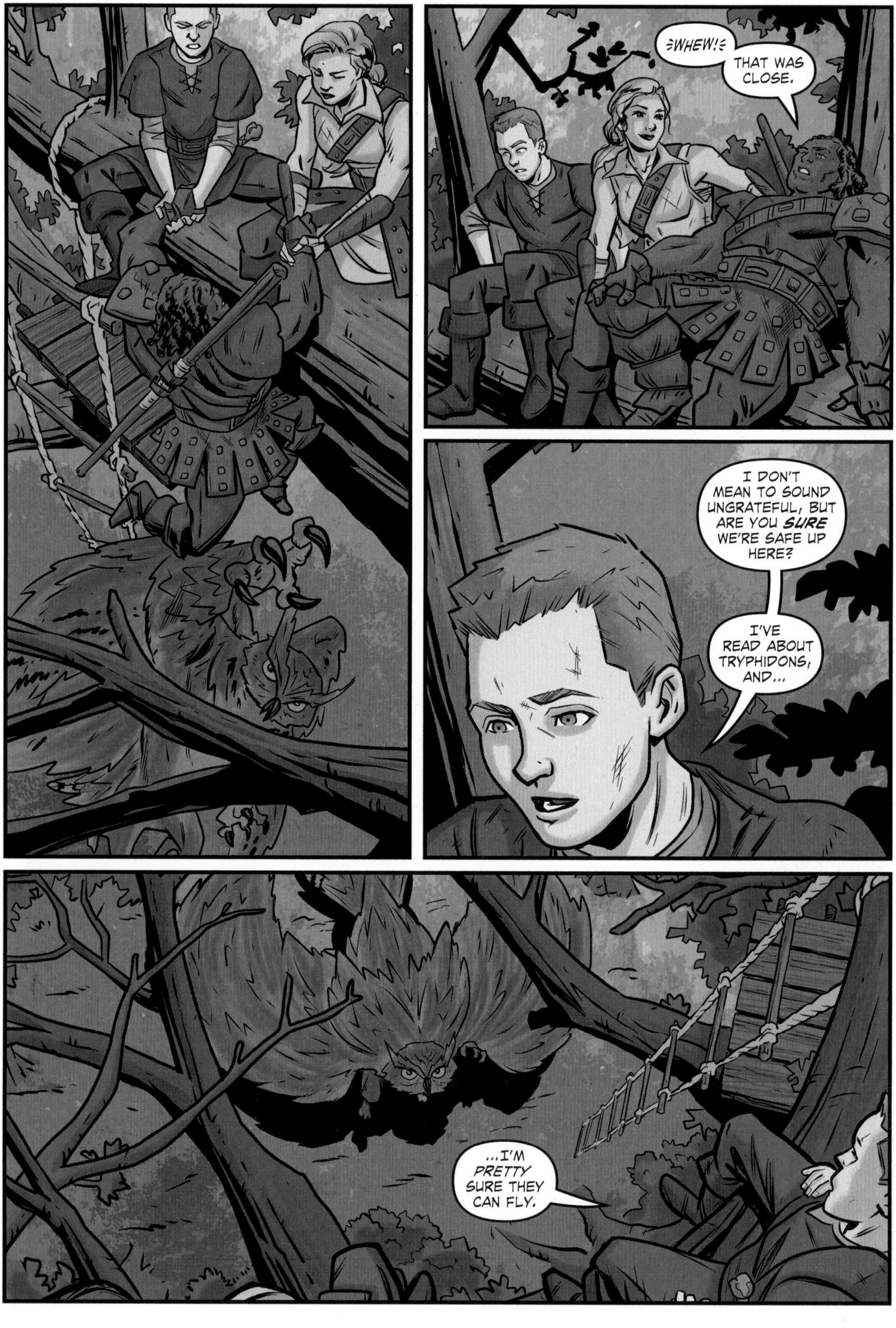

WHEW!
THAT WAS CLOSE.
I DON'T MEAN TO SOUND UNGRATEFUL, BUT ARE YOU SURE WE'RE SAFE UP HERE?
I'VE READ ABOUT TRYPHIDONS, AND...
...I'M PRETTY SURE THEY CAN FLY.

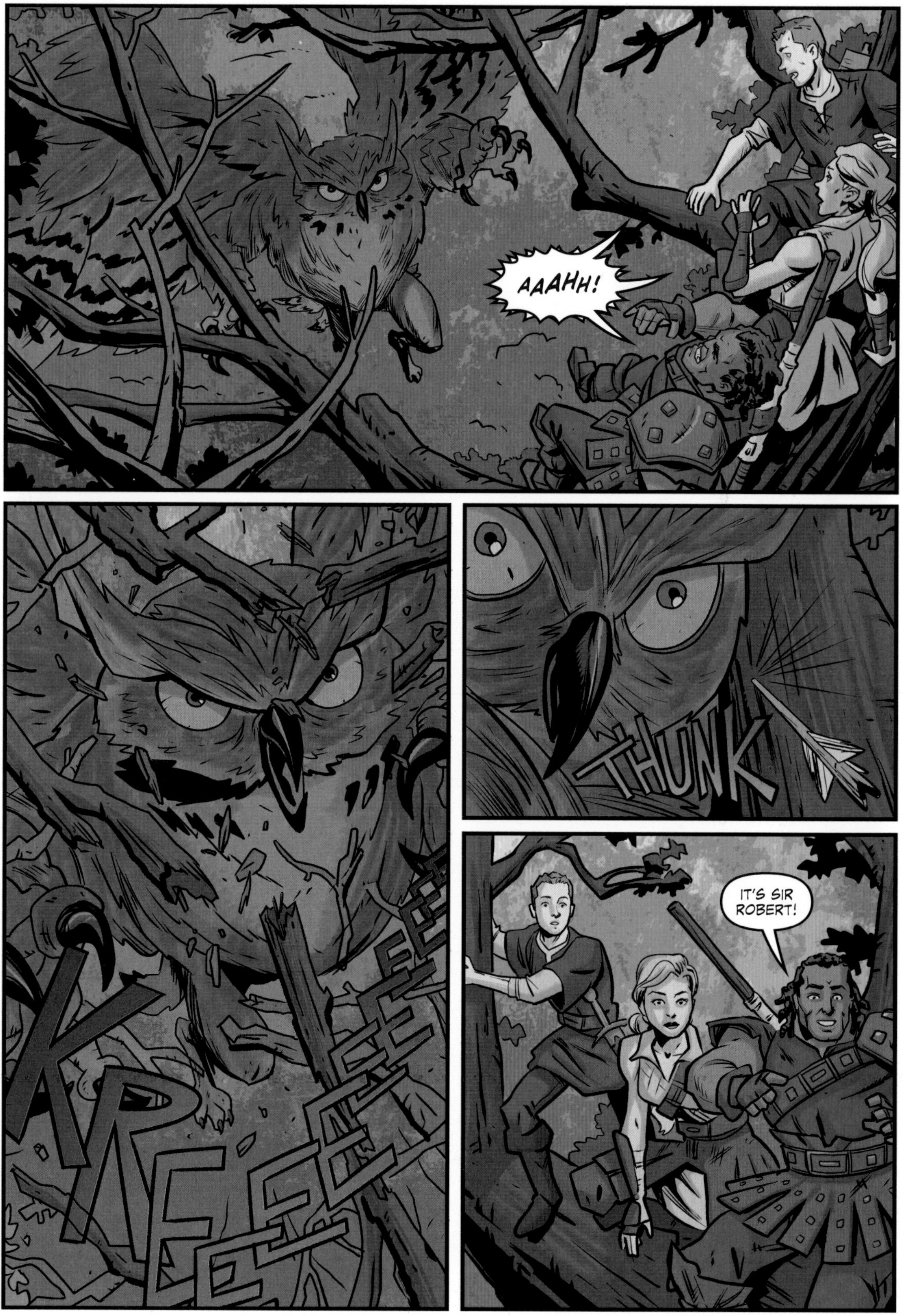
AAAHH!
THUNK
IT'S SIR ROBERT!

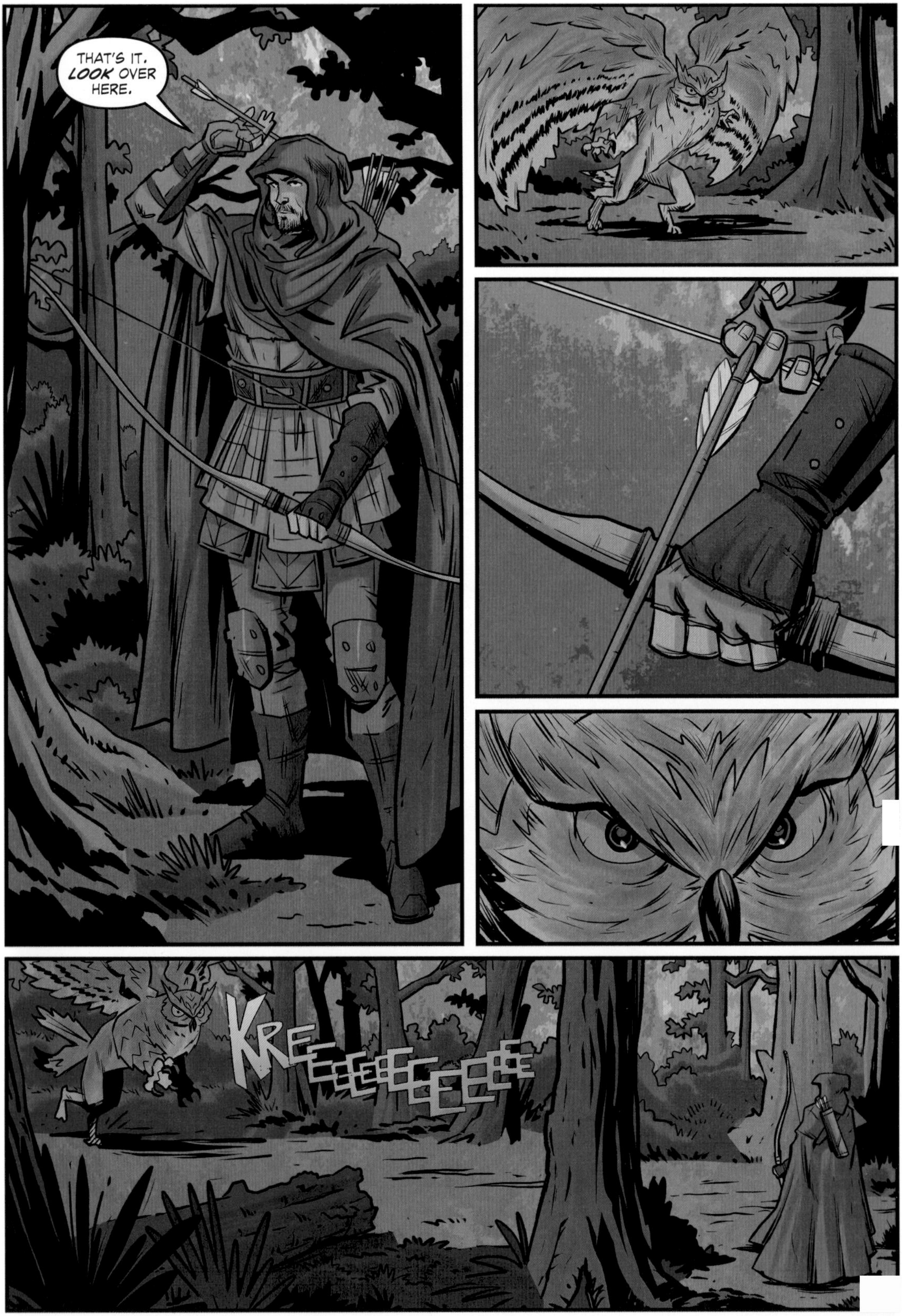
THAT'S IT. LOOK OVER HERE.
KREEEEEEEEEEEEEEE

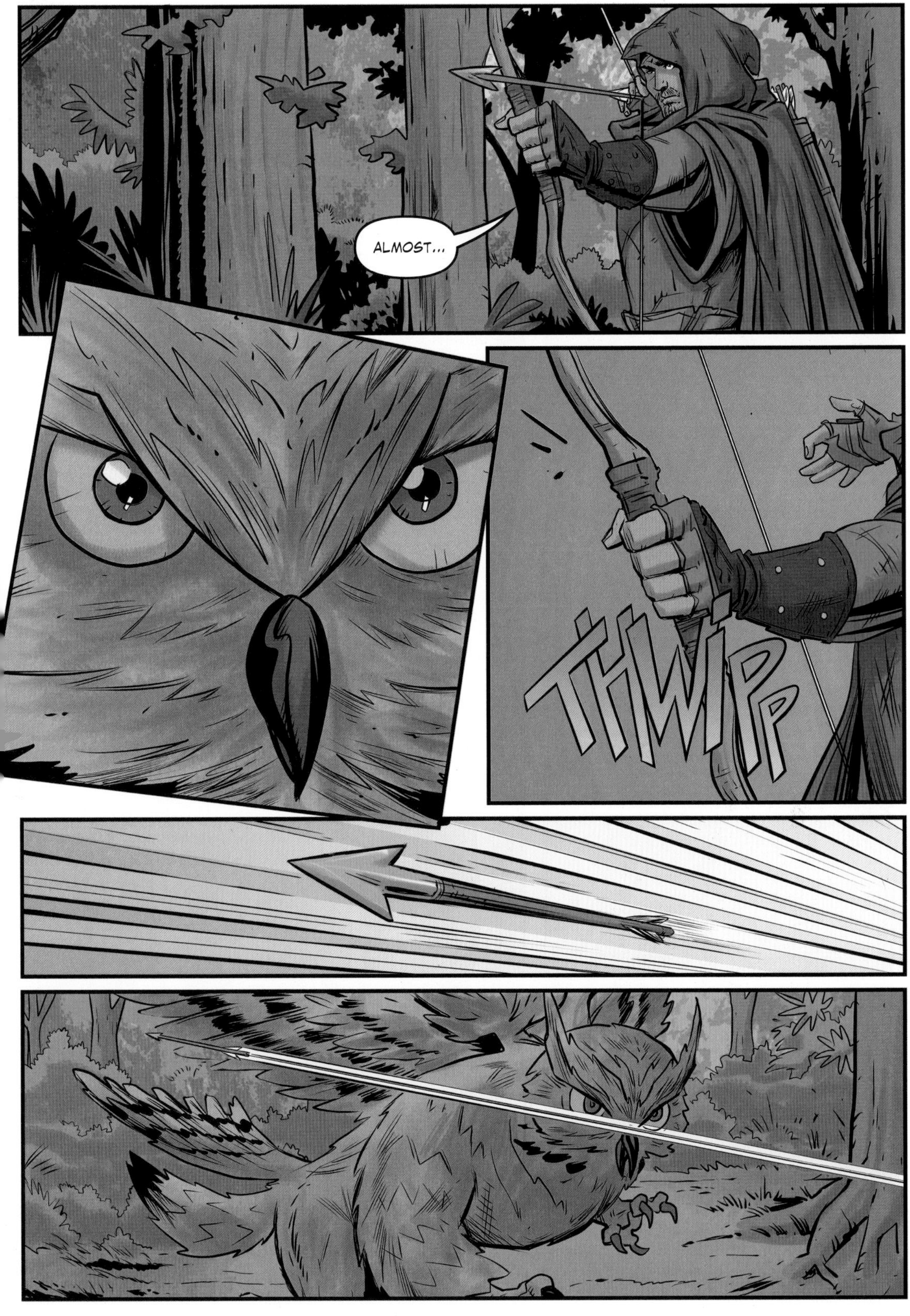
ALMOST...
THWIPP

SNAP

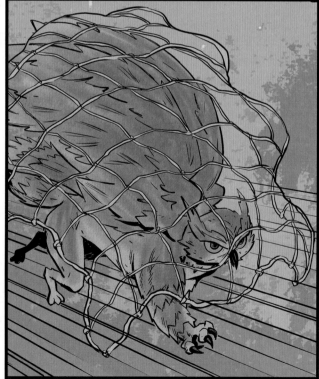

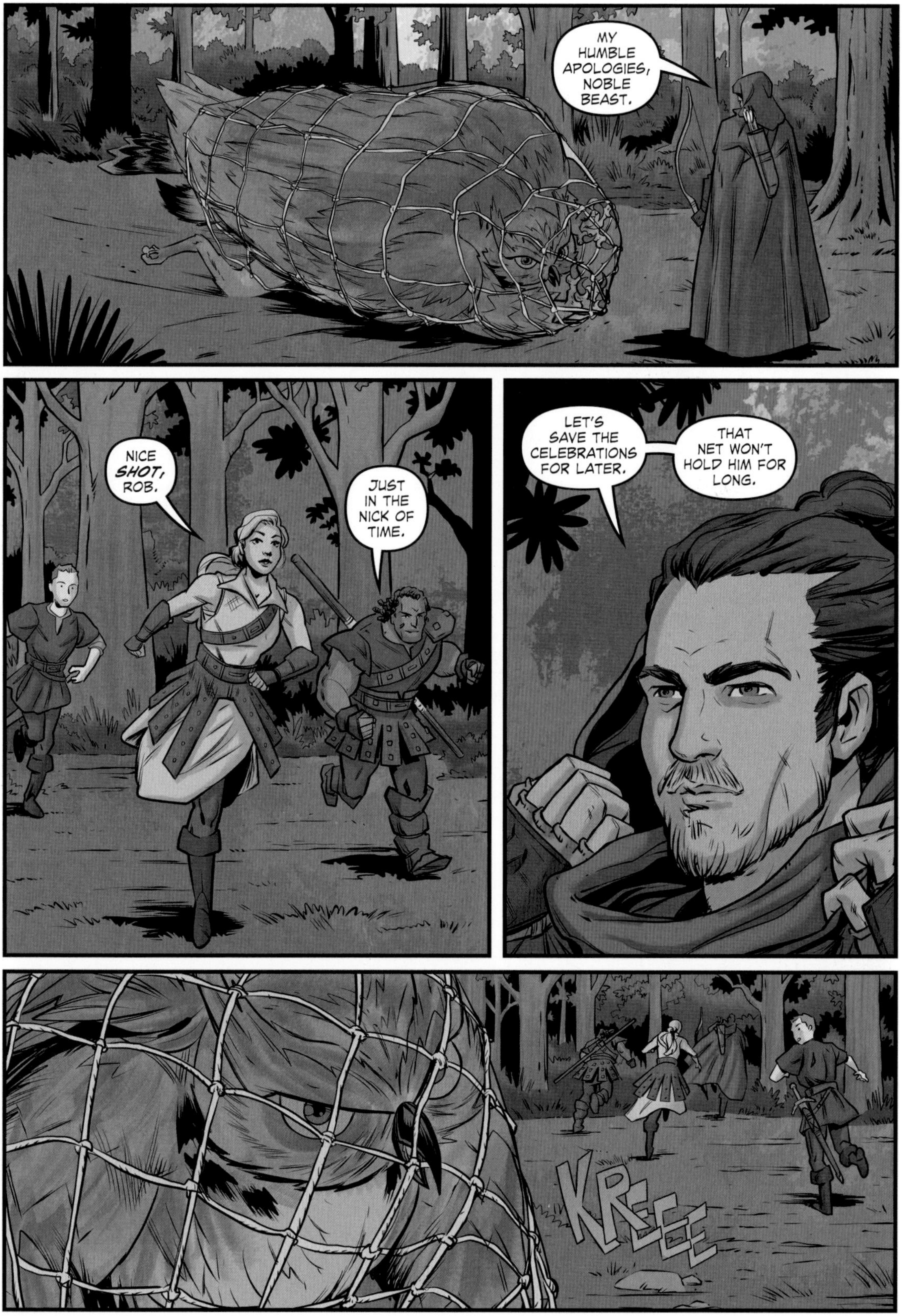
MY HUMBLE APOLOGIES, NOBLE BEAST.
NICE *SHOT*, ROB.
JUST IN THE NICK OF TIME.
LET'S SAVE THE CELEBRATIONS FOR LATER.
THAT NET WON'T HOLD HIM FOR LONG.
KREEEE

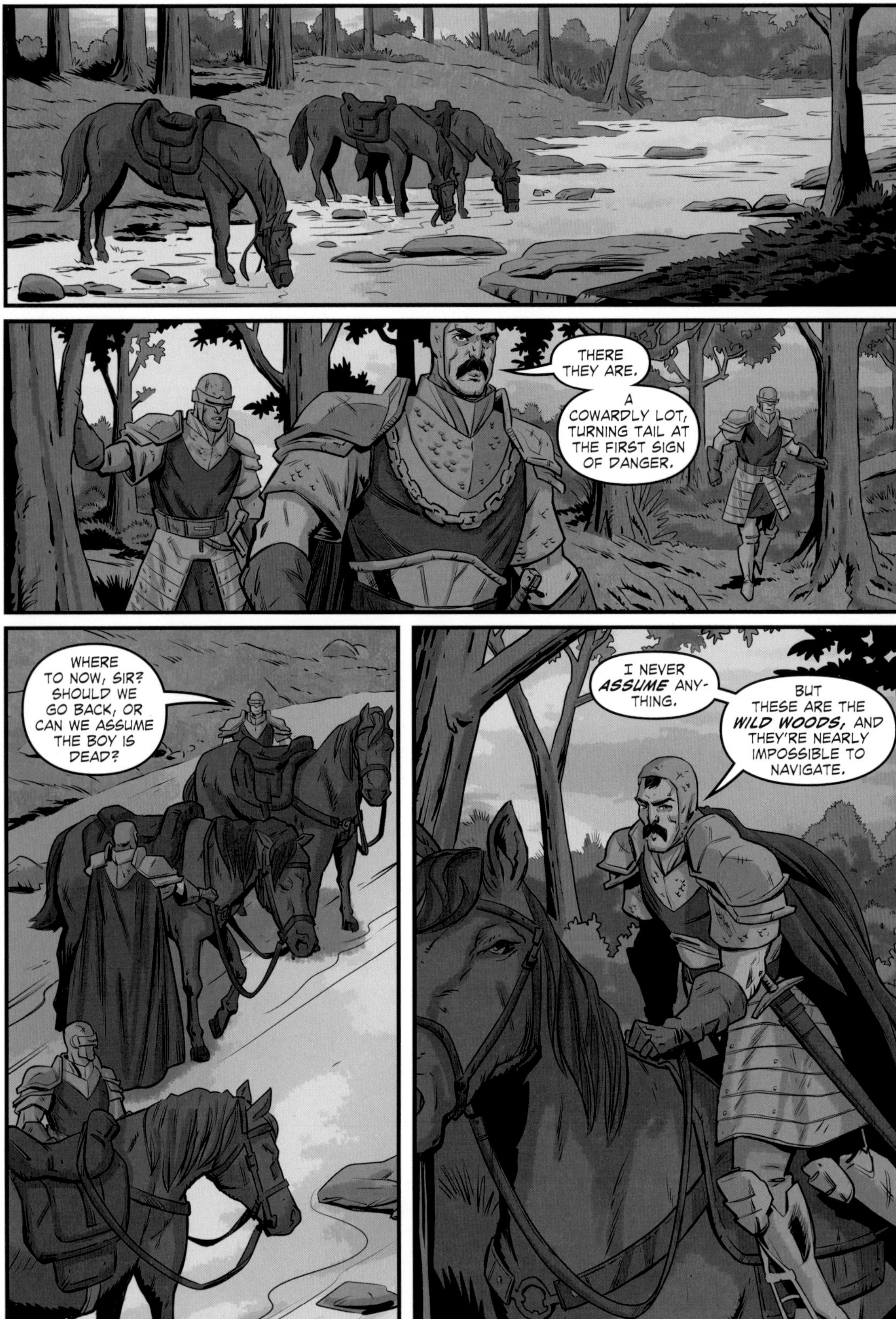
THERE THEY ARE.
A COWARDLY LOT, TURNING TAIL AT THE FIRST SIGN OF DANGER.
WHERE TO NOW, SIR? SHOULD WE GO BACK, OR CAN WE ASSUME THE BOY IS DEAD?
I NEVER ASSUME ANYTHING.
BUT THESE ARE THE WILD WOODS, AND THEY'RE NEARLY IMPOSSIBLE TO NAVIGATE.

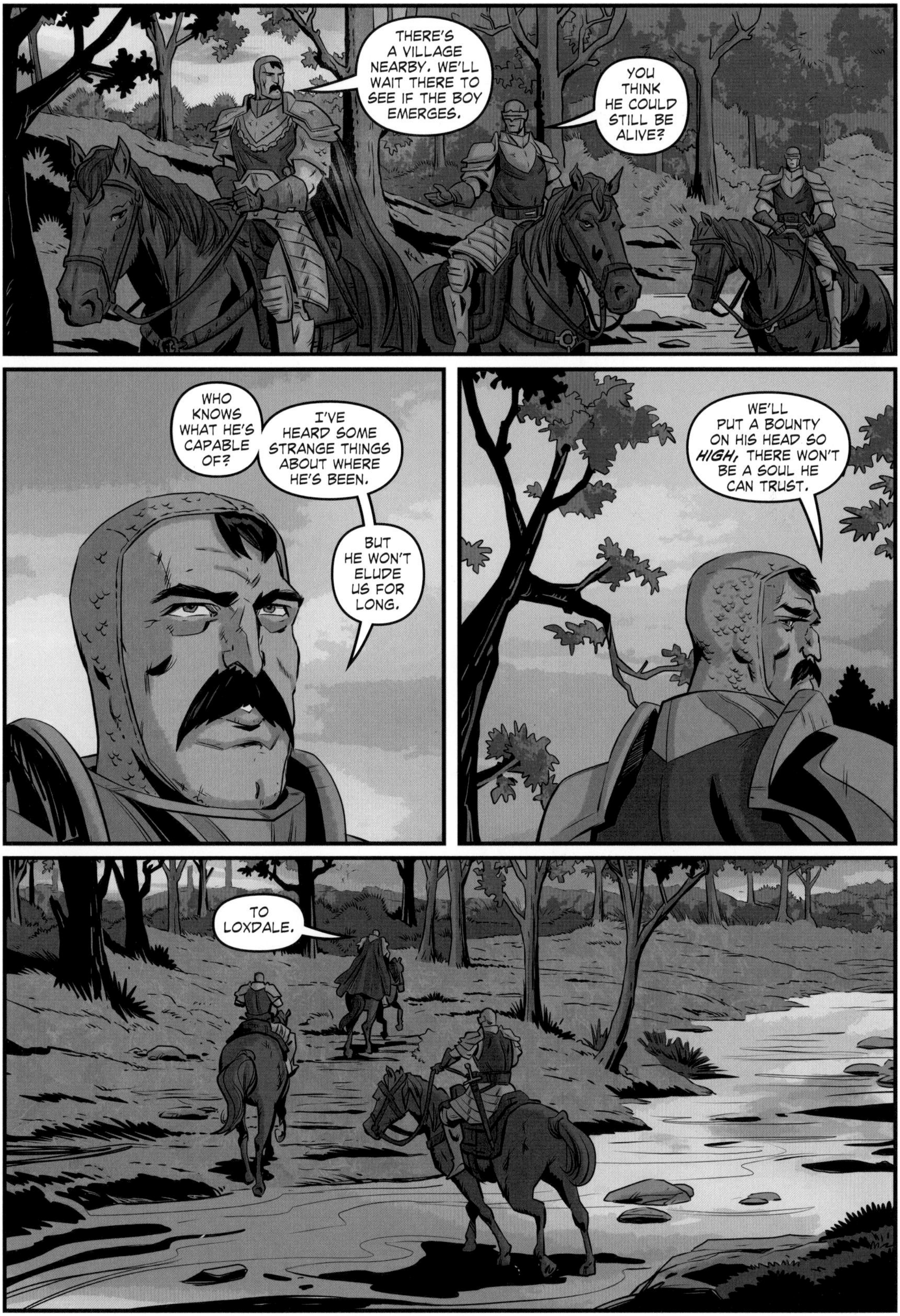
THERE'S A VILLAGE NEARBY. WE'LL WAIT THERE TO SEE IF THE BOY EMERGES.
YOU THINK HE COULD STILL BE ALIVE?
WHO KNOWS WHAT HE'S CAPABLE OF?
I'VE HEARD SOME STRANGE THINGS ABOUT WHERE HE'S BEEN.
BUT HE WON'T ELUDE US FOR LONG.
WE'LL PUT A BOUNTY ON HIS HEAD SO *HIGH,* THERE WON'T BE A SOUL HE CAN TRUST.
TO LOXDALE.

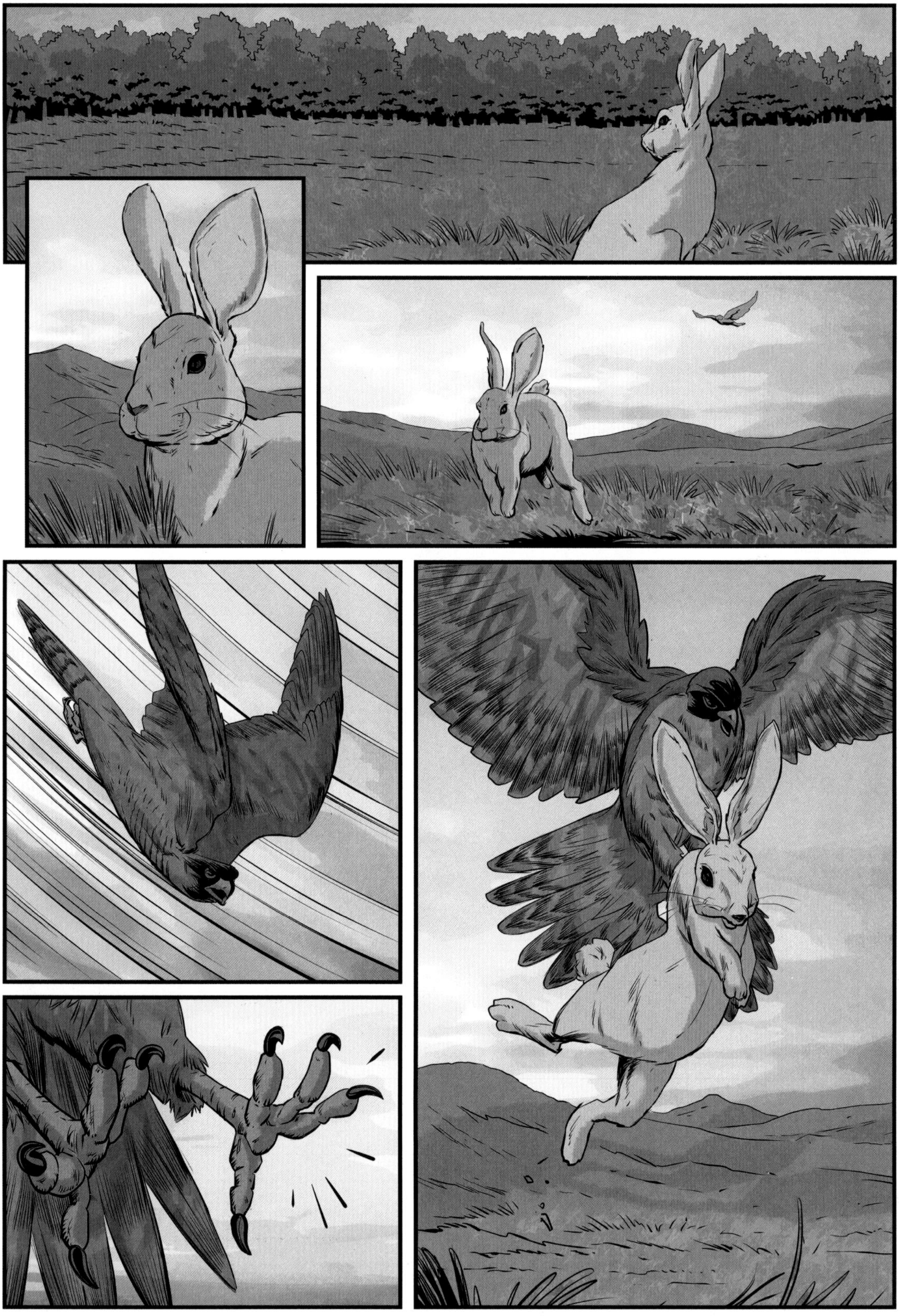

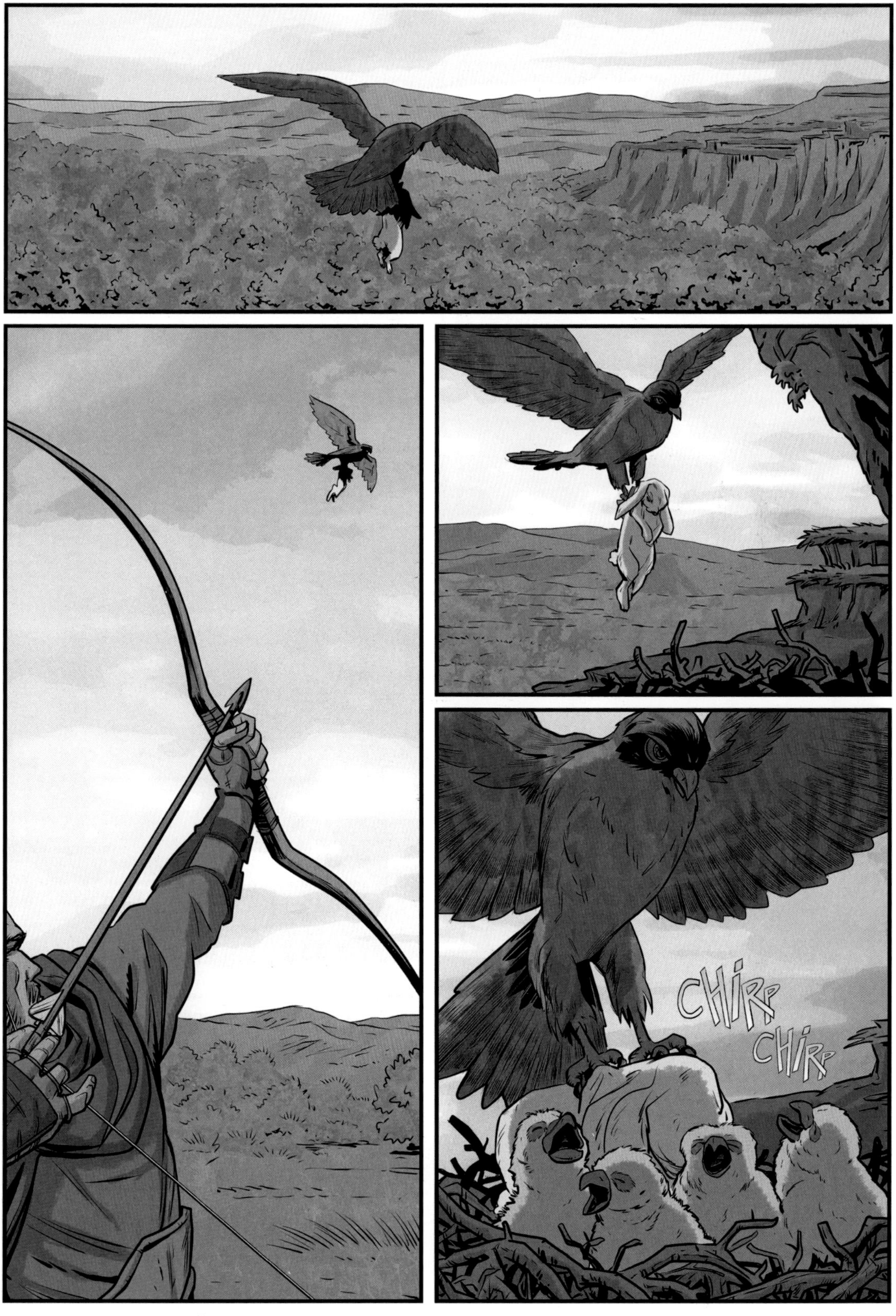
CHIRP
CHIRP

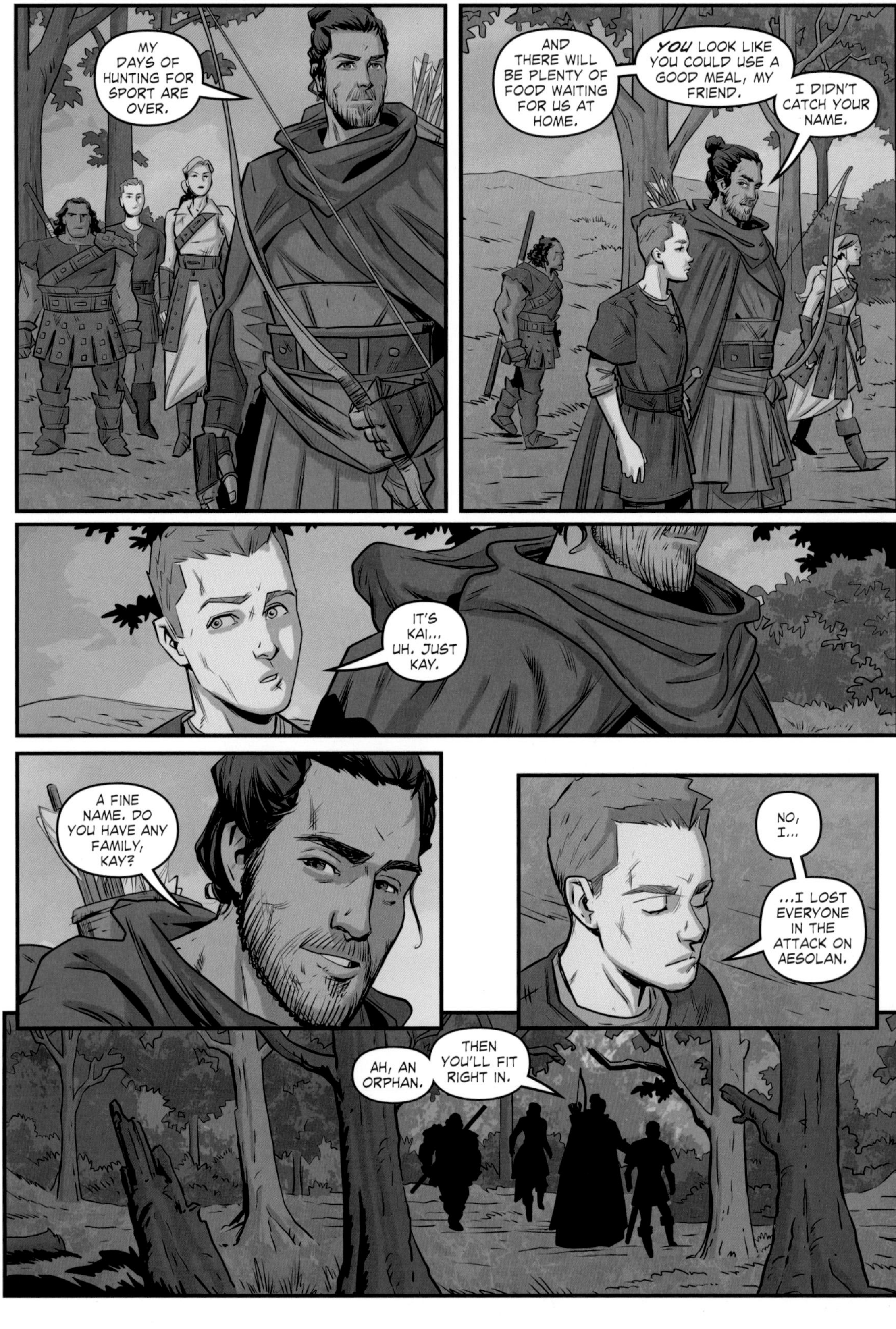
MY DAYS OF HUNTING FOR SPORT ARE OVER.
AND THERE WILL BE PLENTY OF FOOD WAITING FOR US AT HOME.
YOU LOOK LIKE YOU COULD USE A GOOD MEAL, MY FRIEND.
I DIDN'T CATCH YOUR NAME.
IT'S KAI... UH. JUST KAY.
A FINE NAME. DO YOU HAVE ANY FAMILY, KAY?
NO, I...
...I LOST EVERYONE IN THE ATTACK ON AESOLAN.
AH, AN ORPHAN.
THEN YOU'LL FIT RIGHT IN.

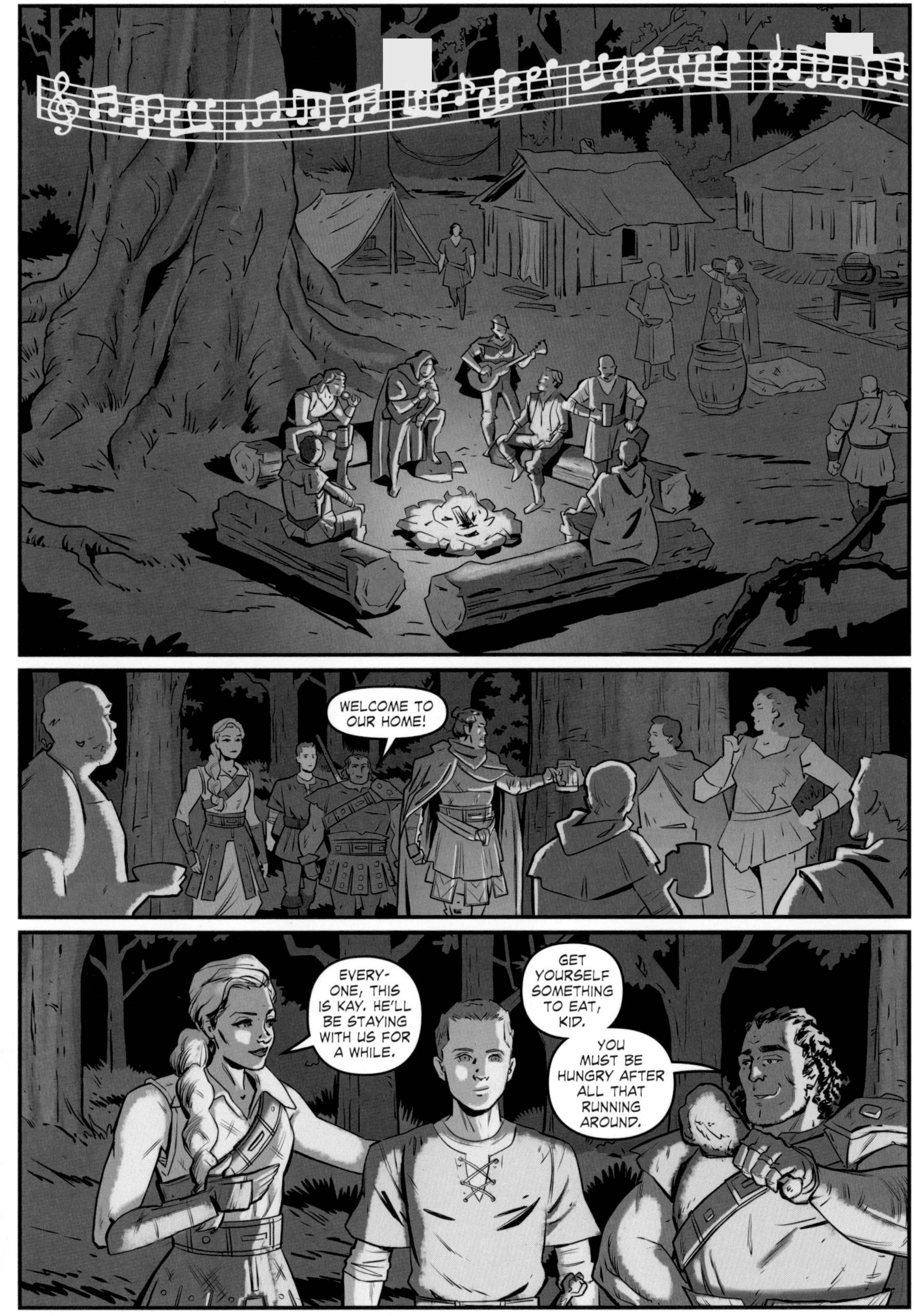
WELCOME TO OUR HOME!
EVERY-ONE, THIS IS KAY. HE'LL BE STAYING WITH US FOR A WHILE.
GET YOURSELF SOMETHING TO EAT, KID.
YOU MUST BE HUNGRY AFTER ALL THAT RUNNING AROUND.

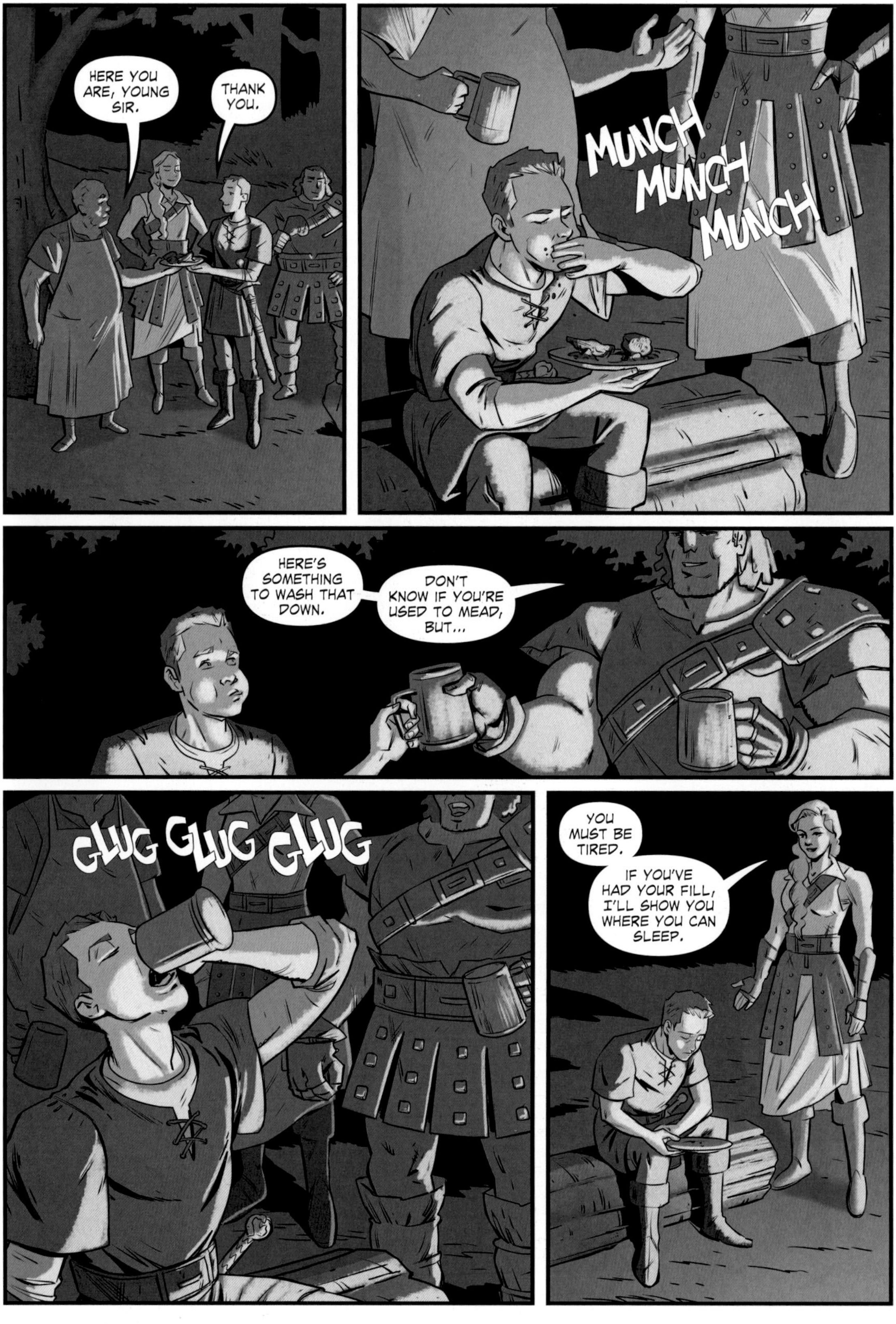
HERE YOU ARE, YOUNG SIR.
THANK YOU.
MUNCH MUNCH MUNCH
HERE'S SOMETHING TO WASH THAT DOWN.
DON'T KNOW IF YOU'RE USED TO MEAD, BUT...
GLUG GLUG GLUG
YOU MUST BE TIRED.
IF YOU'VE HAD YOUR FILL, I'LL SHOW YOU WHERE YOU CAN SLEEP.

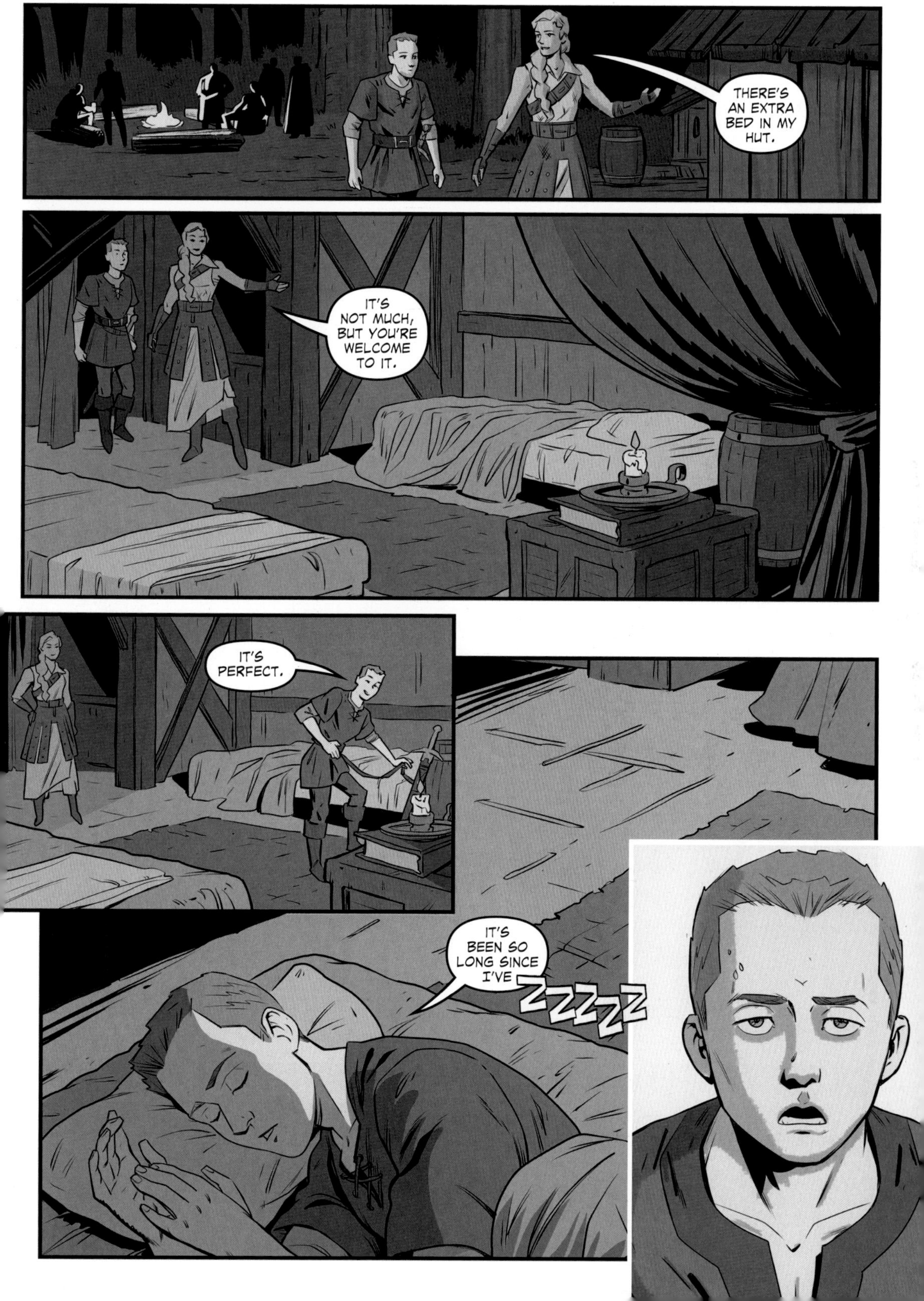
THERE'S AN EXTRA BED IN MY HUT.
IT'S NOT MUCH, BUT YOU'RE WELCOME TO IT.
IT'S PERFECT.
IT'S BEEN SO LONG SINCE I'VE
ZZZZZ

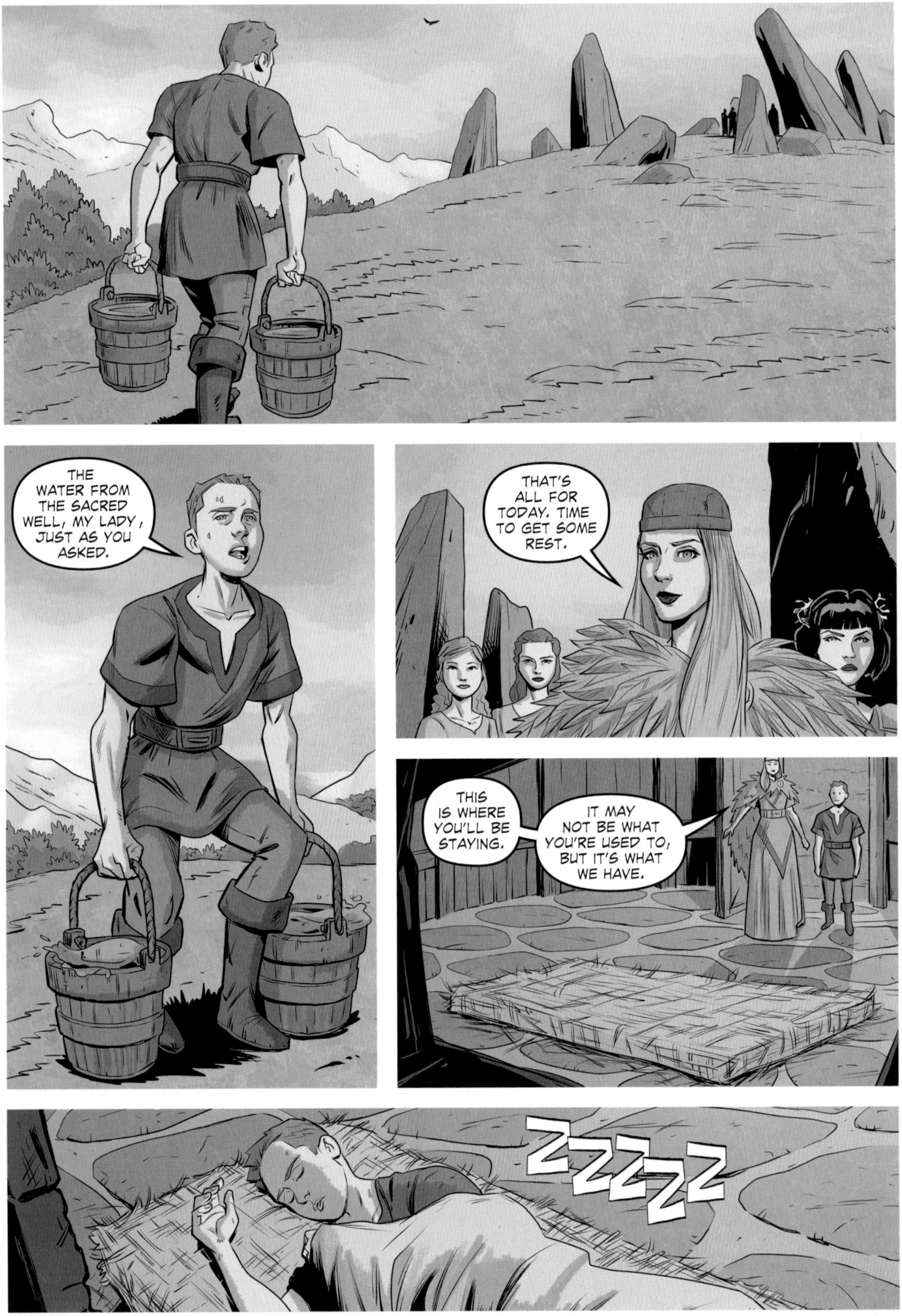
THE WATER FROM THE SACRED WELL, MY LADY, JUST AS YOU ASKED.
THAT'S ALL FOR TODAY. TIME TO GET SOME REST.
THIS IS WHERE YOU'LL BE STAYING.
IT MAY NOT BE WHAT YOU'RE USED TO, BUT IT'S WHAT WE HAVE.
ZZZZZZ

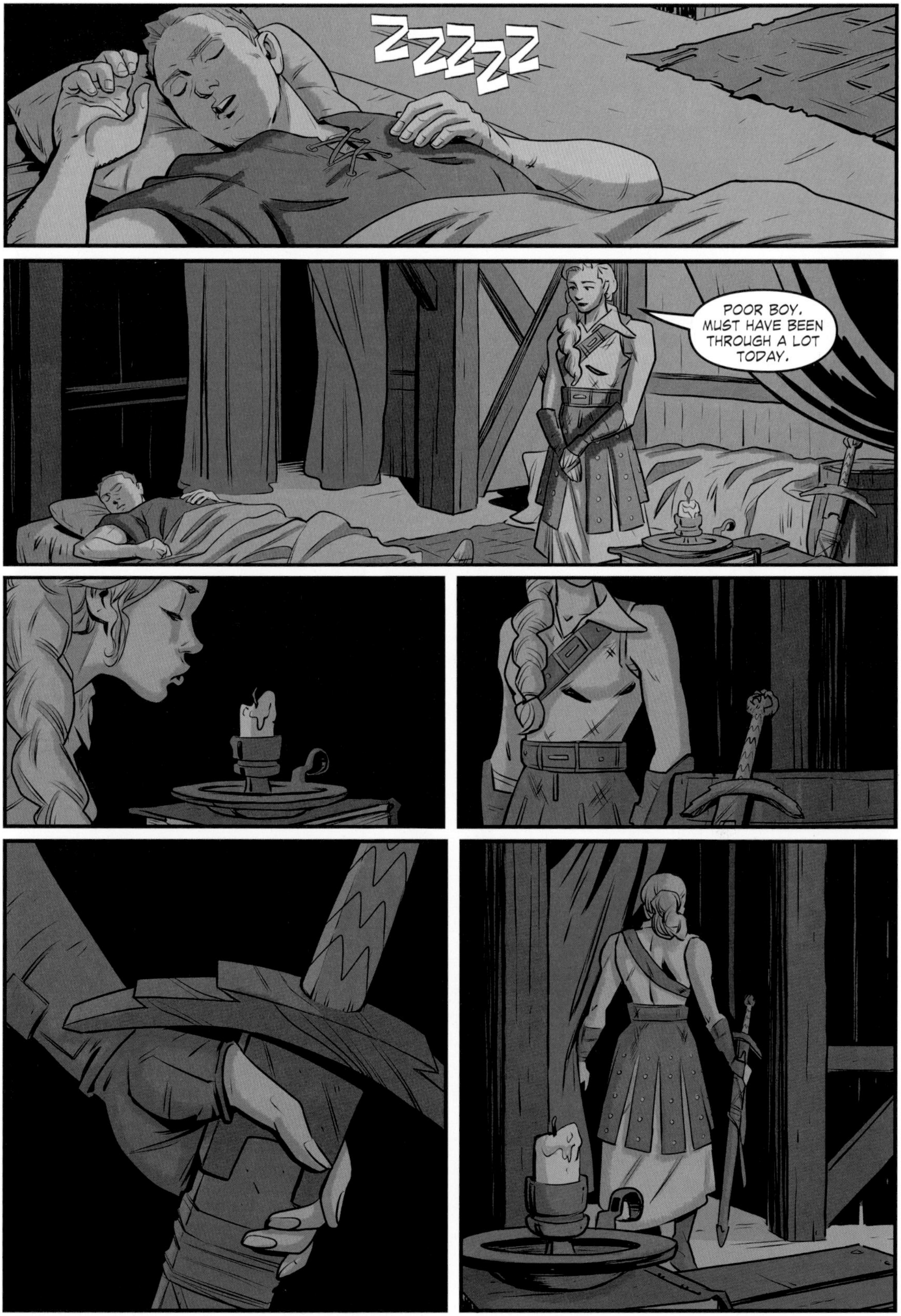
ZZZZZ
POOR BOY. MUST HAVE BEEN THROUGH A LOT TODAY.

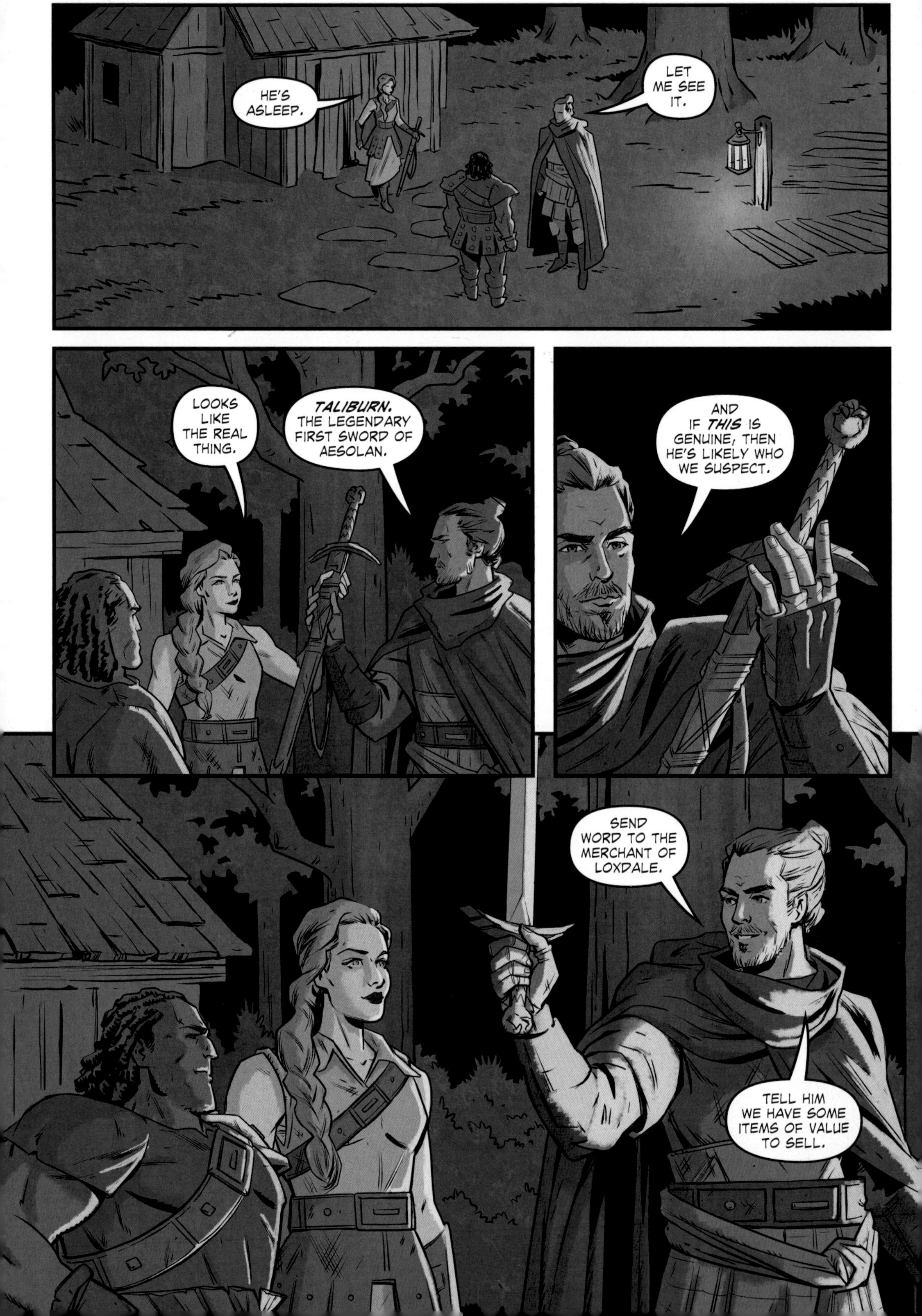
HE'S ASLEEP.
LET ME SEE IT.
LOOKS LIKE THE REAL THING.
TALIBURN. THE LEGENDARY FIRST SWORD OF AESOLAN.
AND IF THIS IS GENUINE, THEN HE'S LIKELY WHO WE SUSPECT.
SEND WORD TO THE MERCHANT OF LOXDALE.
TELL HIM WE HAVE SOME ITEMS OF VALUE TO SELL.

Chapter 4

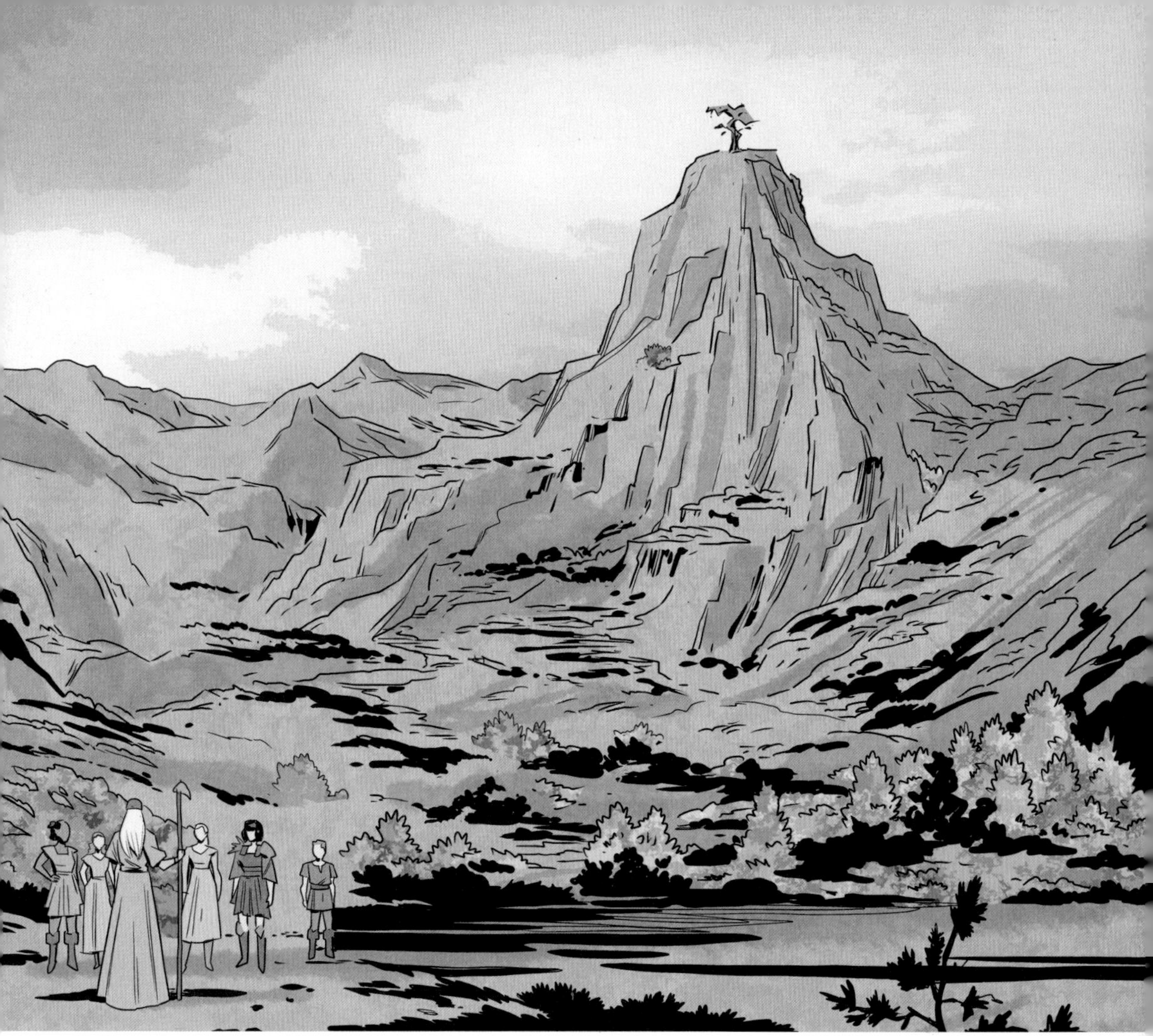

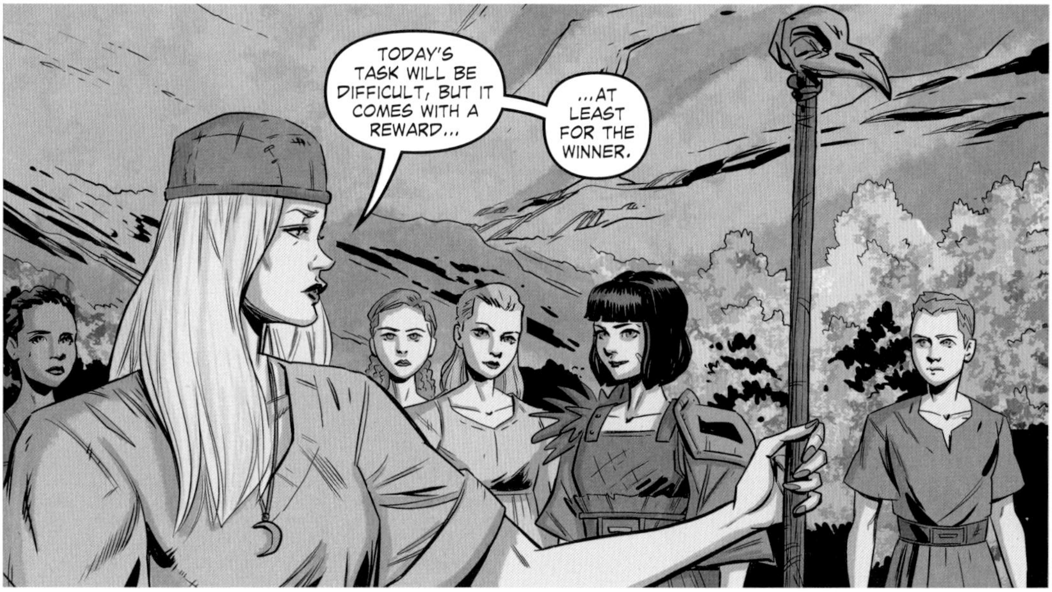
TODAY'S TASK WILL BE DIFFICULT, BUT IT COMES WITH A REWARD...
...AT LEAST FOR THE WINNER.

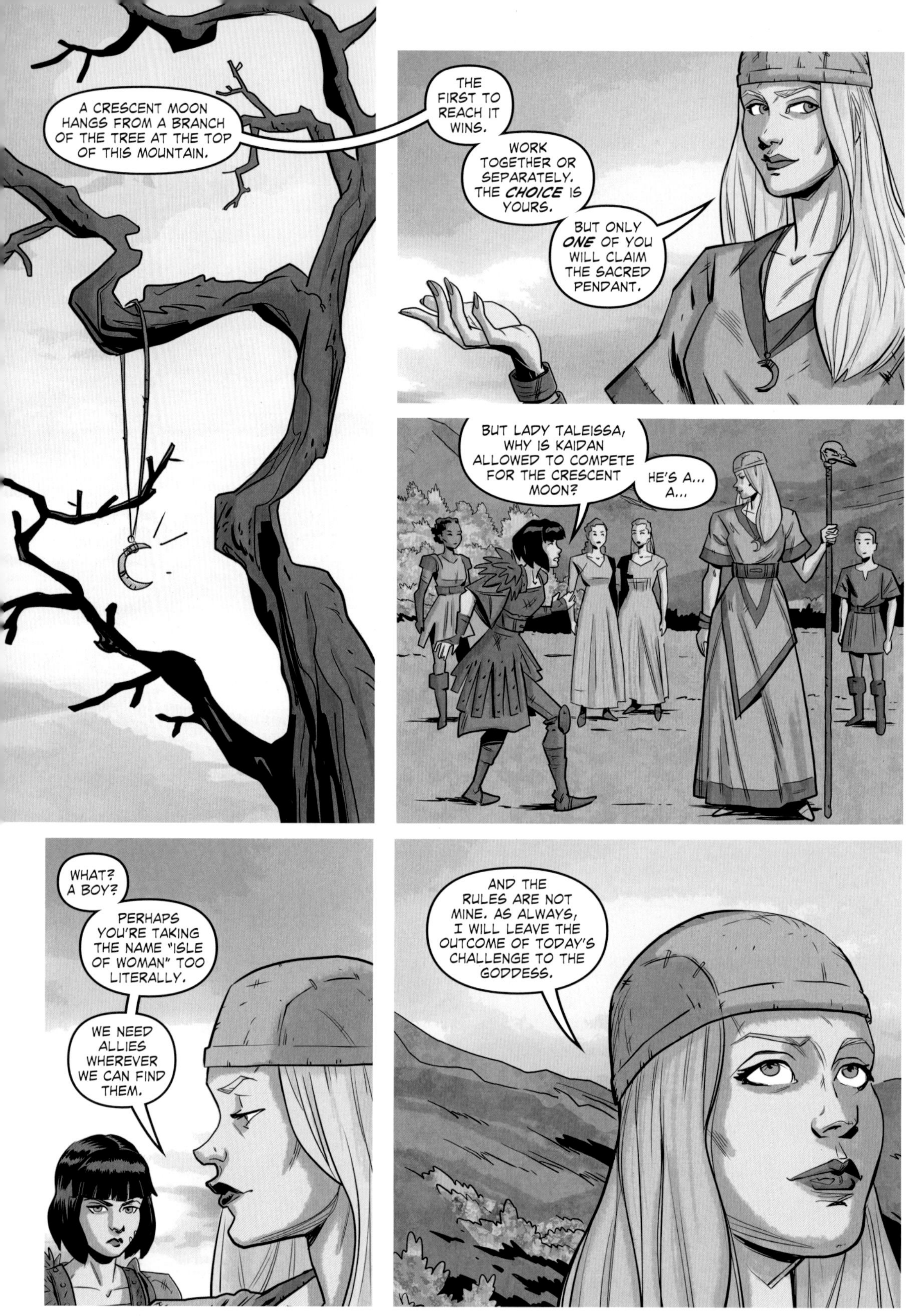

A CRESCENT MOON HANGS FROM A BRANCH OF THE TREE AT THE TOP OF THIS MOUNTAIN.
THE FIRST TO REACH IT WINS.
WORK TOGETHER OR SEPARATELY. THE CHOICE IS YOURS.
BUT ONLY ONE OF YOU WILL CLAIM THE SACRED PENDANT.
BUT LADY TALEISSA, WHY IS KAIDAN ALLOWED TO COMPETE FOR THE CRESCENT MOON?
HE'S A... A...
WHAT? A BOY?
PERHAPS YOU'RE TAKING THE NAME "ISLE OF WOMAN" TOO LITERALLY.
WE NEED ALLIES WHEREVER WE CAN FIND THEM.
AND THE RULES ARE NOT MINE. AS ALWAYS, I WILL LEAVE THE OUTCOME OF TODAY'S CHALLENGE TO THE GODDESS.

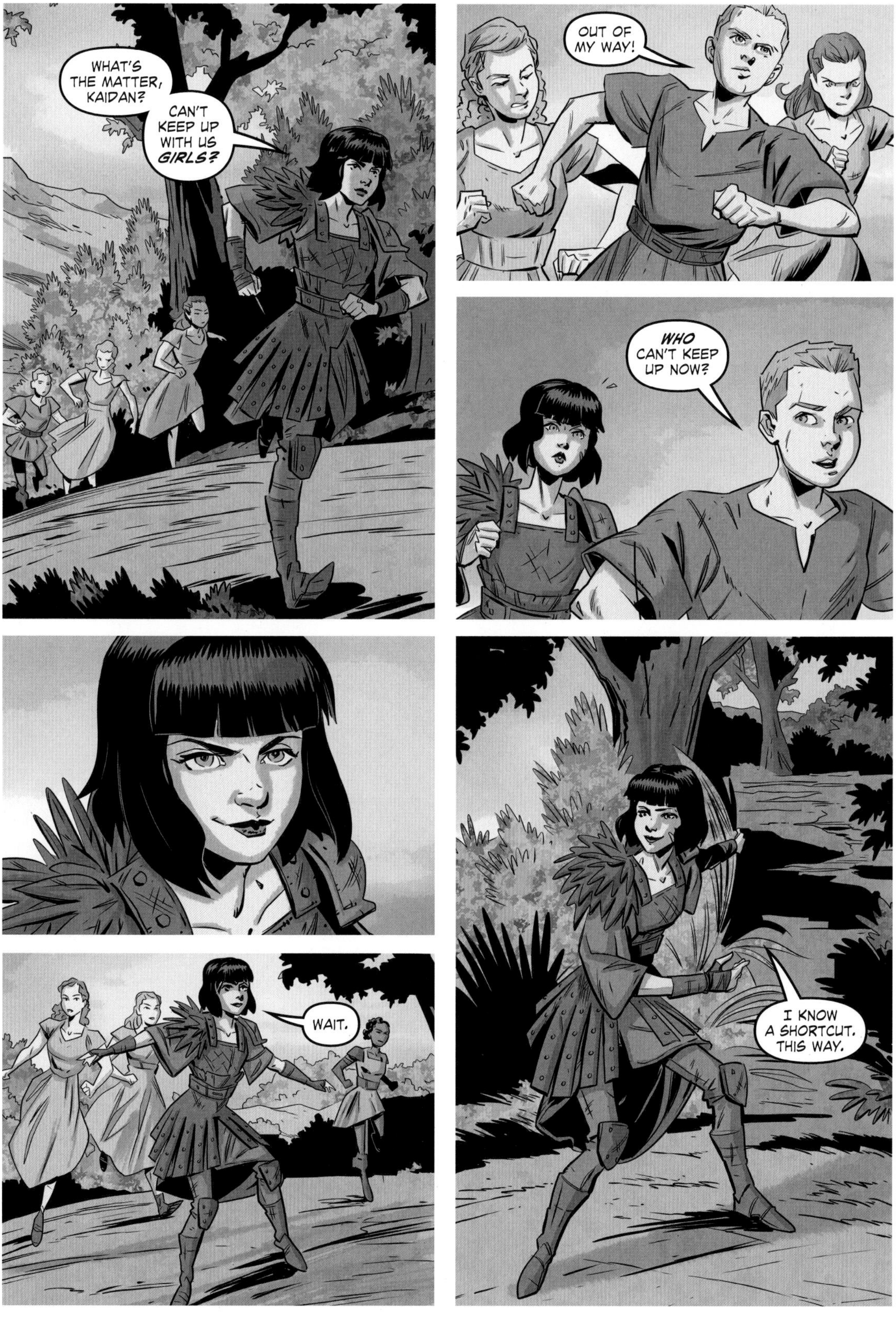
WHAT'S THE MATTER, KAIDAN?
CAN'T KEEP UP WITH US GIRLS?
OUT OF MY WAY!
WHO CAN'T KEEP UP NOW?
WAIT.
I KNOW A SHORTCUT. THIS WAY.

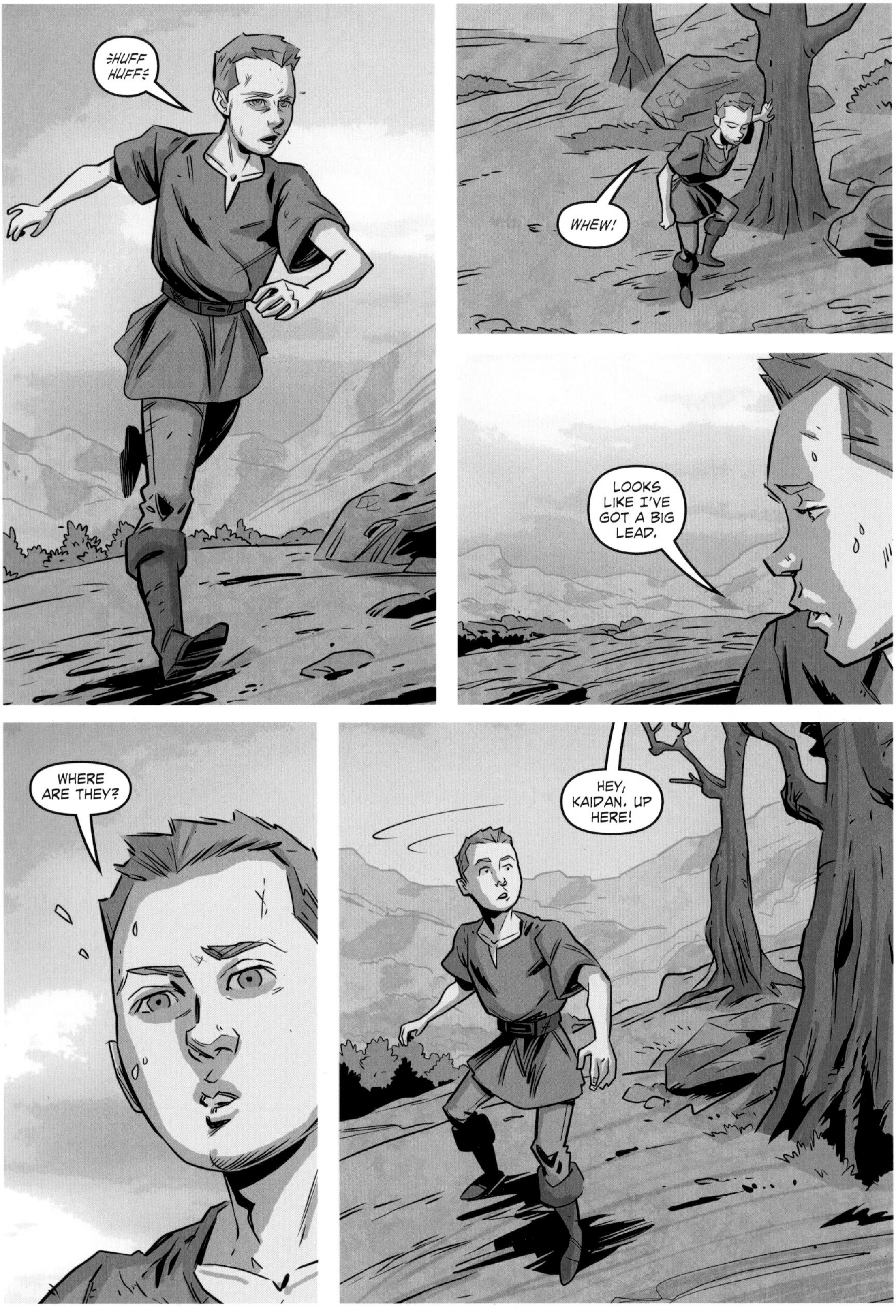
HUFF HUFF
WHEW!
LOOKS LIKE I'VE GOT A BIG LEAD.
WHERE ARE THEY?
HEY, KAIDAN. UP HERE!

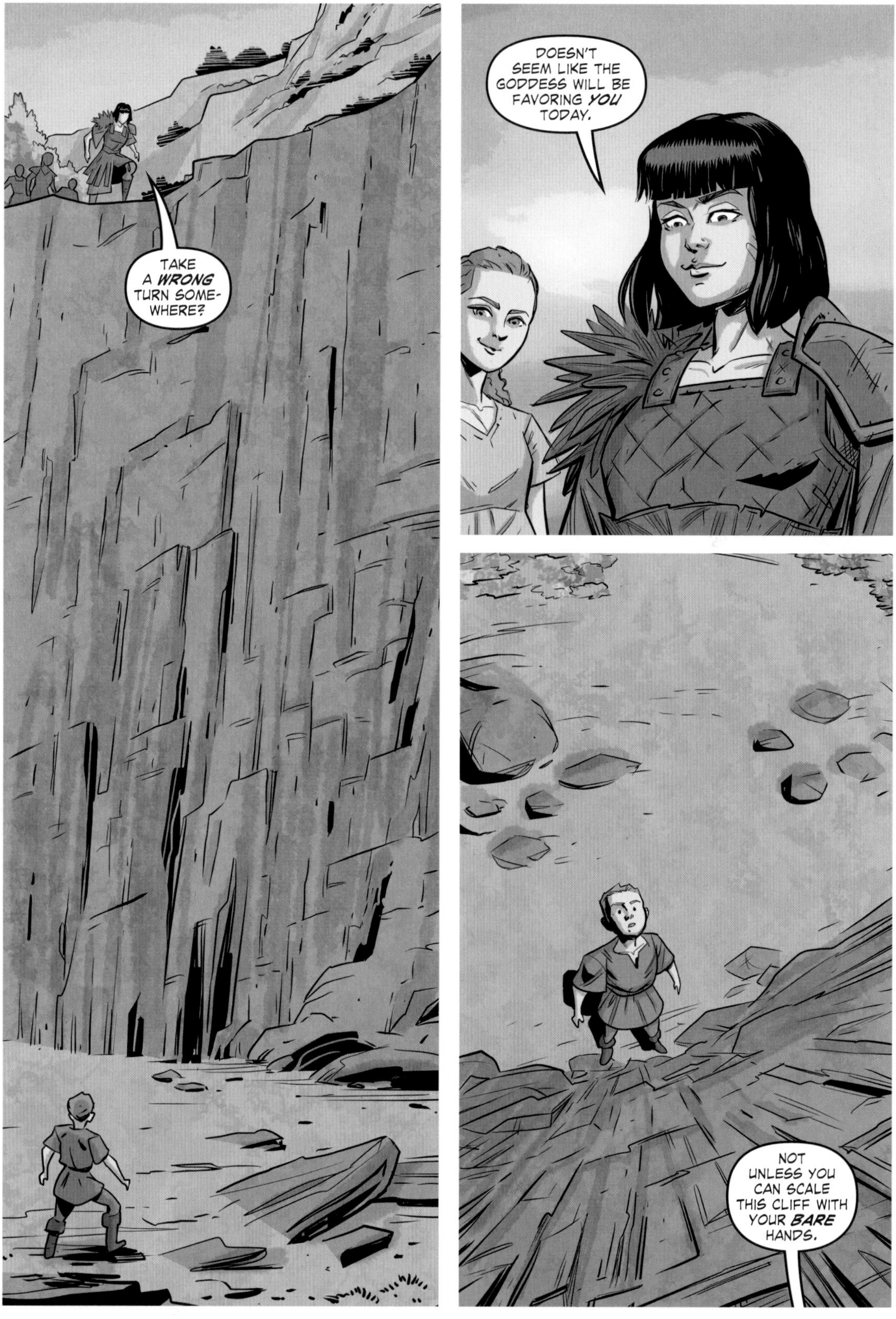
TAKE A *WRONG* TURN SOME-WHERE?
DOESN'T SEEM LIKE THE GODDESS WILL BE FAVORING *YOU* TODAY.
NOT UNLESS YOU CAN SCALE THIS CLIFF WITH YOUR *BARE* HANDS.

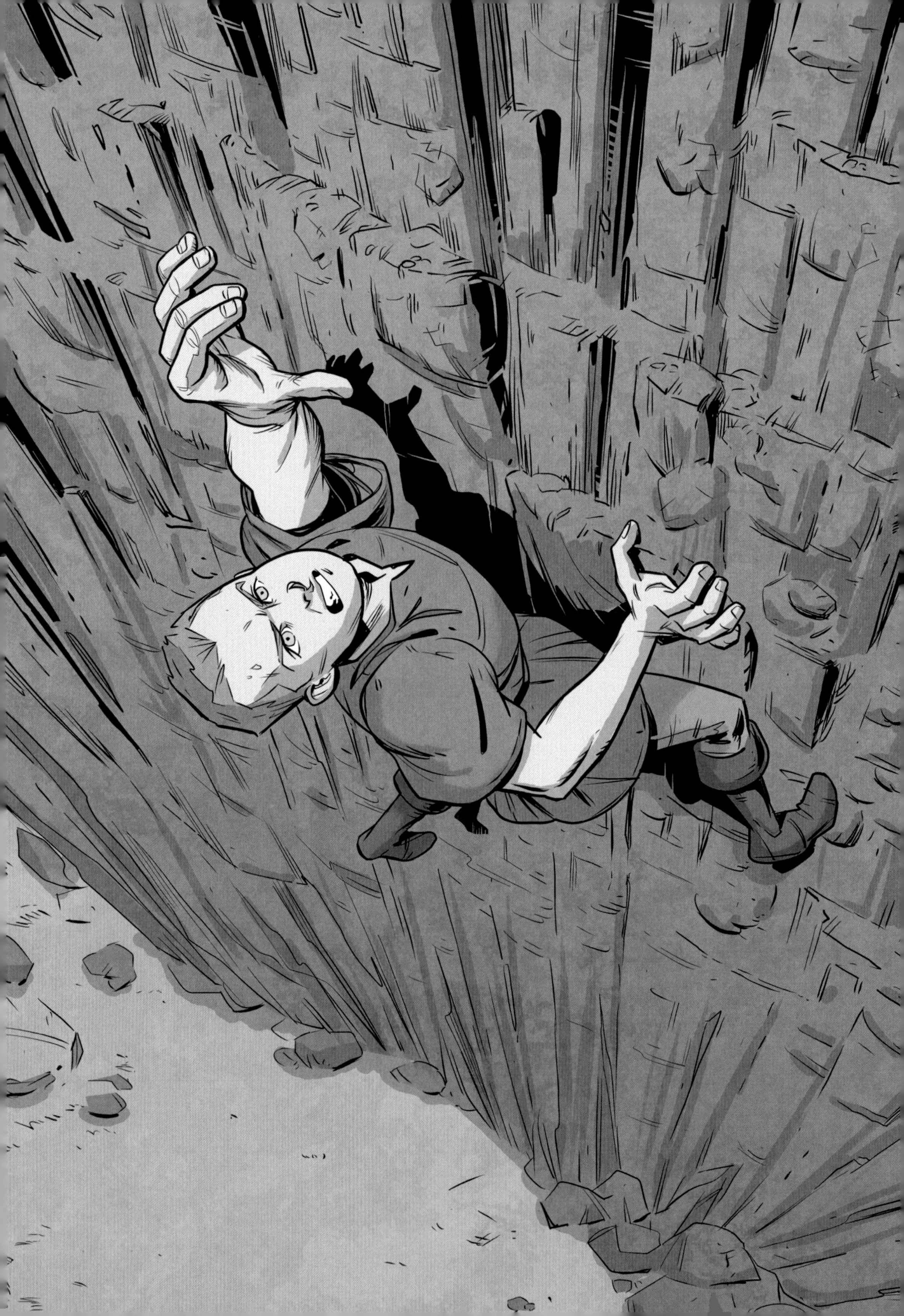

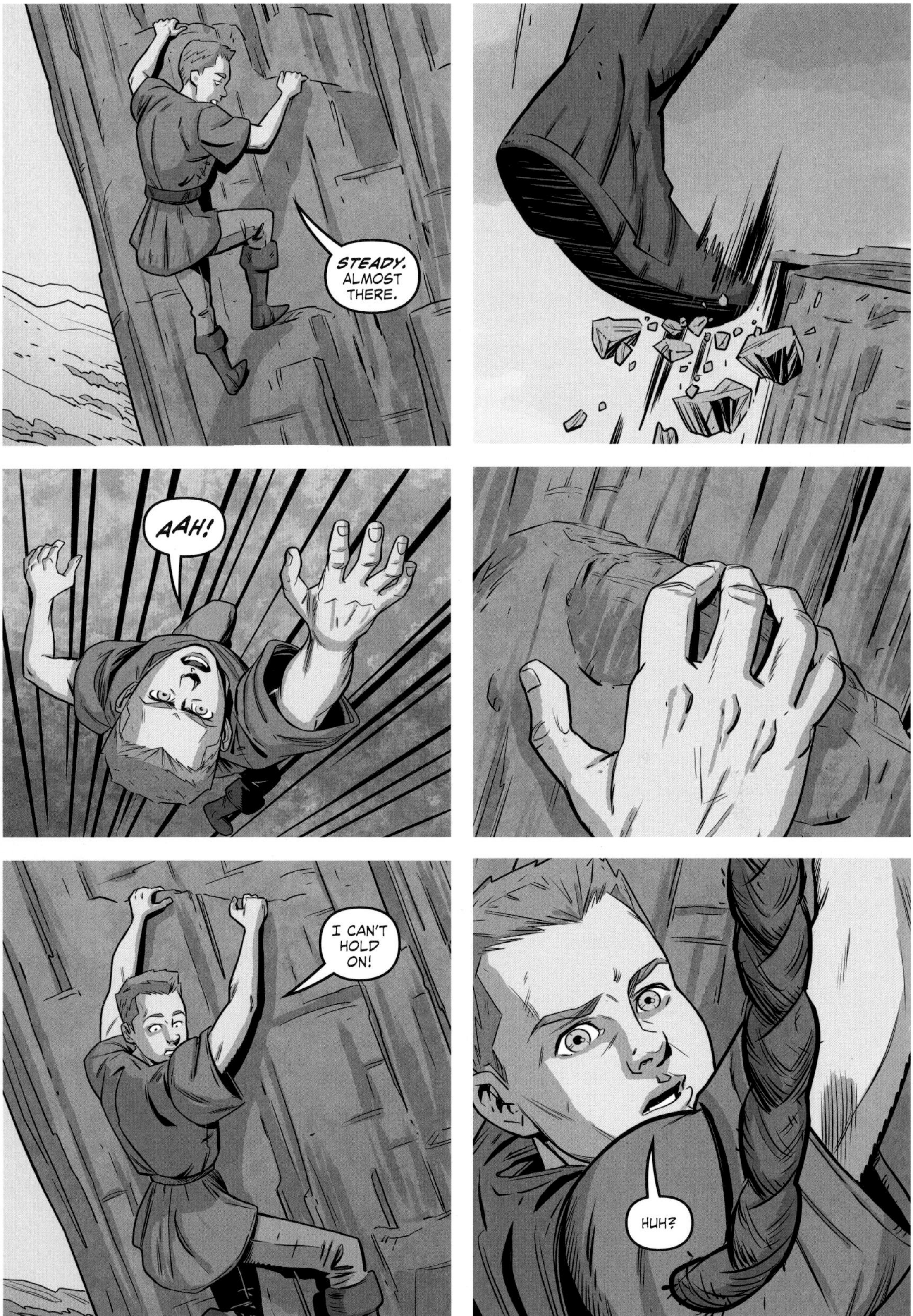
STEADY. ALMOST THERE.
AAH!
I CAN'T HOLD ON!
HUH?

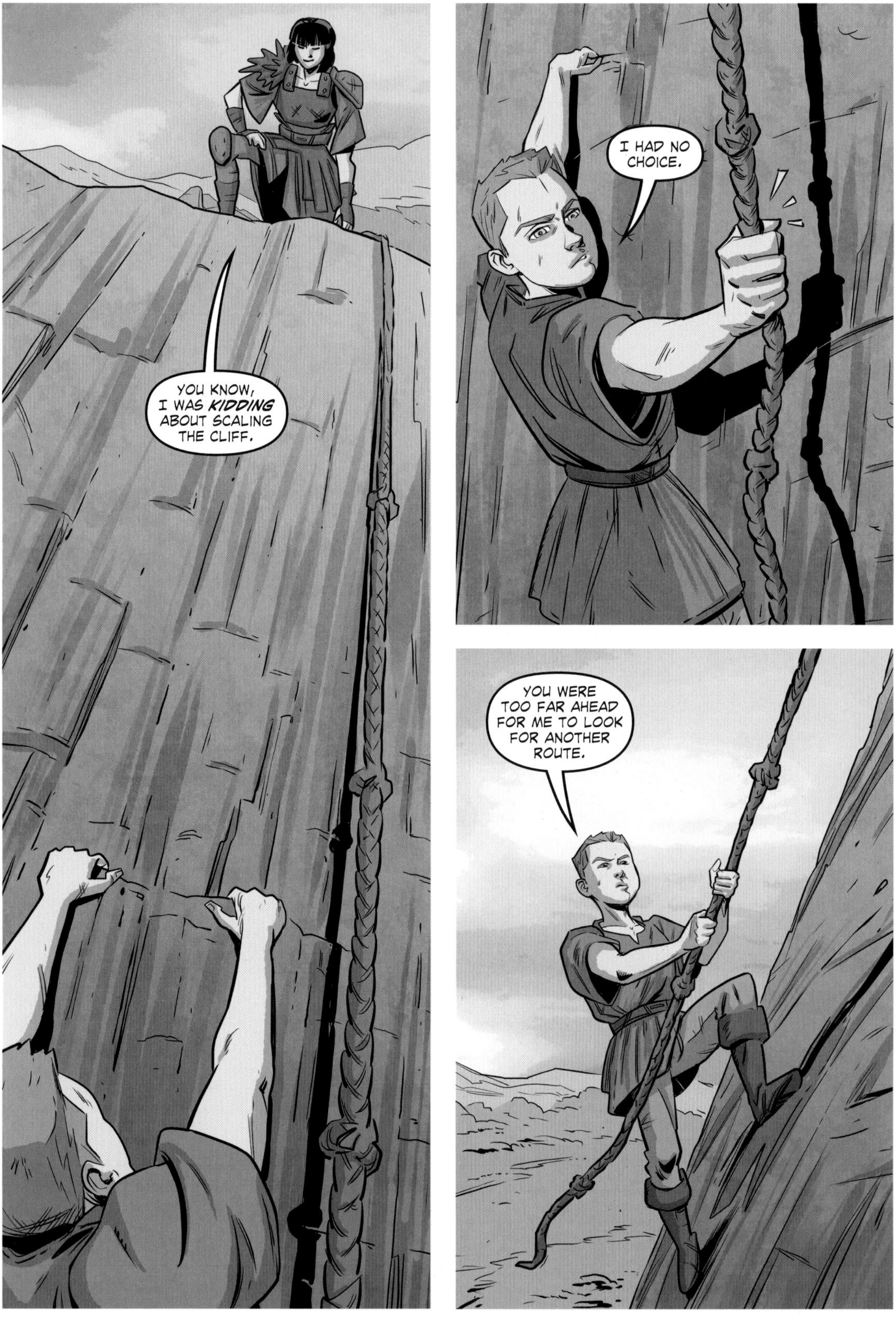
YOU KNOW, I WAS *KIDDING* ABOUT SCALING THE CLIFF.
I HAD NO CHOICE.
YOU WERE TOO FAR AHEAD FOR ME TO LOOK FOR ANOTHER ROUTE.

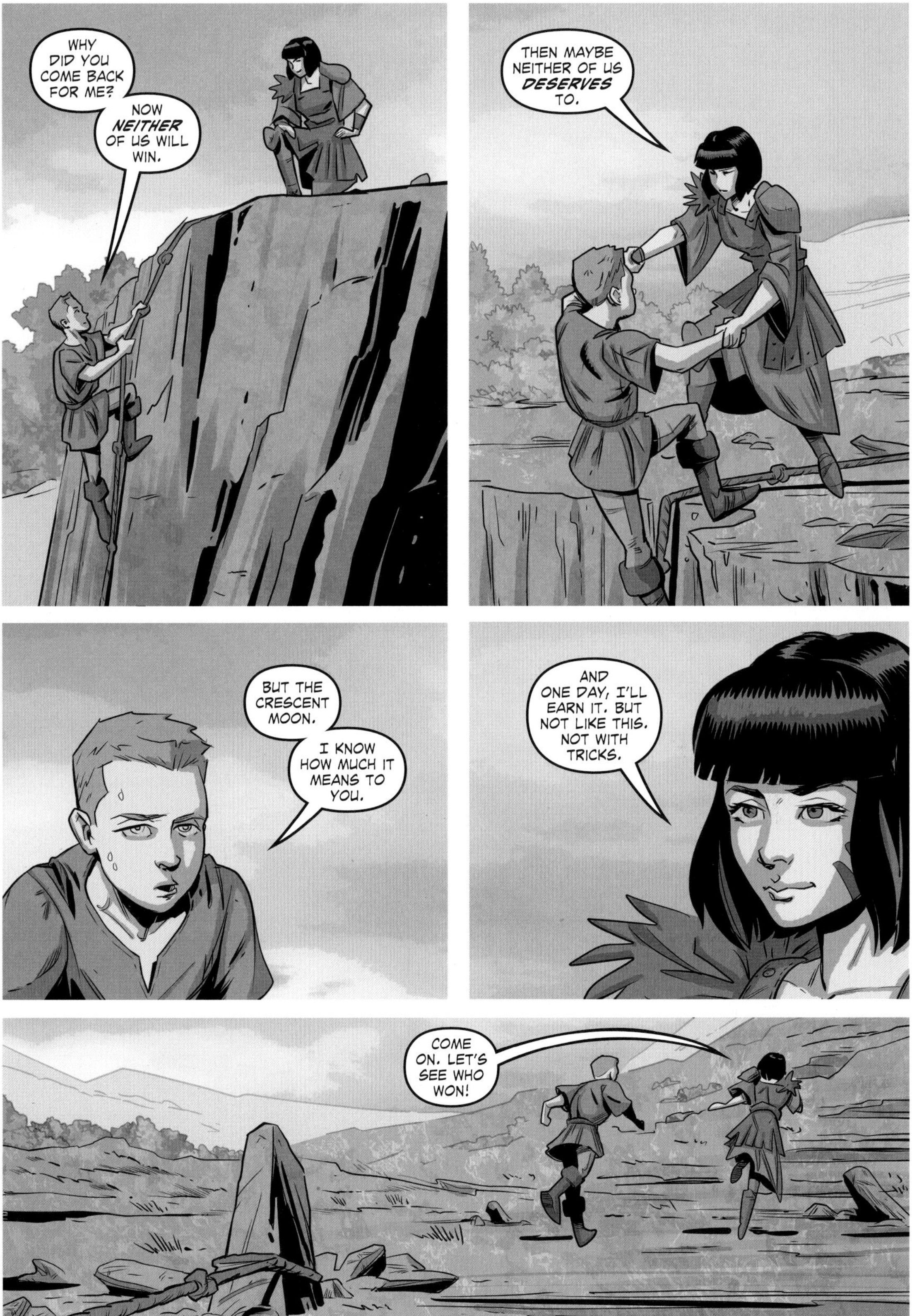
WHY DID YOU COME BACK FOR ME?
NOW NEITHER OF US WILL WIN.
THEN MAYBE NEITHER OF US DESERVES TO.
BUT THE CRESCENT MOON.
I KNOW HOW MUCH IT MEANS TO YOU.
AND ONE DAY, I'LL EARN IT. BUT NOT LIKE THIS. NOT WITH TRICKS.
COME ON. LET'S SEE WHO WON!

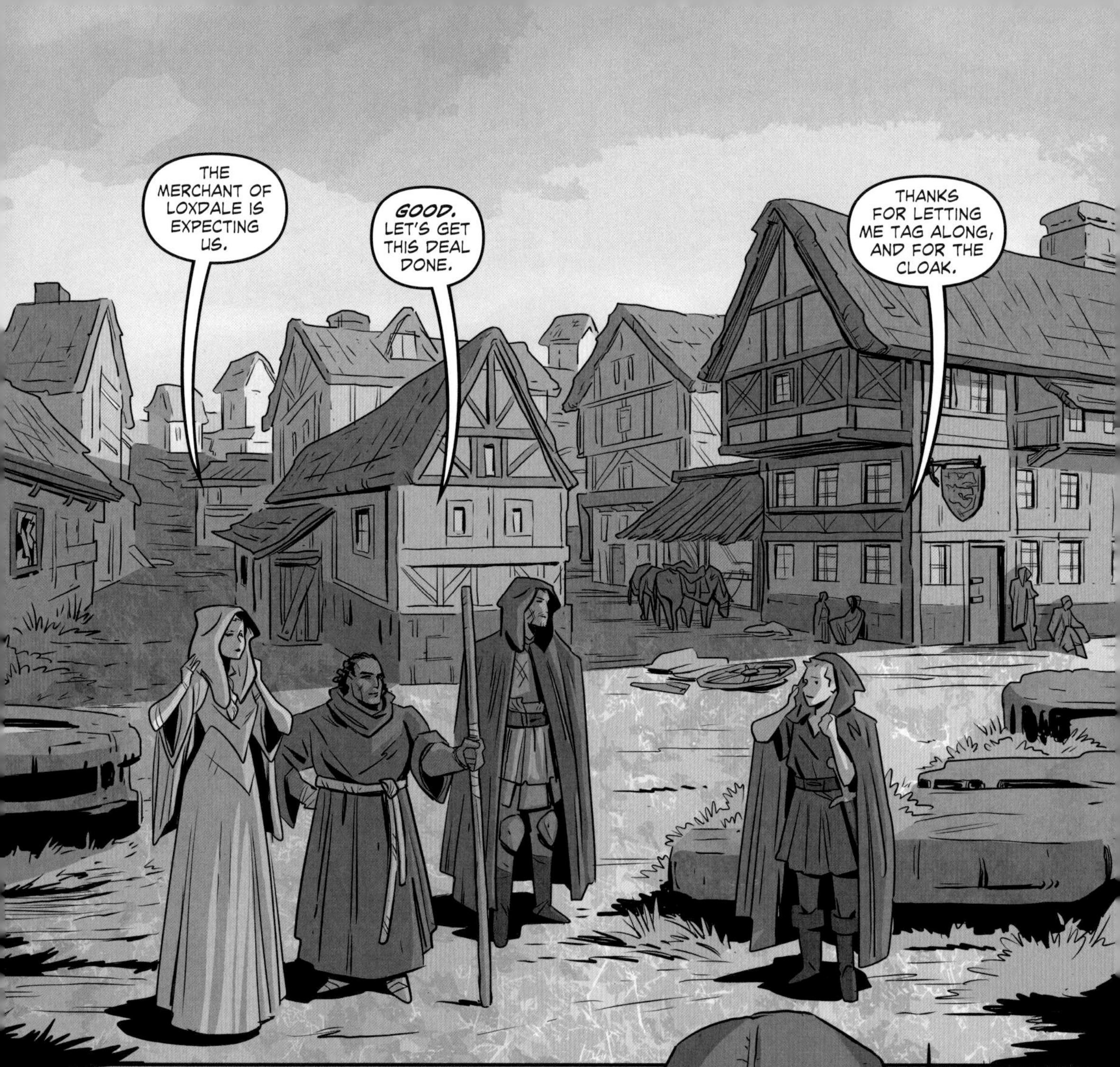
THE MERCHANT OF LOXDALE IS EXPECTING US.
GOOD. LET'S GET THIS DEAL DONE.
THANKS FOR LETTING ME TAG ALONG, AND FOR THE CLOAK.

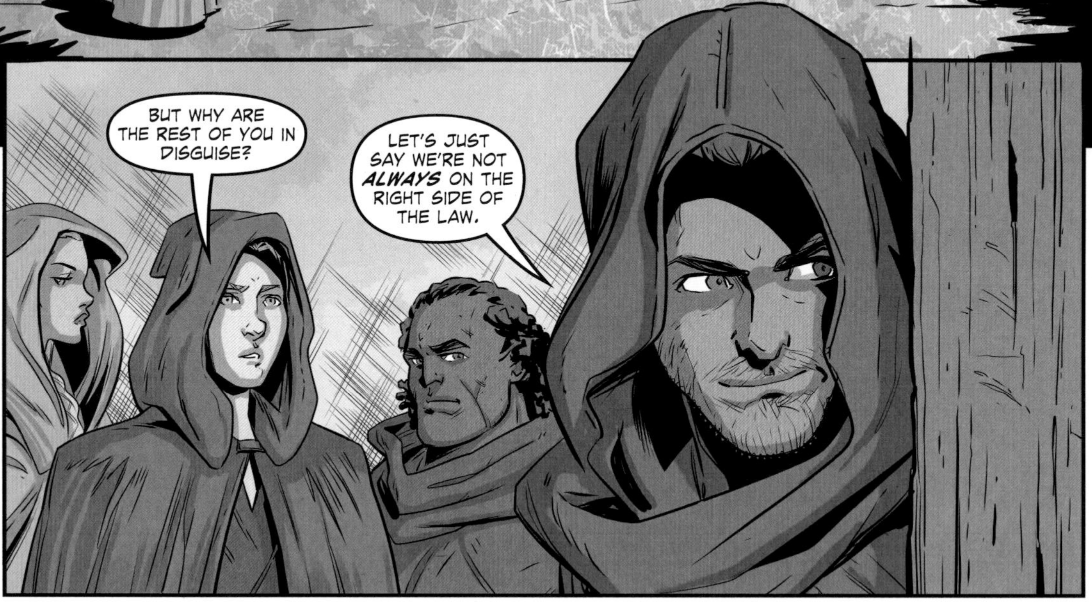
BUT WHY ARE THE REST OF YOU IN DISGUISE?
LET'S JUST SAY WE'RE NOT ALWAYS ON THE RIGHT SIDE OF THE LAW.

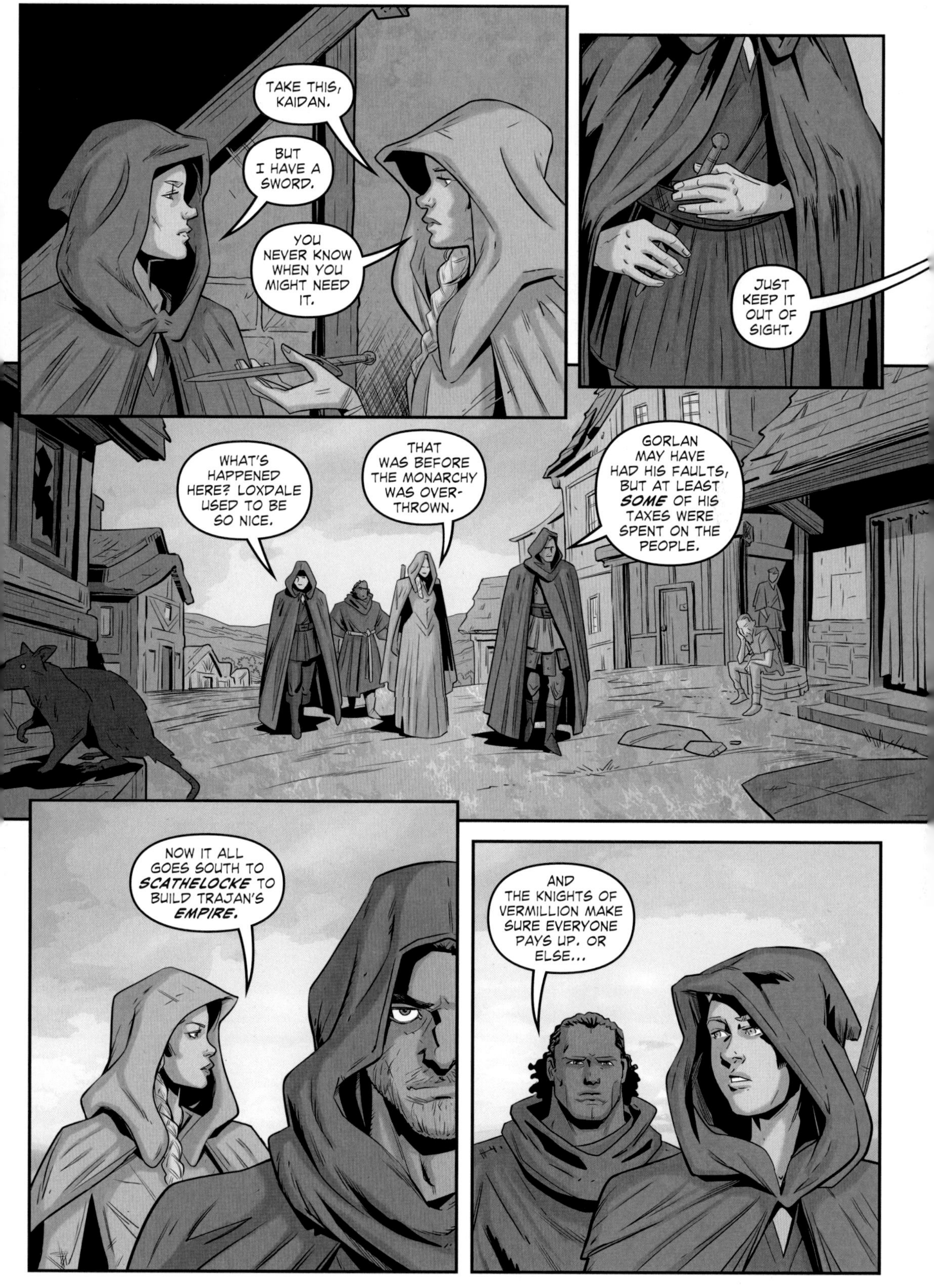
TAKE THIS, KAIDAN.
BUT I HAVE A SWORD.
YOU NEVER KNOW WHEN YOU MIGHT NEED IT.
JUST KEEP IT OUT OF SIGHT.
WHAT'S HAPPENED HERE? LOXDALE USED TO BE SO NICE.
THAT WAS BEFORE THE MONARCHY WAS OVER-THROWN.
GORLAN MAY HAVE HAD HIS FAULTS, BUT AT LEAST *SOME* OF HIS TAXES WERE SPENT ON THE PEOPLE.
NOW IT ALL GOES SOUTH TO *SCATHELOCKE* TO BUILD TRAJAN'S *EMPIRE.*
AND THE KNIGHTS OF VERMILLION MAKE SURE EVERYONE PAYS UP. OR ELSE...

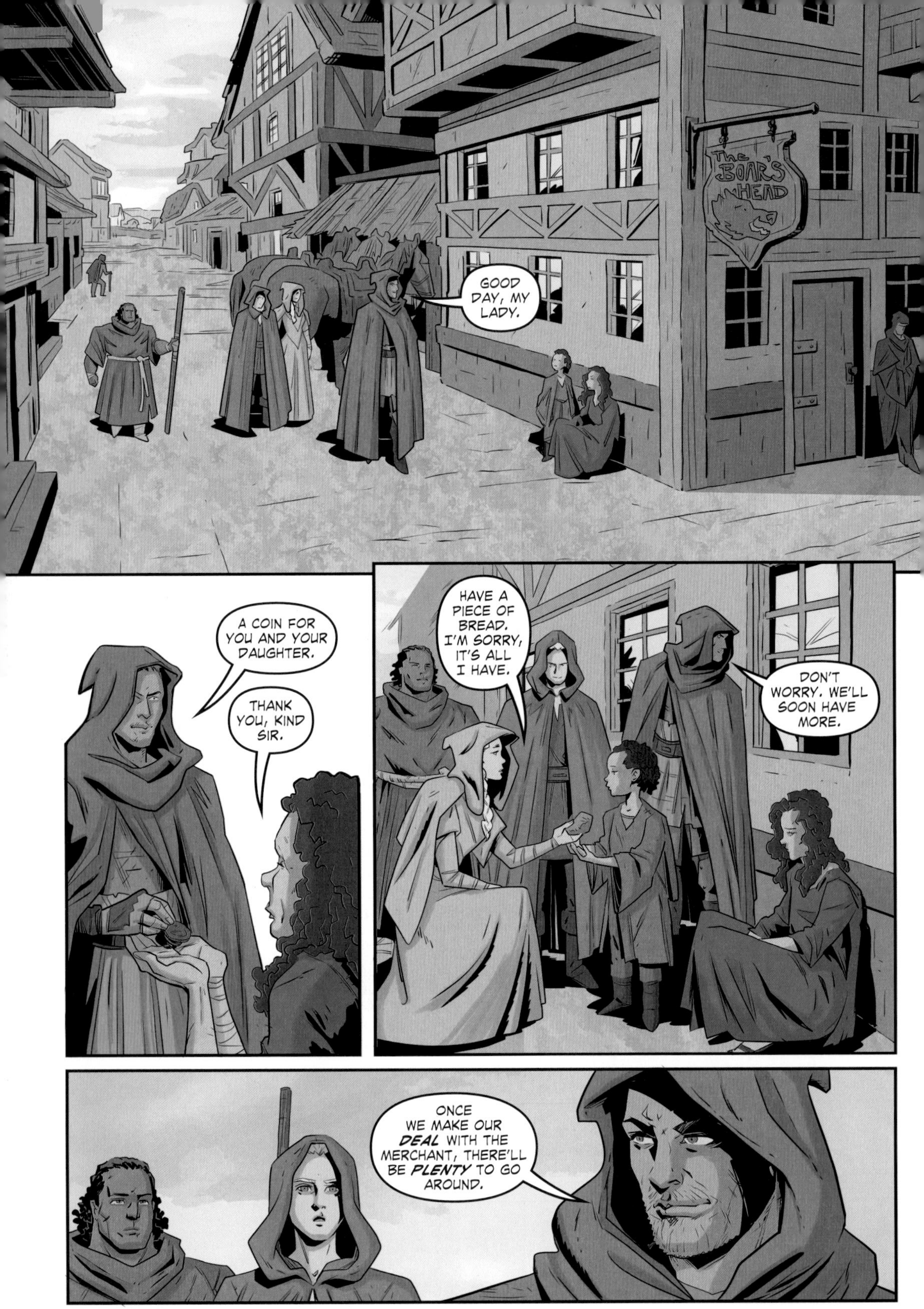

THE BOAR'S HEAD
GOOD DAY, MY LADY.
A COIN FOR YOU AND YOUR DAUGHTER.
THANK YOU, KIND SIR.
HAVE A PIECE OF BREAD. I'M SORRY, IT'S ALL I HAVE.
DON'T WORRY. WE'LL SOON HAVE MORE.
ONCE WE MAKE OUR *DEAL* WITH THE MERCHANT, THERE'LL BE *PLENTY* TO GO AROUND.

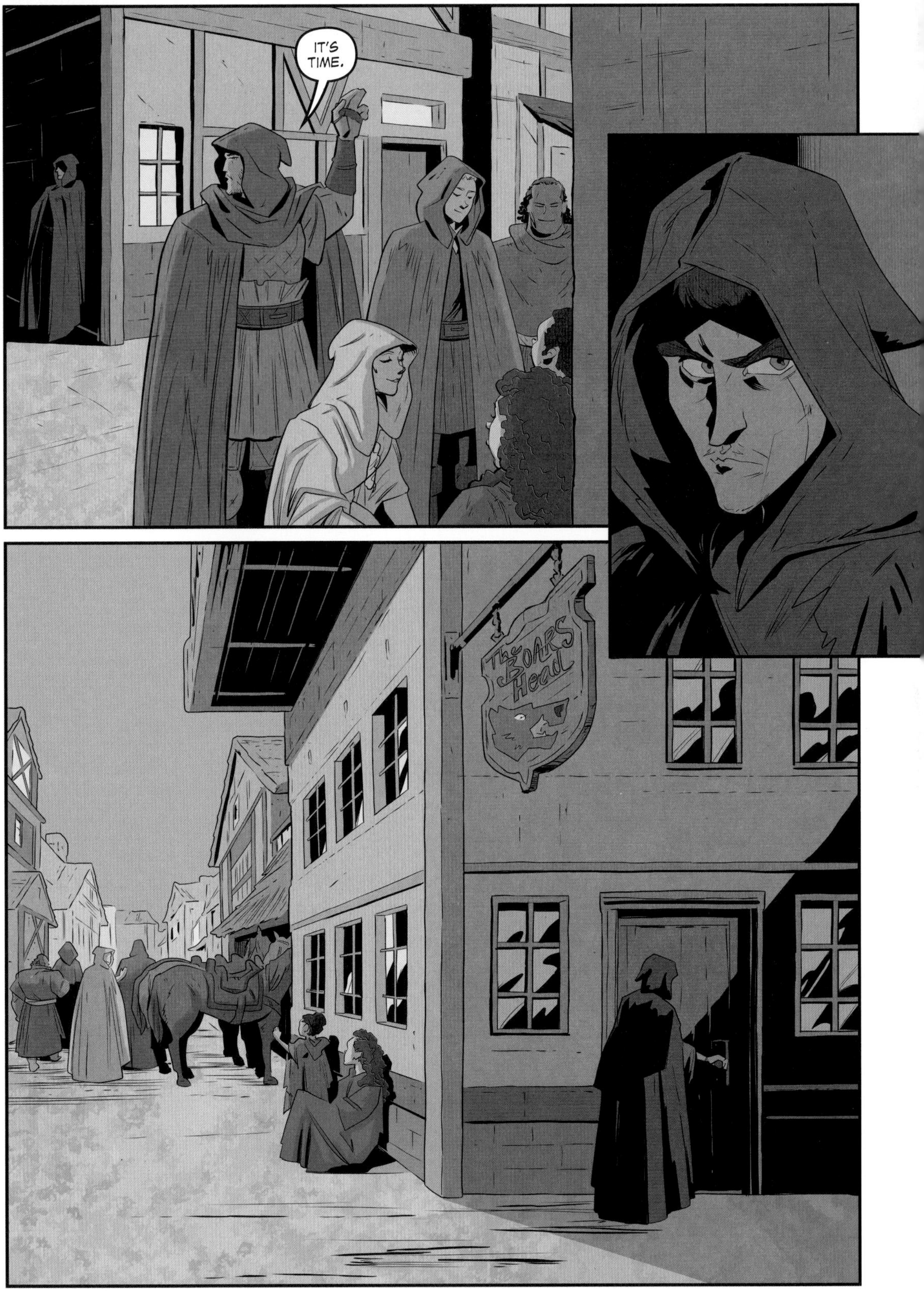
IT'S TIME.
The BOARS Head

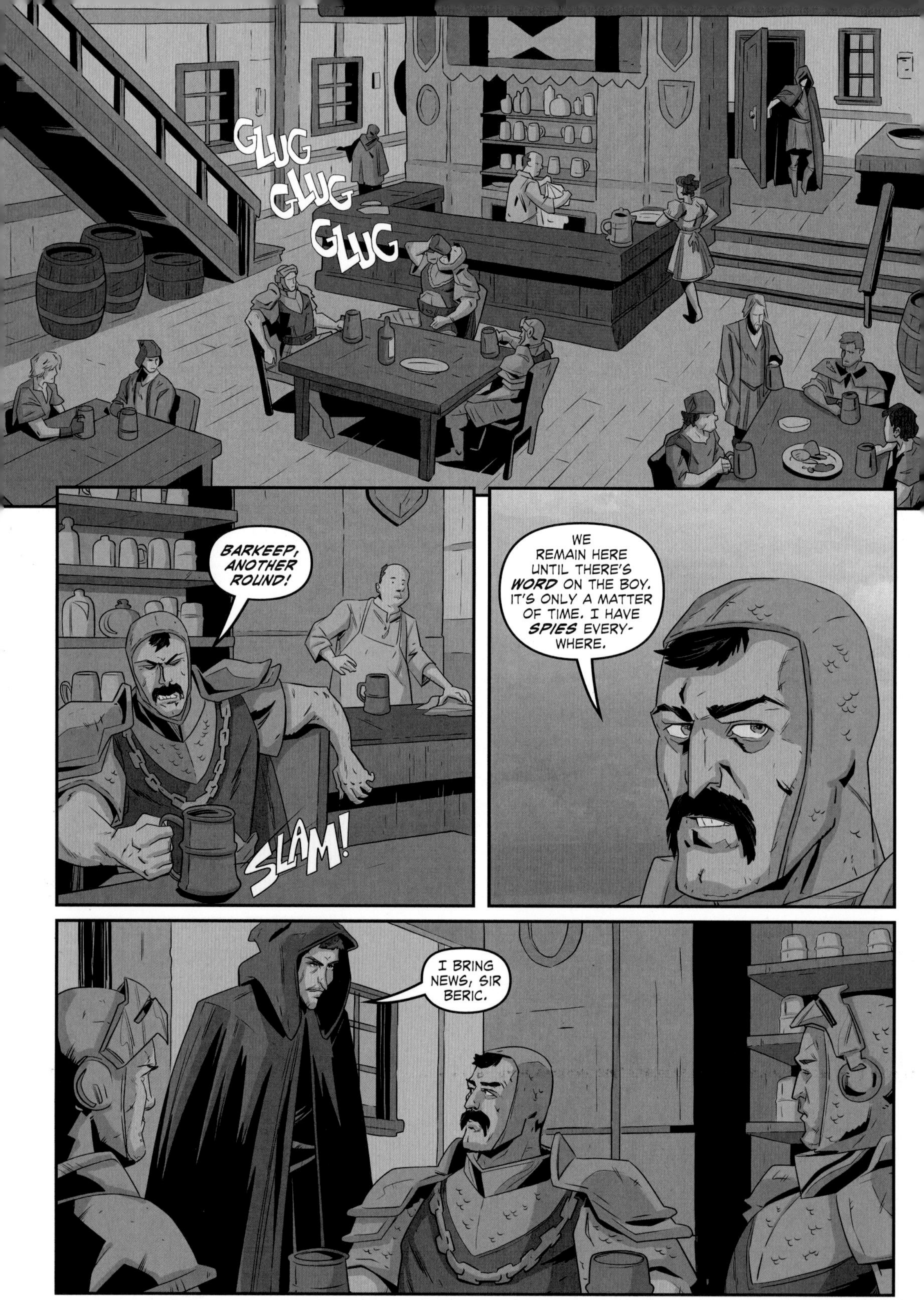
GLUG
GLUG
GLUG
BARKEEP, ANOTHER ROUND!
SLAM!
WE REMAIN HERE UNTIL THERE'S WORD ON THE BOY. IT'S ONLY A MATTER OF TIME. I HAVE SPIES EVERY-WHERE.
I BRING NEWS, SIR BERIC.

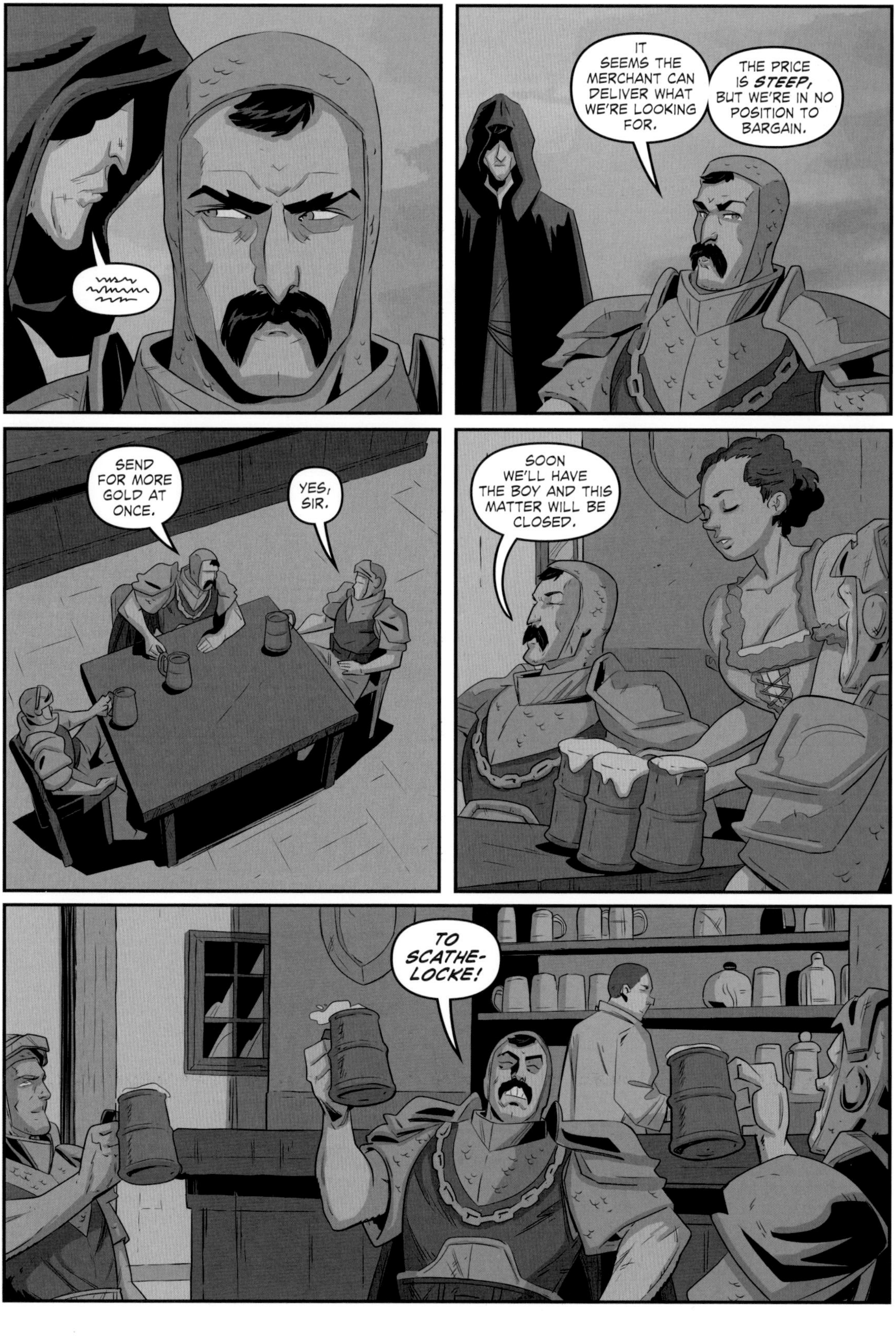
IT SEEMS THE MERCHANT CAN DELIVER WHAT WE'RE LOOKING FOR.
THE PRICE IS ***STEEP,*** BUT WE'RE IN NO POSITION TO BARGAIN.
SEND FOR MORE GOLD AT ONCE.
YES, SIR.
SOON WE'LL HAVE THE BOY AND THIS MATTER WILL BE CLOSED.
TO SCATHE-LOCKE!

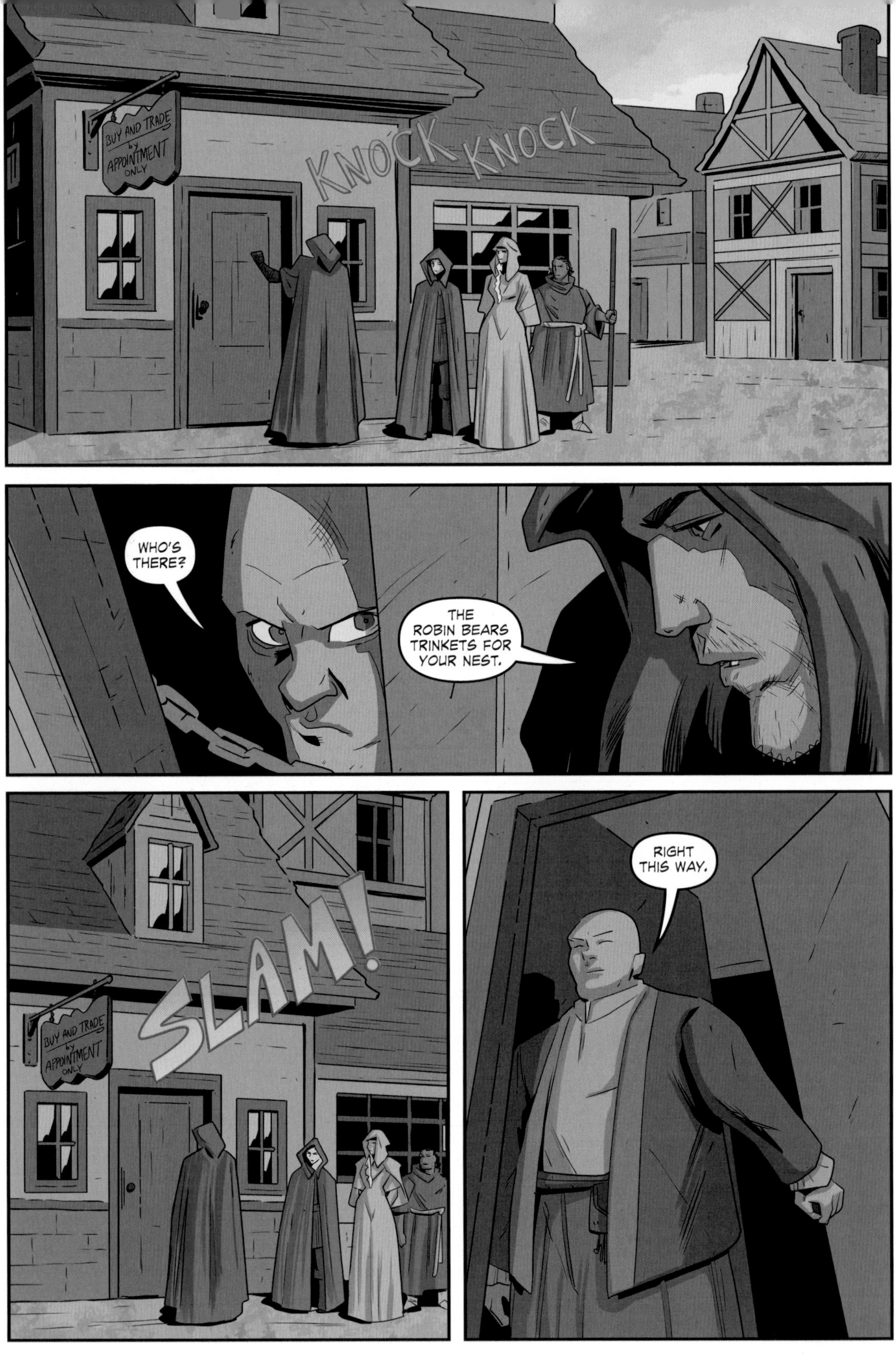
BUY AND TRADE by APPOINTMENT ONLY
KNOCK KNOCK
WHO'S THERE?
THE ROBIN BEARS TRINKETS FOR YOUR NEST.
BUY AND TRADE by APPOINTMENT ONLY
SLAM!
RIGHT THIS WAY.

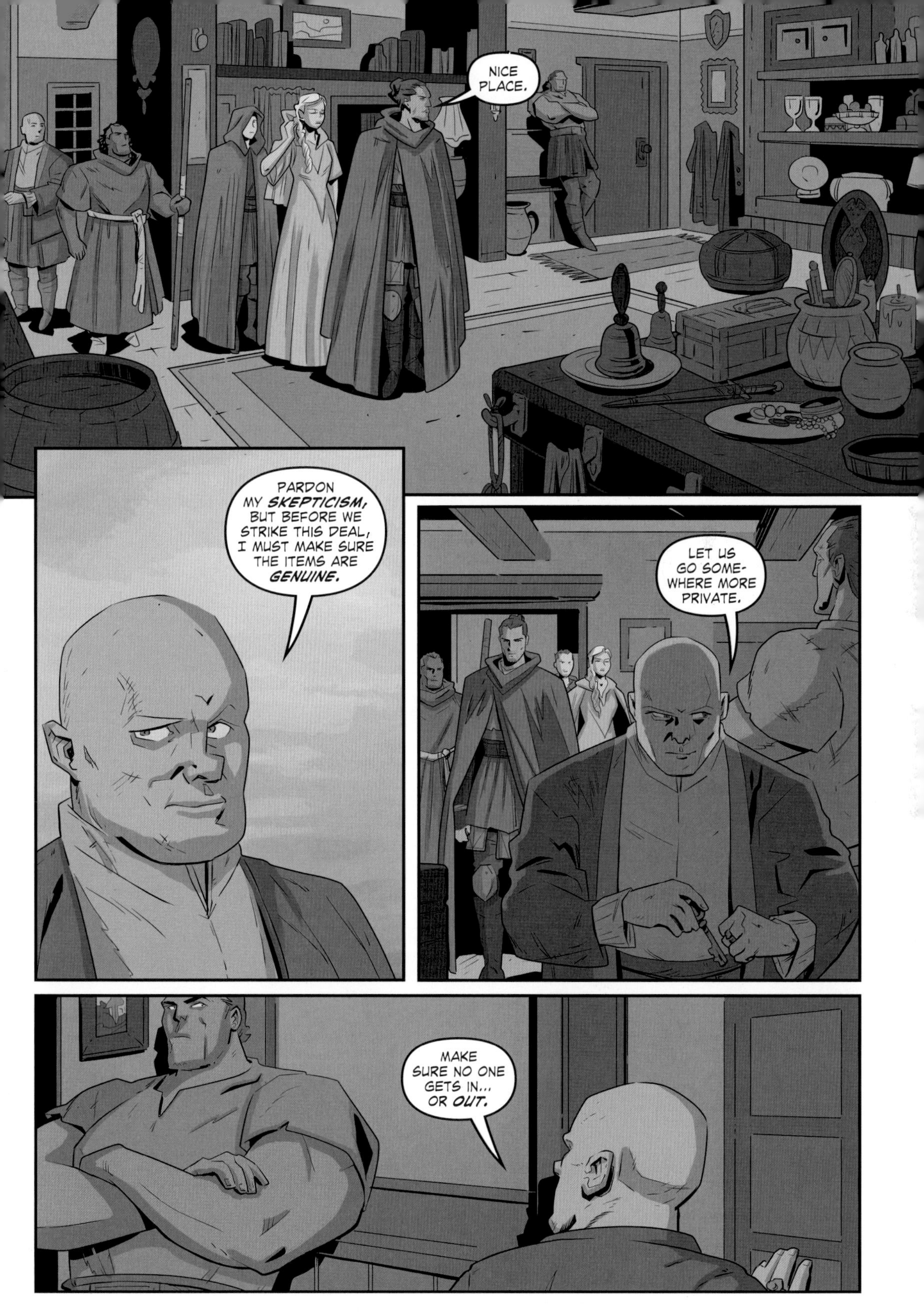
NICE PLACE.
PARDON MY SKEPTICISM, BUT BEFORE WE STRIKE THIS DEAL, I MUST MAKE SURE THE ITEMS ARE GENUINE.
LET US GO SOME-WHERE MORE PRIVATE.
MAKE SURE NO ONE GETS IN... OR OUT.

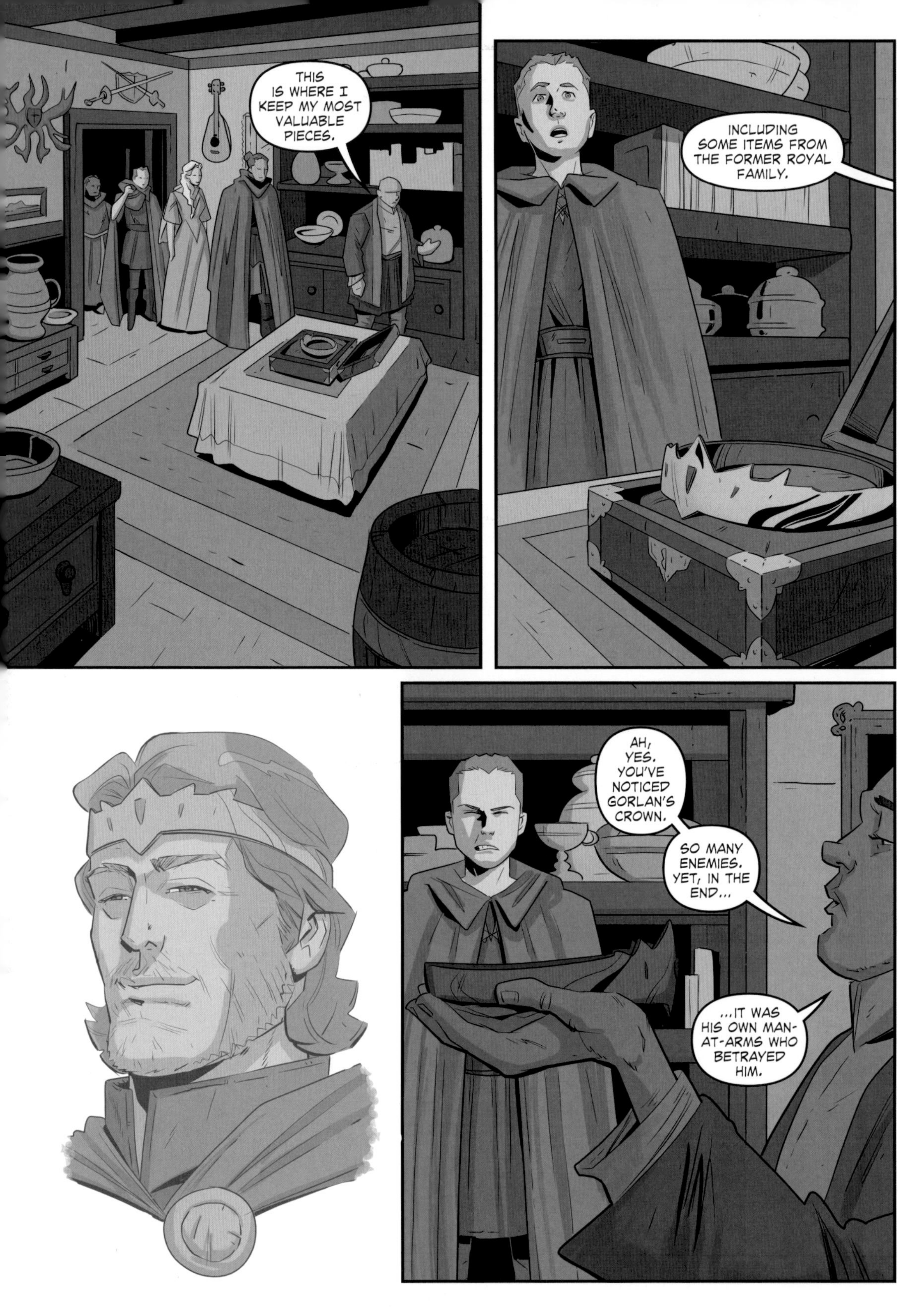
THIS IS WHERE I KEEP MY MOST VALUABLE PIECES.
INCLUDING SOME ITEMS FROM THE FORMER ROYAL FAMILY.
AH, YES. YOU'VE NOTICED GORLAN'S CROWN.
SO MANY ENEMIES. YET, IN THE END...
...IT WAS HIS OWN MAN-AT-ARMS WHO BETRAYED HIM.

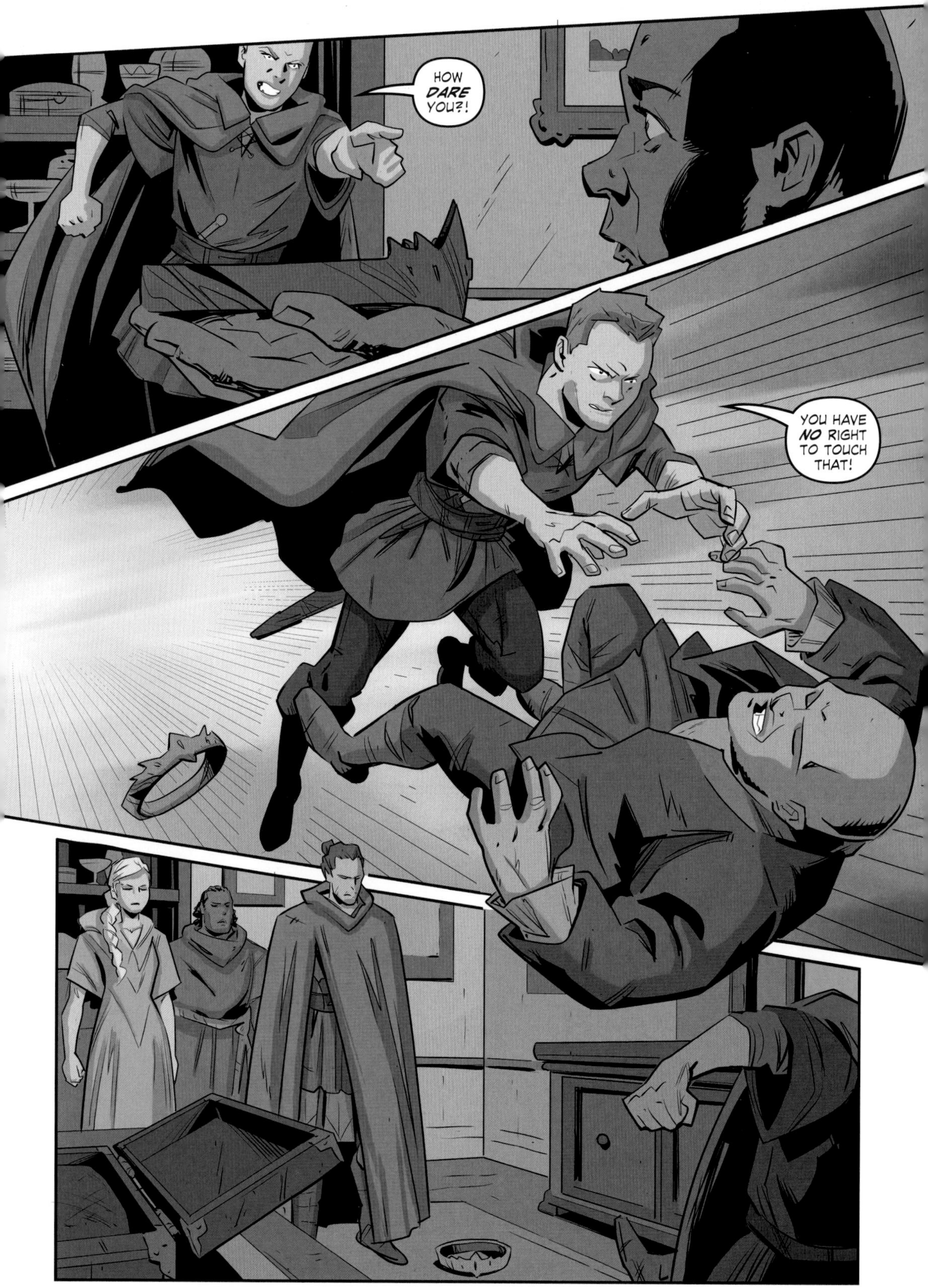
HOW *DARE* YOU?!
YOU HAVE *NO* RIGHT TO TOUCH THAT!

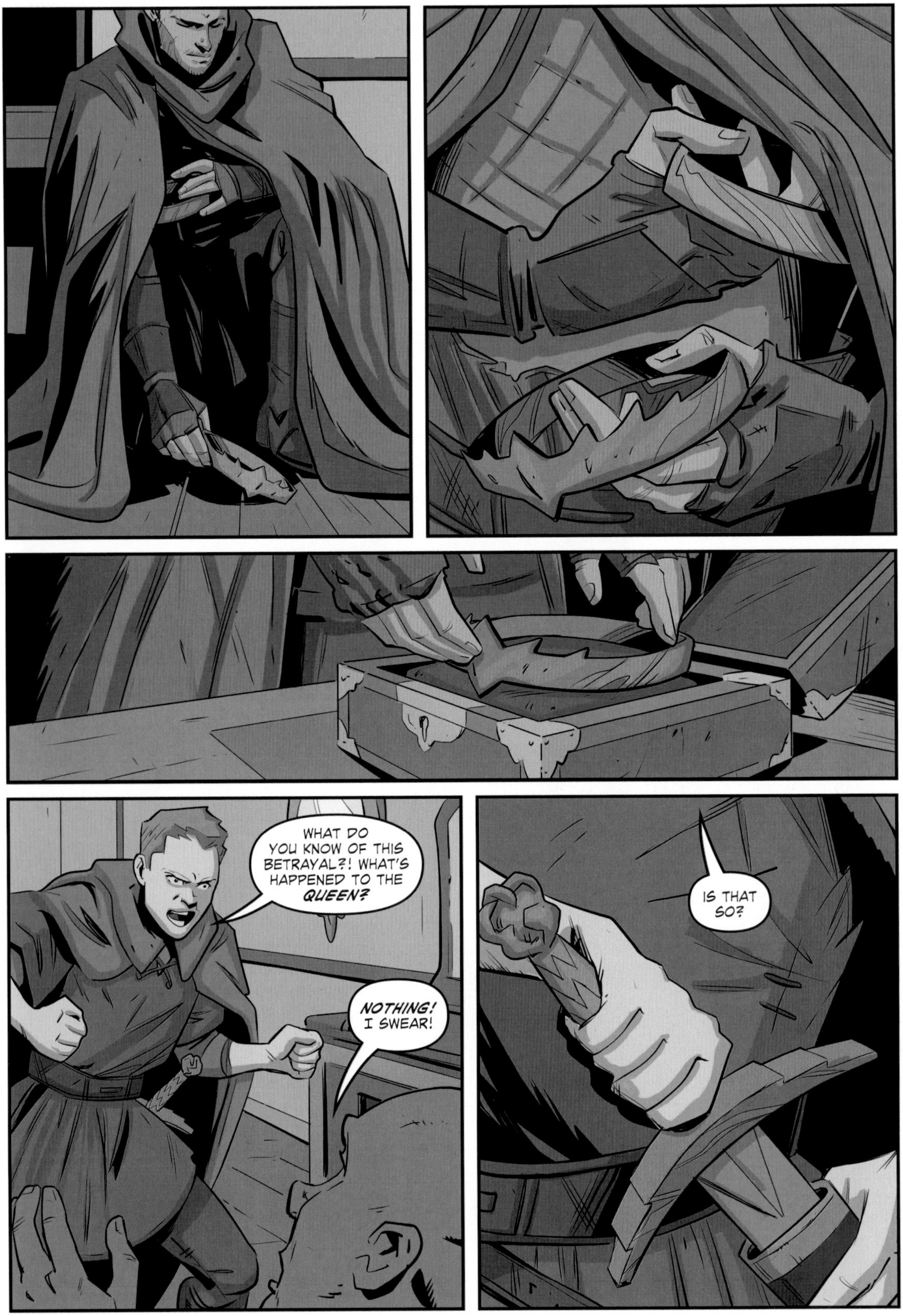
WHAT DO YOU KNOW OF THIS BETRAYAL?! WHAT'S HAPPENED TO THE QUEEN?
NOTHING! I SWEAR!
IS THAT SO?

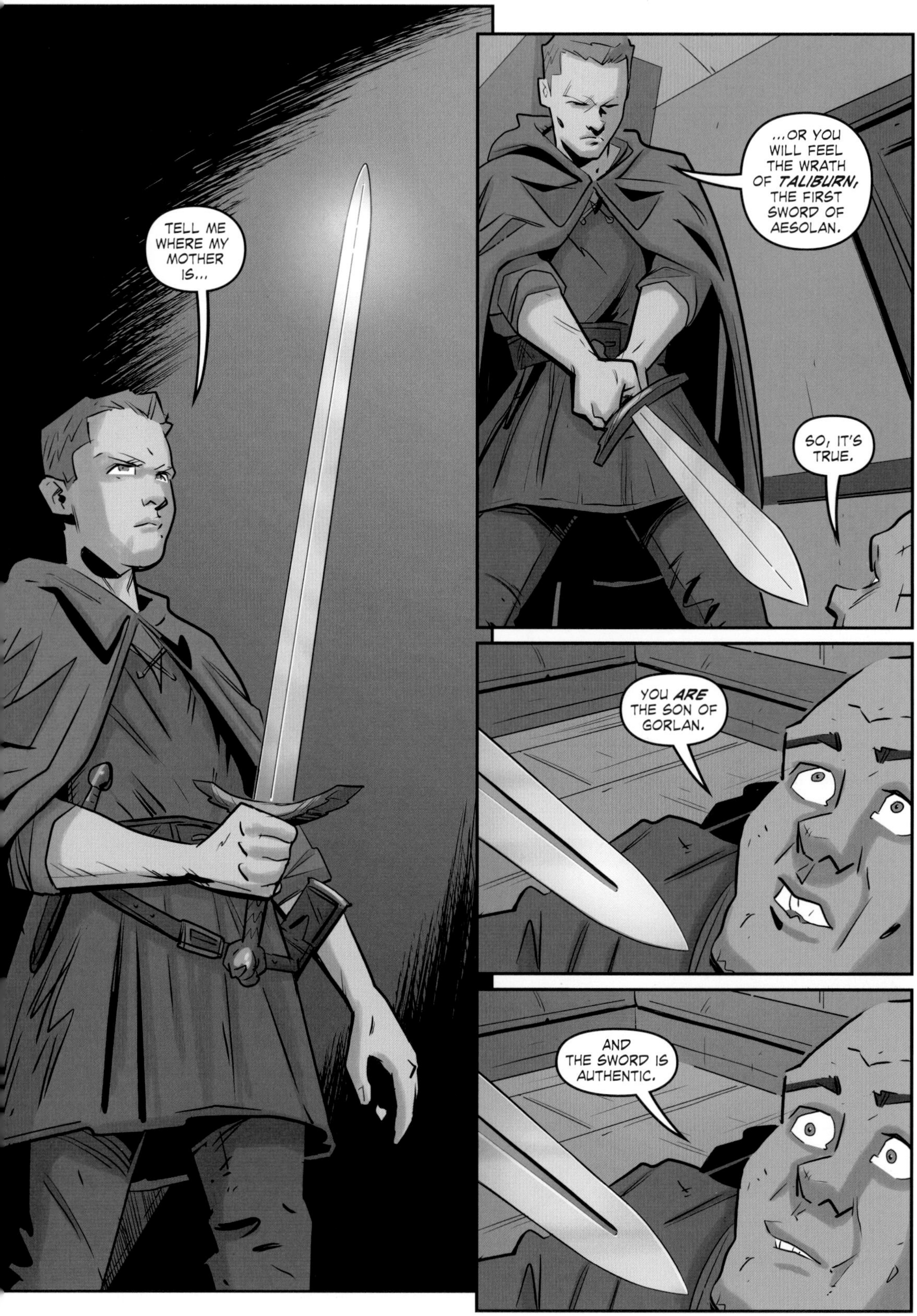
TELL ME WHERE MY MOTHER IS...
...OR YOU WILL FEEL THE WRATH OF TALIBURN, THE FIRST SWORD OF AESOLAN.
SO, IT'S TRUE.
YOU ARE THE SON OF GORLAN.
AND THE SWORD IS AUTHENTIC.

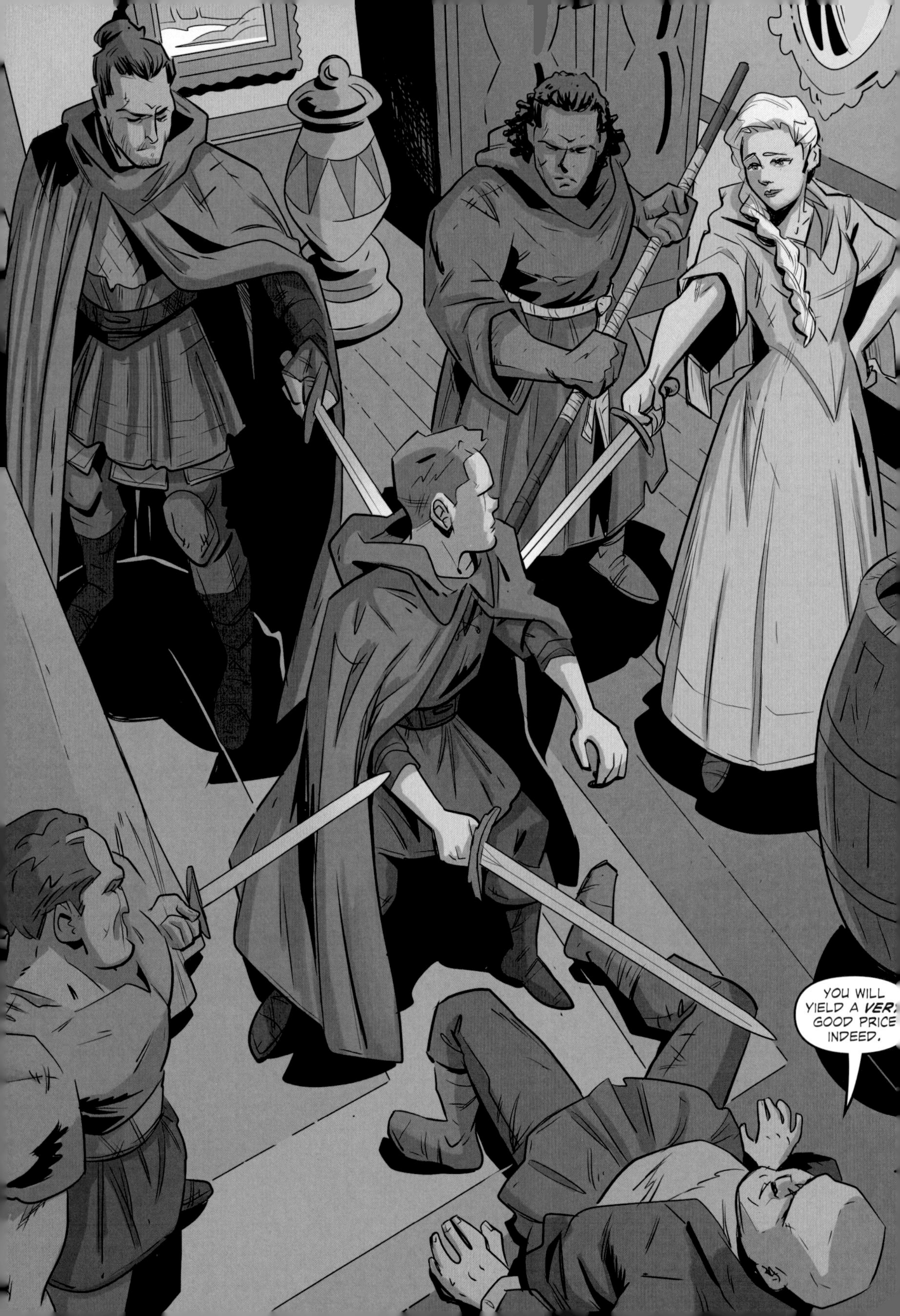
YOU WILL YIELD A VER. GOOD PRICE INDEED.

Chapter 5

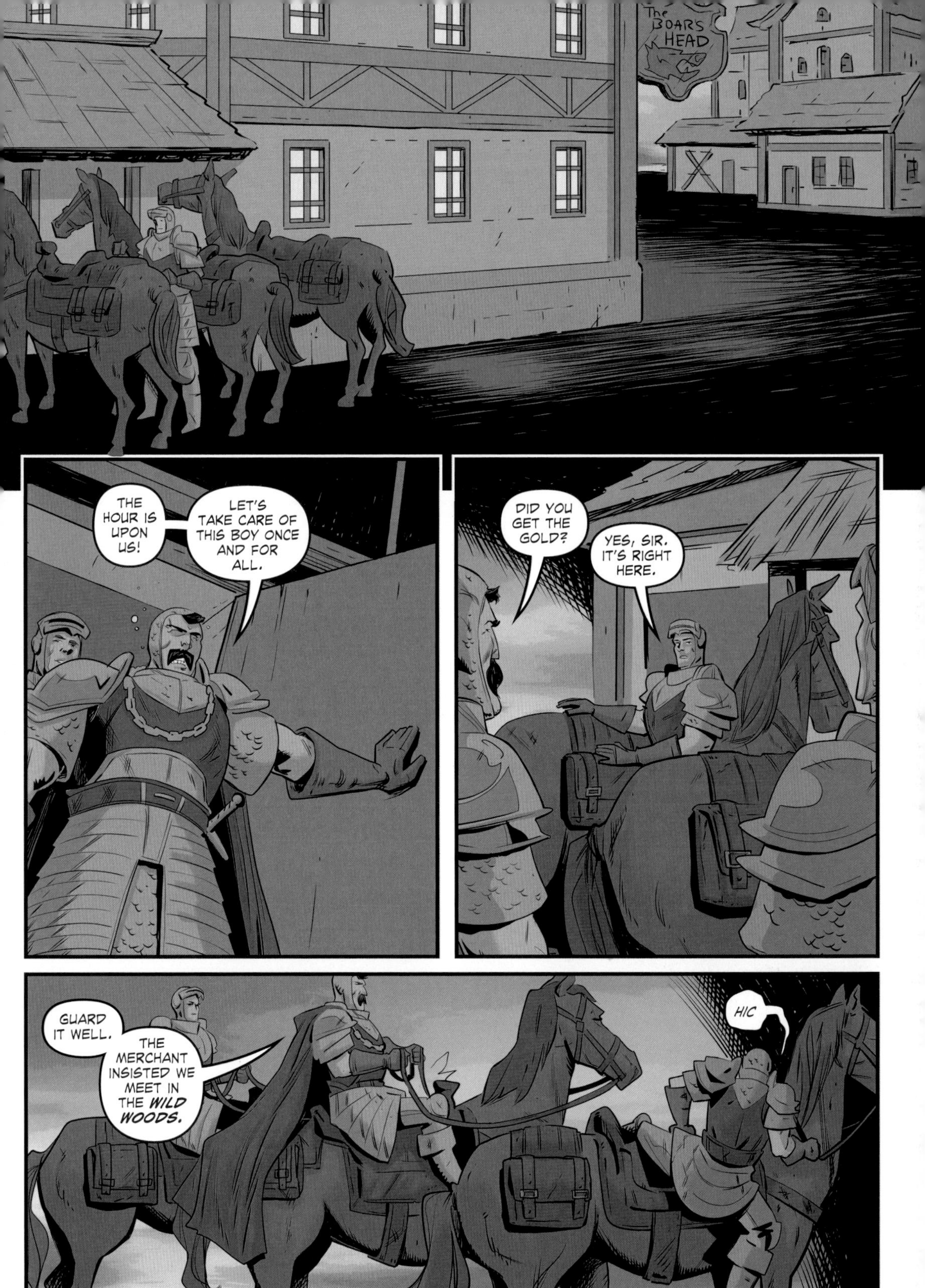

The BOAR'S HEAD
THE HOUR IS UPON US!
LET'S TAKE CARE OF THIS BOY ONCE AND FOR ALL.
DID YOU GET THE GOLD?
YES, SIR. IT'S RIGHT HERE.
GUARD IT WELL.
THE MERCHANT INSISTED WE MEET IN THE *WILD WOODS.*
HIC

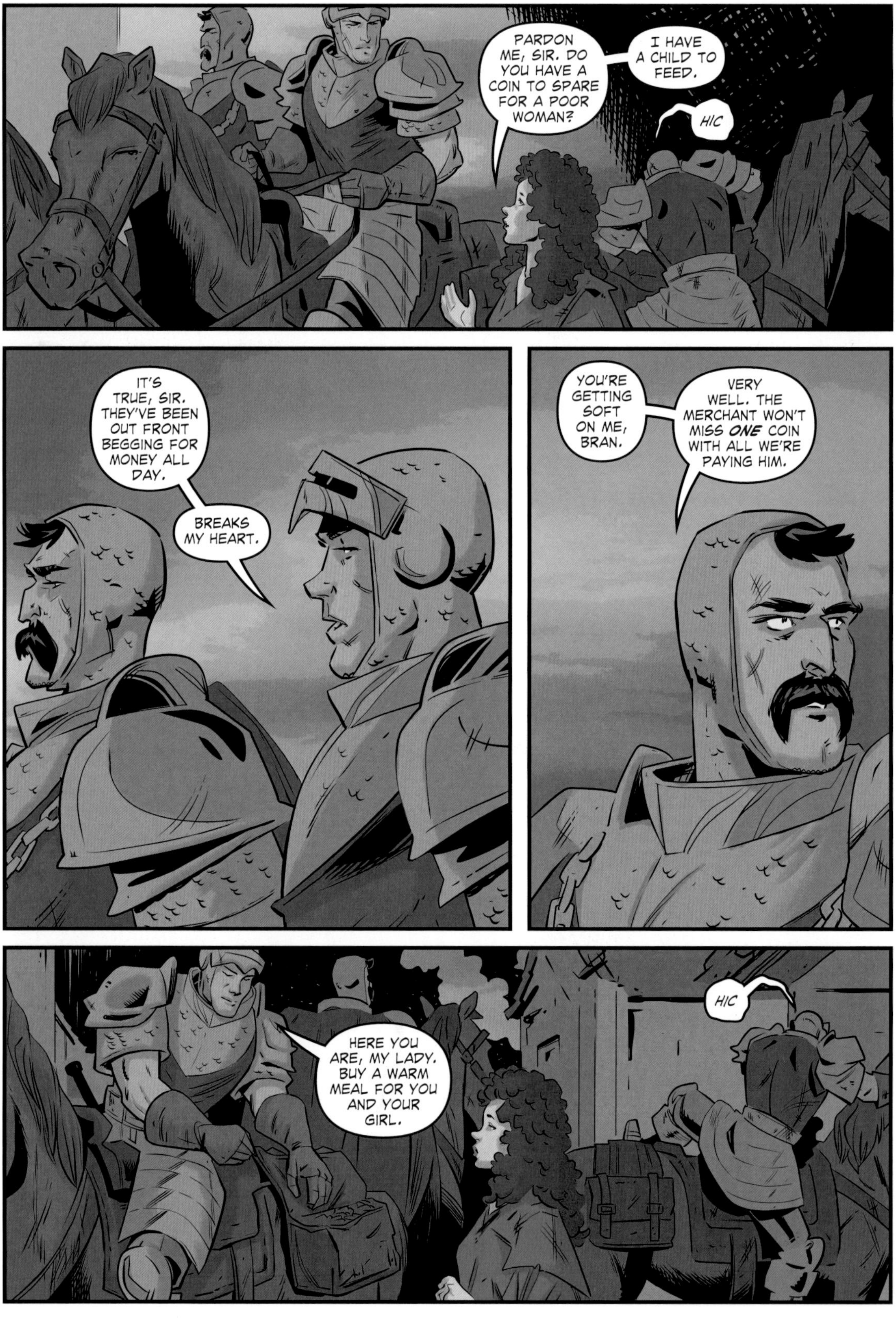
PARDON ME, SIR. DO YOU HAVE A COIN TO SPARE FOR A POOR WOMAN?
I HAVE A CHILD TO FEED.
HIC
IT'S TRUE, SIR. THEY'VE BEEN OUT FRONT BEGGING FOR MONEY ALL DAY.
BREAKS MY HEART.
YOU'RE GETTING SOFT ON ME, BRAN.
VERY WELL. THE MERCHANT WON'T MISS ONE COIN WITH ALL WE'RE PAYING HIM.
HIC
HERE YOU ARE, MY LADY. BUY A WARM MEAL FOR YOU AND YOUR GIRL.

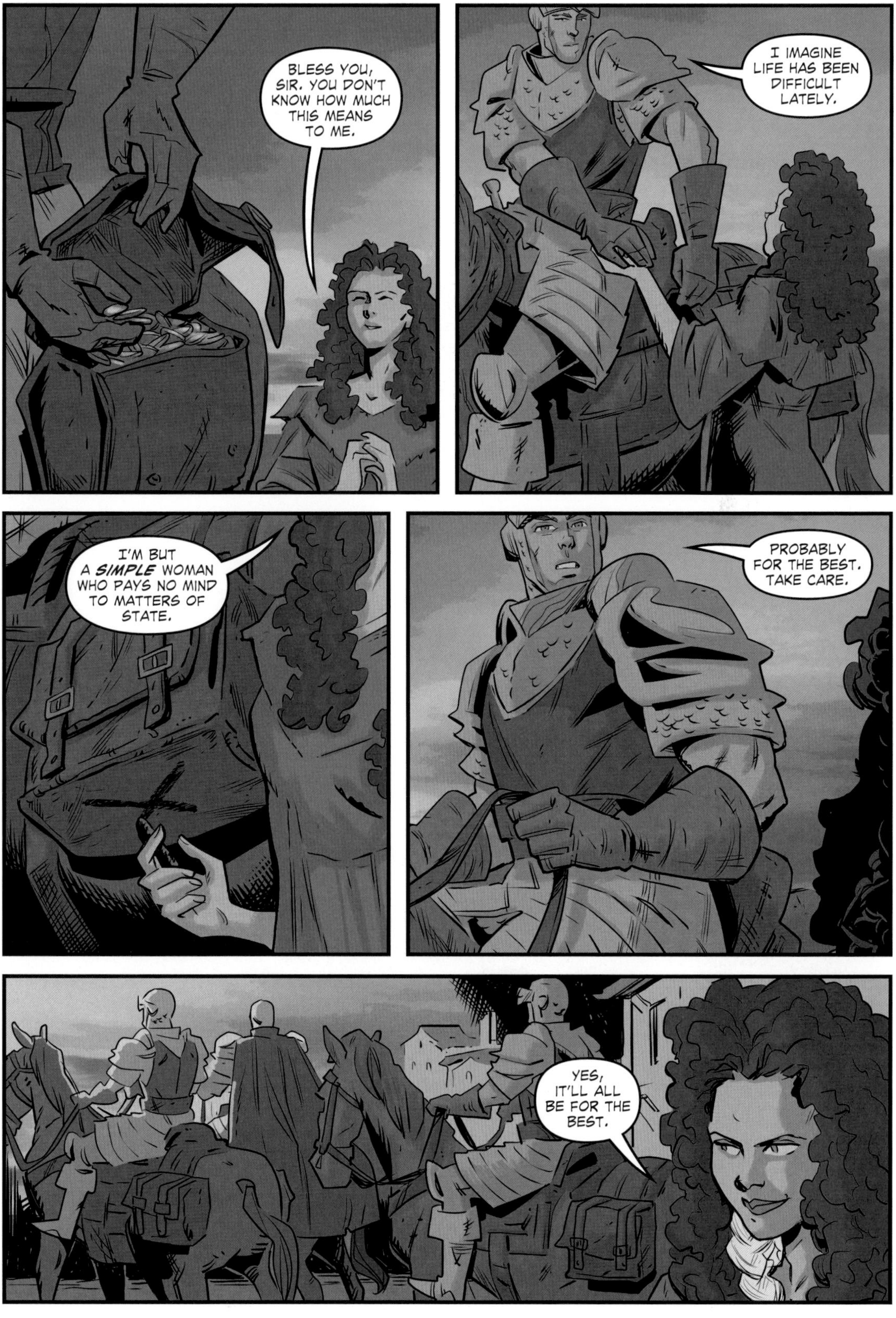
BLESS YOU, SIR. YOU DON'T KNOW HOW MUCH THIS MEANS TO ME.
I IMAGINE LIFE HAS BEEN DIFFICULT LATELY.
I'M BUT A *SIMPLE* WOMAN WHO PAYS NO MIND TO MATTERS OF STATE.
PROBABLY FOR THE BEST. TAKE CARE.
YES, IT'LL ALL BE FOR THE BEST.

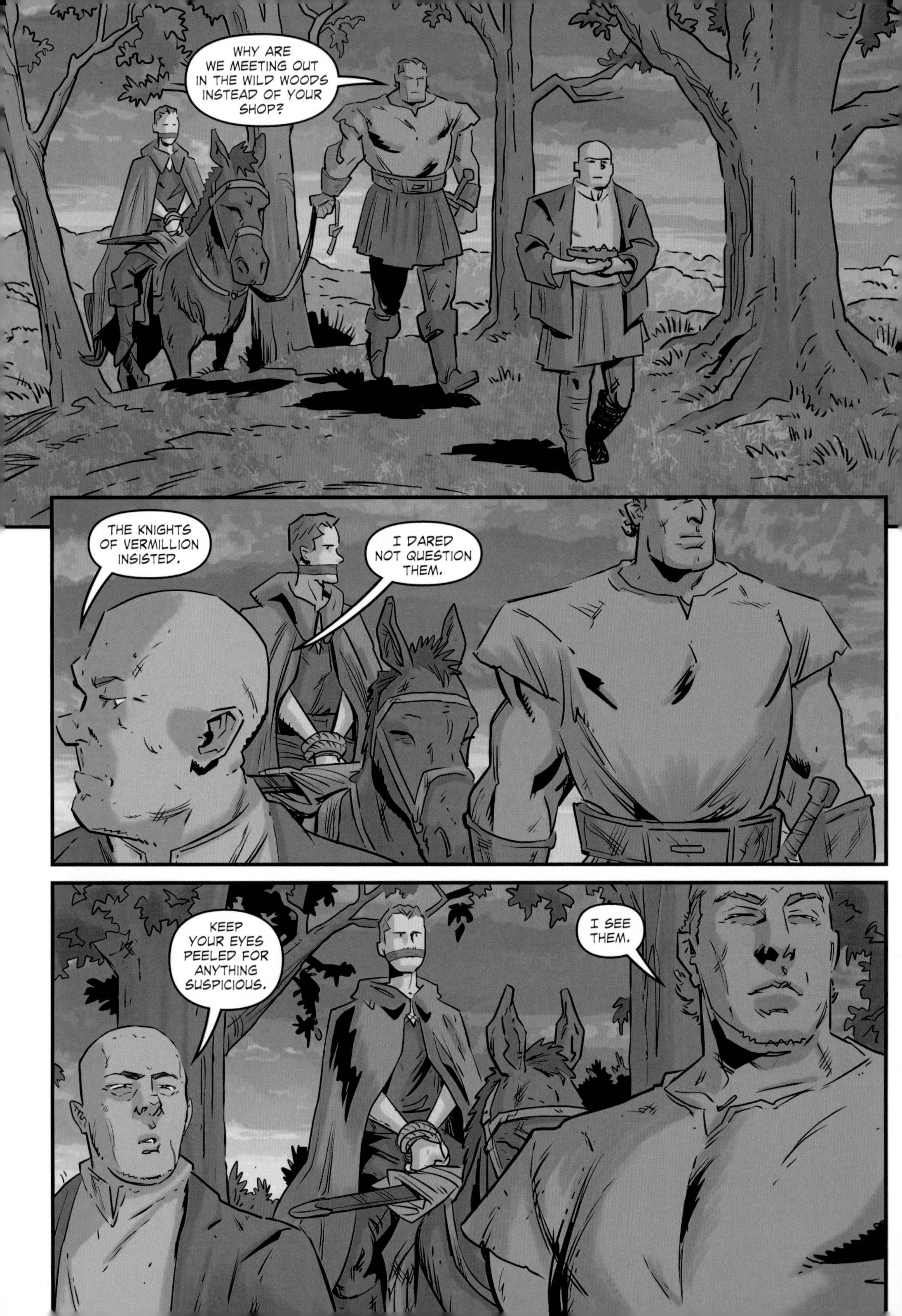
WHY ARE WE MEETING OUT IN THE WILD WOODS INSTEAD OF YOUR SHOP?
THE KNIGHTS OF VERMILLION INSISTED.
I DARED NOT QUESTION THEM.
KEEP YOUR EYES PEELED FOR ANYTHING SUSPICIOUS.
I SEE THEM.

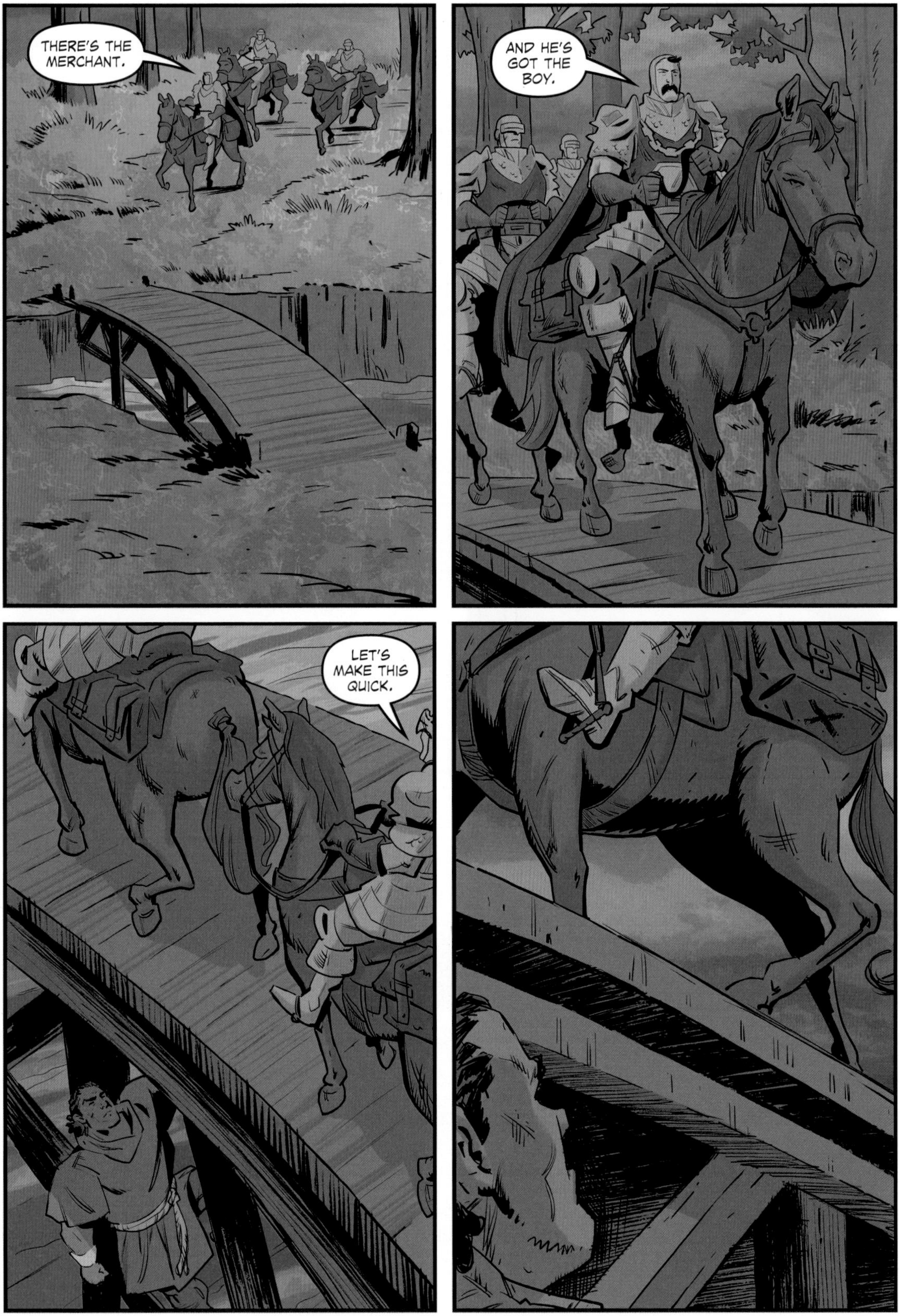
THERE'S THE MERCHANT.
AND HE'S GOT THE BOY.
LET'S MAKE THIS QUICK.

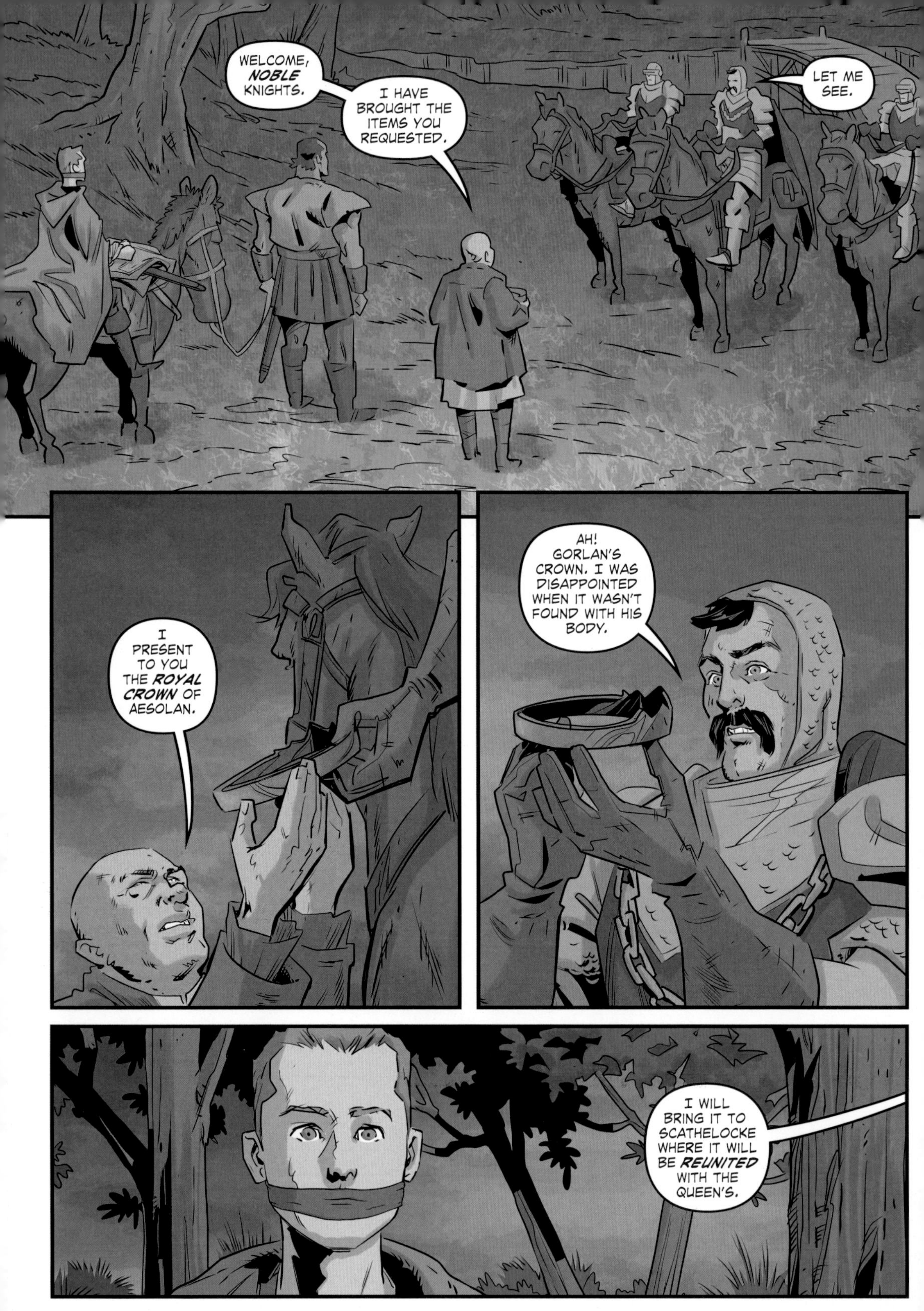
WELCOME, ***NOBLE*** KNIGHTS.
I HAVE BROUGHT THE ITEMS YOU REQUESTED.
LET ME SEE.
I PRESENT TO YOU THE ***ROYAL CROWN*** OF AESOLAN.
AH! GORLAN'S CROWN. I WAS DISAPPOINTED WHEN IT WASN'T FOUND WITH HIS BODY.
I WILL BRING IT TO SCATHELOCKE WHERE IT WILL BE ***REUNITED*** WITH THE QUEEN'S.

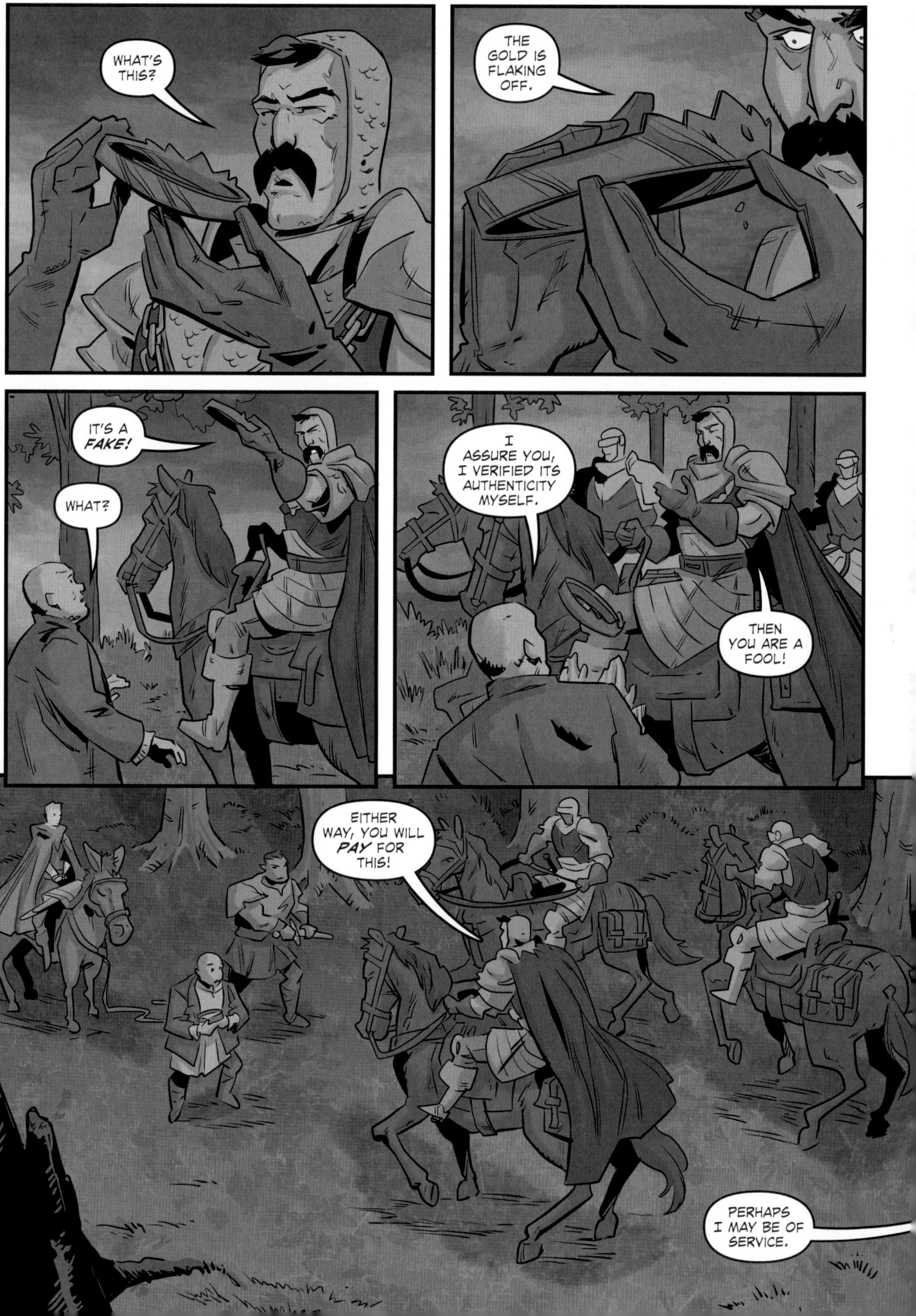
WHAT'S THIS?
THE GOLD IS FLAKING OFF.
IT'S A *FAKE!*
WHAT?
I ASSURE YOU, I VERIFIED ITS AUTHENTICITY MYSELF.
THEN YOU ARE A FOOL!
EITHER WAY, YOU WILL *PAY* FOR THIS!
PERHAPS I MAY BE OF SERVICE.

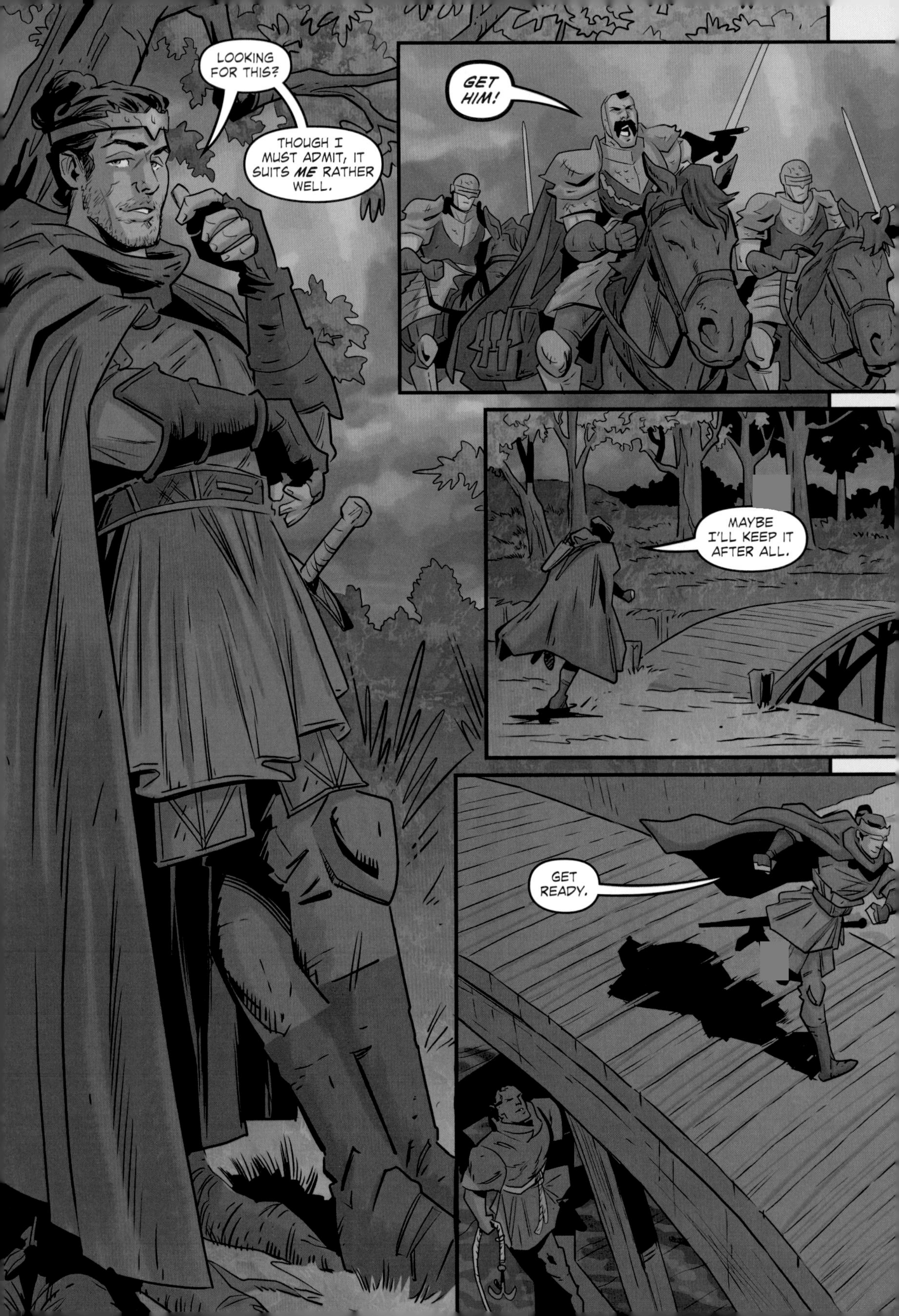
LOOKING FOR THIS?
THOUGH I MUST ADMIT, IT SUITS ME RATHER WELL.
GET HIM!
MAYBE I'LL KEEP IT AFTER ALL.
GET READY.

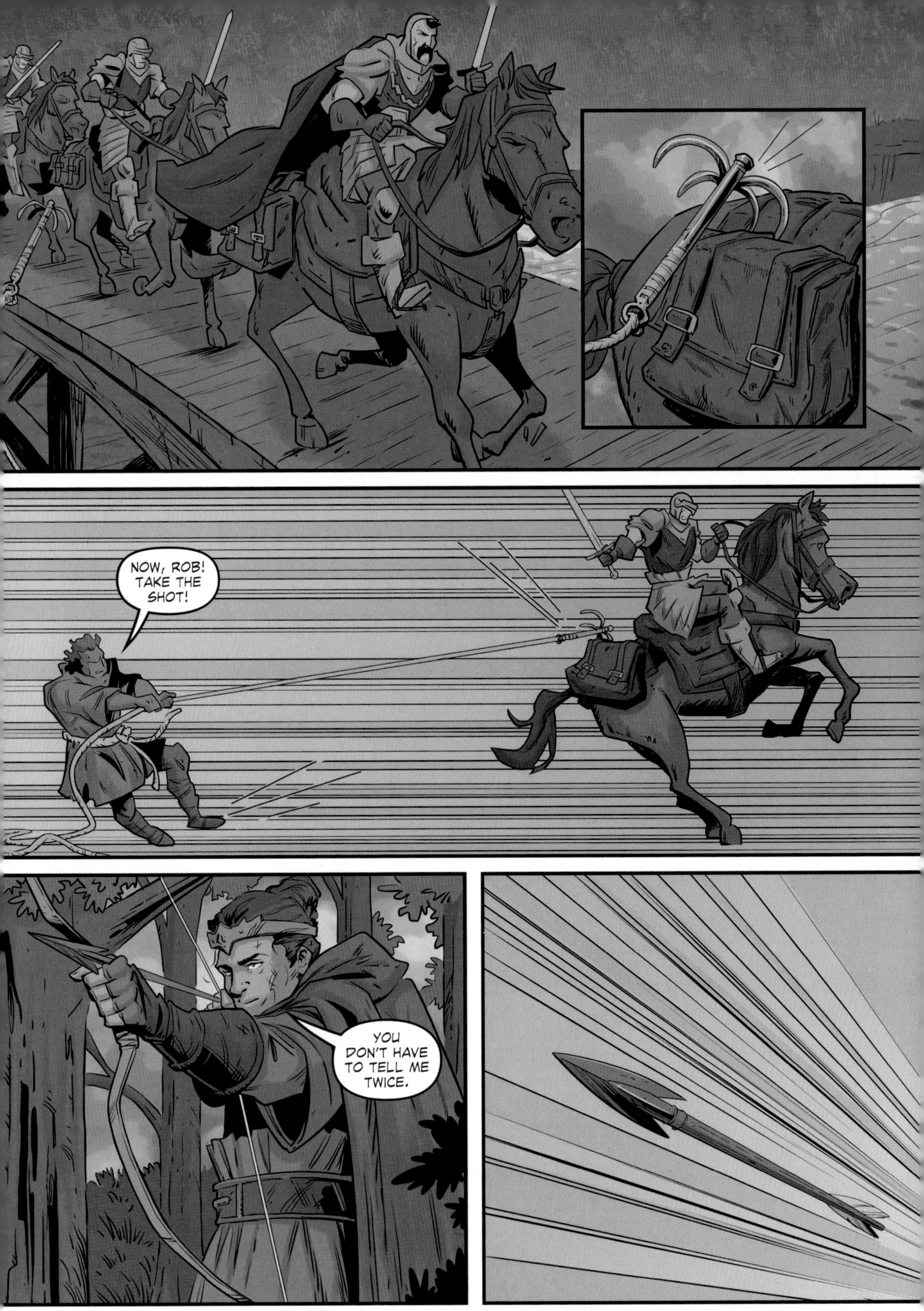
NOW, ROB! TAKE THE SHOT!
YOU DON'T HAVE TO TELL ME TWICE.

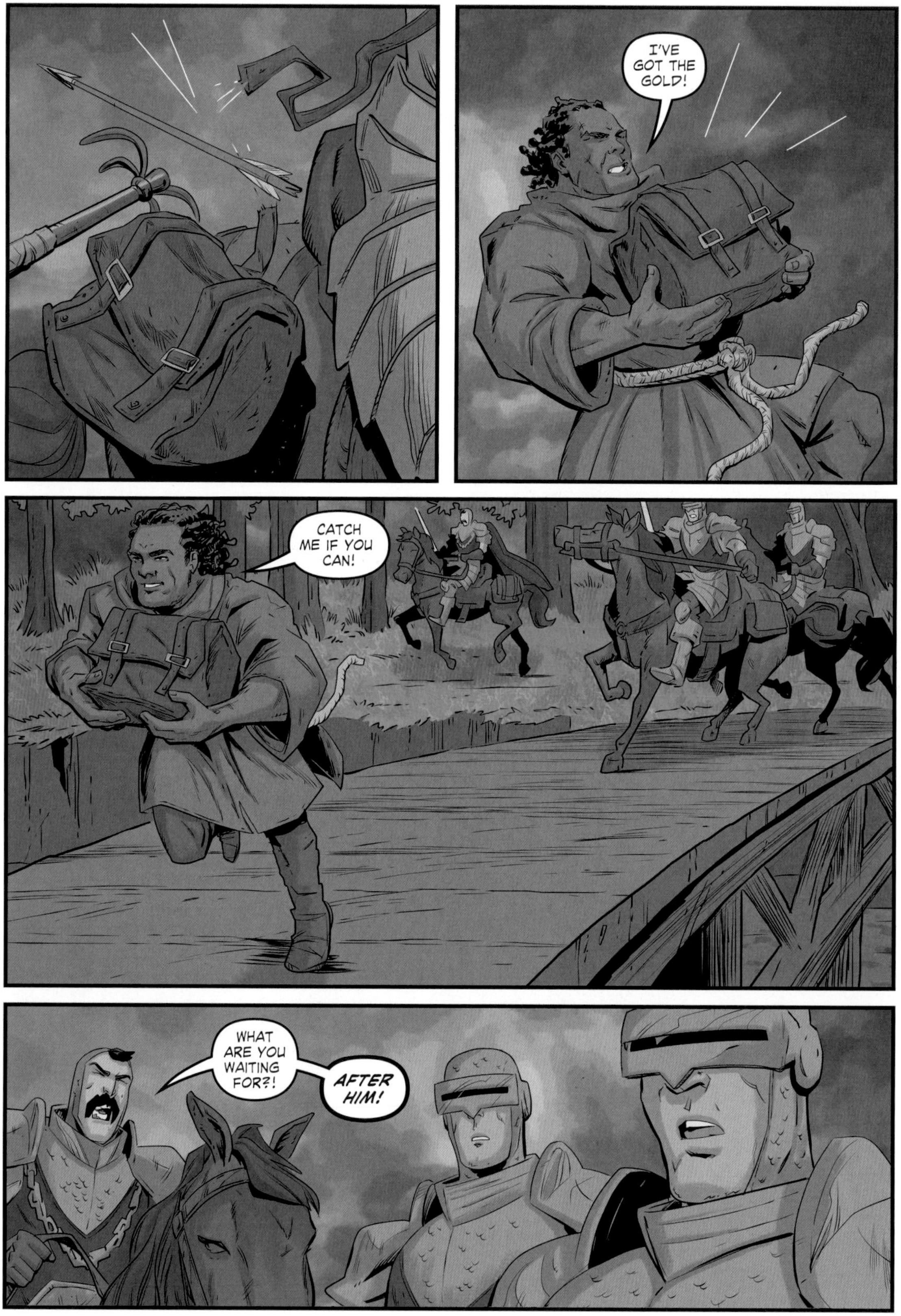
I'VE GOT THE GOLD!
CATCH ME IF YOU CAN!
WHAT ARE YOU WAITING FOR?!
AFTER HIM!

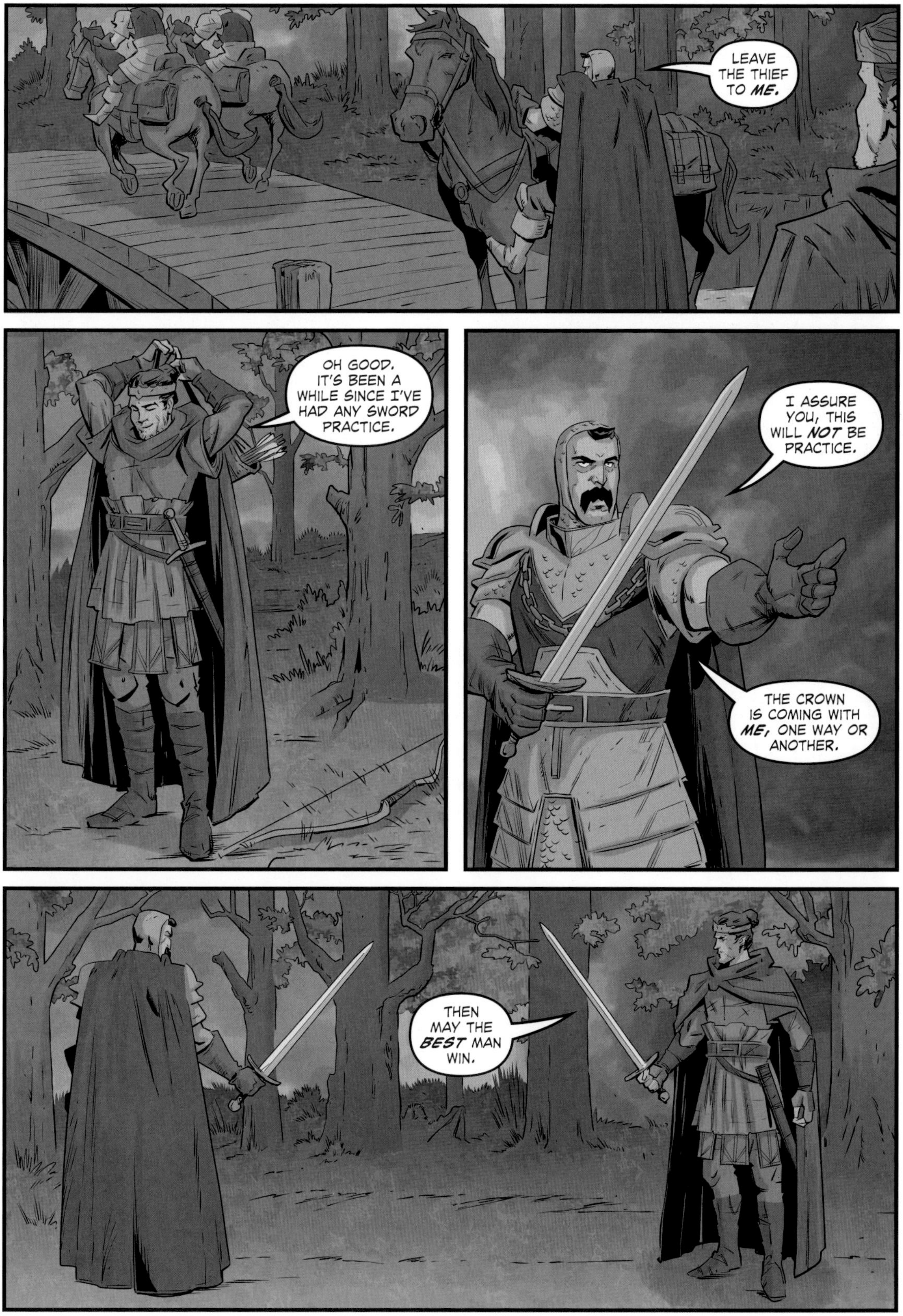
LEAVE THE THIEF TO *ME.*
OH GOOD. IT'S BEEN A WHILE SINCE I'VE HAD ANY SWORD PRACTICE.
I ASSURE YOU, THIS WILL *NOT* BE PRACTICE.
THE CROWN IS COMING WITH *ME,* ONE WAY OR ANOTHER.
THEN MAY THE *BEST* MAN WIN.

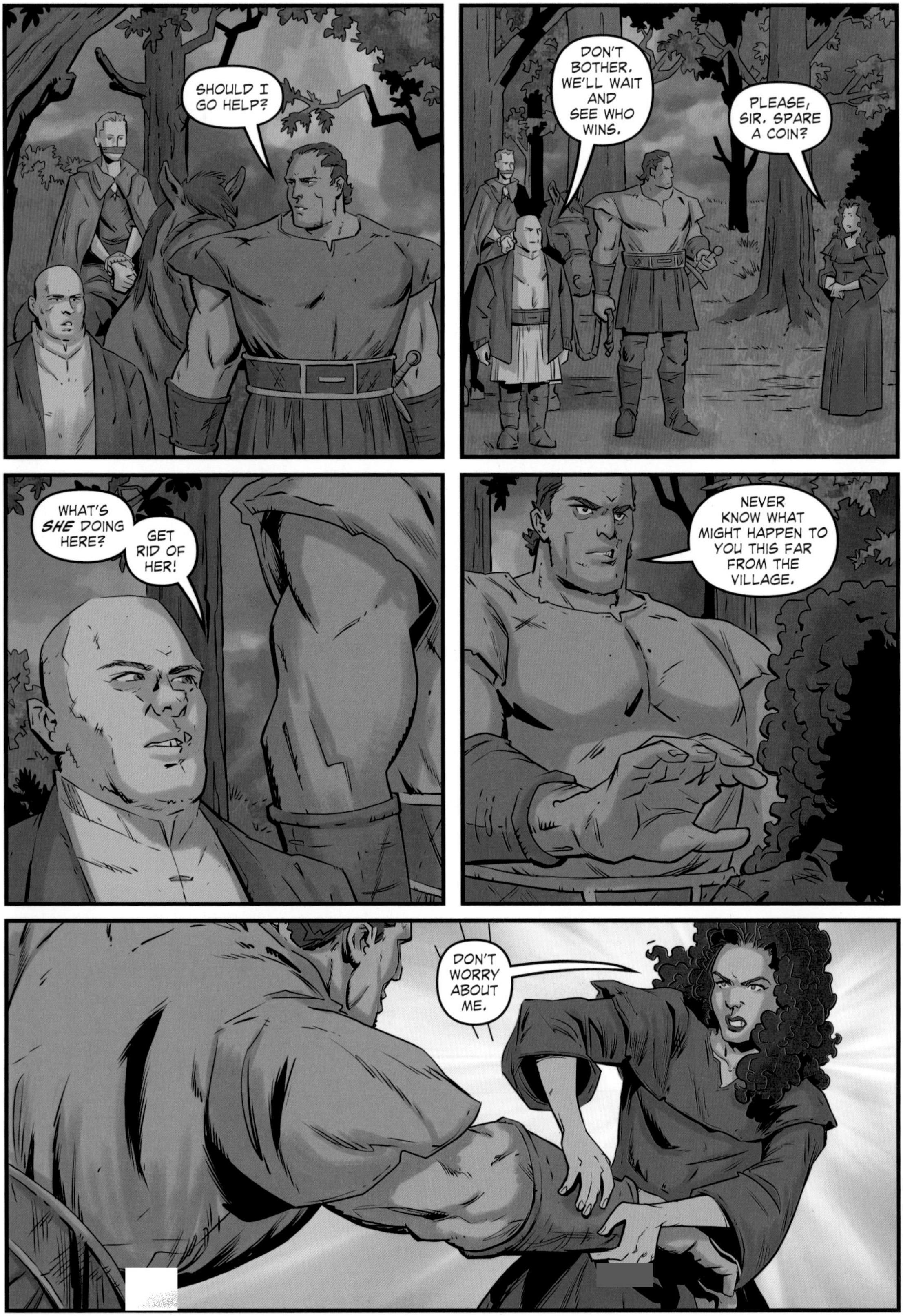
SHOULD I GO HELP?
DON'T BOTHER. WE'LL WAIT AND SEE WHO WINS.
PLEASE, SIR. SPARE A COIN?
WHAT'S ***SHE*** DOING HERE?
GET RID OF HER!
NEVER KNOW WHAT MIGHT HAPPEN TO YOU THIS FAR FROM THE VILLAGE.
DON'T WORRY ABOUT ME.

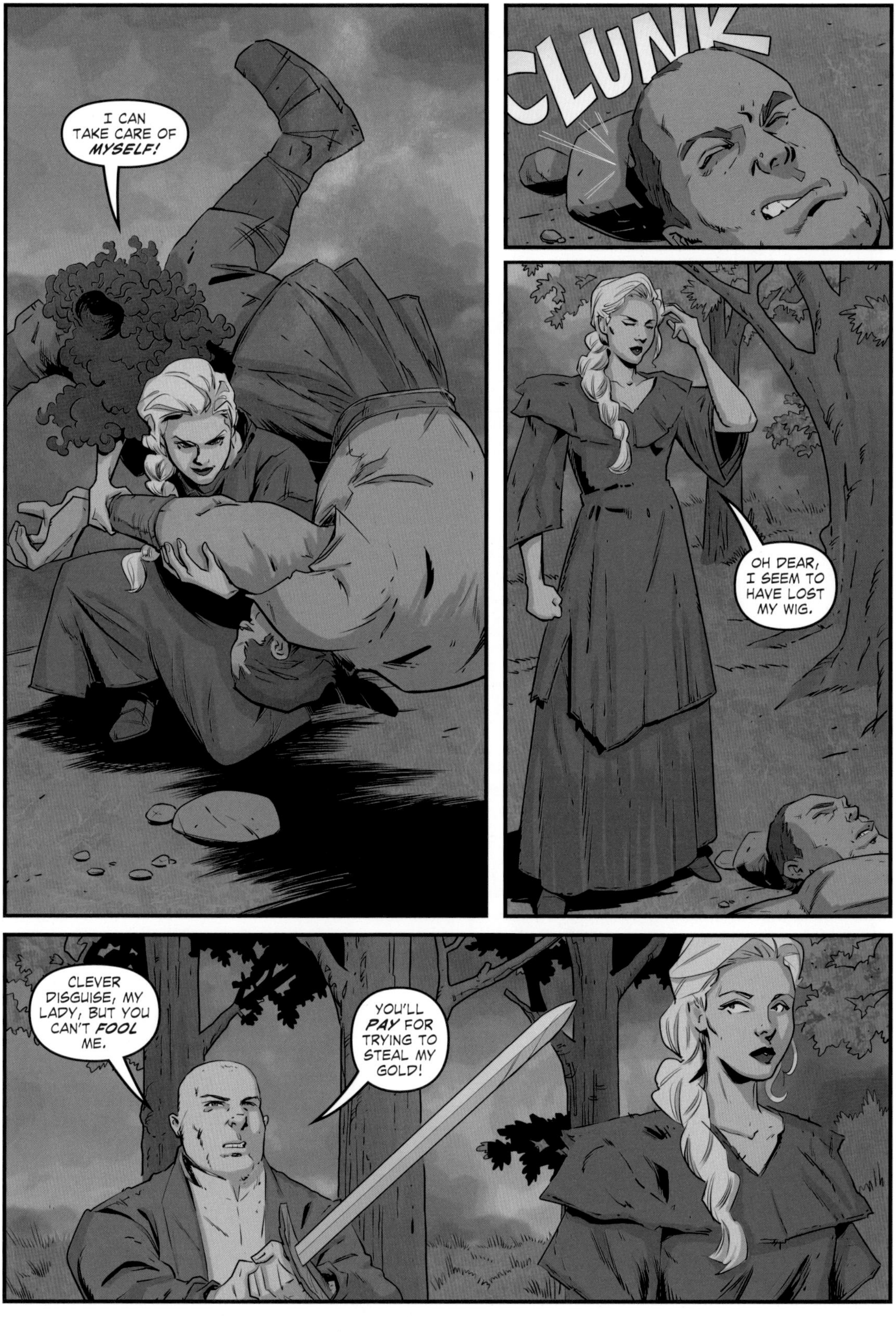
I CAN TAKE CARE OF *MYSELF!*
CLUNK
OH DEAR, I SEEM TO HAVE LOST MY WIG.
CLEVER DISGUISE, MY LADY, BUT YOU CAN'T *FOOL* ME.
YOU'LL *PAY* FOR TRYING TO STEAL MY GOLD!

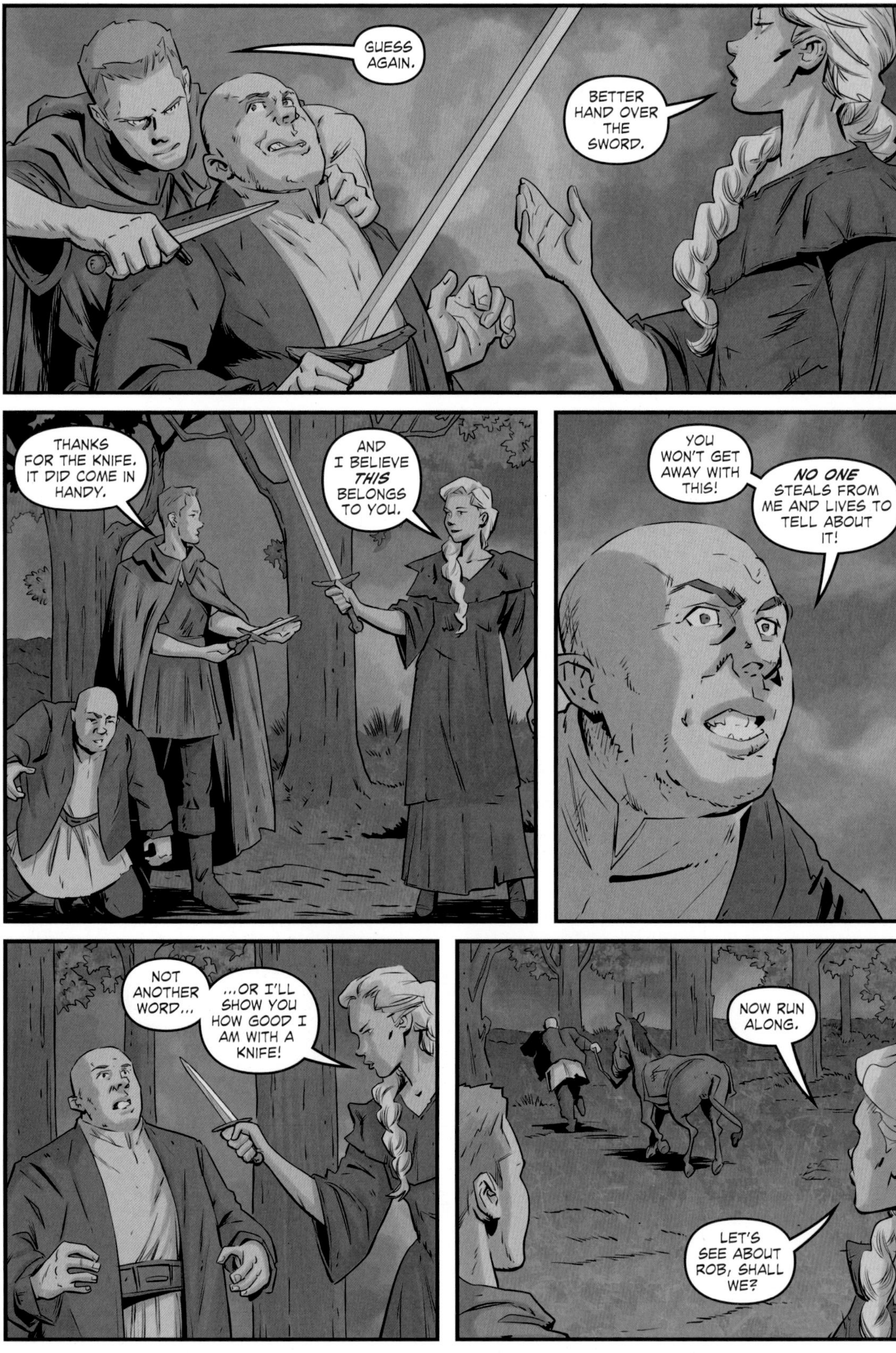
GUESS AGAIN.
BETTER HAND OVER THE SWORD.
THANKS FOR THE KNIFE. IT DID COME IN HANDY.
AND I BELIEVE *THIS* BELONGS TO YOU.
YOU WON'T GET AWAY WITH THIS!
NO ONE STEALS FROM ME AND LIVES TO TELL ABOUT IT!
NOT ANOTHER WORD...
...OR I'LL SHOW YOU HOW GOOD I AM WITH A KNIFE!
NOW RUN ALONG.
LET'S SEE ABOUT ROB, SHALL WE?

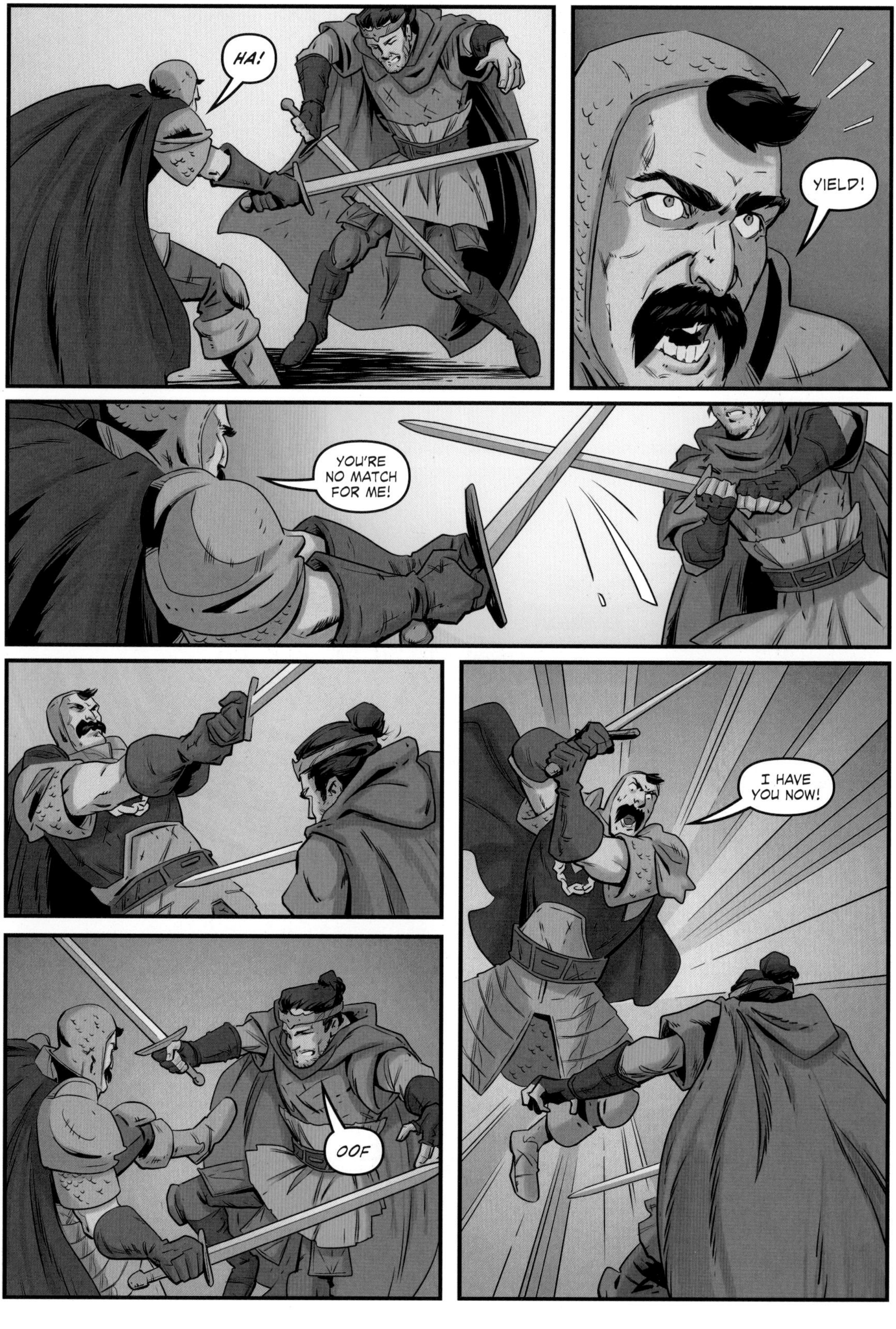
HA!
YIELD!
YOU'RE NO MATCH FOR ME!
I HAVE YOU NOW!
OOF

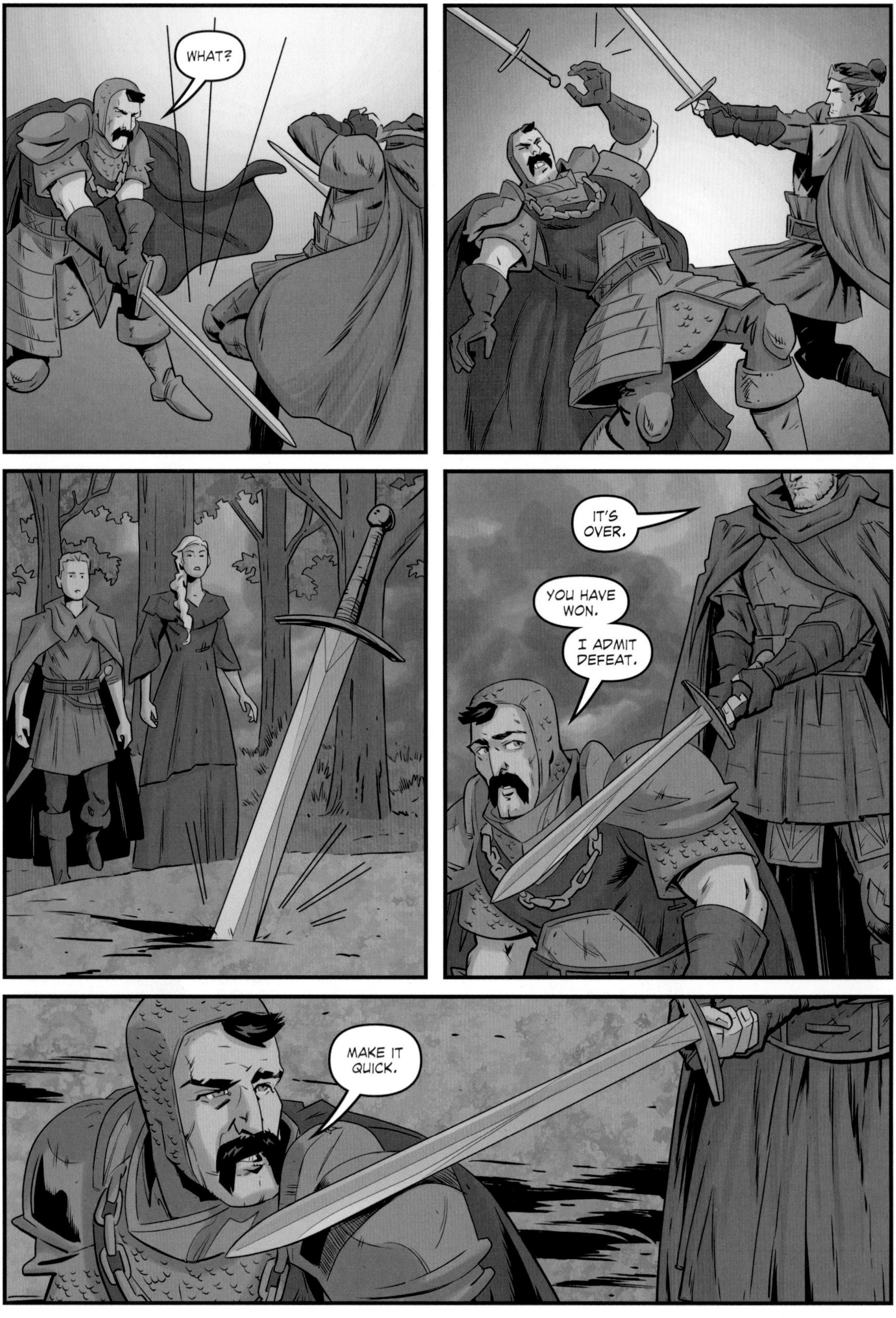
WHAT?
IT'S OVER.
YOU HAVE WON.
I ADMIT DEFEAT.
MAKE IT QUICK.

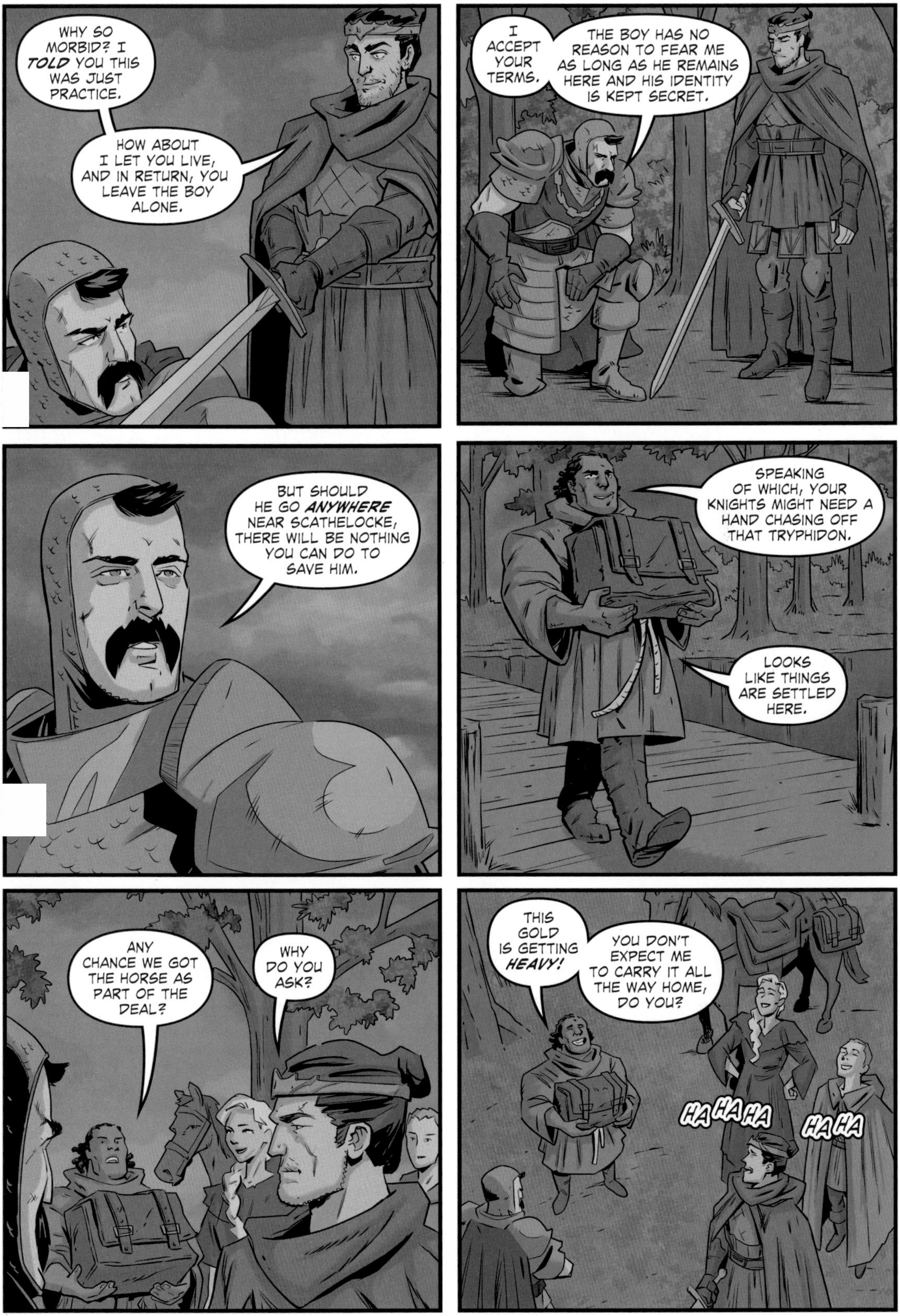
WHY SO MORBID? I *TOLD* YOU THIS WAS JUST PRACTICE.
HOW ABOUT I LET YOU LIVE, AND IN RETURN, YOU LEAVE THE BOY ALONE.
I ACCEPT YOUR TERMS.
THE BOY HAS NO REASON TO FEAR ME AS LONG AS HE REMAINS HERE AND HIS IDENTITY IS KEPT SECRET.
BUT SHOULD HE GO *ANYWHERE* NEAR SCATHELOCKE, THERE WILL BE NOTHING YOU CAN DO TO SAVE HIM.
SPEAKING OF WHICH, YOUR KNIGHTS MIGHT NEED A HAND CHASING OFF THAT TRYPHIDON.
LOOKS LIKE THINGS ARE SETTLED HERE.
ANY CHANCE WE GOT THE HORSE AS PART OF THE DEAL?
WHY DO YOU ASK?
THIS GOLD IS GETTING *HEAVY!*
YOU DON'T EXPECT ME TO CARRY IT ALL THE WAY HOME, DO YOU?
HA HA HA
HA HA

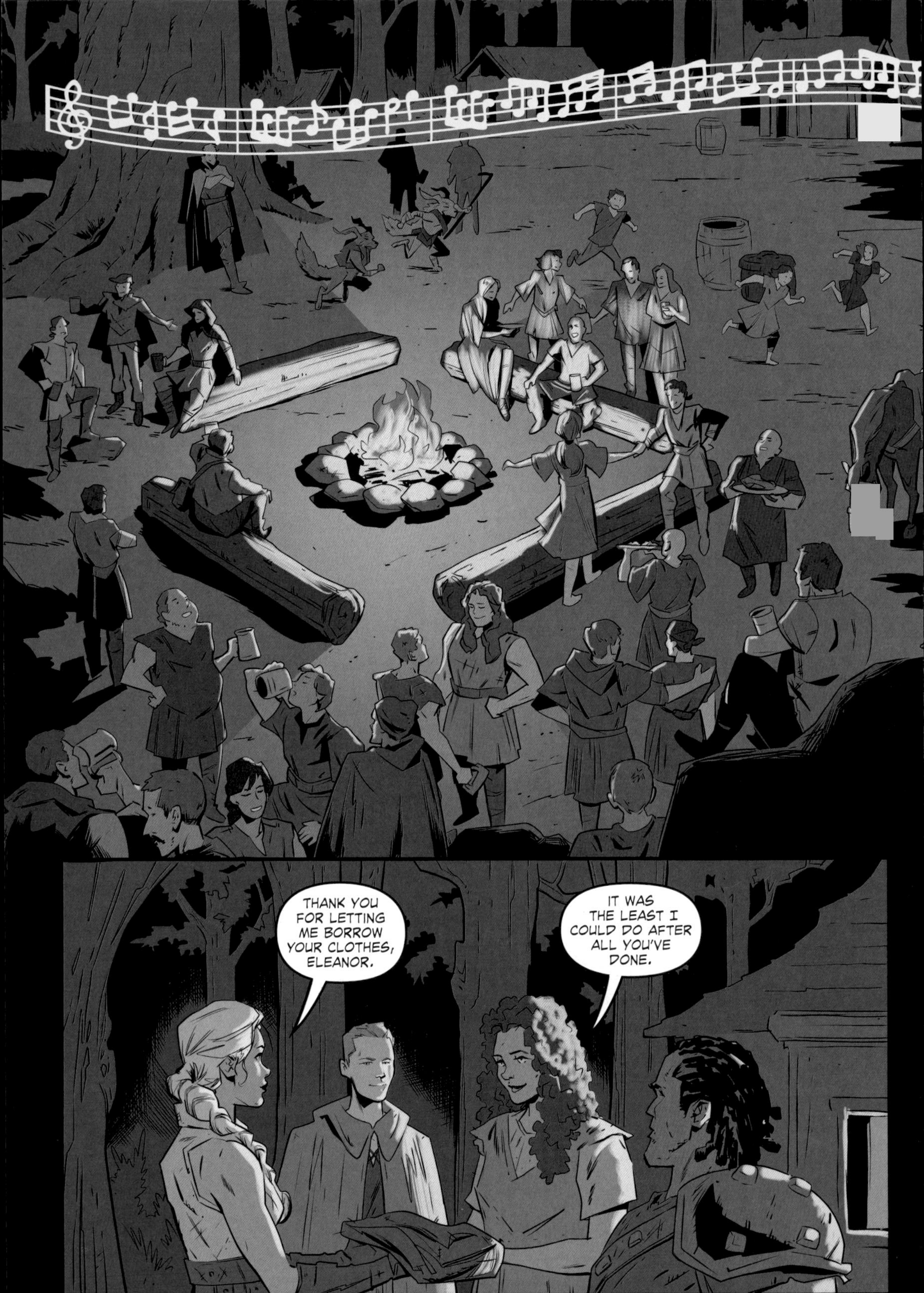
THANK YOU FOR LETTING ME BORROW YOUR CLOTHES, ELEANOR.
IT WAS THE LEAST I COULD DO AFTER ALL YOU'VE DONE.

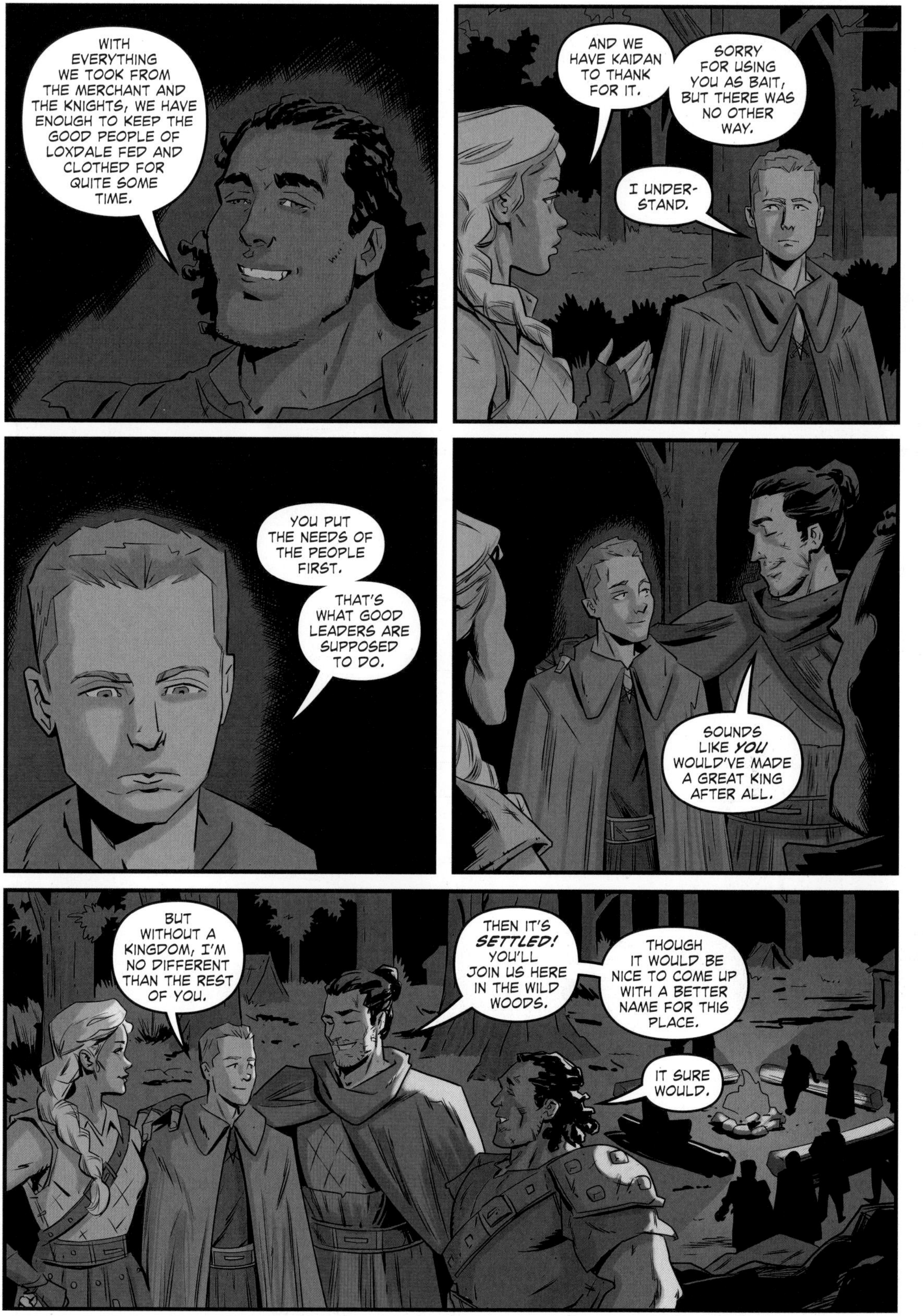
WITH EVERYTHING WE TOOK FROM THE MERCHANT AND THE KNIGHTS, WE HAVE ENOUGH TO KEEP THE GOOD PEOPLE OF LOXDALE FED AND CLOTHED FOR QUITE SOME TIME.
AND WE HAVE KAIDAN TO THANK FOR IT.
SORRY FOR USING YOU AS BAIT, BUT THERE WAS NO OTHER WAY.
I UNDER-STAND.
YOU PUT THE NEEDS OF THE PEOPLE FIRST.
THAT'S WHAT GOOD LEADERS ARE SUPPOSED TO DO.
SOUNDS LIKE *YOU* WOULD'VE MADE A GREAT KING AFTER ALL.
BUT WITHOUT A KINGDOM, I'M NO DIFFERENT THAN THE REST OF YOU.
THEN IT'S ***SETTLED!*** YOU'LL JOIN US HERE IN THE WILD WOODS.
THOUGH IT WOULD BE NICE TO COME UP WITH A BETTER NAME FOR THIS PLACE.
IT SURE WOULD.

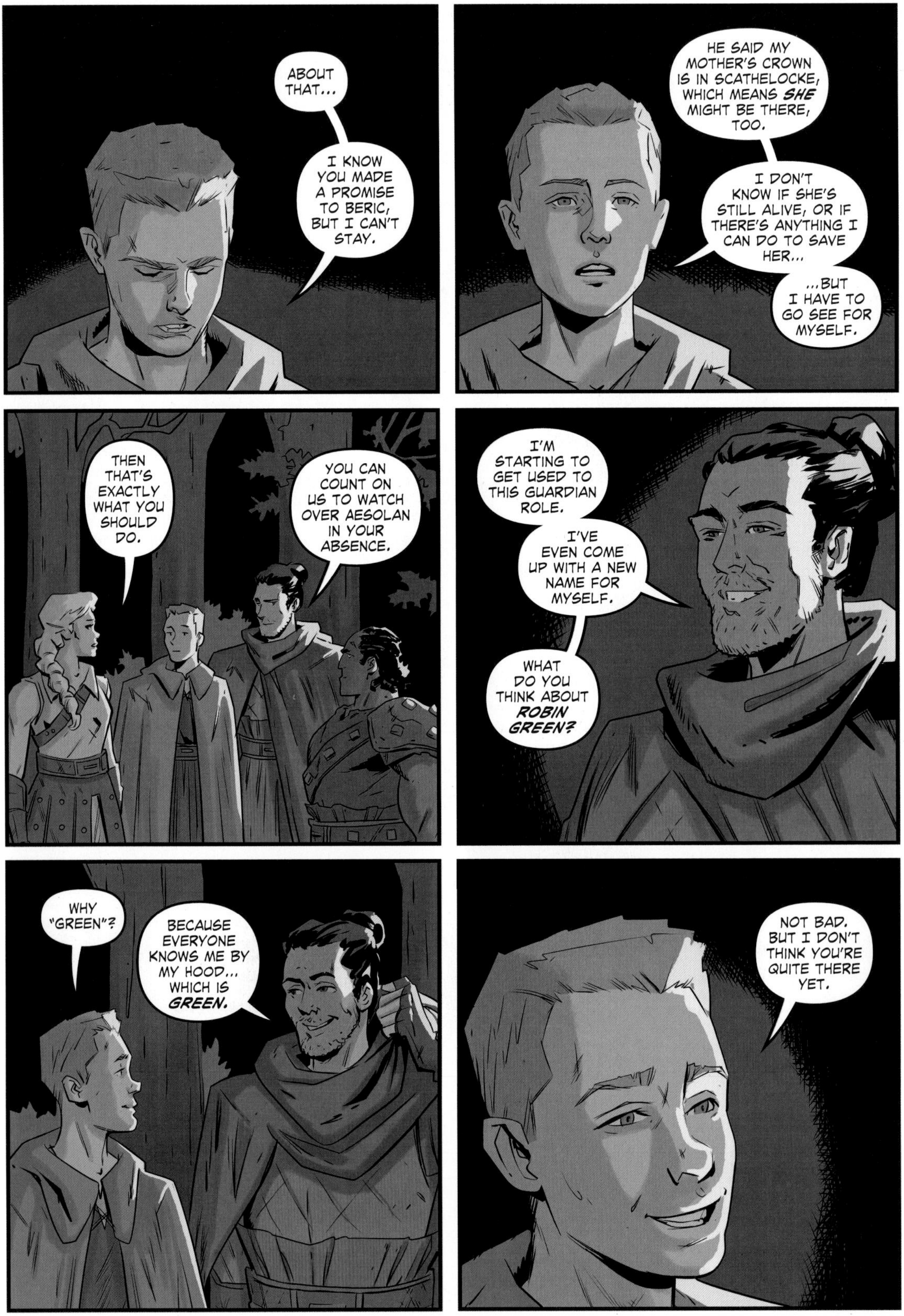
ABOUT THAT...
I KNOW YOU MADE A PROMISE TO BERIC, BUT I CAN'T STAY.
HE SAID MY MOTHER'S CROWN IS IN SCATHELOCKE, WHICH MEANS *SHE* MIGHT BE THERE, TOO.
I DON'T KNOW IF SHE'S STILL ALIVE, OR IF THERE'S ANYTHING I CAN DO TO SAVE HER...
...BUT I HAVE TO GO SEE FOR MYSELF.
THEN THAT'S EXACTLY WHAT YOU SHOULD DO.
YOU CAN COUNT ON US TO WATCH OVER AESOLAN IN YOUR ABSENCE.
I'M STARTING TO GET USED TO THIS GUARDIAN ROLE.
I'VE EVEN COME UP WITH A NEW NAME FOR MYSELF.
WHAT DO YOU THINK ABOUT ***ROBIN GREEN?***
WHY "GREEN"?
BECAUSE EVERYONE KNOWS ME BY MY HOOD... WHICH IS ***GREEN.***
NOT BAD. BUT I DON'T THINK YOU'RE QUITE THERE YET.

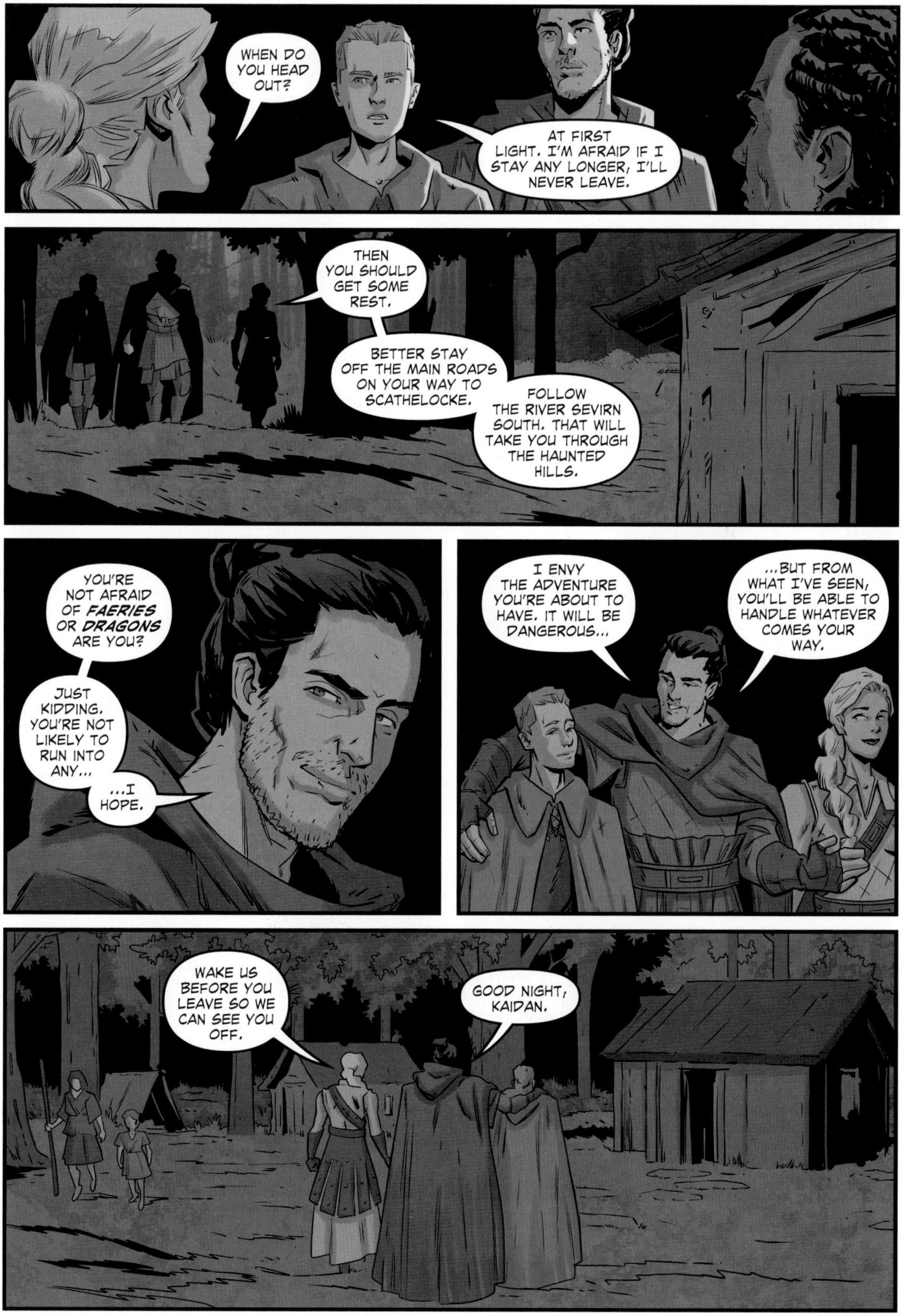
WHEN DO YOU HEAD OUT?
AT FIRST LIGHT. I'M AFRAID IF I STAY ANY LONGER, I'LL NEVER LEAVE.
THEN YOU SHOULD GET SOME REST.
BETTER STAY OFF THE MAIN ROADS ON YOUR WAY TO SCATHELOCKE.
FOLLOW THE RIVER SEVIRN SOUTH. THAT WILL TAKE YOU THROUGH THE HAUNTED HILLS.
YOU'RE NOT AFRAID OF **FAERIES** OR **DRAGONS** ARE YOU?
JUST KIDDING. YOU'RE NOT LIKELY TO RUN INTO ANY...
...I HOPE.
I ENVY THE ADVENTURE YOU'RE ABOUT TO HAVE. IT WILL BE DANGEROUS...
...BUT FROM WHAT I'VE SEEN, YOU'LL BE ABLE TO HANDLE WHATEVER COMES YOUR WAY.
WAKE US BEFORE YOU LEAVE SO WE CAN SEE YOU OFF.
GOOD NIGHT, KAIDAN.

CHIRP CHIRP

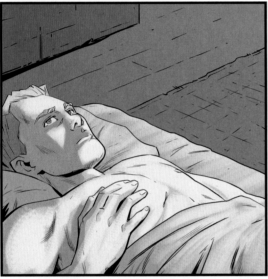

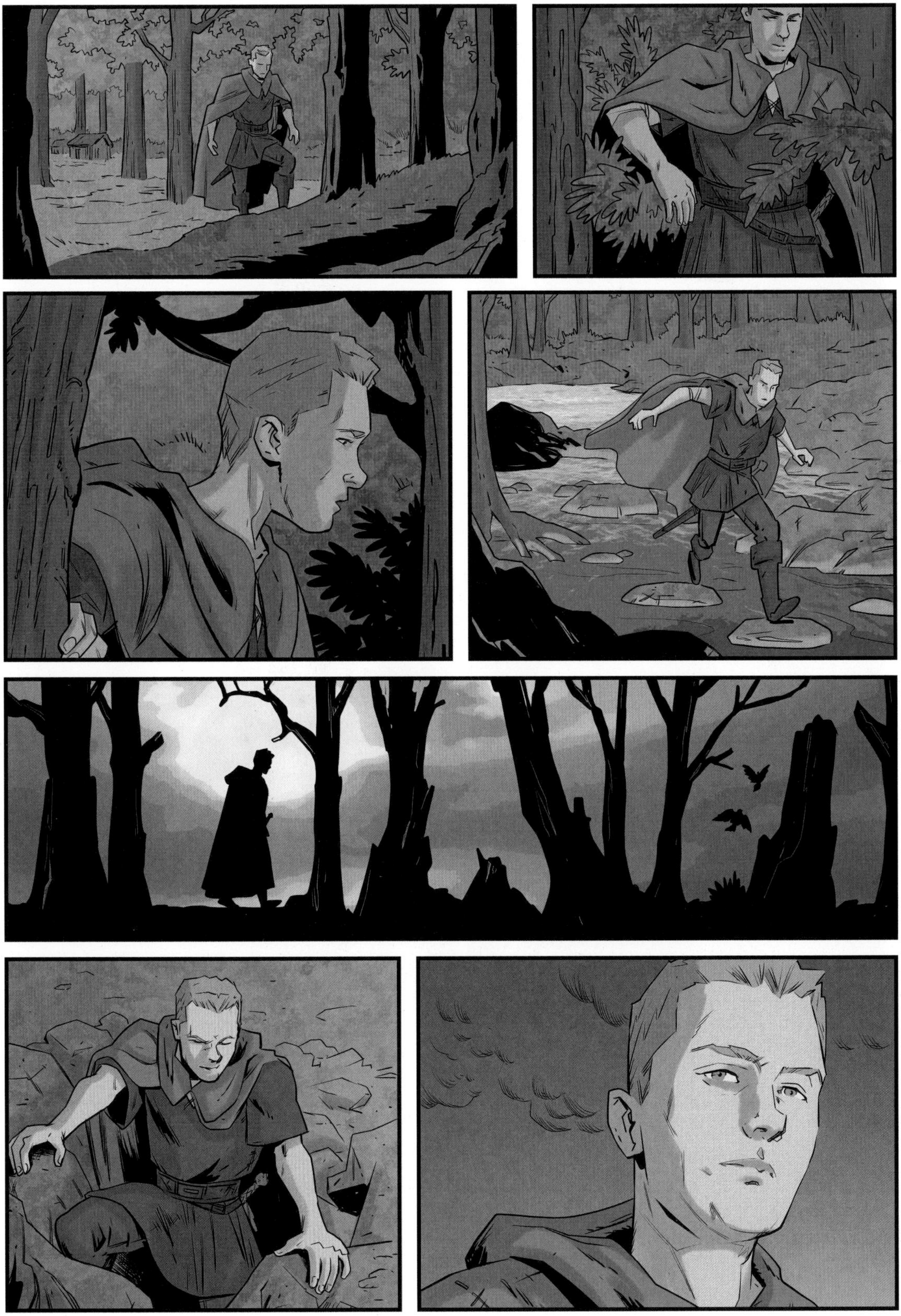

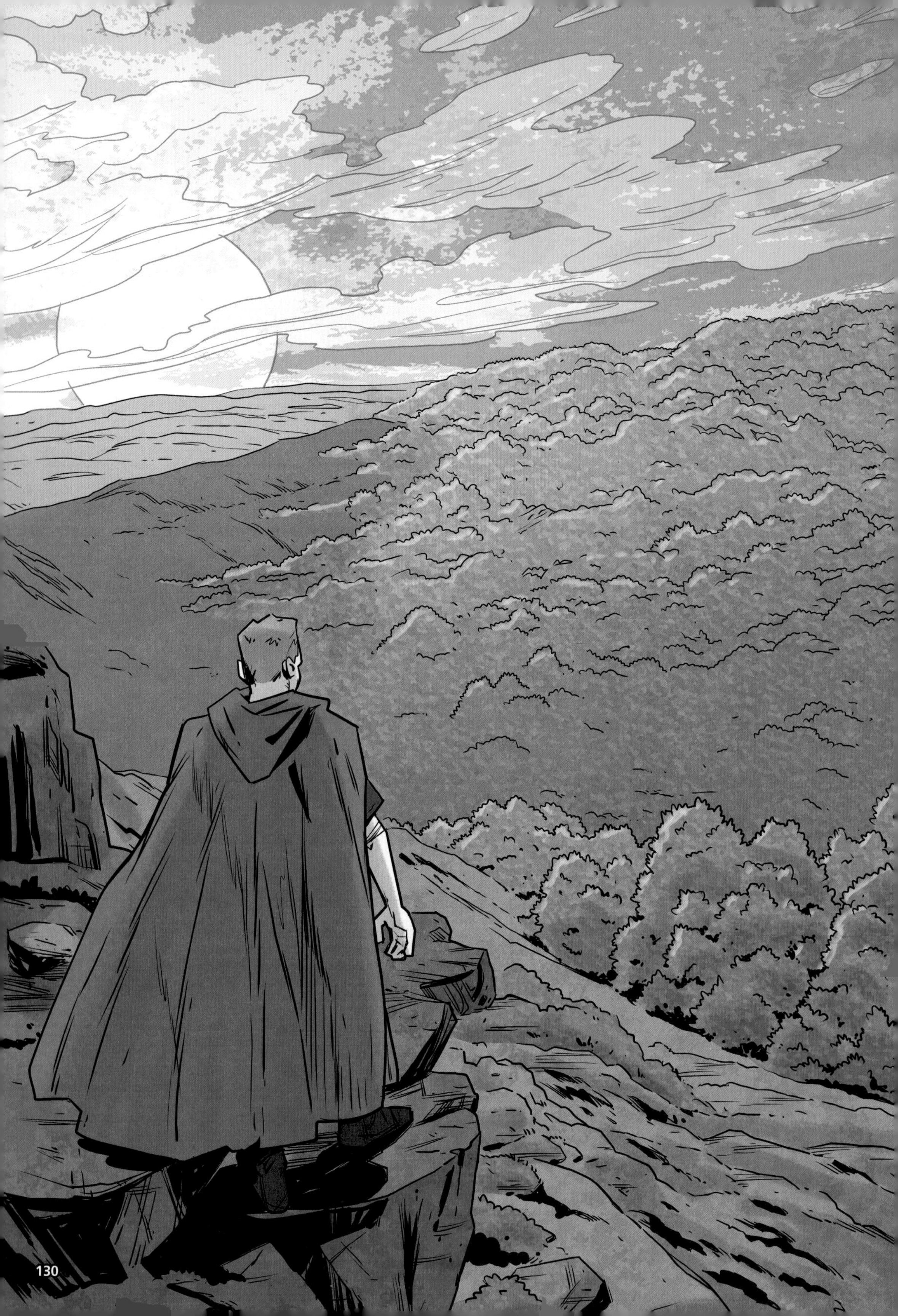

Kaidan's adventures will continue in:
The Orphan King, volume 2

THE HAUNTED HILLS

Character Designs

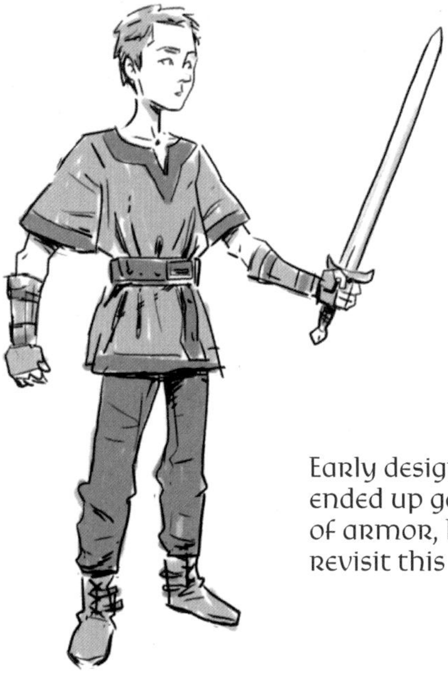

Early designs for Kaidan. We ended up going with a full suit of armor, but maybe we'll revisit this look in the future.

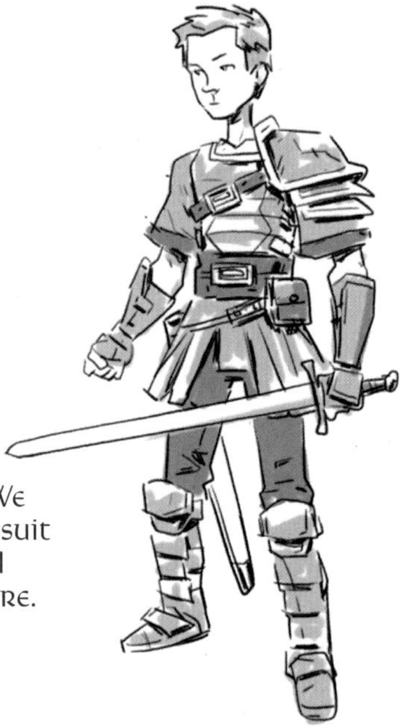

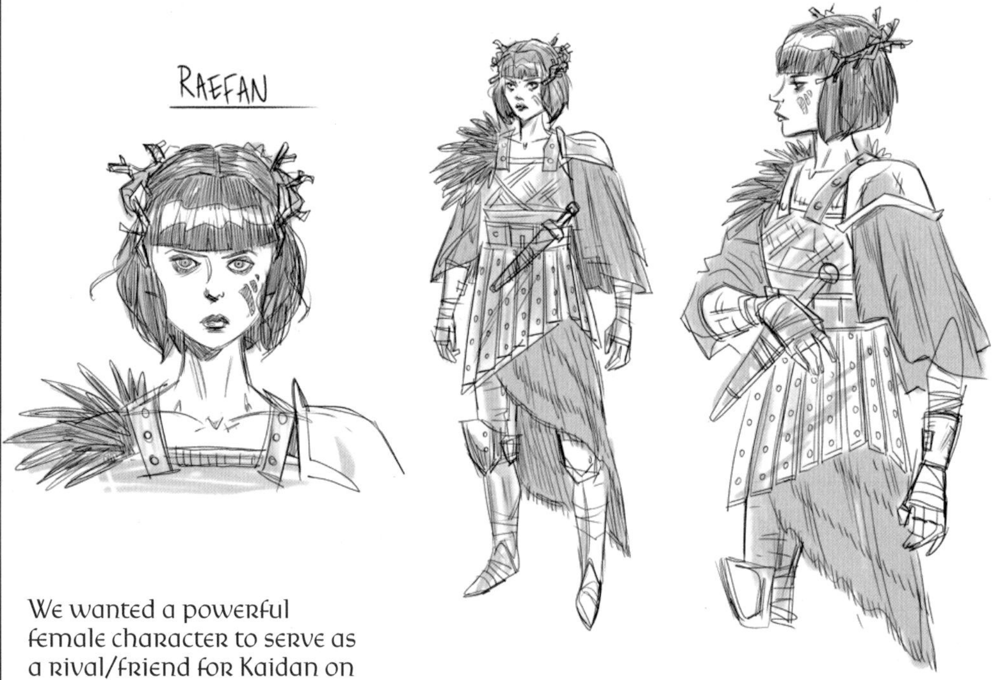
RAEFAN

We wanted a powerful female character to serve as a rival/friend for Kaidan on the Isle of Woman.

KNIGHTS OF VERMILLEON

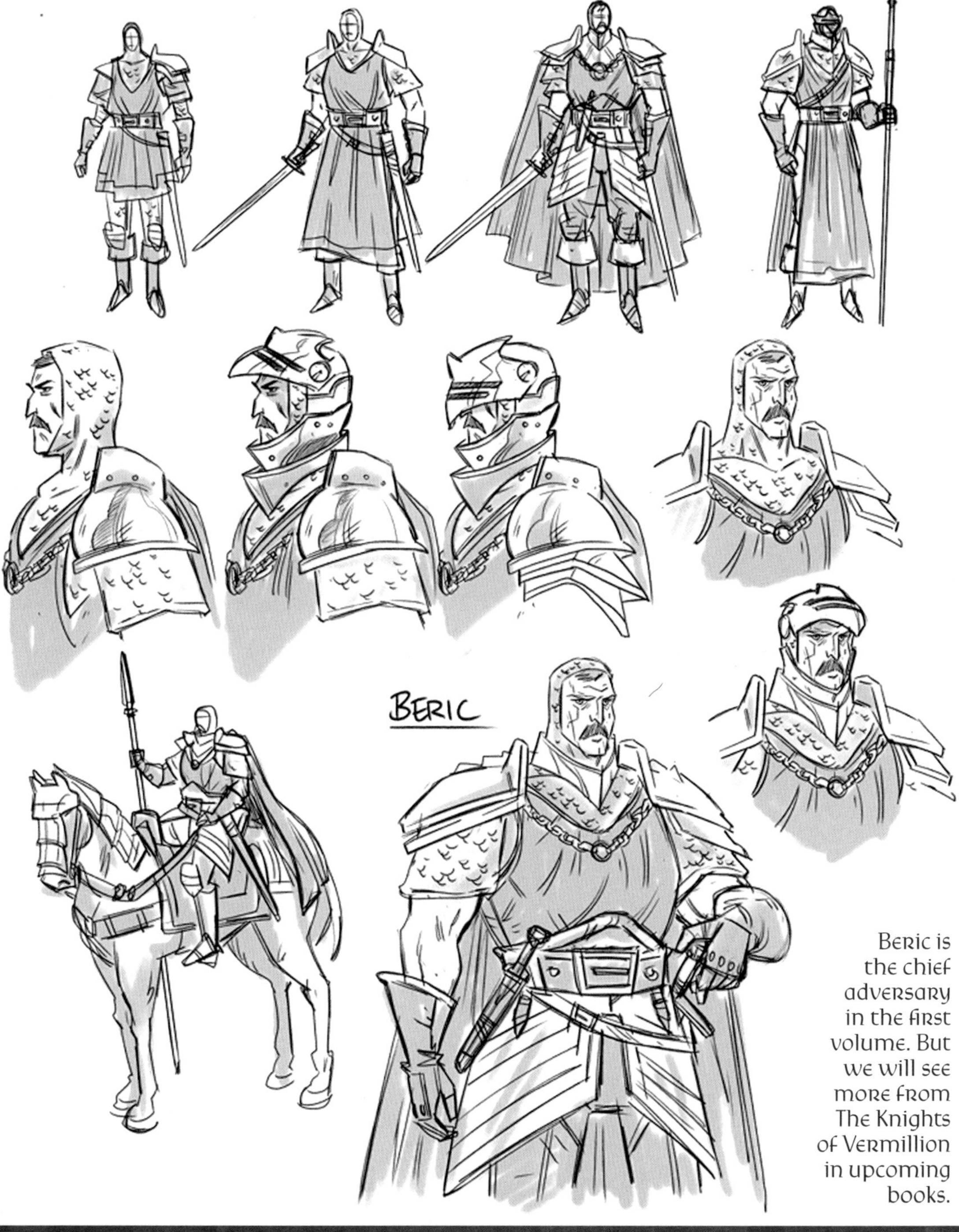
BERIC

Beric is the chief adversary in the first volume. But we will see more from The Knights of Vermillion in upcoming books.

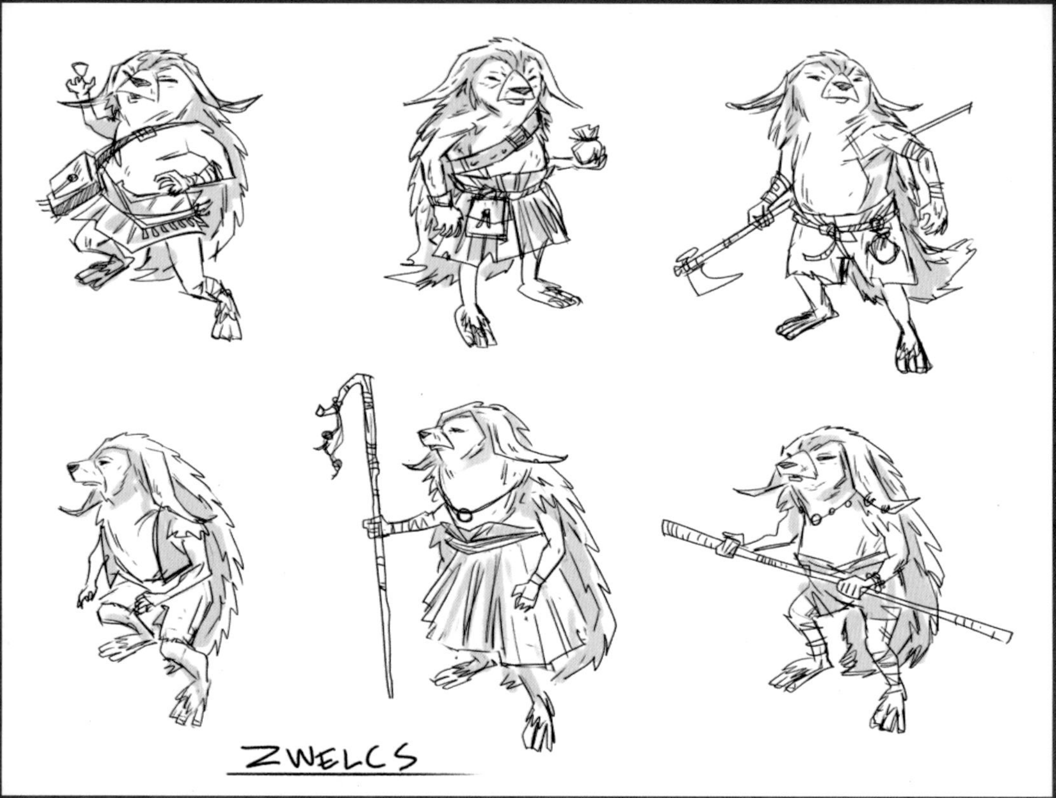
ZWELCS

Our own version of the Robin Hood characters with alternative names. Anne, Robert and Sturdy Jon (who ended up being taller than shown here).

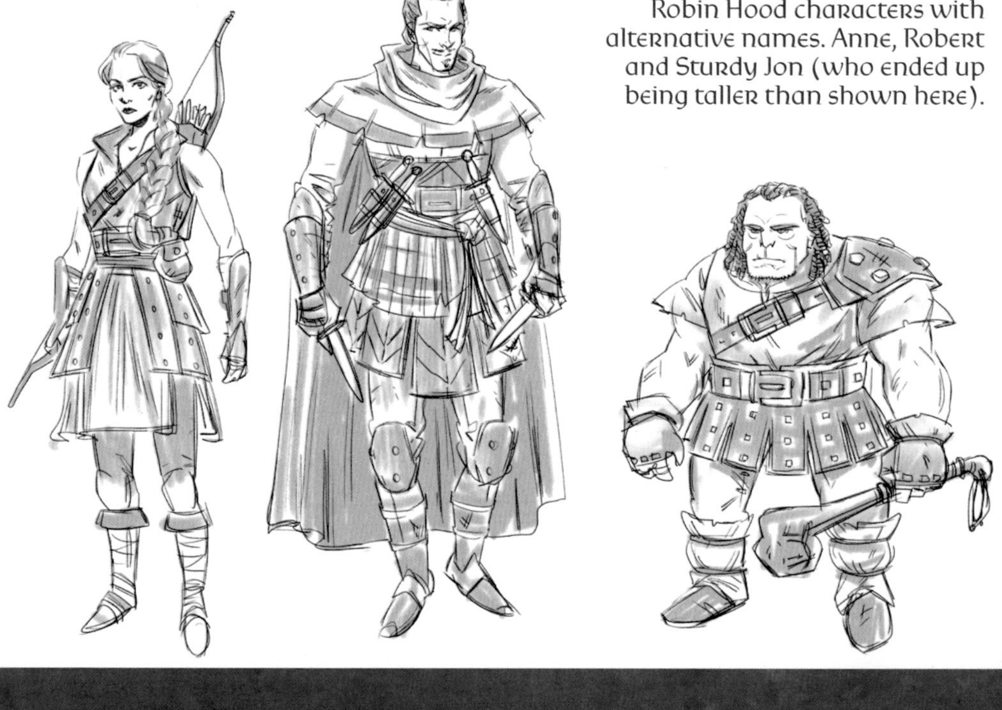

An original creation for this story, the noble Tryphidon is a mix between a wolf and a horned owl.

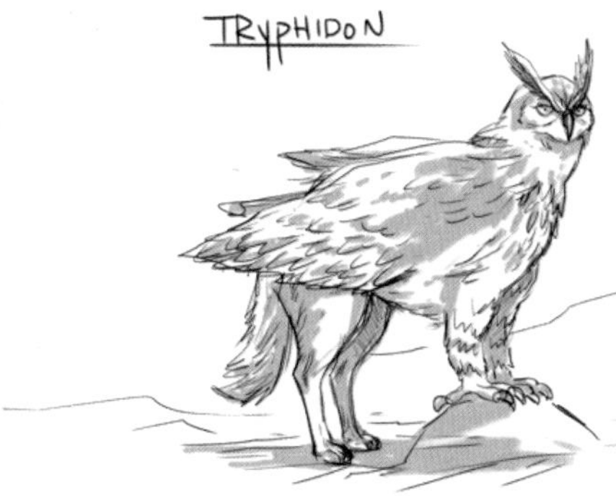
TRYPHIDON

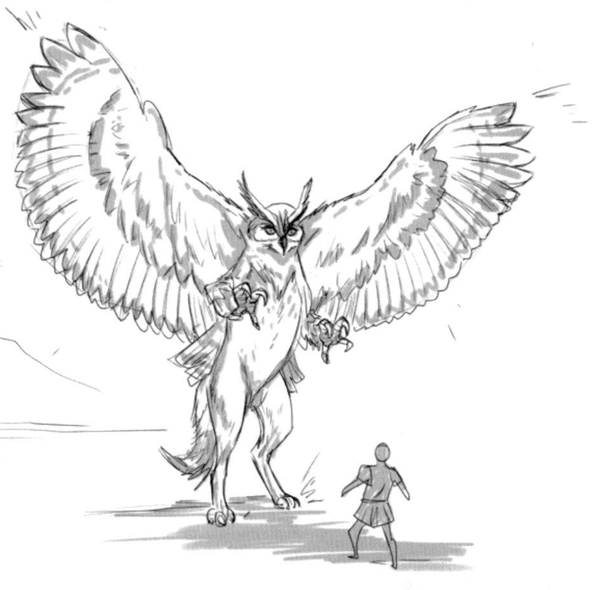

Below: Cover concepts for digital issues 4 and 5

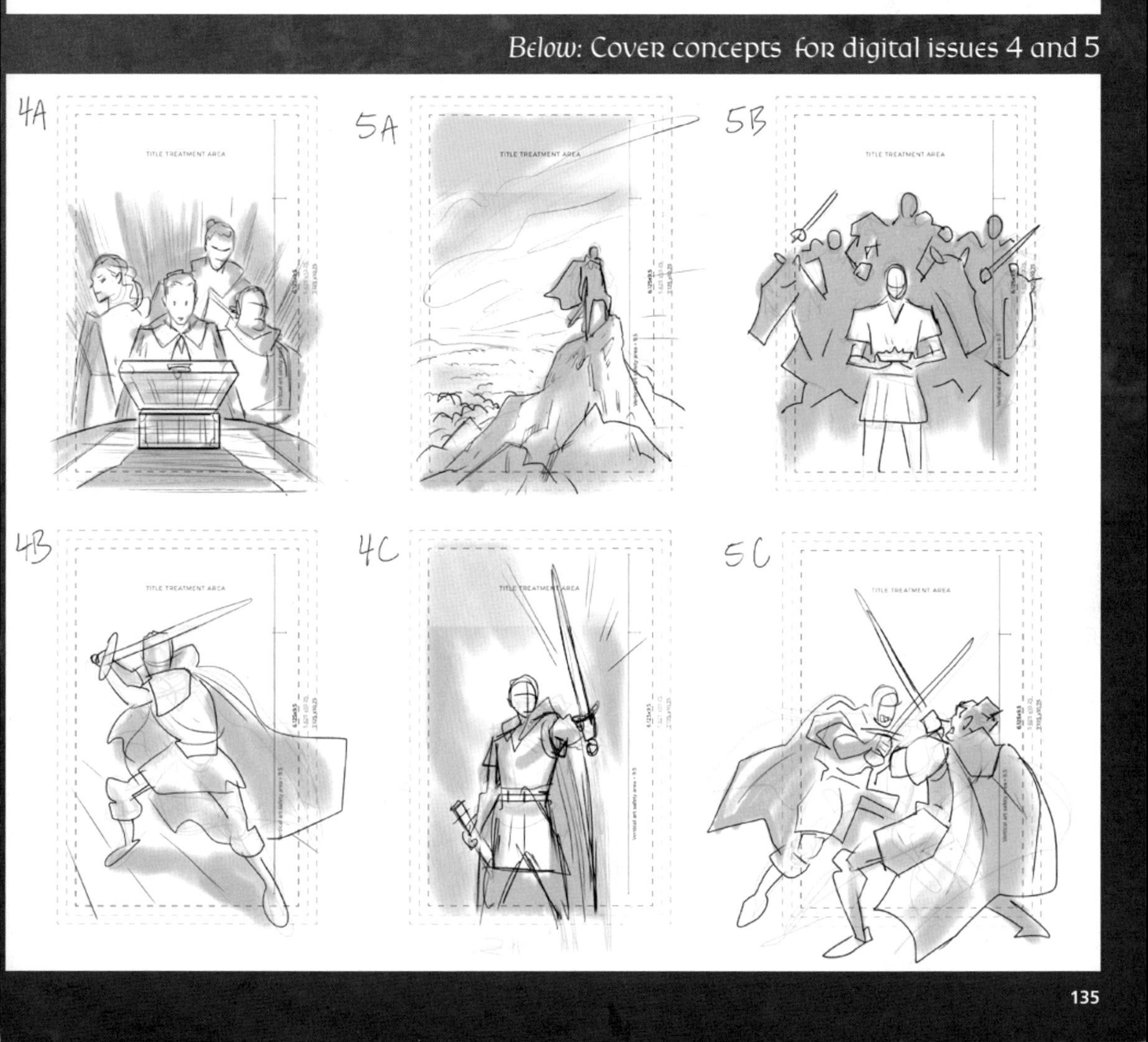
4A
5A
5B
4B
4C
5C

Cover Gallery

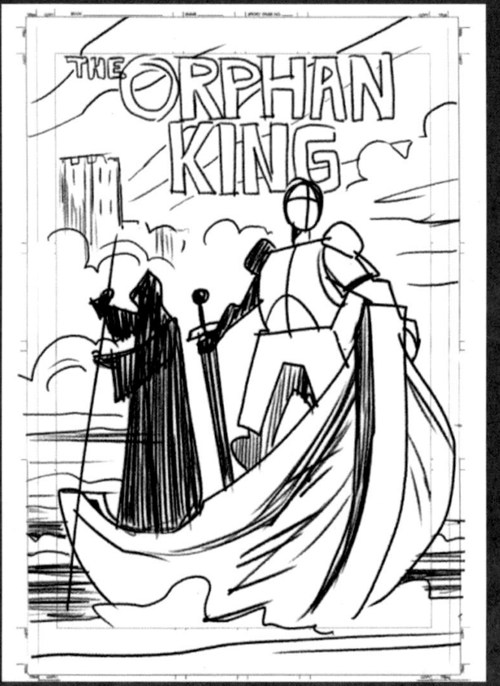
THE ORPHAN KING

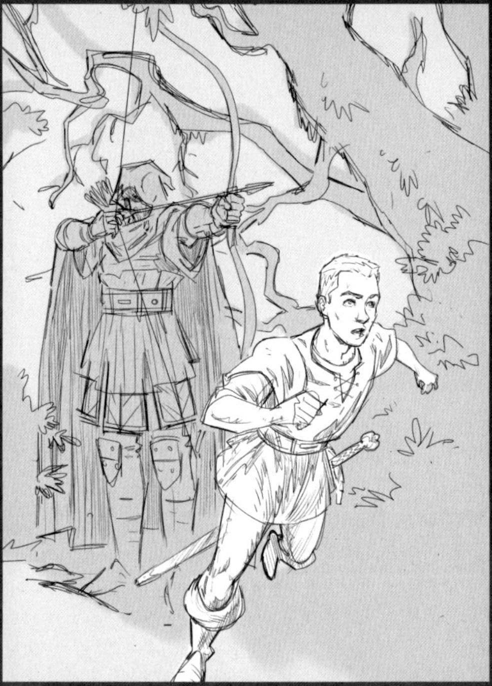

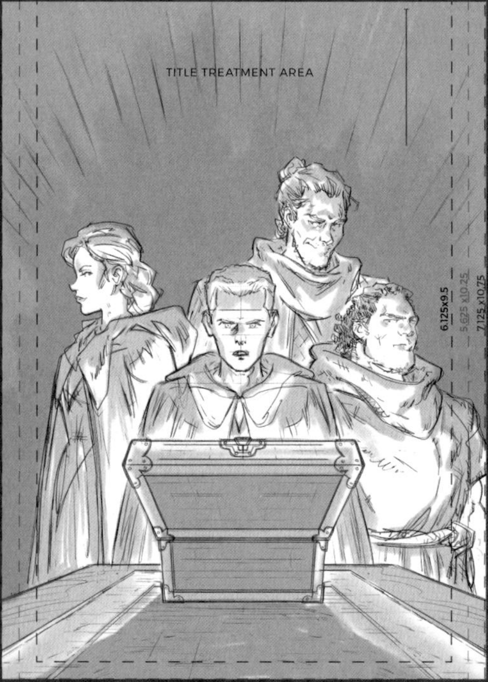
TITLE TREATMENT AREA
6.125x9.5
5.625 x10.25
7.125 x10.75

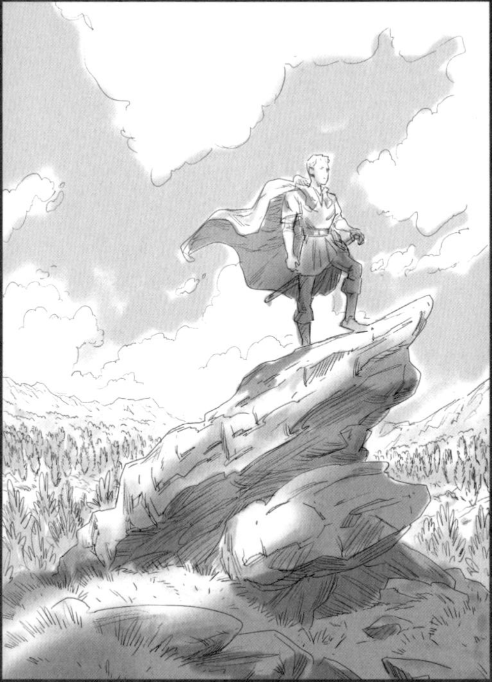

Above: Cover sketches for digital issues 1, 3, 4 and 5
Pages 137 – 141: Digital covers #1–5; artist: James Boyle
Page 142: Premier Edition cover, regular edition; artist: InHyuk Lee
Page 143: Premier Edition cover, dark variant; artist: InHyuk Lee

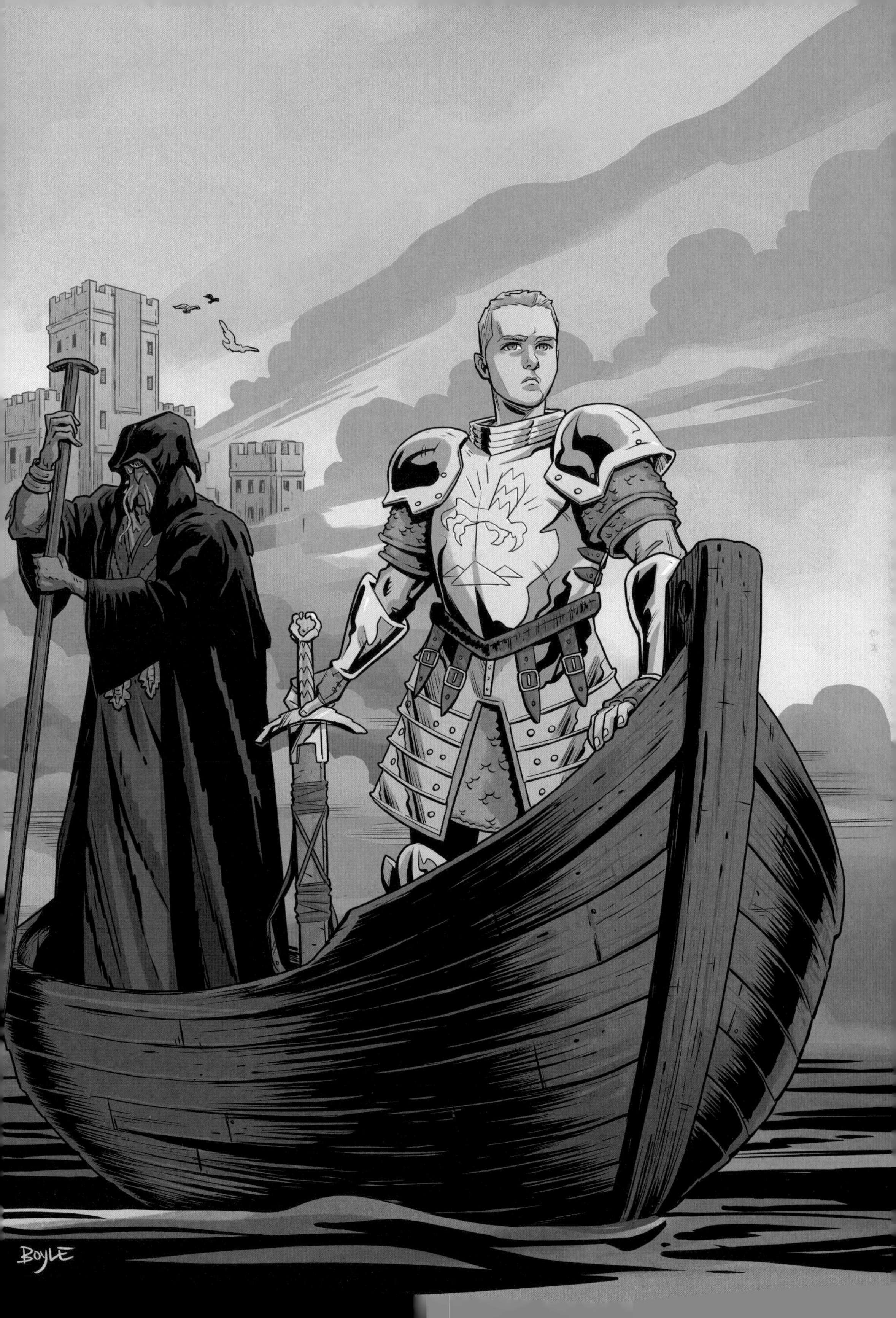
BOYLE

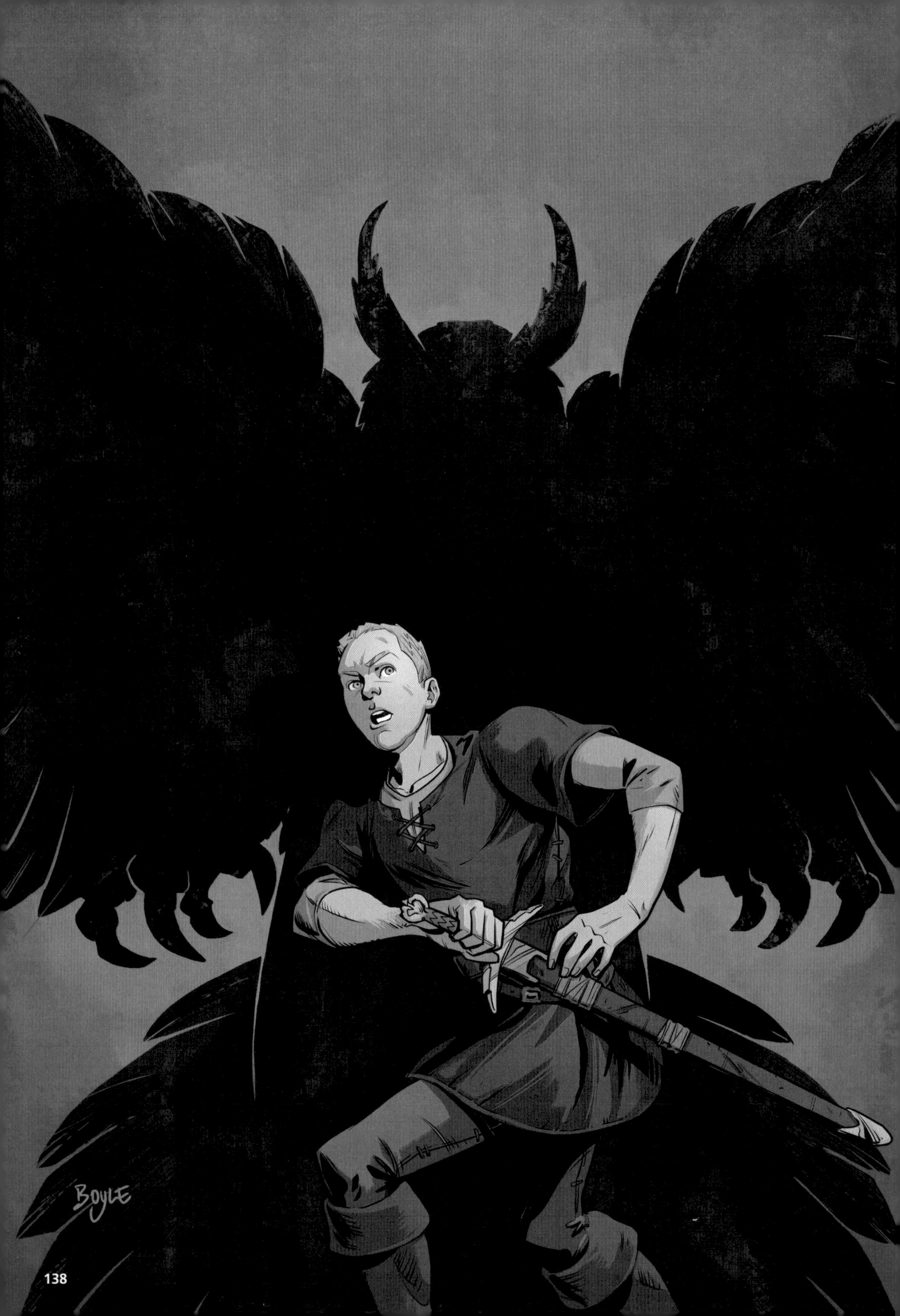
BOYLE

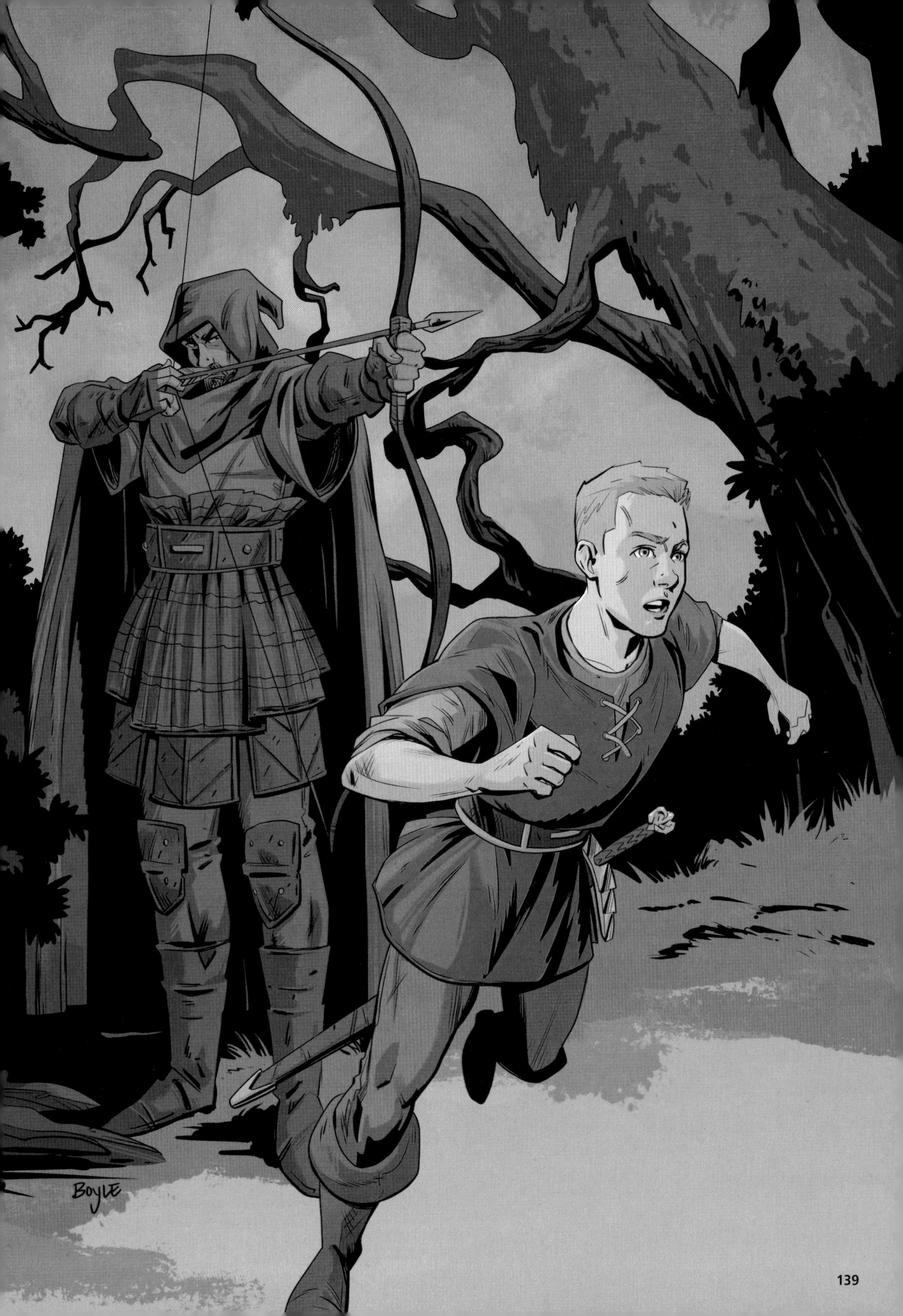
BOYLE

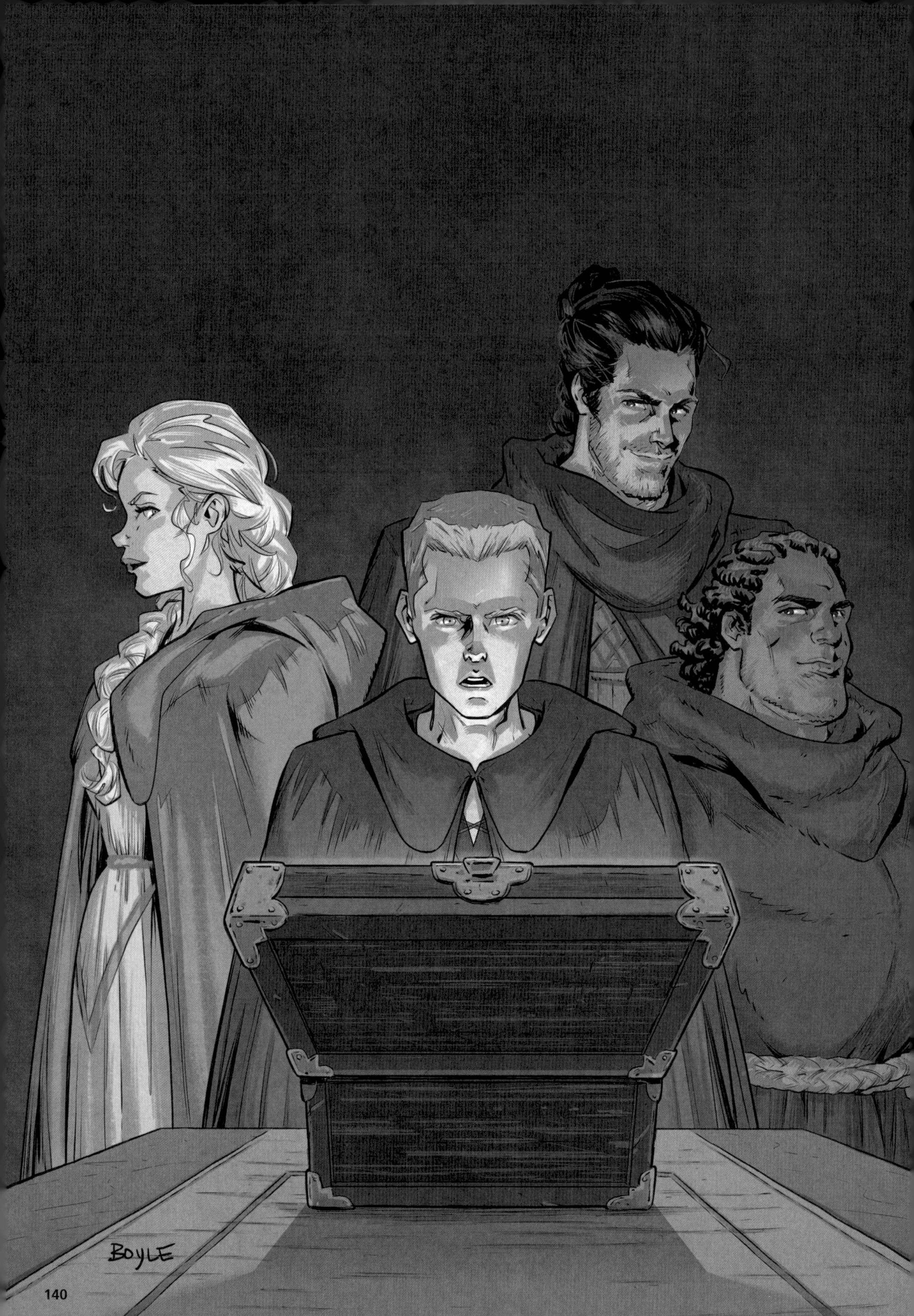
BOYLE

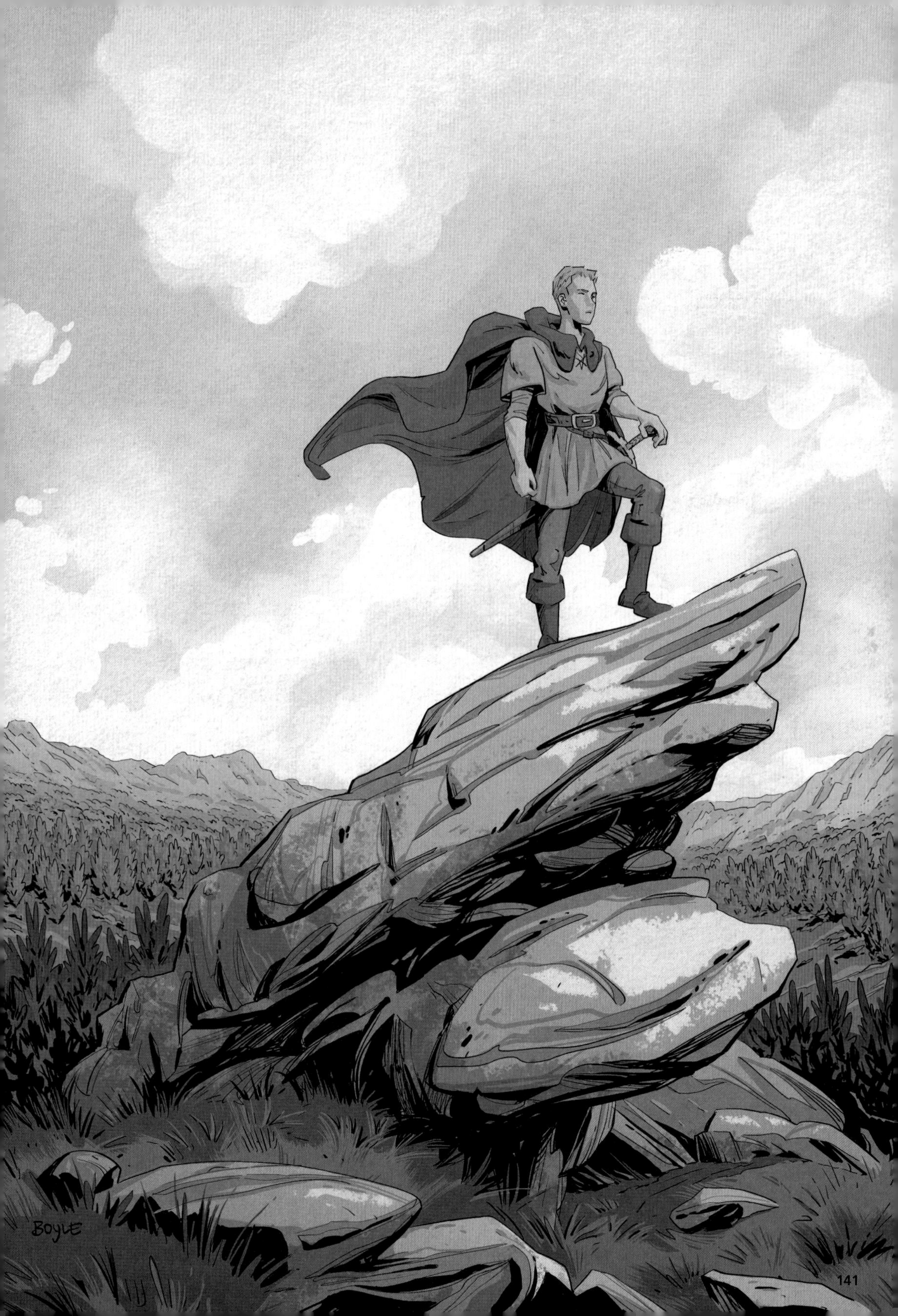
BOYLE

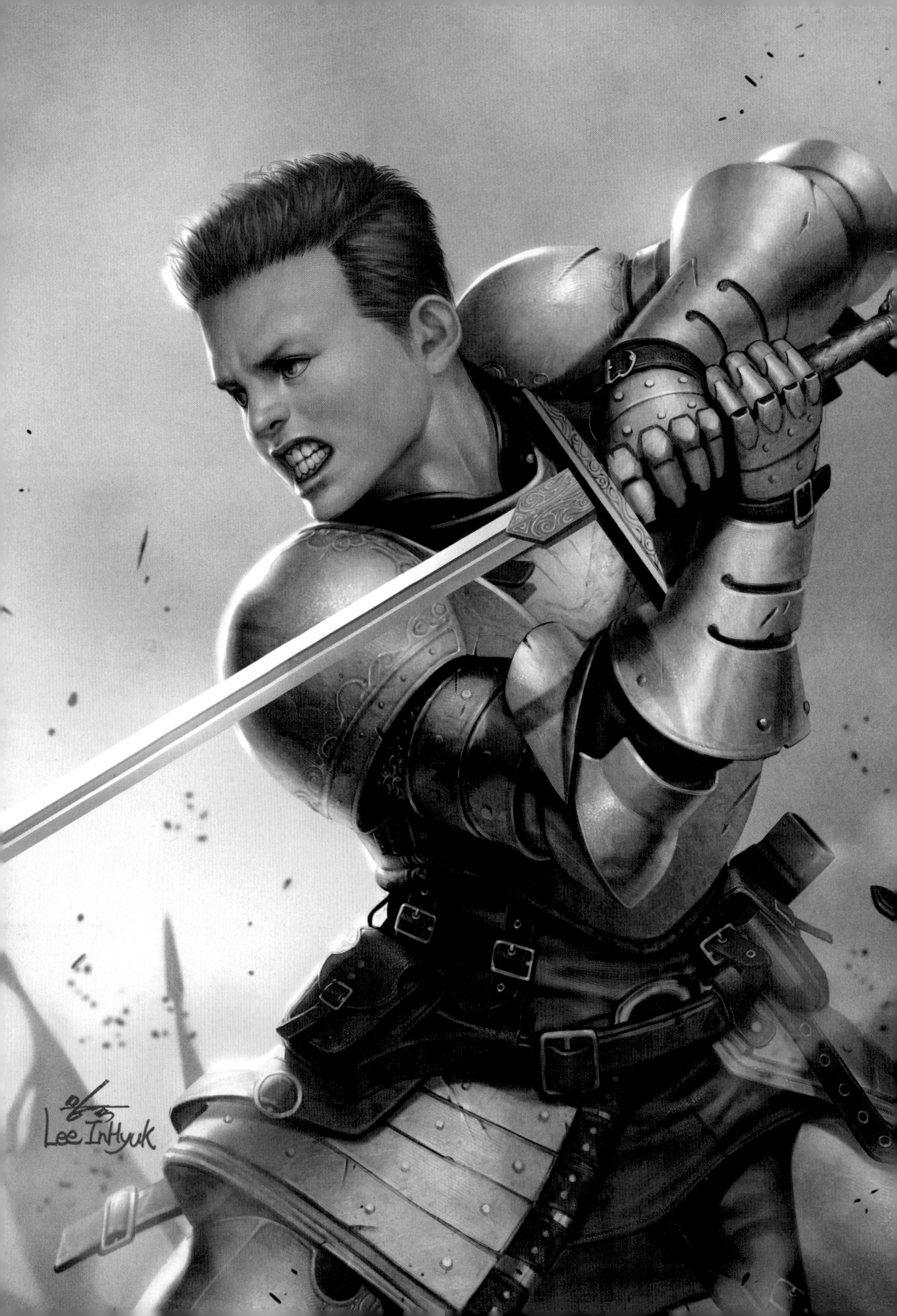
Lee InHyuk

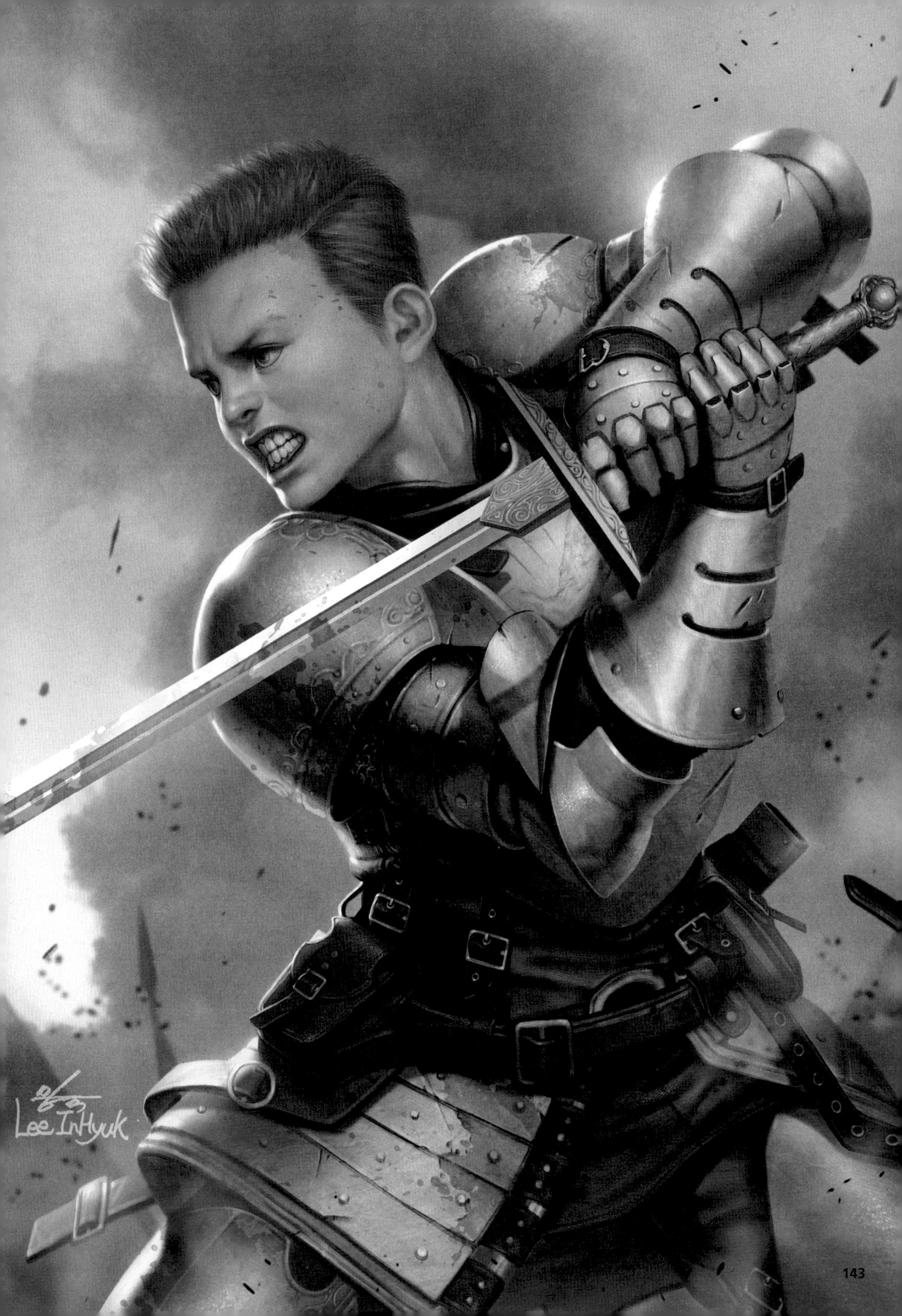
Lee InHyuk

Tyler Chin-Tanner

From his early careers in teaching and humanitarian aid work, Tyler Chin-Tanner took the leap into his lifelong passion for comics attending The Kubert School from 2003 to 2006 and co-founding A Wave Blue World with his wife Wendy in 2005. Publishing through AWBW, Tyler is the author of a number of graphic novels including New York Times featured *American Terrorist* and *Mezo*, as well as the editor of several anthologies such as *All We Ever Wanted*, *Dead Beats*, and *Maybe Someday*.

James Boyle

James Boyle is an illustrator, comic artist and art teacher. His work has appeared in a variety of publications, both print and digital. In addition to being the co-creator of The Orphan King, James is the artist behind The Philly Tarot Deck. He lives in a noisy house in southern New Jersey and enjoys quietly playing guitar from time to time.